Missing
Steps

YORK VAN NIXON III

ISBN: 0615817939
ISBN-13: 9780615817934

CONTENTS

Missing Steps is a work of fiction. This revision is dedicated to Camille Alleyne Van Nixon.

CHAPTER 1:

Despair

During moments such as this, copper moon rays usually disappeared before anything happened, except tonight. Indecision had finally lost patience. At last the indolent flame would be drowned in welling wax. In sympathy, shadows folded arms and bore witness.

Minutes till daybreak, the air had become dank. Propped up by pillows against a mahogany headboard, Kory lay naked in bed. Vomit spattered his withered legs after he'd tasted gun-cleaning oil on the barrel of his nine-millimeter Glock. This was not the first time he had sat alone with a pistol in one hand and the picture of his only child in the other. Until now, the breached hollow-point bullet had been ejected from a gun usually kept under his pillow for the past thirty years.

But early Sunday morning, tolerance waned. Agony ignored repeated handfuls of multicolored pills taken to numb nerve pain from multiple sclerosis. Now the simplest movement was too painful—like brushing what was left of his hair.

On the bedroom window ledge, an exhausted cricket made its last chirp. Kory's bloodshot eyes closed for dreamless sleep. Peace supplanted further pretense for being alive.

Kory Vanon was only four years old the year he lost faith. It became obvious one Epiphany Sunday morning when the sun failed to illuminate a passage from John 8:12 in the stained-glass window: "I am the light of the world. Whoever follows me will never walk in darkness, but will have the light of life."

Above the nave, whirling fans made hive-like murmurs of parishioners' unfinished breakfast conversations. Overly Sunday-dressed families, shrouded in various shades of mourning, waited for the first ecclesiastical chord from a recently purchased organ.

To the right of the invocational lectern, Mr. Wingfoot, their rumored effete organist, donned in a crisp white surplice with matching white-rimmed glasses, tiptoed to the bench and softly sat down. After a twist of his wrist and an exaggerated nod to God, his hands shuffled between two suspended keyboards while his right leg danced over a pedal board—punctuating rhythms that rose from a reedy forest of pipes inside a hidden room to the left of the apse.

Long, slippery pews, still smelling of linseed oil that had been lovingly rubbed on during the week by hairnetted, raspy-voiced women, filled with the elite. John Wesley African Methodist Episcopal Zion Church, two blocks from Logan Circle and in the heart of an island within Washington, D.C., was a house of worship for people who had been out of slavery four generations—although not long enough to have forgotten the rattle of chains.

Doctors, lawyers, proprietors, artists, and, of course, the postal worker, which was the best blue-collar job in America for a "Colored Man" in the fifties, prayed to a floor-to-ceiling mural left of the sermon lectern that depicted a blond-haired, blue-eyed Jesus Christ kneeling on a rock in the Garden of Gethsemane. His countenance resigned to the judgmental beam from the lamp of the Almighty. To this day, Kory saw himself during moments of the sermon comparing his little brown hands with the pallid arms of the Son of God, whose embrace he never envisioned hugging him after all the sins he hoped to commit.

While snuggled in the Vanon family pew between his mother, Elaine Vanon, and his brother, Ephen, Kory usually drifted back to his bedroom and soared through his imaginary world. But this was a special morning. His grandfather would deliver Kory's favorite sermon, "I Can Sleep on a Stormy Night." Kory always looked forward to this sermon. It reminded him of the times he stayed with his grandfather, when he read fairy tales in which children were the center of attention and the stories always had a happy ending.

Granpa, as his grandchildren called him, loved to read to all thirteen almost as much as he liked to preach his dictum of responsible living to their parents. This was Stephen George Vanon at his best: on most Sunday mornings, his room-filling baritone voice portended all the consequences suffered if the edicts of the Apostles' Creed were not followed; the alternative was nightmarish damnation.

The Right Reverend Vanon began his sermon with the lights of the sanctuary dimmed to that of the faint glow from a single flickering candle. From his fifty-foot-high pulpit, under a spotlight directed from heaven, he painted a tree-shrouded, late-nineteenth-century Victorian house, which was not visible from the street, except when intermittent lightning torched a frozen January night sky. Deep inside a pitch-black house, past endless locked doors and at the end of a dark hallway, a slowly dripping candle reflected the sleepless movements of a troubled man writhing beside his dying wife.

Without warning he was jolted out of bed by the sound of a thunderbolt that struck a lightning rod on one of the roof turrets, but that brief dawn quietly retreated and left the house silhouetted in front of a swirling black sky. The heart of the dispirited man pounded. His soul trembled. He feared his house would be destroyed. Not knowing what else to do, he fell to the cold wooden floor. On his bare knees, he begged God to forgive him for doubting his faith. Lightning and thunder ceased. Stephen George Vanon stood silent as he stared into the souls of those sitting in the back pews.

His stentorian voice thundered again: "The soul of man is in peril. All weekend Christians, heed my admonitions. Your Judgment Day is today. Fall on your knees, and beg our master for forgiveness with your most heartfelt contrition. Yes, I can sleep on a stormy night. When I am denied my rights, I know God will make all things equal in the Promised Land because I did the right thing in spite of the injustice of my oppressor. Yes, my friends, I dream of a world where people are judged not by the color of their skin but by the virtue of their deeds. My friends, we must have faith in Jesus to lead us to everlasting freedom."

After nudging him, Kory's mother whispered, "Wake up. I want you to sit up and listen to your grandfather's sermon." But Kory was not asleep. He was more than listening to his grandfather's voice; he was enjoying the fantasy Granpa had created just for him. Sometimes his grandfather would peer over his gold half-rimmed spectacles and raise the ends of his thick moustache to send a secret smile in his direction.

He loved Granpa. It was only when his grandfather was around that he felt safe and happy. "Kory, I said sit up," his mother said again, giving him a pinch on his ear this time. Kory sat up and looked at Ephen, who was smirking with satisfaction as he brandished the toy he had smuggled to church in his suit pocket. It was the Black Knight, and it belonged to Kory.

There was little he could do, he thought. If he protested, his mother would take it from them, thereby denying either one any chance of playing with it while the lights were lowered. Despite the challenge, Kory was more interested in listening to "I Can Sleep on a Stormy Night." But sibling rivalry got the best of him: the battle-dressed knight was his, and he was determined to have it. He tried to snatch it from his brother. Ephen simply placed it on the far side of his body, where Kory's short arms could not reach. Most children, when tormented by an older sibling, use pleading to get their way. Kory never gave his brother the satisfaction of tears; crying for him was something only to be done alone in the deafness of closets. Determined to win, he whispered in Ephen's ear he had found pieces of the broken Egyptian vase hidden in the coal bin. Kory told him if he did not give him the toy, plus his dessert tonight, he would tell their mother while he was taking his bath, the usual time for Elaine Vanon to release her unhappiness. Notwithstanding Kory's age, he understood his mother's need to numb her memory of her failed marriage to a brutal and insecure man with a sense of morality, unlike those of the men in the Vanon family.

Love and tenderness became infrequent visitors to Kory's home. Their usual regrets for not coming to dinner, or any other part of the day, were previous engagements with more deserving families.

Kory discovered children like him were not the ones in his bedtime stories. Every day he looked for a happy ending, but it never came. Somehow he must have been born a bad child. Life became one long penance to atone for the sins of his parents. Somewhere a dirge played while the child inside died.

CHAPTER 2:

Fire This Time

A box of kitchen matches exploded. Fourth of July–like sparks raced up the basement closet walls. "Uh-oh!" The two brothers shrieked with fear and excitement as flames reached the bottom shelf filled with wrapping paper. It quickly flared to stacks of plastic shoe boxes.

Ephen was still angry from the spanking he had gotten the night before. The bruises were paltry compared to the emotional lashes from his mother. The responsibilities of single parenting had overwhelmed her instincts of motherhood.

So he took his revenge on her favorite possessions. He had climbed to the top of the kitchen cupboard to find matches that were supposed to be unreachable. But, not unlike many children, he always found a way to match his knee-high mind to his mother's heights of depression.

Within seconds, the fire grew hotter than his revenge. Ephen ran to the kitchen and returned with a small pot of water. It did little to dowse the bonfire of dresses, coats, and melting plastic. Ephen looked into his little brother's face and whimpered, "I'm getting out of here. Mommy will kill me for this."

Kory held back his fear. "You're in a lot of trouble, but I swear I won't tell." Ephen made sure he didn't; he escaped the basement apartment and left Kory sitting alone in the burning closet.

For a short while, Kory just sat there, listening to the popping sounds exploding mothballs made. He was also mesmerized by the colors dancing around the smoke-darkened closet. Soon his little lungs began filling with deadly smoke, and his eyes were burning so badly he could not keep them open. "Mommy! Mommy! Mommy!" he yelled. His mother was too far away to hear. Kory's cries were not as loud as the band playing the all-night cabaret.

Through blackness and choking smoke, and behind a closed door, Kory heard Phoenicia, his grandmother, calling their names. She followed the sounds of his coughing and cries for help. He felt her grab him by the arm. She lifted him to her breast. "Are you hurt? Where's Ephen?" Kory told her that Ephen had run out of the house with only his socks and undershorts. "Are you sure, Kory?" He nodded his head, but his grandmother was not sure she could rely on a report from her crying four-year-old grandson.

Phoenicia carried him to the back door and told him to run to his grandfather upstairs. He ran only as far as the old garden hose hanging against the wall and stopped. Kory turned around and watched his grandmother as she disappeared into a black cloud through the basement kitchen door. Somehow Kory knew this was the last time he would ever see her face. Inside his heart, the spring of adulthood had been wound more tightly. A funeral drum beat as he took his first step to morality.

Kory resolved saints perish as often as sinners—although they are more likely to leave behind loved ones who accept an explanation for pain as the "will of the Creator."

Waiting for mercy, Jesus hanged in silence; it arrived with thorns and eternal blame.

CHAPTER 3:

Facing the Mirror

Though Elaine Vanon was never blamed for leaving her children alone Sunday morning, she was obliged to rent an apartment three blocks from her father's house. His eight-bedroom home lacked a room large enough to hide her guilt.

There she was, only twenty-one years old, two toddlers, no husband, a college dropout, few friends, and jobless. Because she was the youngest, everything was done for her, except matching the accomplishments of her older siblings. Her husband even had to show her how to scramble an egg. Had her father not forgiven Elaine for the death of his wife, the broken heart of a young woman struggling to cope with the challenges of parenthood would never have healed. But mended things are seldom as good as they once were; even cutting the umbilical cord leaves a scar.

Elaine Vanon's atonement began after she accepted the nurtured imperfections in herself and took responsibility for each and every tragic mistake.

Before her marriage, Elaine had been an overly romantic teenager. She spent many after-school hours reading and composing love poems. The day she accompanied one of her older sisters to the library, she was introduced to a world of endless ideas and fantasies. Even after she was estranged from her husband, she managed to steal a few hours away from her responsibilities to escape into the pages of a novel.

As fortune had it, a few years later, while waiting at the checkout desk, Elaine overheard one of the librarians discussing an ad in *The Washington Post* for the recently vacated position of junior librarian. The head librarian took a long look at Elaine before handing her an application. "I know you. You've grown up. We used to call you Pippi Longstocking because of your very long pigtails and the knee-high socks you used to wear. I see you here at least three times a week, so I assume you love to read. Tell me—we've been trying to figure out if you are Italian." An old, white-haired janitor shuffled his feet as he delivered lunch for the librarians. Elaine thought about how much he reminded her of her paternal grandfather. She turned her attention back to the head librarian and smiled. "That's a good guess. My grandmother is from a small city in Europe."

So Elaine got her first job, at the Central Library in downtown Washington, DC. She worked there two years before anyone besides the slow-walking, invisible black custodian realized she was actually a light-skinned black woman, "passing" and taking advantage of the ignorance of racial diversity held by all but the most discerning whites.

Elaine Vanon enjoyed her work. Even though her salary was meager, she always brought home the best children's books available for her two growing sons. In her small apartment, she learned on her own how to be a parent and what it meant to have responsibilities that she could not leave in the lap of someone else. The dreams she had of marrying one of the men who appeared in the poetry she wrote every night were gone. As much as she wished to walk away from her children, her father did everything to prevent his daughter from placing her two sons for adoption. And at the urging of her parents, she agreed to change her name and that of her two sons to the family's name, Vanon. This infuriated the boys' father, but

Elaine knew her children would stand a better chance in life carrying her family's surname.

On nice days Elaine ate her lunch in the park surrounding the library. One day Rosemary, one of her closest friends, who was the color of a copper penny and not able to "pass" for anything but black, happened to be walking near the park and saw Elaine sitting on the grass, enjoying her lunch and reading a copy of *Troilus and Cressida*. Elaine had no idea that the always-suspicious head librarian watched her share lunch with one of her best friends.

Upon her return, the gossamer veil shrouding racism was raised. When asked directly, Elaine proudly declared her race. "The Central Library only employs white girls at the desk," declared the head librarian.

Elaine held her head high as she closed the chapter on her first job. Later that night she cried while her two sons slept in the next room, oblivious to the color of their skin.

After two days she gathered the courage to tell her father what had happened. Having experienced similar humiliations as a young man, he knew firsthand the slap of bigotry. Being a man of the cloth, he had learned to turn the other cheek but not to look the other way. Recently appointed to the bishopric, he hired his daughter to work in his small home office. This gave her the flexibility to be home with her children when they were out of school and facilitated emotional and financial support from a father who never turned his back on his youngest daughter, despite the fact she had taken from him the only woman he ever loved.

CHAPTER 4:

Fixing Roller Skates

Forgiving never meant forgetting one whose universe ends at the tip of his nose.

"Kory, Ephen has been hit by a car," Billy yelled from the other side of the fence.

"You're lying. I'm going to send you home crying, like I did last week," Kory warned just before he made another basket in his friend's backyard.

"I'm not kidding. He was hit by a car on Champlain Street after he made the turn from Kalorama Road on his roller skates. He's hurt real bad. His head is cracked in half, and blood is everywhere."

Kory jumped the fence and ran through the alley until he reached the front of his mother's duplex. There his mother stood; her face told him Billy had not lied.

"He's dead, Kory," she said as she reached for him.

"I don't believe you!" Kory pulled away from her. "He's not dead. He wouldn't leave me alone again. He promised! He promised!" Kory started running toward the scene of the accident.

"Don't go there," she pleaded through her sobs.

"You can't stop me. I'm going to see Ephen."

After running the six blocks to Champlain Street, he saw, sitting alone in the gutter just before the intersection, one of his brother's mangled roller skates, and below the crest of the hill, streams of his brother's life baked on the hot pavement as he got closer to a whispering crowd. Ephen was lying motionless on his back, head covered with a blood-soaked sheet and feet bare.

"That's his little brother there," someone yelled in the crowd.

"Poor little thing. They don't have a father," bleated an old lady with curlers in her hair and wearing a quilted housecoat, defying the searing heat that afternoon.

"Everyone stay back until the ambulance gets here. Kid, I said stand back," ordered one of the few white faces in the crowd, who happened to be wearing a badge and gun.

"I want to see my brother. He'll be all right. Just let me help him get up."

"You can't help him now." The policeman placed a hand on Kory's shoulder.

A screaming ambulance all but drowned out his voice as Kory pleaded. "Ephen! Ephen! It's me. Get up! I found your roller skates. Mommy is going to be mad at you."

Kory kicked the policeman in the shin. He ran to his brother and knelt down. "I can fix your skates. Mommy won't know you broke them again." He dangled the bent skate over the bloody sheet. "Ephen, you've got to get up before she gets here. You're going to get another spanking." He searched under the sheet for his brother's hand. Just as the policeman was about to grab him, Ephen moved his head.

"He's still alive," yelled the other white face in the crowd, standing next to the car with the bloodied windshield.

The ambulance medic pulled back the bloodstained sheet and revealed the little boy's battered head as it slowly flailed side to side. Ephen's skull had been fractured; lumps of bloodied gray brain matter oozed through the cracks and clumped on the oven-hot pavement. As the police officer held the sheet to block the afternoon sun, the ambulance worker checked for a pulse. They applied compresses to his head, legs, and arms, and loaded him into the ambulance. As it screamed away with its flashing lights, little Kory was still standing in the middle of the street, holding his brother's skates. "Ephen, please don't die. You promised…"

An hour later, the Toiles, Elaine Vanon's father's oldest and closest friends, who lived directly across from Children's Hospital, offered to lodge Kory and his mother for the night. He slept in the guest bedroom with his mother holding him tight against her heart.

CHAPTER 5

Hands from Above

Dr. Grayson, head of neural surgery, spoke with Kory's grandfather minutes before going into the operating room.

"Bishop, we'll do everything medically possible. But to be honest with you, your grandson's fate will be in the hands of someone with better skills than mine. Sorry to say, your little grandson doesn't have much of a chance surviving surgery. He has massive trauma to his brain and compound fractures to both legs, and his right arm is broken in two. Even if he were to make it off my table, chances of him speaking or walking again are remote."

The Right Reverend Vanon had to speak to Ephen's doctor without Ephen's mother. The reality of losing her firstborn child kept her ridden with fear between the creases of a tear-stained pillow. Colonel Israel "Butch" Toile, an army surgeon, had given her a sedative to calm her. The injection was strong enough to knock her off her feet but too weak to stem her desire to flee and, for brief moments, thoughts of suicide. She held Kory tight to stay alive.

After Ephen's doctor left the waiting room, Colonel Toile and Reverend Vanon found a tiny chapel down the hall. There they knelt, until the bishop's often-introspective friend reached out across the silence.

"Stephen, I treated hundreds of similar injuries like this during the war. I've seen boys with half of their heads blown away recover and lead normal lives. But, as Dr. Grayson said, he's in the hands of God." Colonel Toile placed his hand on the bishop's shoulder.

"Butch, please pray with me," Bishop Vanon said. He had to clear his throat. "Lord, please give my little Ephen the strength to live through the night. You've taken the one person I loved more than life itself, which I still do not understand. Please don't take the life of my grandson, who has only begun to live."

As a glimmer of dawn streamed to the peak of a golden cross sitting on the tiny altar, Bishop Vanon appeared to have frozen in supplication with his head buried in his folded hands. Colonel Toile, completely exhausted, was sitting in a pew. Reverend Vanon had not moved once from his knees all night.

A voice whispered from the doorway. "Reverend Vanon, Dr. Grayson needs to see you right away," the nurse said.

"Has something happened?"

"I'm sorry, Reverend. I can't tell you anything except that the doctor wants to see you right away in the recovery room."

"Stephen, if he's there, Ephen must have pulled through," said Colonel Toile. He looked into Reverend Vanon's eyes for affirmation.

"Butch, I know he's going to be alive when we get there."

When the elevator door opened to the seventh floor, Bishop Vanon and Colonel Toile were met by wails coming from the end of the hall, from a woman clutching the knees of a surgeon still fully masked, who diffidently tried to console the hysterical mother with his gloved hands.

"Oh, God, please don't take him. He's all I have. Why, God? He's just a baby. It was my fault, Jesus. Please take me. I can't live if he dies," wailed the mother. She was wearing a party dress. A nun held her from behind.

"Father, have mercy on your children." Bishop Vanon looked toward the white acoustic-tiled ceiling just before the entrance to the recovery room.

"We're here to see Dr. Grayson," the colonel stated to the duty nurse.

"Just a minute, please. I'll page him for you. If you would like to take a seat, he shouldn't be long."

"Thank you. Is there a coffee machine nearby?" inquired Colonel Toile.

"Yes. Just past the elevators and turn right."

"Get something for yourself, Butch. I'm not moving from here until he comes out."

"Stephen, you haven't had anything to eat or drink in almost twenty-four hours. As a physician, I am directing you take something before we have another person in your family in the hospital."

The Right Reverend Vanon looked exhausted; his eyes were puffy, and the white stubble of a beard was apparent.

"Butch, I don't need anything but good news right now."

"How about a cup of broth?"

"I'll have a cup of hot cocoa. It's Ephen's favorite," said his grandfather. He leaned his head against the wall and closed his eyes.

As he retreated inside himself, Reverend Vanon went back in time. He was inside the emergency room of Freedmen's Hospital. It was the never-ending day his wife died from smoke inhalation caused by a fire that started the morning his daughter failed to return home from a night of revelry. His prayers were unanswered that morning.

"Here you are." The Colonel handed the hot paper cup of cocoa to his friend. "Why don't you try to get this down? In the meantime, I'll call the house and check on Elaine and Kory."

"Butch, you are a good friend. Don't know if I could have held together without you here."

"Stephen, one would never know it. You seem to be getting all the support you need from outside this hospital, or maybe from some place above the hospital." He winked.

The bishop took a sip. "I thought you were going to call Mattie."

The colonel could not help yawning before he spoke: "Maybe I should be drinking the cocoa! I'll be back shortly."

It was a quick walk to the phone booth. "Mattie, how is everyone?"

"Forget about us for the moment. How is Ephen?"

"We're still waiting for his surgeon. Ephen is in recovery."

"Amen to that. I haven't slept a wink thinking about you being there, trying to support Stephen."

"As usual, he is holding his own and that of others."

"Well, I wish I could give you a good report on Elaine and Kory."

"Has something happened?"

"Yes. Would you believe Elaine went out with someone about two hours ago without even telling me where she was going?"

"Nothing would surprise me about that confused young lady. Do you know with whom she left?"

"He said his name was Buzz. He looked like a young Cab Calloway but without the refinement."

"And how is Kory?"

"He cried himself to sleep last night. Later, when I went in to check on them, he kept saying in his sleep he had the roller skates. This morning, I prepared a good breakfast for him, but he would only drink a glass of milk. He said his mother seldom cooks breakfast for them. Those poor children! Elaine should be horsewhipped for the way she neglects those two boys. Sorry. How is Stephen holding up?"

"Like a rock on the outside. But we know since Phoneica died, he has poured his heart out into his grandsons."

"Well, it's almost lunchtime. I'm going to see if I can get Kory to take his nose out of your medical books and eat some lunch."

"That boy is quite a reader. It's amazing he can even pronounce the terms in some of my books at his age. I wish we had a son like him. God is truly whimsical in giving those who really deserve it the least. We could have made a good home for those boys."

"Butch, we've talked about this many times. I'm sorry I was never able to give you children. I think we are a bit old to be raising two troubled boys at our ages."

"Sorry I brought it up. Ah…I see Ephen's doctor heading this way. I'll call you as soon as we have an update."

"Tell Stephen I've been praying all night."

"He wouldn't believe that hogwash. I think he knows you are godless."

"Is that what he told you?"

"No. That's what I told him."

"How dare you!"

"Listen, this is not the time for this. I'll talk to you later." Colonel Toile hung up before his wife had a chance to fire back.

"Well, Dr. Grayson, how is my grandson?"

"A team of doctors has reviewed his chart. All our medical knowledge indicates your grandson should be dead. He's still not breathing on his own, but his blood pressure is approaching normal. Our greatest concern now is the swelling on his brain. If we don't reduce it, he may have permanent damage. We need to operate again, but I need permission to proceed. This will be a very complicated operation. Is his mother here yet to sign the consent form?"

"No, she's still sedated. I'll sign whatever is necessary."

"Okay. We'll prep him for the surgery. Just see the duty nurse, and she will give you the consent forms."

"Thank you for the good news."

"We're not out of the woods yet, but your grandson has more than a seventy percent chance, which are better odds than when he first got here. I'm always amazed at the power of faith."

"Are you a religious man, Dr. Grayson?"

"No, Reverend. But do I believe God directs my hands every time I go into the operating room."

"Amen," said Reverend Vanon, with a look of relief.

"Stephen, you haven't touched your cocoa. Why don't you take a few sips before it turns cold?" said the colonel. He placed the cup next to the signed consent forms.

"Butch, you are becoming a nag in your old age. Ugh, this is terrible cocoa."

"I believe the sign on the machine said HOT; maybe it was meant to be drunk before you reached your next birthday."

"What a profound idea. I'll have to put that in one of my sermons."

"I can hear you now: 'My brothers and sisters, is your cup of faith half full or half empty?'" said the colonel. He took another Benson & Hedges cigarette from its gold-and-gray box.

"You'd better stick to medicine. While you're at it, Doctor, please let me have one of those awful cigarettes of yours."

"I thought you gave up cigarettes for your pipe again."

"Time to switch again."

"How do you know when it's time to switch?"

"That's the easy part. I always switch for Lent, but lately I find my throat telling me it would appreciate receiving irritation from a different source."

"Maybe you should give them up entirely."

"A man needs sins to repent. Surely you don't expect me to destroy the equilibrium of the Holy See."

"You make it sound so simple. It's as if you've reduced the desires of man into a regimented formula that can be redacted into dates on the calendar. You had better be careful. Someone may come out with a manual and eliminate your job."

"It's called the Bible, Butch."

"The Bible! Now that sounds like a good title for a book. Do you think anyone will read it?"

"Hope not—if they all did, then all those years in the seminary would have been for naught. Reading the Bible is no great intellectual challenge. Trying to make it sound interesting to paying customers is."

"Now you are starting to sound like me."

"God perish the thought! You and Mattie have turned cynicism into a monastic tryst of self-indulgence."

"We go to church."

"And we thank you for coming. Why do you, and particularly Mattie, go to church?"

"Well, you know I believe in God, whereas Mattie, being a mathematician, hopes one day to find the cardinal reason for faith."

"Thank you for that, Butch. I've been waiting forty years for someone to admit that. Has she ever considered pondering the ordinal reason for faith? Therein lies the essence of faith and man's association with God."

"There are times when you make faith sound so simplistic that I think even she could throw away her slide rule for the Golden One."

"I appreciate your attempt to bring some levity to all that has happened in the past twenty-four hours." Bishop Vanon took another sip of the tepid brew and grimaced.

"There you go again, belittling my lightness of being. I was trying to be serious. We can't all be as fortunate as you to have had such Calvinist parents."

"Butch, there are times you are full of sh...I mean dog mess. They were not Calvinists. In fact, they believed man should spend his lifetime preparing for heaven, whereas the Calvinists, with their selective salvation, all but made that pursuit futile."

"Thanks for the dissertation. Isn't your clerical collar removable?"

"Where are you headed with this? Of course it is."

"Stephen, you are not saying what you are feeling right now. I know you are angry with Elaine, but you refuse to express it."

"Please don't be offended, but this is an area where it may be difficult for you to empathize without ever having been there."

"Just because we don't have children doesn't mean we don't understand what you're going through."

"This has nothing to do with understanding. It's all about how parents naturally blame themselves for whatever their children do. When something like this happens, I can't stop wondering what I or Phoenicia did or did not do that caused Elaine to make so many inimical choices."

"Stephen, regardless of what you did, she is an adult, and she made her choices. Maybe this is one of those times when God chose for her."

"Maybe, Butch. I hope God makes the right choice now."

"Reverend Vanon, please follow me."

"Where are you taking me?" he asked as he jumped to his feet.

"Dr. Grayson called the duty desk to ask to have you follow me to the recovery room."

"How is my grandson?"

"You'll be able to ask his doctor in a few minutes."

"But you are able to answer me now."

"Jesus has been up all night, Reverend."

"Amen," said Reverend Vanon.

"You will see his love today," said the nurse with a scrubbed smile that reflected light bouncing off the cross hanging from her neck.

There was his little grandson in the dimly lit room. He was shrouded nearly head to toe and surrounded by machines and tubes pumping life into his motionless body.

"Reverend, we were able to stop the bleeding and reduce the swelling. It's too early to know if there will be any permanent impairment, but we are very optimistic, given what we've seen so far. Because of his age, his brain is better able to adapt to any changes than yours or mine. He needs to sleep right now, so I have prescribed a heavy sedative to promote a deep sleep. We will try to wake him around eleven o'clock tomorrow morning. I don't think he's in any real danger now, so I suggest you go home and get some rest."

"Thank you, Dr. Grayson. I know you have done your best. We'll have to wait for God to finish the job."

Dr. Grayson looked at the huge gold cross hanging from Reverend Vanon's neck. "What can I say, Reverend? That is your purview."

Colonel Toile dropped the Reverend Vanon at his house on Sixteenth Street and proceeded home. As he swung open the wrought-iron gate, Mattie, who was wearing a very large hat and her ever-present handbag hanging from her wrist, appeared at the door.

"Where are you off to?"

"Butch, Kory's missing!"

"What do you mean, missing?" He threw his cigarette onto the pavement.

"He isn't anywhere in the house. I also checked in the alley and around the corner at the store where he likes to buy his candy. They said he bought two candy bars about half an hour ago."

"You should have been watching him."

"Butch, I can't watch him every second. There are things one must do outside of the vision of others. But let's not argue. I think you should call Stephen."

"That poor man. I just dropped him off, and now you're telling me I have to tell him while one of his grandsons is fighting for his life in a hospital, the other is missing from the care of his best friends."

"Just call him, please. I'm going to check at the store one more time before we drive around the neighborhood."

Mrs. Toile started the car and waited for her husband.

"Mattie, he didn't answer his phone, which could mean he is fast asleep."

They drove to Kory's neighborhood and asked the children if they had seen him. Most of the children on the block knew Mrs. Toile as the no-nonsense principal of Morgan Elementary School, a few blocks away.

"Hi, Ms. Toile! Kory was here about twenty minutes ago. He borrowed Billy's roller-skate key to fix Ephen's skates. We thought Ephen was dead."

"He's not dead, everyone. It will be a while before you see him again, but he should be back in school in a few months."

"Mattie, what did you say Kory was moaning in his sleep?"

"Why didn't I think about that? He's probably at the hospital."

"Keep your fingers crossed we'll find him there and not have to call Stephen."

They drove in silence. Mattie chain-smoked cigarettes. The colonel just closed his eyes and thought about all the "ifs" in the rear-view mirror.

CHAPTER 6:

Search for Cain

Imagine the universe and the mind of a child.

"Where's my big brother?"

"What's your brother's name?" asked the young woman wearing a candy-striped habit behind the reception desk.

"Ephen!"

"Ephen? What's your brother's last name?"

"The same as mine! I'm Kory Vanon, his little brother. Uh…he's waiting for me."

"Hmm, just a minute, and I'll check what room your brother is in."

As the young woman searched, Kory sat on the floor and worked on Ephen's roller skates.

"I found your brother…Where did you go?"

"Here I am. You found him?"

"Yes, I found him, but where are your parents? You're too young to see your brother in the recovery room by yourself."

"I'm six years old and in the first grade."

"Yes, you are a big little man, but I can't let you see your brother without an adult. He's very sick. Those are hospital rules."

"But I told him I would fix his roller skates and bring them to the hospital. Please let me see him. He's going to cry if I don't give them to him." Kory pretended to hold back tears.

"I'm sorry, but there's nothing I can do. As I said before, your brother is still in the recovery room."

"Okay. My father is outside in the car. He'll take me to see my brother."

"Please bring your father back to this desk so I can talk to him first."

"All right, I'll get him."

Because Kory was so short, he simply waited for her to turn her back and walked unnoticed to the elevator.

"Can I help you?" asked a nurse dressed in a traditional Florence Nightingale white habit.

"I can't reach the elevator button. I'm going to see my big brother."

"And where is your brother?"

"He's in the recovery room. My father is waiting there for me. But I don't think I remember where it is."

"It's on the seventh floor. I'll press the button for you."

"Thank you. You look like the angel in *The Littlest Fairy* that my grandmother used to read to us before God took her away. Are you an angel?"

"Just for today. Okay, here's my floor. Now, when you get to the seventh floor, promise me that you will walk out as soon as the door opens. Will you promise me that?"

"I promise. Thank you, Lady Angel," he said, waving good-bye to her as the elevator door closed.

Kory jumped into the hallway when the door opened. He had hoped to avoid being seen, but a little girl in a wheelchair, holding a Betsy Wetsy doll, said, "Look, Mommy, he's got roller skates."

"And where are you going, young man?" asked a nurse behind the counter.

"Do you know where my daddy is? He's supposed to be reading a story to my big brother so he can go to sleep."

"Who is your brother?"

"Ephen. I mean Ephen Vanon."

"Let's see. Ah, yes, he's in recovery. You'll have to wait for your father to come out. Children aren't allowed there."

"Why not?"

"Because it's hospital policy."

"What's a policy?"

"It's like a rule, which means you have to obey it."

"My mother says rules are made to be broken."

"Your mother should not have told you that."

"My mother does whatever she wants."

"It sounds like it. But you still have to wait here until your father comes."

"Is there a playroom for kids?"

"Yes. It's just past the elevators, before the canteen."

"Thank you. I'll wait for him there until he comes to get me."

"I'll tell your father where to find you when he comes out."

CHAPTER 7:

The Key

Again Kory took advantage of his size. He went unnoticed by most hospital staff as he made his way around the corridor until he spotted a minister sitting in a waiting room, working on a sermon.

"Hi, my name is Kory. My grandfather is a minister like you, but I can't find him. He told me to meet him at the recovery room. I think I'm lost. Would you take me there, please?"

"Why, sure! Who is your grandfather?"

"Bishop Vanon."

The minister stood. "I know your grandfather quite well. He's spoken at our church many times. I'd love to see him again," he said as he took Kory's hand.

"Maybe he went to see my mother." Kory put on his best innocent smile as he looked up to the tall minister, recently recruited to do his bidding.

"Here we are. But I don't see your grandfather. Why don't you sit here while I check with the nurse?"

"Okay. I'll stay here until you find him."

As soon as the minister turned his back to talk to the duty nurse, Kory pushed open the heavy recovery-room door with all of his strength and used his feet to kick the roller skates inside. He hid behind a gurney draped with a sheet until he was sure no one was looking. It did not take long for him to find his brother's bed. He whispered in his ear, "Ephen, it's me, Kory. Wake up. I fixed your roller skates, but they're still a little wrinkly. Billy said he'd give me an axle that will make them like new. Are you glad?"

Ephen did not respond. The only sound in the room was a constant hiss from the respirator next to Ephen's bed.

"Why won't you talk to me? Mommy said she would take us to the beach when you get better."

Kory got in bed beside his brother, rolled the wheels on the skates, and continued to talk to Ephen. It wasn't long before he was fast asleep.

A nurse checking the respirator noticed an unusual protrusion under the sheet and discovered Kory clutching the roller skates to his chest with a half-eaten candy bar in his other hand. She phoned Bishop Vanon. The Toiles met him in the lobby and followed him to the recovery room.

"Steve, please forgive for me letting Kory out of the house."

"Mattie, it wasn't your fault. I know my little grandson. There's nothing in this world that could stop him from doing something once he has made his mind up. Kory has the resolution of an adult and the cleverness of an angel with a dirty face. Look at all that chocolate around his mouth," he said as he gently lifted Kory to his shoulder. "It's time to take him home with me."

"Steve, why not let us take him with us? You need to sleep," said Mattie. She reached inside her large handbag to find a tissue to clean Kory's face.

"I greatly appreciate all you've done, but it is time for me to step in and provide the stability Elaine can't. If you were to take him home tonight, he would just run away again. His brother is unconscious, and his mother is nowhere to be found. In his way, he's just trying to please everyone and bring some order to his world. His methods may be a bit unorthodox, even for a six-year-old, but you must admit they are effective."

"Hi, Granpa. Are we going home now?" Kory asked in his sleepy voice.

"Yes. With the help of the Lord, Granpa is going to make everything all right."

As the Toiles drove back in their smoke-filled car, Mattie stopped puffing on her cigarette long enough to ask her husband a question: "Do you think Kory will grow up to be a manipulator like his mother?"

The colonel rolled down his window and flicked his burning Benson & Hedges cigarette into the wind. "Not quite. She could learn a thing or two about life from him."

It was almost a year before Ephen was well enough to leave the hospital. Kory had started to enjoy being the only child in the house.

The two boys never saw the inside of their old home on V Street again. Their mother, with the help of her father, purchased a modest house in a quiet neighborhood in uptown Northwest Washington, D.C.

The Petworth section of Washington in the early 1950s was still mostly Jewish, with well-kept lawns. There, children could play in the street.

While her sons got used to their new surroundings, Elaine Vanon busied herself making a real home for them. Now they would have separate bedrooms and a large yard with many trees for the dog Kory wanted. The new house also afforded Elaine privacy and space to escape from her children when she needed to—something that happened all too often. By the time Kory and Ephen reached fifth grade, they saw little of her except at dinner, and that was limited to her setting the table with whatever she felt like cooking that night. She seldom ate with them.

Since the boys were close in age, rivalry and jealousy often defined their relationship. But when there was a dearth of support, which was often, the two often-combative brothers buried their differences in times of need. Their errant parent forced them to rely on each other, albeit in a mostly one-sided way: Ephen depended on his younger brother's succor, whereas Kory had resolved to confront life solely with creative machination after the death of his grandmother. He was satisfied to spend eternity unable to seek advice from anyone except an inner sage. Discovering his ability to look inside himself so early in life assured Kory a trustworthy mentor. From then on, within every shadow glimmered a phospene reminding him that he was unique and alone in the universe.

CHAPTER 8:

Apron Strings

Perhaps J. M. Barrie had it right in his magnum opus *Peter Pan*. Growing up should have been an option to every newborn before its umbilical cord was severed. Once done, the search began for the warmth and security of being oblivious to all sounds except a proximate heart echoing through a primordial broth seasoned with universal consciousness, an ether dispelling the notion of tabula rasa and affirming the oneness of everything and the absurdity of black space.

Kory Vanon entered the world innocent of prior acts but not necessarily without forethought of possibilities. The loss of his childhood following the death of his grandmother commenced frequent treks inside to reshape what others accepted as a preordained reality; doing so set boundaries but did not preclude yielding to the power of raging hormones responding to pheromones filling the air and titillating the senses of a typical adolescent.

Blossoming protrusions under tight-fitting blouses, little more than bee stings on peaches a few months earlier, demanded more concentration than homework or sports. Those budding debutantes induced fantasies in "red-blooded" boys, who stole away to their comic book–filled bedrooms to flip through the lingerie section of a discarded Sears catalog before dinner.

Kory's mouth always watered when he thought about the sweet taste of red candy lipstick the girls practiced with, before they replaced it with a brass bullet–size sample of the real thing, provided by the neighborhood Avon Lady, whose Interlude perfume wafted inside the imaginations of boys as they played King of the Mountain and made up tales of what they had already done or hoped to do.

Yes, Kory loved everything about girls—especially the ones who wore the new miniskirts with Slingshot shoes and danced the D.C. Swing to the music of The Temptations' top-ten hit "The Way You Do the Things You Do."

Seldom lost for words by the time he entered high school, Kory usually found a compliment for every girl he espied, even the ones other boys ignored. What they missed, he discovered: the less popular girls were often friends with the gorgeous girls in school. They provided valuable information about future conquests he hoped to add to his list, hidden in a black book under his pillow. His system worked well for him, but it did little to endear him to his male classmates. When he was not wooing a new girl, walking home alone was better than herding with the boys.

During the hours when his hormones were not dictating life, being in his own company—reading whatever he could find or playing the piano in his basement hideaway—filled the vacant time slots left by the absence of perfume glissading across his brain. And when utterly bored, he hurried through his homework with little desire than to finish.

Most of his assignments were unimaginative, so he was seldom motivated to do more than required, which kept him near the top of his class but never made him the teacher's pet. With the exception of advanced math, he was already well versed in most subjects offered at the public high school he attended for one year. Before he transferred to a prep school, Kory had read his entire set of encyclopedias more than three times. And when it came to English class, he spent more time writing short stories than parsing the requisite American literature he had read the year before.

In dating, Kory never courted Patience; therefore, when the time to begin driving neared, he availed himself of the opportunities to practice at Highland Beach (an exclusive African American bayside resort), where parents allowed their children to drive unlicensed around the five miles of flat private roads. So as soon as he reached fifteen years and six months of age, he was eligible to take the driver's education course at his high school. He could barely wait for the semester to end so he could pick up one of his girlfriends in the new, shiny black Renault he had been promised—if he made the honor roll again.

One late Sunday afternoon in 1965, Kory was in the recreation room, practicing the new hit by Ramsey Lewis, "The 'In' Crowd," from the sheet music he had purchased Saturday afternoon, when his mother knocked on the door. With the exception of calling him for dinner, she usually forgot he was down there.

"Kory, may I come in?"

He took off his glasses before he answered. "Sure, Mother. Is something wrong?"

She stood in the doorway with her hands on her hips. "This is quite a little hideaway you've made down here. How would you like to take a break from your routine and go to a cocktail party with me this afternoon?"

"Uh...sure!"

"Now that you're driving, I think you are old enough to handle yourself around drinking adults. Your Auntie Susie is having a party, and she said that you are welcome to come. Do you think you can drag yourself away from your music long enough to drive to her house for a few drinks?"

"If I didn't have a car, would you still ask me to accompany you?"

"Normally, a remark like that from you would anger me, but now, since you've grown up so much, I don't feel so guilty about not being the best parent in the world. Let's think of it as two friends going out for a good time."

Kory knew his mother's car was being repaired, so he pretended to believe her. "I can learn this new song anytime. What time is the party?"

"You have just enough time to take a shower," she said as she picked up his sheet music. "I have this album in my collection. If you're careful with it, you may borrow it."

"Thanks, but it's more fun to play it on the piano." Kory played a few bars.

"That's pretty good. You have a good touch for jazz, although I wish you would continue your classical training."

Kory quickly played Chopin's *Minute* Waltz for his mother and then started Beethoven's *Moonlight* Sonata.

"You could have been a classical pianist—if you hadn't cut some of the nerves and tendons in your hands in that stupid bicycle accident."

"I find classical music technically challenging, but jazz takes me into outer space."

"And that's where most jazz musicians are living—in outer space. Most of them live from day to day and die in poverty."

"Well, Beethoven, Mozart, and Bach never made enough money to properly support their families."

"You are so much like me. You have a smart answer for everything."

"I'm not responsible for the genes I inherited, am I?"

Now slightly exasperated, she turned her back to him. "Take your shower, young man!"

"Whatever you say, Mother!"

Kory wanted to appear older for the party. A two-piece dark gray suit topped with a burgundy ascot enhanced the illusion. But the charade was not complete until he sneaked into his mother's bathroom while she took a chicken from the freezer for the next night's dinner. Her eyebrow pencil gave continuity to his fledgling moustache, an advancement of nature's handiwork.

Auntie Susie was not a relative. She was his mother's best friend, who always treated him like the son she'd never had. When Kory had been in junior high school, he had frequently stopped by, since her house was only two blocks from his school.

As he held the car door open for his mother, something caught his eye. "I thought you didn't like Phoenicia's pearl necklace."

"Now that you are becoming a young man, always remember a woman has the right to change her mind anytime she pleases," she said, as she ran her fingers around one of the few pieces that had once belonged to her mother.

Kory did not answer her immediately. He thought about a reply as he walked to the driver's side and sat down.

"If that's true, then does that mean I can sometimes forget to do something you asked me to do, because I think you might change your mind?"

His mother gave him a look children are very familiar with, the one that contained a thousand words of warning.

"Do you think you we can get Susie's without a debate?"

"I mean, I was just asking a question, Mother."

"And you have your answer. Now drive!"

The car lurched forward as he quickly released the clutch. "Yes, ma'am!"

"Why can't you be more like your brother?" she said, as she waved to a neighbor pruning her roses: the same retired elementary-school principal whom Kory had played a mean prank on three Halloweens ago. He blew up her bed of roses with a well-placed cherry bomb. Sometimes when the boys played in the alley, a stray ball would end up in her flowers. She usually refused to return them, despite the apologies they gave and their offers to clean up the mess they made.

He shifted into second gear as they passed the entrance to Rock Creek Cemetery. "Because I'm more like you. You did say that, did you not?"

Kory grinned inside when he considered adding, *Unless you have changed your mind.* But he knew that would be pushing his luck, and he would have nowhere to run if she decided she had heard enough.

Elaine Vanon had never been in her son's car. She looked a little out of place riding in such a small vehicle. His mother was a very elegant woman. From the time she was a young girl, everyone had commented on how pretty she was. And all through school, she had always been voted the most attractive girl at Dunbar High, whose students were children mostly from the "Black Elite" of Washington, D.C. If they were not from the best families, then they had to be so light in complexion that success would be guaranteed for those who looked most like their grandparents' previous owners.

Elaine Vanon had both of those advantages. She had the world at her feet, but the youngest child in a competitive family frequently makes bad choices, and she had. It would have been easy for her to have had her choice of any man she wanted to marry from her circle. Instead, she had defied her family and dated a man from another high school, whose social standing and physical characteristics were eschewed by families who worked hard to insulate their little society from those they did not consider worthy of admission to their exclusionary world.

Elaine broke the silence. "I must say, you keep your car as immaculate as your bedroom."

"I'm glad it pleases you," Kory said, as he changed gears to slow down at the light in front of the Basilica of the National Shrine of the Immaculate Conception.

"You even drive well. It's good you took the driver's education course."

"I think I learned more about driving from you at Highland Beach and watching the way you responded to changing conditions on the roadway."

Elaine Vanon looked at an old woman who was dressed in a powder-blue maid's uniform and waiting at a bus stop. She reminded Elaine of Kory's paternal grandmother. "That's one of the few skills I got from your father that's worth keeping."

"He never offered to teach me or Ephen to drive," he said, as they crossed the railroad bridge near the Catholic University of America.

"How could he? He's too busy trying to impress one of his new girlfriends to worry about his children."

"Mother, why did you marry him?" Kory searched her face for an answer.

"I was only nineteen and gullible. Your father was a very charming man. But once I got past the wrapping paper, I was left with a box of disappointment. I don't wish to berate your father to you. It's up to you to decide what kind of man he is and what kind of man you will be. I pray you do not make the rebellious mistakes I did. Kory, always remember it is very romantic to fall in love with the first person who tickles your fancy, but when the honeymoon is over, things such as character and family background become more important."

"It wasn't all bad. You have me."

His mother looked at him, ran her fingers through his hair, and kissed him on the cheek.

"What was that for?" he asked.

"That was for me."

Kory did not have a reply for that one.

It was obvious something was going on at Auntie Susie's house. There were expensive cars parked in every usually available space on her street. As they approached the walkway, they could hear music and laughter coming from the garden. The front door was open, and the smell of liquor, cigarettes, and perfume greeted them at the threshold. Elaine Vanon introduced her son to a few of her friends seated in the living room and quickly left him on his own. He walked to the rear of the house and took a seat at the bar in the sunroom so he could watch the adults play their games.

Kory was smoking a Winston cigarette from one of the many packs lying on the highly polished oak bar, when he felt the arms of someone around his shoulders. He recognized the perfume and knew it was his Auntie Susie. When he turned around, he saw she had the usual happy, glazed look that most adults get when they have been drinking scotch.

Auntie Susie gave him a kiss on the cheek. "Why are you sitting here alone? Do you want something to eat? How about something to drink?"

"I'm a little thirsty," he answered.

"What would you like to drink? I have everything," she said, as she went behind the bar.

"How about a beer?"

"Your mother would kill me if I gave you one. Who gives you beer?" Auntie Susie demanded.

"My father's mother—that is, Grandma Bertie—lets me sip her Ballantine Ale."

"She drinks Ballantine Ale? Oh, your mother told me your father's mother was from southern Maryland. Women from there drink home-made wine and ale. Now, if I give you one, you have to promise not to tell your mother."

"If she sees me drinking it, I'll just tell her I got it for myself. Anyway, an hour from now and after she's had a few drinks, I doubt she'll care."

"Kory, try not to be so hard on your mother. She does the best she can. You know that you and Ephen are her life."

He looked at Auntie Susie in disbelief. Kory decided not to negate what she said and enjoyed his glass of Champale.

"Wow! This is really good! I promise to drink it slowly."

"I can tell you are not experienced in sneaking a drink—like I was when I was your age. If you take your time, your mother will surely catch you."

He upended his glass. "That was better than any soda I ever had, Auntie Susie!"

"I'm glad you liked it," she said, as she poured a Coke for him into a red tumbler. "Remember how good it tasted, because you'll be drinking soft drinks for the rest of the evening."

"I could handle another!"

"I'm sure you could, but not in my house, young man." She placed a rose-colored crystal bowl filled with mixed salted nuts on the bar.

"Just kidding, Auntie Susie." Kory stared across the garden. "Who's the lady in the red dress sitting on the stool?"

"Her! That's Ramona. We grew up on the same street. Your mother doesn't like her, for some reason."

"Does she always wear such big earrings? She looks like a movie star."

"Her nickname is Carmen. She's very popular with the gentlemen," she said with exasperation.

"I sure would like to meet her."

"Ramona! Bring yourself over here," Auntie Susie commanded.

"And who's this young man?" Ramona asked, as she sat down beside Kory and crossed her shapely legs, which were covered with red stockings. He could see just a hint of her black garter peeking under the hem of her tight red dress. He took a big gulp of his cold Coke and tried not to look.

"Ramona, this is Kory—Elaine's son," Auntie Susie said.

Her earrings jingled as she threw back her long, black, wavy hair. "My, my, my. What an attractive young man he is!"

"I like your earrings. You look like Carmen Jones," Kory remarked.

"I like him already. Anyone who compares me to Dorothy Dandridge is on my good list."

Kory added, "You're prettier than Dorothy Dandridge."

Ramona began rubbing his leg. "And how old are you, Kory?"

"I'm old enough. I mean, old enough to drive," he stumbled.

"And he drives, too." Her hand was still on Kory's thigh.

Auntie Susie admonished, "You better leave him alone. You're old enough to be his mother. And speaking of mothers, Elaine is walking up behind you."

Ramona turned around. "Elaine, I want your son."

Kory started to cover his ears, expecting to hear his mother hurl the most vituperative words at Ramona.

Elaine Vanon said with a very smug look, "Take him. Maybe you'll learn something."

After taking her hand off of Kory's leg, Ramona started to say, "You bit—"

Auntie Susie broke in, "Watch your mouth, Ramona. You know you're wrong, and you deserve what she's saying to you."

"I was just fooling around," Ramona cowered.

"Ramona, you don't fool around with my sixteen-year-old son. He probably thinks you're serious," Elaine exhorted.

Hoping to diffuse the situation, Kory said, "No, I didn't. I knew it was just a game. I told her she looked like Dorothy Dandridge."

"You must be referring to her backside," Elaine said.

"All right, Elaine! You've made your point. I'm sorry if I offended you and your son," Ramona said, as she stood up and smoothed down her tight dress.

Elaine broke in, "You owe Susie an apology as well." Ramona got up and walked away in the direction of the garden.

"Let her go, Elaine. I'll deal with her later," Auntie Susie said. She poured another Coke for Kory, who was still watching Ramona.

"Who is that tramp with tonight?" Elaine asked.

"Come on, Elaine—it's over." Auntie Susie poured Elaine a drink. "If you must know, she's with Ted Hagans, the owner of the Dunbar Hotel."

"I know him. Does he ever go anywhere with his wife? He asked me to dinner a few times. I told him I don't dine with married men," Elaine said.

"The owner of the Dunbar Hotel is here?" Kory asked.

"Ramona just perched her backside in his lap," Elaine remarked.

"A friend of mine told me they have a training program for desk clerks. I wonder if he would hire me for the summer."

"Kory, that hotel is filled with some of the worst people in society. I don't any son of mine in the mud."

"It would only be for the summer. I can take care of myself."

"What do you think, Susie?" Elaine asked.

"Ted would not let anything happen to him. I've got too much dirt on him. If you'll let Kory apply there, I know I can convince Ted to hire him; besides, the Dunbar has escaped its past. Ted remodeled the hotel last year and threw the miscreants into the street—even the ones who paid their rent on time. Now most of them live in the Whitelaw Hotel. You know the place—two doors from Duke Ellington's house."

"Okay. But make sure he knows I'm still a little apprehensive about Kory working there," Elaine added.

Auntie Susie introduced Kory to Ted Hagans. When she told him Kory wanted to work in his hotel, he agreed so quickly that Kory worried Ted would not remember him, given that the well-dressed man with the prematurely gray patch of hair was having such a hard time holding his tall glass filled with Cutty Sark scotch.

CHAPTER 9

The Dunbar Hotel—A Lesson in Room Service

The heart of the African American community in the District of Columbia beat loudest along U Street. Even though desegretion opened many "Whites Only" doors, those with sepia palms wanting admission tickets to theaters and nightclubs seldom ventured downtown, unless it was for a slap in the face to remind them the Nation's Capitol was still a Southern city; instead, "separate but equal" venues were within steps of where Duke Ellington and other entertainers lived and played.

Richmond, Virginia, the former capital of the Confedercy during the Civil War, was less than one hundred miles from a Congress that would eventually mitigate its hypocrisy by passing the Thirteenth Amendment to the US Constitution. Three years prior to its passage, Washington, DC, with a long history of comparative racial tolerance, boasted a first by freeing its slaves by an executive order from President Abraham Lincoln in 1862. More than one hundred years later, in 1966, despite Washington being legally open to all residents, it was still culturally divided. Kory barely noticed. While white teenagers enjoyed *American Bandstand* on television,

DC high schoolers watched and went to *Teenarama* to see their idols in the brown flesh.

The last time Tina Turner had appeared on the local TV show, Kory had not been able to get a ticket. But during summer vaction in 1966, the sultry, long-legged chanteuse of "River Deep—Mountain High" was doing a matinee show at one of the premier stops along the Chitlin' Circuit: the Howard Theatre, just off Seventh and Florida Avenue.

Because Kory's summer job had him training on weekends and working shifts Monday through Friday, this was his last chance for fun before classes resumed in the fall.

After two weeks of training with three other interns, all related to the owner, he was assigned the midnight tour with the night auditor, even though math had been far from one of his favorite subjects.

So there Kory was, only sixteen years old and working at the largest black-owned business in Washington, DC. Auntie Susie's appraisal of the hotel had been slightly exaggerated: despite "The Dunbar" having been renovated, it was still the last choice of black entertainers and professionals who could stay at the Hilton and other well-known hotels downtown. Regular guests in the midsixties were often entertainers needing to save money. But there was another class of guests, what Kory's mother called "the unrefined": an eschewed olio of black society composed of philandering couples, pimps, prostitutes, bank robbers, and immoral evangelists—the people he had only heard about. Upper Northwest Washington, where Kory had grown up, was a world away from those living day to day.

It did not take long to realize the advantages of coming to work at midnight. During his initial training on the day shift, he had checked the typical tourists in and out. But at night emerged the personalities who slept most of the day; their pupils were unusually dilated when they checked in just before dawn.

Couples rendezvousing for a tryst were usually in the first wave of guests. Most avoided eye contact. But as daybreak neared, pimps and ladies of the evening threw down hundred-dollar bills on the hotel desk. The ladies smelled of cheap perfume as they sashayed down the hall in their micro mini skirts. The ones who checked in without a pimp liked to flirt with the new kid behind the desk. Some teased and taunted him because they knew from their street experience that he was young and ignorant of their lifestyle. One lady in particular loved to raise his blood pressure when she came in from "The stroll," as she referred to the streets where she plied her trade. Every other word she spoke was vernacular.

"Hey there, young stuff! Every morning I come in here, and you always justa working away on that thang. Whatcha doing with that big ole machine anyway?"

Kory straightened his tie before he answered. "It's called an NCR 9200 computer. I put in all the hotel's transactions of the day every morning."

"A computer? Like in *The Twilight Zone*?" she asked as she filled out the hotel registration card.

"Yes, something like that," he said, pretending to be engrossed in his work.

The lady of the evening slid the partially completed registration card to Kory. "You mean you even put in that I got a room at this place yesterday morning?"

Kory pushed his glasses higher on his nose as he read her registration card. "That's right, uh, Miss Phyllis Smith."

"That ain't my real name. I use it on the street. You know, if the cops bust me for walking too close to cars and stuff. Hey, young boy, you know that I'm a working girl, don'tcha?"

"Well, I kinda guessed that. You always come in around four a.m., and you usually pay with a fifty or hundred-dollar bill. It looks like you're making a lot of money out there."

"You got that right, Suga. I'm a thorough bitch. I made more money tonight than your lanky ass will make all week." She pulled a roll of bills from inside her bra and waved it under his nose. The whiff made him sweat.

"That's all right—I like what I do. How about you?" After the words left his mouth, he wished he had not gone so far.

"What-chou fucking talking about? I ain't gotta answer to no muva-fucker. And I ain't got no goddamn pimp."

"What's a pimp?"

"Young boy, you don't know shit from shinola! A pimp is a lowlife who'll take a ho's money and beats her with a pimp stick. That's a coat hanger he uses if she don't make her quota."

"That's a good reason to be by yourself. Don't you ever get lonely sleeping up in that big bed every night by yourself?"

"Baby, most times my feet are so tired, the only thing I want to do is soak in the tub with some bubbles up to my neck," she said as she checked her makeup in the mirror of a cheap white compact.

"So what do you do for fun when you are not working the streets?"

"I like screwing young boys like you—if they can get it up."

"Miss Smith, it is against hotel policy for employees to fraternize with guests." Kory took off his glasses and began cleaning them with his handkerchief.

"To frat…? What in the hell are you talking about? You must be one of those college boys."

"Ah…you guessed right. I start college this fall," he said with a straight face.

"A young boy like you couldn't handle a real woman like me."

"Is that a challenge, Miss Smith?"

"Get off of this 'miss' shit. My real name is Paulette. College boy, do you want some or not?"

Kory picked up her registration card, tore it into pieces, and threw it into the trash can. He also opened the register, counted the money she had paid for the room, and slammed it on the counter.

"What's wrong, young boy? Did I scare you? Ain't you going to give a lady a room here tonight?"

Kory grabbed a key from under one of the red-tagged room numbers on the pegboard. "Here is a key to an out-of-service room. If you really meant what you said, I'll meet you there in twenty minutes."

She rolled her tongue over her lips. "Don't make me wait too long now, young boy."

Paulette walked to the elevator and winked at Kory. He could hear footsteps coming from behind the back-office door. The night manager, who was also the head night auditor, often talked about spending some of his hard-earned money on Paulette.

When Kory told him he needed to take the bill to the manager of the Five Blind Boys, a well-known gospel singing group on the Chitlin' Circuit, the head auditor, Mr. Winston, told Kory he had overheard part of his conversation with Paulette. Kory also knew Mr. Winston sipped coffee laced with cheap scotch all night. His eyes were slightly red, but he appeared to be in a cheerful mood.

"Mr. Vanon, the Five Blind Boys' bus does not leave until eleven o'clock. Why don't you tell me the real reason you want to go upstairs?" Mr. Winston took a big sip from his coffee cup and lit a cigarette.

Kory stood in front of the night auditor's desk with his hands in his pockets. "There's no use trying to lie about it. Miss Smith, whom I know you are familiar with, invited me to spend a little time with her. She's not even going to charge me."

"You have the nerve to stand in front of me and expect me to allow you to neglect your duties just to go upstairs and get in bed with the very lady I was considering spending my paycheck on?"

Lost for words, Kory threw up his hands, expecting to be fired.

"Mr. Vanon, I'm going to say this just once—so you better listen closely."

Kory breathed a sigh of relief inside. "I think you are going to say that I deserve to be tossed out of the training program, but you are going to give me a second chance because I'm a teenager unable to control his hormones," he said contritely.

A wide grin spread across Mr. Winston's face. He took Kory's time card out of its slot and threw it on his desk. "Mr. Vanon, if you don't screw her brains out, you're fired."

"I'll do my best, sir."

"Hey, and one last thing: Mr. Hagans sometimes comes early on Monday to count his money. Listen up for the phone in case he makes it in before six."

"Yes, sir!"

Kory pressed the elevator bell three times before it dawned on him that the dark sunglasses–wearing operator was known to disappear around this time of the morning. It was rumored he had two prostitutes working for him in the hotel and that he sold half-pints of liquor to anyone willing to pay his bootleg price.

By the time he ran the eight flights, he was panting, not from the run but from anticipation. He took a deep breath and knocked stiffly on the door of room 369.

"It's not locked, baby," she whispered. Kory opened the door.

"Give me a minute. I'm still wet."

There was Paulette, nude and drying her flawless skin as she sat on the edge of a cerise duvet with Dunbar Hotel monogrammed in gold letters. Her damp skin glistened in the dimly lit room. With the exception of Tina Turner, he had never seen another woman for whom the miniskirt must have been invented. His fantasy had stepped out of his teenager's imagination and placed itself inches from his sweating fingers. Never had he expected to find this much perfection in one room, waiting for him enjoy it. Kory was only sixteen years old, tireless, inexperienced, and ready to learn.

"Take your pants off and let me see what you got, young boy. Don't take too long. I'm hot and juicy for you, baby. You probably shaking in your knees, ain't you, young boy?"

Kory had had little contact with his father when he was growing up. And when his father had died the year before, Kory's only inheritance had been his father's physical endowment. Kory was one of the boys in the locker room who never wrapped himself in a towel coming out the shower. He dropped his pants. "Well, take a look. Do you see my knees shaking?"

"Young stuff, I haven't looked at your knees yet. Don't need to look no further. Honey, you should have a license for that thang."

"You on the bed is all the license I need!" he said.

There was no foreplay. This was about a teenage boy's lust. She positioned one pillow under her rear and pulled him on top of her. Even though her skin was still wet from the shower , she still exuded sex from every pore of her body. He was on fire. It was as if someone had turned on an oven under his skin and set it on high. He rammed himself inside her and cupped his hands around the most perfectly formed buttocks he had ever held. They were tight with muscles. Kory prayed she would use them with her years of experience to take him to places he had only dreamed of in the privacy of his bedroom.

They started in the middle of the bed and soon rolled over onto the floor. Paulette ended up on top. Then he rolled her over and thrust so hard that his knees bled from the friction the carpet created. Several times Paulette tried to get on top again, but no sooner was she on top than Kory rolled her over again and again—until they ended up in the closet.

After thirty minutes of banging around in close quarters, Kory's feet knocked the sliding closet door off its hinges. It fell so hard that it cracked the screen of a new color television. The sound of the gas coming out of the smashed television made them take a breath and laugh—although Kory wondered how he was going to explain its destruction to housekeeping.

Paulette was lying on Kory's chest. "You are pretty good for a college boy."

"Does that mean I still need more lessons?"

"Yes, young boy, you still need more training," she said as she got up to go to the bathroom.

"I do have a name, you know," he said as he picked up the fallen closet door.

"I know your name, but I'm going to call you Sugar Stick from now on," she said as she closed the bathroom door.

Kory returned to the bed, still throbbing with desire. He knocked on the bathroom door and asked if he could come in. She told him she was only brushing her teeth. He walked up behind her and looked at himself standing behind her in the mirror. She smiled at him and rubbed her rear against his crotch. Kory entered her from the rear until she moaned for him not to stop. He picked her up with him still inside her, carried her back to the bed, and enraptured her body until the phone rang. It was the front desk.

"Kory, this is Winston. 'Thunder-Cloud'—that is, Mr. Hagans—just stumbled through the lobby en route to his office. You better get down here fast."

Paulette had turned to her side after the phone had rung. She had pulled the sheet only over her shoulder, leaving her chocolate cheeks exposed. Kory still yearned for more, but there was not enough time for him even to take a shower. He dressed quickly and wrote her a note thanking her for the good time he'd had. The message also told her she could stay in the room for another day, since he still needed more of her professional instruction.

When Kory returned that evening, Paulette did not answer the door of room 369. Someone he had never seen before invited him into the room where, just the night before, he had experienced more pleasure than he had known existed.

"Hi, baby! This is my sister Karen. Karen, this is my new man, Kory."

Karen may have been Paulette's sister in the street life but certainly was not by birth. She was an attractive girl with red hair, green eyes, short legs, and large breasts—in other words, average.

"Kory, Karen has been dying to meet you. I told her how much fun we had last night. So I told her that maybe the three of us could party together—if that is all right with you."

Judging by the way the two girls smiled at each other, Kory knew they were about to take advantage of his youth and inexperience. He was determined to rise to the occasion.

Playing coy, he replied, "Sure, let's party. Which club should we hit first?"

"We're talking about partying *here*, baby. But you're the man. You tell us what you want us to do. Karen brought her trap so she can get into pocket, baby."

"What's a trap?" he asked.

The two of them laughed. Paulette said, "*Trap* means her money. It's also called *choosing money*. If a working girl who is down with the life wants to leave her pimp and go to another man, she gives the new man her money."

"Thanks, but I'm not a pimp. Whatever money a woman makes, she should keep for herself. Considering what she had to do to get it, she deserves to keep every penny. Let's have a good time. I already have a job."

"You mean you don't want me?" Karen asked.

"Oh, I want you. I just don't want your money," Kory said.

"Whatever you say, baby. You're the man," Paulette said.

"Anyone thirsty? I can go down the hall to the machine and get us some drinks if you like."

"How about some champagne? Karen will pay for it," Paulette added.

"That sounds okay to me." He picked up the telephone and dialed the hotel operator. "Bette, this is Kory. Connect me to the Captain's Table, please. Hello, this is Mr. Vanon at the front desk. Please send two bottles of champagne to room 369. They'll be paying the waiter at the door."

Kory took off his clothes and walked to the bathroom. He turned on the shower and said in a very commanding voice, "Playtime, ladies?"

The three of them had been in the shower for only a few minutes when there was a knock at the door.

"That was unusually quick service. The word must have gotten around the hotel already," Kory said.

"Is that a good thing?" Paulette asked.

"Too soon to say, but there's one thing I've learned so far about this hotel."

"What's that?" they asked.

"The Dunbar is a small city unto itself, where rumors are born from the echoes in the hallways. There's always someone watching and listening. Karen, don't let him come in. Take the tray and pay him at the door."

Kory had barely gotten the hang of having sex with one woman before that night. The three of them went out to dinner and returned to the hotel two hours before Kory had to return to the front desk. It was a very long night of work before he got off and returned to the room to find both girls asleep. Now all Kory wanted to do was to crawl into bed between his two ladies and sleep for a few hours before it was time for him to be up again and hard at work.

By the end of the summer, Kory admitted he did not belong in the same life as those who hid from sunlight. Additionally, it had become difficult to concoct reasons to give his mother for why he came home so late after work in the morning. Fortunately, most days she had left for work by the time he finally arrived.

That same summer, his grandfather married the now-widowed Mrs. Toile. Having grown up in the same house where she had lived from childhood until her first marriage, she was unwilling to move into Kory's grandfather's large house on Sixteenth Street. His new step-grandmother believed she saw the ghost of Kory's grandmother in every corner of the house. Her discomfort was apropos for him, now that his grandfather wanted someone in the family to live in the usually vacant family home. It took Kory a lot of persuasion to convince his mother, but she finally gave in.

CHAPTER 10:

Charon's Helping Hand

All students entering Emerson Preparatory School were required to take a battery of tests, including the culturally biased Stanford–Binet, or IQ, test, on which Kory scored at the top of the class, despite his meager study habits.

At his last school, most teachers, at best, had had master's degrees; many at Emerson had doctorates. Dr. Nader, his English professor, in addition to being a published Shakespearean scholar, spoke five languages fluently, a skill he had used as an interpreter for two former US presidents. This was a bonus, given that many students were children of diplomats from embassies just doors away. It was Dr. Nader's love and mastery of Shakespeare that most impressed Kory. Like many students who tried to manipulate their teachers, he tested his English professor the second week of class. When called on for his homework, Kory offered an incredulous excuse for not having his assignment and said he would have it tomorrow. Dr. Nader responded, "Mr. Vanon, 'Tomorrow, and tomorrow, and tomorrow, creeps in this petty pace...it is a tale told by an idiot full of sound and fury signifying nothing." The gentle old scholar always found ways to use Shakespeare to explain everything—particularly his cherished students' mistakes and achievements.

When Kory started college, he had to study a fraction of what his fellow students did. With his sponge-like memory and ability to regurgitate chapter and line with any of his professors, Kory could have relaxed his way to a degree. The boredom returned. One day, while checking the notices on the bulletin board in the lobby of the psychology department, he read, "The National Institutes of Mental Health is conducting experiments on the effects and affects of LSD and other hallucinogenics on cognition...," which translated into the inevitable dissonance between what was perceived outside and what was actually sitting on one's shoulder. *Unbelievable*, he thought—clinical-grade lysergic acid diethylamide, and they were willing to pay him to scramble his consciousness. Most of his peers who experimented with this class of drugs did them usually on weekends. Kory had incorporated them into his life and had taken them on a daily basis for over a year. The warped visual and auditory perceptions that usually kept most "trippers" ensconced in a safe place during their eight-hour departures from normal space had become integrated into his routine perception. Instead of simply enjoying the heightened perception of flowers and melodic transition, he preferred to play chess without the pieces on the board. And when he was not moving pieces in his mind, he enjoyed reading the thoughts of kindred and tortured souls, like Carlos Castaneda, Will Durant, Søren Kierkegaard, and, appropriately, Dante Alighieri—whose quests for self-examination gave him company when he stepped into his personal hell, a reality that bubbled from the river Styx and drained into a wormhole that eventually released him into a universe where all of his questions were answered—if only for a few hours.

Once, in psychology class, the instructor asked each of his students what was the most useful skill they had acquired since they started college. Kory answered that it was his ability to examine and sort out all the trash inside his mind. He yearned to discover anything repressed. To his surprise, he got a nod of cautious approval from his psychology professor when Kory told him about his experiments with perception via LSD—a hot topic in the late sixties.

Fortunately, his formal studies of the mind provided a safety net for the dangerous excavations of his soul. Before dropping acid, he planned his trips by constructing a spiritual itinerary that contained a posthypnotic suggestion to guide him out of the eight-hour tour of his personal hell. At first the demons were frightening. He relived long-repressed childhood horrors, including his mother's abuse by his father. By the middle of the semester, it became apparent to him that much of the garbage he lugged around was necessary to maintain the integrity of his personality. Kory found regular purging of his psyche left him empty and eventually withdrawn. Cycles developed where he would descend to the bowels of his now-malleable mind, withdraw for days, and then reinvent himself on his latest platform, minus one level of crud.

After one extended period of soul searching, Kory found it necessary to barricade himself in his grandfather's house for two weeks. During that time he spoke to no one except the voices bouncing from the walls of his mind. They were whispers from mentors and long-dead ancestors. He particularly had frequent conversations with his grandmother, who had perished in a basement closet fire just below the room where he spent most of his days.

Since he was now on a macrobiotic diet, his needs for food and drink were nil. His weight had dropped from 170 pounds to a ghastly 130 pounds. Add a long beard and the black halo of an Afro, and he appeared not too different from many other young people seeking "consciousness three." Of course, that was on the surface. Kory was on the brink of insanity. He had purged his soul and starved his body to the point where he was existing on air or whatever calories his body could scavenge from his diminishing musculature.

The doorbell rang every day. He usually ignored it. One late morning in the middle of summer, his grandfather, the Right Reverend Vanon, stopped by to pick up some papers that were in the study he maintained in one of the larger rooms on the second floor. Kory heard the cascading sound of keys—not those of a typical key ring carried by the average person, but the unmistakable sound of his grandfather's key chain, which must have held over thirty keys. He always wondered why his grandfather carried so many. The old, pious gentleman told him many were to the churches in his diocese and the homes of friends.

"Kory! It's Granpa. Are you in there?"

Hoping he would just leave, Kory continued sitting in the green wing-back armchair facing the fireplace and remained silent. But his grandfather had keys to every door in the house, and he used one to come in and break Kory's solitude.

"Didn't you hear me calling you?"

Kory felt too weak to stand. "Hi, Granpa. I just got up fifteen minutes ago. I have an exam tomorrow. I...er...stayed up all night cramming. How are you?"

There was his grandfather, standing in the doorway, with all the lights in the hallway streaming from behind. He was dressed in his usual black suit and clerical collar with the purple band indicating his bishopric, and jingling his mass of keys as if he were ringing a bell to inform heaven of the travel plans of a recently departed member of his flock.

"I'm fine, Kory, but you don't look well. What have you done to yourself? I hope you are not doing drugs. You know the Nixon administration is watching me after I called the president 'antiblack.' Did you see my picture on the front page of The *Washington Post* denouncing President Nixon last week?"

"Sorry, but I haven't read a newspaper in months," Kory said as he rubbed his legs to wake them up.

"The NAACP doesn't need its chairman's grandson arrested for drug use. They'll use anything to discredit me and our movement," he said, peering over his glasses.

"Why do you keep bringing that up? You know I'm into health foods. I just need to eat a little more protein to get my weight up. It's hard to get enough protein without eating meat. And you know I stopped chewing flesh last spring. But I was not aware Big Brother was watching us. If I see any lurking in the hedges, I'll invite them in for a soy burger."

"This is not a laughing matter. Do you have any idea what a scandal could do to the cause of the NAACP? And what is that smell?"

"Oh, just incense, similar to the type they use in Catholic churches."

"We're Methodist. That kind of gimmickry is not needed in the house of God. And I'm sure even the Catholics don't use anything that smells like that. What is it called?"

"Sufi Sense!"

"Sufi! Are you referring to the sect of Islam?"

"Yes. They contemplate problems like the sound of one hand clapping and such."

"Ha! Is this another one of your antireligious experiments? I respect your questioning of the religious institution, but don't forget everything we have has come from the African Methodist Episcopal Zion Church."

"I know—you never let me forget it. Granpa, I just can't accept things on face value. I need to know why I need to have faith. Can man exist without faith? Established religion has been around only a fraction of the time man has walked upright."

His grandfather moved to the mantel, where the eyes in the portrait of his departed wife seemed to move back and forth with their conversation. He smiled at her and brushed an unseen speck of dust from the frame. "Yes, and before man found God, he was lost."

"If that is true, then why are soldiers dying in rice paddies in Vietnam? Why are our African brothers in Nigeria killing one another for the oil American companies covet? Why can't a black man in the sixties walk into a downtown restaurant and be greeted like a customer, instead of being mistaken for a servant who's wandered into the wrong room?"

"Kory! Kory! Kory! All that anger. It will never do you any good until you have found a way to focus it to work within the system. You young people clamor for change today, but it has taken centuries of struggle to get where we are now. Do you think we don't want change today? I hope to live long enough to see more of the Jim Crow laws erased so that by the time you are my age, your grandchildren will be free from the systemic and psychological vestiges of slavery."

"Granpa, how did you manage to control your anger? When I sense racism, it makes my blood boil. This will probably anger you, but I'm convinced Christianity's promise of an afterlife has intoxicated us with hope and thwarted the de facto emancipation of our people."

"You may feel that way, but had we not religion, we as a people would have found it impossible to survive without the promise of a better life—albeit in heaven."

"That all sounds very nice, but at the end of the road to heaven waits a white God with blond hair and a blue-eyed son. I have a real problem with that concept. If we were to put a suntan and curly hair on him, I might warm to the idea."

"How is your Latin?"

"Better than most, I suppose."

"*Nigra sum sed formosa.*"

"'I am black, but I am beautiful.' Sounds like a variation of the 'Black Is Beautiful' motto we see on many black-pride posters."

"Actually, it is from a thousand-year-old statue of the black Madonna and Child. Many scholars believe the Virgin Mary was originally depicted as a black woman with Negroid features."

"I read something about that. It is believed the concept of the Madonna and Child was stolen or borrowed from the Egyptian Isis and Child, which was usually painted black. I forgot about that, but it does not change my opinion of Christianity, despite its possible African origins."

"What do you have against religion, Kory?"

"Granpa, there is just so much hate in this world, and so much of it is sanctioned by the church. I just find it difficult to be a part of it."

"Do you think I didn't feel the same way when I was your age?"

"Did you really?"

"Of course I did, Kory. We live in a very complex world today, where we are all thrown together in a society that has made choices for most of us. But there are those of us who will be instrumental in determining our future. You've heard me speak often of my friend Dr. W. E. B. Dubois. Have you ever—"

"Are you referring to his concept of the Talented Tenth? I'm very familiar with that and similar concepts by Friedrich Nietzsche and Søren Kierkegaard."

"If that's true, then why are you squandering your gifts with drugs? Kory, you have a good mind. Why haven't you finished your studies by now?"

Kory stood and walked to the bookcase and turned his back as if he were looking for a book.

"There you are again—whenever I talk about reality, you seem to float away to some chapter in one of your books. Kory, all of the answers are not there. I grant you that I find our conversations engaging. And I know you are trying at times to needle my faith. Some of your premises have caused me to reexamine some of my beliefs. You are correct: the difference between religion and faith has become muddled. Even I at times forget God is everywhere, and not only in the church, for the faithful. But those questions do not allow me to ignore the responsibility I have to my family, the church, and my people."

"I'm not avoiding responsibility. I guess I'm reluctant to make a choice until I have more information."

"Kory, you could spend the rest of your life reading; the result will be that you will have led an a priori life, bereft of the pleasure of actually experiencing it. I have found the more I read, the more questions I have. You have to sample life every now and then. If you find it was the wrong decision, it should be then that you try something else. Change cannot take place without action."

"But what about the change that occurs when you have discovered your connection to the universe?"

"That's a good thing. But you need to share your discovery with the rest of the world. If not, you'll die a very unhappy and forgotten man."

"Granpa, I know many times I act like a spoiled child. I sometimes forget how lucky I am to have someone like you in my life. You've given me the opportunity, with your seemingly endless patience, to tackle life at my own pace. I'll always be grateful for that."

"Well, I hope our talk will encourage you to get out of this den. You really need to get out more. You haven't seen any of your friends in months. Even your mother is worried about you."

"I doubt that. She just doesn't want to be blamed if something bad happens to me, and you know it."

"Well, your mother does her best. She has had very little happiness in her life because of the wrong choices she made. I pray every day you will find the way to a life that will bring you joy."

Such conversations with his grandfather convinced Kory to continue his self-discovery. Months later, when he thought he had gone too far, he found solace when traveling through hell at night, knowing he would be able to speak to an emissary of God in the morning.

CHAPTER 11:

Mac in the Mirror

All through high school and college as well, Kory had few relationships with young men his age. When he was not wooing a new girl, he found being alone preferable to pretending to be part of a crowd—with one exception: an unusual guy he met on campus one evening during the intermission of a Nigerian Ibo harvest dance performance at Cramton Auditorium on the Howard University campus.

As he drew Labanotation sketches of the dancers' movements from his seat, the usual soreness in his legs from dancing every day nagged him more than ever. Pain had become a constant companion after he had started ballet and jazz classes his freshman year. But tonight was worse than usual. Despite frequent shifts in his seat, he failed to find a position to lessen tingles fulgurating from his toes to his groin. So before the curtain was completely down on the first act, he was stretching his legs outside in the sticky midsummer night air.

After walking the perimeter of the green two times, he felt his hyper-awareness of his legs diminish, but the soreness and tightness remained. Since there was no performance that night in the Ira Aldridge Theater adjoining Cramton Auditorium, the deserted entrance, not far from the stadium, made a discreet place to sit and stretch his legs out of view of curious eyes.

The cool marble landing in the front of the theater became a dance floor after he removed his wooden clogs. Using a massage technique he had learned from a girlfriend studying reflexology, Kory located pressure point number fifteen on his foot, which accessed spinal and vertebral neural pathways. He rubbed the area with the joint of his thumb until he felt a warm sensation in his spine and legs. And with his eyes closed, he concentrated on the increasing warm sensation instead of the pain produced with each stroke.

Then a voice came out of nowhere: "You must be a dancer to stretch like that." A dark figure was finding its way up the unlit path beside the stadium fence.

Kory could not see the face, but he answered with an unconscious sense of recognition. "I do a little song and dance. How about you?"

"I'm studying modern, but I can't stretch my legs like that."

The owner of the voice finally passed under lights bright enough for Kory to see his observer. There he was in his full persona: "trucking" down the sidewalk, wearing massive bell-bottom pants, a leather vest, an Afro hairstyle parted down the middle, and Roman-style sandals.

"They call me Mac," he said, giving Kory the New Nation handshake, complicated to explain but easily done by young men of his age.

"My parents named me Kory. Haven't found a reason to change one of the last things they agreed upon. What others call me, I couldn't give a shit."

Mac stood in front of Kory and smiled. "I like your rap. Sometimes people accuse me of trying to be too different."

Kory looked into his eyes. "Maybe you are!"

"Deep inside, I know I am. When I bring it to the surface, I tend to overdo it." Mac patted his hair as if he were looking into a mirror.

Despite Mac's unexpected personal revelation, Kory quickly reflected, "You can only be yourself, unless you want to drive yourself crazy trying to fulfill the insecure ego failings of someone trying to make you in their image."

Mac lit a Bidi East Indian cigarette and inhaled deeply. "You speak like the wise man I talk to in Washington Square. He was once a dancer, but now he calls himself Lord Shiva." Mac tilted his head back as if he were expecting some inspiration from the cosmos.

"So does he now dance in the name of creation or destruction?" Kory asked as he continued his exercises.

Mac stood and flicked his cigarette into the air high enough to clear the telephone wire over the street before falling into the gutter. "Was that supposed to be a joke? To tell you the truth, that's probably why he sometimes seems conflicted when you try to ask him a question about himself. He's the most sagacious when giving advice to someone else. But that's enough about him. Where do you come from?"

"I'm a Washingtonian. What about you?"

Mac sat down on the sidewalk. "North Portal! Know where it is?"

"My father's house was at Sixteenth and Tuckerman."

"Okay, so we're from the same part of town. I'm surprised we've not run into each other before." Mac adjusted his sandals.

"So am I, but it's a big city. I believe things happen when they're supposed to. My family name is Vanon. We're third-generation Washingtonians."

"My mother's family has been here for three generations, but Dad is from Virginia—something my mother is always berating him about. I wish my parents had never met."

"That's a heavy thing to say. For all we know, if they had not married, the world may have ceased to exist," Kory posited.

Mac folded his legs into a half-lotus position. "The world would be a better place if my mother had never been born."

"Too bad we can't pick our parents; that will be the first thing on my list for the new world when I reincarnate."

Another entity seemed to take Mac over. "I wish I could reincarnate now. I hate my life. I want to die and be reborn with a singing voice like Larry Graham's. Then I could get all the beautiful-smelling girls I want." He proceeded to make panting sounds like a dog chasing after its prey.

"I bet you do okay for yourself in your present form."

"Yeah, but they all want to play games. I just want to love them for a few hours." Mac took out another Bidi cigarette.

"Your desires sound pretty familiar to me, but the Larry Graham baritone—I'm not sure about that. What kind of voice do you have now?"

"Check this out!" Mac grabbed an imaginary microphone from the air, did a double turn on his heels, and belted out the first two bars of Sly and the Family Stone's "Stand." Kory thought Mac would certainly need to reincarnate to come anywhere near Larry Graham, but his movements were fluid and original. His new acquaintance was certainly different from any other person he had met on the campus and the planet, as a matter of fact, which was probably why Mac was not a student there. His purpose on campus was the same as Kory's—girls.

Mac was strictly uptown Gold Coast. He was the only child of a judge and a D.C. school administrator, so whatever he wanted, Mac got—at least from his parents, even if it was not good for him. Not surprisingly, Mac, like Kory, had gone to private school, but Mac had enjoyed the indulgence of privileged education longer than Kory. He was studying to become an actor, singer, and dancer at a very expensive private college in New York City. Even though the two of them had never met before, they would find out a few months later that their families were well acquainted with each other. In fact, their fathers were members of the same men's club, and Mac's mother was a colleague of Kory's aunt. At any rate, it was an immediate friendship.

It wasn't long before Mac and Kory were cruising all of the college campuses and hot spots for young, unsuspecting female game. But despite all of their similarities—love of the arts, girls, and drugs—and the fact that they were only a few months apart in age, their maturity levels differed markedly. For the most part, Kory had been on his own since his late teens, whereas Mac had never worked a day in his life and never intended to work until he hit it big on the stage. He wasn't looking for money—just attention.

One year went by. Mac had all but taken up permanent residence at Kory's grandfather's house, which was convenient for Mac, since he had so many car accidents and moving violations that his driving privileges were limited to going to class and back. His loving parents coddled him in every attempt to damper his frequent temper tantrums, so they permitted him to drive regularly in the evening so long as he was home by 1:00 a.m. That agreement was not honored very long. Mac would arrive at Kory's door in the early evening with enough marijuana for the two of them to play chess until the early hours of the morning.

Between going to class and rehearsing in the dance studio, Kory eventually had little time to go out and just cruise around for entertainment and girls. Instead, people of all configurations dropped by to see him. It was as if everyone knew if you needed to see Kory, he was in residence at his grandfather's house on Sixteenth Street. If you were able to stay around long enough, whatever or whomever you were looking for would end up in his living room.

Kory was convinced Mac had become more interested in the girls from his dance classes, who were always dropping by, than in their chess games. That was fine with Kory, but he was worried about Mac. This was an age of free love, when most people were looking for casual sex and not good old-fashioned romance. Mac yearned to fall in love, and he did—time after time and girl after girl—but he never found that perfect girl he dreamed of every day. Kory tried to convince Mac such a creature lived on another planet. Coincidentally, it was just six months later when Mac became a member of that exclusive segment of society whose reality existed only inside their heads. Hamlet said it well: "Oh, God! I could be bound up in a nutshell and count myself a king of infinite space, were it not that I sometimes have bad dreams."

When Mac was not performing for his audience in Washington, he competed for the spotlight in New York City—and if you cannot find it there, it probably does not exist. Any afternoon, Mac could be seen chatting up some nirvana-seeking young lady in the streets of The Village or looking for new material for his persona from some of the long-lost souls who haunted Washington Square.

Included in his immediate circle of friends was the female lead singer of one of the most popular groups in the country, known for performing such hits as "Stand" and "Everyday People." According to an eyewitness, who was not seen again he was loaded into an already overcrowded ambulance after a heroin overdose during the last days of the Woodstock concert, Mac had attended a party in The Village, where he arrived about two hours before everyone else. He never wore a watch, and even if he had, he was always on Mac time. The host was preparing a psychedelic punch, mixed with grain alcohol, Hawaiian Punch, and measured doses of LSD. Mac was known for being impulsive, and his instant-gratification personality would become his mental undoing. The punch chef used a very large brandy snifter as a cauldron to mix the mind-altering brew. What happened next came as no surprise.: Mac sees a drink. Mac is thirsty. Mac drinks the drink. Poor Mac!

Before he could be stopped, Kory's unfortunate friend had swallowed more than half of the contents in the snifter, which was being prepared for a party of at least fifty people. It took more than a week for Mac to put enough of his brain together to say a full sentence, and when he did, it was in spiritual doublespeak. Luckily, this happened during a time when many people were searching for a guru. In fact, many naïve people thought Mac had reached a higher plane, when he was really in need of a massive dose of Thorazine.

Kory had many spiritual awakenings as well, but he always kept one foot firmly planted in reality when he stuck one of his toes in the river of Zen. Mac, now the intrepid Swami Man, as some forlorn personalities sometimes called him, shaved his head to the glisten of a tan bowling ball, dressed in white flowing linen, and spoke to his disciples in what sounded like an East Indian accent by way of some undiscovered island somewhere between Jamaica and Trinidad.

Years went by. Most of Mac's friends finished college, and their use of drugs diminished with the arrival of adult responsibilities. But poor Mac was still stuck in a time continuum where nothing seemed to matter, particularly if it were gray. Thirty years later, Mac could still be seen walking down Sixteenth Street, talking to the pigeons and spirits perched on the oak-tree limbs. The last time Kory pulled his car over to the curb to say hello to Mac, Mac spoke to him, in the same quasi–East Indian accent, about his need to meditate harder so he could reach the nearest quasar, where he would at last be at peace with the universe. Mac was not aware he had reached that section of timeless space many years ago, but he was still trucking along. He was one of the few souls Kory would like to see again in another life. His ability to force one to question what is and what is not reality helped Kory to open his mind to alternate possibilities of existence. Mac was probably one of the few people who understood his aloneness— although he never felt lonely. Even today, when Kory looks into the mirror, Mac is there with his forefinger pressed against his pineal eye.

CHAPTER 12

The Circle

"Everything's real cool, Daddy-o," slathered the gray-haired beatnik wearing a black beret and sitting behind a nearly empty pitcher of draft beer in the walk-down back room of Tassos, a public house just one block from Embassy Row, at the corner of Seventeenth and O Streets, just far enough from uptight society to make a difference.

In the summer Kory took evening classes at Emerson to fight the boredom. One evening, around eight o'clock, he heard the sound *doom, dum-dum, doom* as he stepped onto the front-door landing to his school.

"Hey, Kory! We're going to hang out in Georgetown," yelled Jean-Paul as he straddled the wall separating the two stairways of the adjoining painted white-brick federalist row houses.

Kory heard it again: *doom, dum-dum, doom.* "No, thanks. I've got to meet a friend at the Circle."

"You mean you actually know people who hang out there? I hear there're some real far-out people going there. Is it true people sit on the grass and smoke pot while listening to folk music?" Jean-Paul asked.

Kory threw his books in the trunk of his car. "Don't really know about that. I've only been there a few times. But I'll let you know if I see any really far-out people on the grass."

Kory walked only one block west on Massachusetts Avenue, to the front of the Federal Savings bank. Then he heard it again: *doom, dum-dum, doom.* It was the sound of ten or more conga players, along with other Dupont Circle musicians, warming up to prepare the night air for the change from the Embassy Row crowd of the daylight to the freaks of the growing counterculture of the '60s.

When he stepped into the Circle, he was transported into the latest handiwork of social evolution, where the sons and daughters of middle- and upper-class families experimented with creating or finding their places in a society that had grown indifferent to the natural exploration of youth. Years of Dr. Spock, *Captain Kangaroo, Howdy Doody*, five-cent Coca-Colas, and family cocktail hours, as well as two terms of Lyndon Johnson, had produced a new generation willing to explore again why their parents' society had reached a stage of democratic evolution that produced compliancy in the voting booth and guilty priests in the confessionals.

When they were not playing in the Circle, many of the musicians, as well as some of the crowd who were aware of its existence, would end up at Tassos. No one Kory ever met seemed to know how the bar had gotten its name, but it seemed appropriate. The dark and dingy beer-soaked walls were like the bottom of an old brewery keg. Kory was not old enough to legally order a beer at Tassos, but the waitress would slip him a cold one when the bar was crowded.

For the first two weeks, the regulars all but ignored him. He would just find a seat close to the round table at the back, open up a book, and absorb the conversations of wannabe and soon-to-be social architects of Amerika.

One Thursday evening, when Tassos offered a free jazz concert featuring local musicians, a guy known as Jimmy around the bar and the Circle approached Kory. He was not one of the intellectuals, as they liked to refer to themselves; he was just an unusually good-looking guy trying to get laid as often as he could. In some ways he could have been considered a predator. He saw the way Kory was dressed and approached when Kory was outside the bar, sitting on his British-racing-gren Austin-Healey and smoking a Winston cigarette. Jimmy had gotten out of the navy two years earlier and spoke with a heavy Boston accent. He often wore a Harvard University T-shirt, although he had never finished high school. Engaging him in conversations more than a few minutes revealed his limited education, despite his natural wit and rapid-fire repartee.

Jimmy was always in motion, going from one audience to another. If he could not cull a wide-eyed girl from the first group, he quickly moved on, claiming he had to visit a friend or pickup his girlfriend.. Jimmy didn't even own a car but talked often about the red convertible Cadillac he had been saving for over the past two years. He lived frugally in a one-room apartment, with a bathroom down the hall and a hot plate to prepare his meals. During the day, when the real students were supposed to be in class, Jimmy worked as a stock boy in the Peoples Drug Store warehouse, but he always looked like a graduate student hunting for a research assistant—even when he was stacking crates of #2 pencils.

"Hey, my man! Like your car. I bet you have all those little white girls shitting their pants when you drive by. My name is James, but everyone calls me Jimmy."

"How's it going? I'm Kory. I've seen you in the bar. You look like you've been coming here for a while."

"Tassos is usually my first stop of the evening. I check out about four or five different places, to tell you the truth."

Kory lit another cigarette and offered the pack to Jimmy.

"Never touch them." He smoothed over his well-oiled hair as if there were someone admiring him. "You look like a college student. Which school do you go to?"

"Uh, G.W."

"George Washington! Now that's a good school for chicks. I'm dating a girl who is a dance major there right now."

"Cool. What's her name?" Kory was really gambling, since he was actually still a junior in high school.

"Sweet Jennifer, the love of my life—at least this week. So where are you from? I bet you're from upstate New York."

"No. Uptown Washington."

"Same thing. What are you studying at George Washington University? I'll bet you want to become a lawyer like your father."

"No, I'm studying psychology."

"What does your father do?"

"I don't have the slightest idea. We haven't talked in years."

"Too bad. I never knew my father except from the stories my mother used to tell about him when his ship would stop over in Boston en route to another port of call. The old man was a rolling stone, as they say, and quite a ladies' man. I guess that's why my mother fell for him. The son of a bitch was never even man enough to marry my mom. And sometimes at night, I would go into her room and find her crying herself to sleep. She didn't tell me why she cried until the night before I was to leave for boot camp. When my old man was in town, he would get drunk and then beat her up before he left. If I ever see him, I swear I'll cut his heart out and feed it to the rats."

Trying to be sympathetic, Kory said, "Man, sorry to hear that. How's your mother doing now?"

"She died while I was stationed in the Pacific. They had already buried her by the time I got word."

"Well, Jimmy, thanks for sharing all of that with me. I know it must be hard for you to talk about it."

"It gets easier every time. But enough of all this down stuff; what are your plans tonight? How about hanging out with me? I'll show you some of my spots."

Jimmy seemed like a harmless guy, but Kory was leery of overly friendly people, despite his lack of experience. Even though Kory had had a mostly sheltered life uptown, his cynical mother had unknowingly given him the ability to distinguish those wishing him harm from the majority of people he met, who would help him grow.

"Thanks for the offer, but I'm waiting for this chick I saw in here last Thursday to show up. Her name is Adèle, a French girl who arrived only two weeks ago. She was with another French girl. I believe her name was Marie."

"Marie! Kind of tall, thin, and blond?" Jimmy added.

"Sounds like the same girl. You know them?"

"Oh, yeah! I went on a date with her about a month ago. She was a little too bookish for me, but her friend, she's a real doll—innocent and doesn't know a word of English. How do you plan to talk to her? Do you speak French?"

"Just a little. I had a few years of Latin, though. I hope I can at least understand a little. Anyway, Marie speaks English quite well."

"Yeah, but you won't have any idea what they're saying about you."

"Sounds like fun. Well, see you around. And thanks again."

Kory went back inside. The jazz trio had just finished their second offering, "Blue in Green," when he spied Adèle and Marie, both wearing blue miniskirts with blue, white, and red paisley ties and white go-go boots. They surveyed the room as they looked for a table. Kory waved and pointed to the empty seats at his booth.

"Hi there!" Kory got up and pulled out two chairs.

"Itzz Kore, no?"

"You remember my name. And you are Marie, and this is your friend Adèle. I believe you said you were from Besançon, France." The two girls giggled and looked at each other. "You pronounce that pretty well for an American. Most of the people here cannot even come close. Do you speak French?"

"I wish I could. They forced me to take Latin." Marie spoke to Adèle in rapid-fire French. Adèle's eyes intrigued Kory. They were not a common blue; they were the multicolored hue common in Eastern Europeans. As she spoke with her eyes and gestured with her hand holding a Gauloise cigarette, Kory felt they were talking about him, and he hoped Adèle found him attractive. He also prayed all the lurid stores he had heard about Frenchwomen were true.

"*Salve!*" Kory said hello to Adèle in Latin.

"*Ubi habitas?*" replied Adèle.

"*Habito* in Washington, DC," said Kory. "*Amo* jazz. It's hard to find jazz clubs outside my hometown," Adèle said to Kory in Latin.

"I hope you will make this your home for a while," Kory replied in Latin, with a big smile.

The band assembled for their second set. The next piece, because of its length, would also be the last of the evening—"Maiden Voyage," by a young new piano prodigy named Herbie Hancock. The title was fitting.

"Wow, that was great," said Marie.

"How did you like it?" Kory asked Adèle in Latin.

"It was beautiful," Adèle answered.

"Okay, you two." Marie held her watch close to the candle on the table. She unknowingly revealed a recently healed scar on her left wrist. "It's twelve thirty. I have a class to teach in the morning."

"Oh, you are a teacher?" Kory noted the time on his watch and the light as it danced in Adèle's eyes.

"Yes. I teach at the International School for Girls. Adèle also has class. She is studying English at Berlitz and teaching French there as well."

"It's a school day for me tomorrow as well. I have an exam on the Ionian School of Philosophy."

"The Ionian School?" asked Marie.

"Well, the Ionians were not actual psychologists, but their questions about the mind are considered to be the rudiments of modern psychology."

Marie again spoke in French to Adèle. He assumed she was translating what Kory had said.

"You are a psychology student?" Adèle asked Kory in French.

"*Oui!*" He was able to follow most of their conversation.

The two girls stood up. "Can I offer you a lift home? My car is just outside." Kory searched Adèle's eyes for an answer.

Marie answered, "We live only a few blocks away. But sure, if you don't mind."

"It would be my pleasure."

As he pointed to his car, Adèle said, "*Très bonne voiture.*"

"*Merci!*" He could not believe how uninhibited they were as they nonchalantly wriggled into his very low-sitting sports car in their miniskirts. His young heart raced, and other parts of his body moved as well.

His unexpected passengers lived just off Thomas Circle, in an old apartment building that was about three blocks from Kory's grandfather's church. As a child, Kory had often passed it and wondered what the inside of such an old building would hold. He had never expected it to one day contain the images of his adolescent fantasies.

"Thanks for the ride. You should come by for dinner one night when you are free," Marie said with her big sister–like smile.

"I would love to. Just tell me which night, and I'll be there with a bottle of wine."

"How is Sunday at eight o'clock?"

"That's perfect. I'll see you then."

"*Bonne nuit!*" said Adèle.

"Good night," Kory said to Adèle, hoping she did not see in his eyes how much he wanted to kiss her.

In front of the building, the two girls had said good night with traditional international kisses on his cheeks. Their scents mixed with the night air as he drove with the top down back to Tassos. It was nearly one o'clock. Kory hoped he could get another beer before calling it a night. He was too excited to think about sleep now. Luckily, he found another seat in a booth close enough to the round table to follow the conversations, now that the music had ended.

"Cool, man. Have you heard of the *Washington Free Press*?" belched Big Jim.

"No, man. Is it a free newspaper or something?" slurred Art, a really tall guy, who was all of seven feet, two inches and preferred modern dance to basketball.

"Listen, Art, these guys are ready to set this country on fire with stories you'll never see in the government-owned *Washington Post* and *Evening Star* newspapers."

"What kind of stuff have they printed lately? I've been too busy with my thesis to read a newspaper."

"Last week, they featured the number of casualties in Vietnam. They said the government has been lying to us all this time about our involvement. Would you believe they uncovered a secret war budget? Somewhere around a hundred million dollars is being spent on covert CIA operations to overthrow the government of North Vietnam."

"That's far out. Some of that money could be better spent feeding and educating the poor people who live just in the shadows of the White House. I grew up just a few blocks from the Capitol. Those overfed politicians need to take a walk with me in my old neighborhood."

Kory had heard this story before. He found it hard to listen to anything except his own thoughts. After taking one last swallow of beer, he headed home. Despite the hour, there were still many people out. He took a quick turn around the Circle. A crowd had gathered around the fountain. It was difficult to make out the music. Judging by the long hair of most of the freaks sitting around the rim, he thought it must have been folk music; not quite the Peter, Paul and Mary variety, which was usually quaint ballads. This music was about war and its horror: the sons who would never return and the "wickedness of the US imperial empire."

Five minutes later, he turned into his street. His parking space in the rear had not been taken, as it frequently was during a weeknight when he got home at this hour. The alley was deserted, and the house seemed darker than usual. As he walked up the rear stairs, he knew this would be a long night. Getting to sleep right away was out of the question. He went to the bookcase, now overflowing with hundreds of books, mostly read, and saw an old friend: It had been at least three years since he last read Proust's *Remembrance of Things Past*. As he returned to Proust's Combray, Little Marcel's self-absorption reminded him what he had felt for most of his life: no one could love him as much as he had learned to love himself.

CHAPTER 13:

Uncorked and Smitten

Nothing worked to distract him from Sunday. Whether he tried to memorize Leon Festinger's cognitive-dissonance paradigm for psychology class or finish his paper on Aldous Huxley's *Brave New World*, all those pursuits were futile, when all he suffered from was a simple case of love at first sight.

Around noon another problem came to mind: how would he choose the correct wine for two French girls who had probably grown up drinking some of the best wines in the world? Since he was underage, the only store he knew that would sell him wine was Cairo Liquors on Seventeenth Street, a few blocks north of Tassos. It was owned by Huey and Gary, two guys who enjoyed the young, braless girls on the arms of long-haired guys buying cheap Boone's Farm wine to go with their marijuana. Kory needed something to impress the girls. Then he remembered one of the older guys in the Circle, with whom he played chess and who owned a modest liquor store within walking distance of Kory's grandfather's house.

Dale Burke was too young for the beatnik area and too gray around the temples for the new hippie invasion. The only son of a black Pennsylvania minister and a Native American mother, he turned the heads of some of the older ladies and men in the Circle with his reddish lion's mane of hair and chiseled features.

"Hi, is Dale in today?"

"Are you a friend of Mr. Burke?"

"Well, not exactly. We play chess in Dupont Circle."

"In that case, I'll see if he's in," said a very tall guy who had so many freckles, if someone had taken a magic marker and connected the dots, he would have been a black man, except for the green eyes and scattered tuffs of red hair, which was all that was left of his youthful plumage.

"Kory! What a surprise to see you. Couldn't wait for me to make it to the Circle for your daily trouncing?" Dale removed his glasses and let them hang by the cord around his neck.

"I believe you resigned the last two games. But who's counting, unless you're playing for money?"

"Was that a challenge, young man?"

"Tell you what: two lovely French ladies are cooking dinner for me Sunday. So I've come here seeking your expert advice about the right wine to bring. Now, if I win, you have to give me the wine. But if I lose, I'll buy three bottles and still get drunk in the arms of French heaven."

"Sounds serious. What are they cooking?"

"She said *Boeuf* Bourguignon if I pronounced it correctly."

"Not bad. That's beef stew to you and me. Good stuff if it's cooked correctly. You'll need a hearty Burgundy and possibly something fruity for dessert."

"You're the master. What do you have in those categories?"

"Do you want French or California wine? Unless you want to spend a lot of money, I would suggest a Napa Valley Burgundy from a small but excellent vineyard; I happen to be the local distributor for them. Now, for dessert, I would recommend a fruity Chardonnay from Sonoma."

"Okay. Put them on the counter, and let's play. I know you must have a chessboard back in your office. A guy like you needs to practice!"

"Such impertinence from a nice young man. I'll cut those words from a magazine and place them in the bag containing the wine with your bill."

"Wow! Haven't seen this many boards since I was at Googy's Studio in the Village."

"Oh, you know about that place. Some top-flight players there. Bobby Fisher even graced the place with an exhibition last year. I was one of the twenty people he beat while he tied his tennis shoes between yawns."

Kory looked at the shelf above Dale's desk. "Where did you get all of these boards?"

"For the most part, Sean runs the store while I carve chessboards. It's a hobby and side business. Wish I could sell the store and just make boards, but I just can't find enough customers for my boards to make the move—if you'll forgive the pun."

"Are you sure you didn't mean 'forgive the pawn'?"

"Touché! I like a person who's able to think on his feet. Let's see how fast you can lose to me today."

Kory pointed to a board on the bottom. "That is beautiful. Real ebony and ivory, is it not?"

"You've a good eye. That's one of my favorites. Would you like to play on it?"

"Show me your pieces!"

Dale pulled from the top shelf a box of hand-carved Staunton Burgundy and Chardonnay pieces that must have cost a small fortune. Seldom had Kory seen detail and finish like that outside museums and New York City chess studios. Dale took pawns from both sides, put them behind his back, and placed his two closed fists on the table.

"Looks like the lady is with me." Kory rotated the board to the white pieces.

Dale adjusted his half-frame glasses to the tip of his aquiline nose. "After your first move, it won't make a difference."

"Thanks for the commentary. It reduces your concentration, but not mine." Kory grinned as Dale's forehead furrowed, following his opening to the center.

"Mr. Burke, there's a gentlemen here to pick up the board you promised this afternoon," his employee said from the doorway.

Dale's nostrils flared. "Can't you see I'm busy, Sean? Sorry! Tell him to come back at six o'clock. The veneer needs two more hours to dry."

"As you wish, Mr. Burke."

"Dale, unless you see an escape that I don't, you'll lose your queen in two moves."

"Give me a minute. Crap! How did you sneak that one on me?"

"You were busy trying to decide which of my pieces I had decided to give you, while I was busy kicking in your back door to run off with your lady."

"How about another game?"

"Don't have time today. But since I now know you're so close to my home, I can drop by after class on Monday."

"I won't go so easy on you next time, young man. I'll walk you to the register."

"Register?"

"Just kidding. Enjoy the wine."

Sunday evening Kory stood at the girls' apartment door, holding three bottles of wine and his excitement inside.

"*Bonsoir, dames.*"

"*Très bon, monsieur.* Your French is improving. Have you been practicing?" Marie took the bottles of wine and kissed his cheeks.

"Just a few words I picked up watching movies. Where's Adèle?"

"Don't worry. She'll be out in a few minutes. I do not know why she's spending so much time in the bathroom today."

"I hope the wine goes well with dinner."

"Let's take a look at what you have. Oh, California wines. I love trying them. We're tired of people trying to impress us with French wines. It's like inviting you to Paris for a hot dog. There she is!"

"Good ev-en-ing," Adèle said. She hesitated on every syllable.

"You look great…I mean, you…"

"*Merci*…thank you," she said, giving him a kiss on both cheeks.

Marie returned from the kitchen after putting away the wine.

"Kory, you're a little early. Would you excuse me for about ten minutes so I can finish the cooking? I'll need Adèle for a few minutes, but I promise to send her back to you before you fall asleep."

"Sorry. I have a habit of always being a little early."

Their ninth-floor, two-bedroom apartment looked like that of a student or teacher: books everywhere and stacks of papers waiting for attention. There were small oil and watercolor paintings and sketches of what were probably landscapes and houses from their hometown in the northeast of France. Facing the window, which had a skyline view of the city , was not a sofa but beautifully arranged Oriental rugs on the floor, with overstuffed cushions against the wall. Sitting beside the record player was an album by the popular French songstress Edith Piaf. Kory's Latin allowed him to read more French than he spoke. "*La Vie en Rose*." He later found out this was one of Marie's favorite songs. Kory wondered why someone as young as Marie would want to identify with pain so obvious in a language he barely understood.

Adèle placed three small plates on the little dining table against the window and said something in French to Kory that he did not understand. She smiled, threw up her hands, and returned from the kitchen with Marie.

"She was trying to find out if you like escargots." Marie was a little red in the face from the hot kitchen.

"I've only had them in garlic butter."

"Good, then you'll love these. They're cooked in real French butter."

After dinner the three of them lounged on cushions and talked of everything from *Alphaville*, a radical French film similar to the theme of George Orwell's book *1984*, to blues singers like the great Lightning Hopkins and a few Kory had never heard of until that night. When they got to philosophy, Kory's hostesses demonstrated the French penchant for revisionist history.

On the subject of existentialism, Kory posited that Kierkegaard was the father of the concept, whereas his very inebriated ladies from France vociferously asserted that Jean-Paul Sartre's version was the only guidebook for those seeking self-actualization, and a sure way of infuriating their staunch Catholic families. Now the language barriers had become perfumed veils. At some point, words were all but ignored, since their conversation had become animated laughter, with the help of three empty bottles of California wine.

Around eleven o'clock, Kory suggested they take a drive and enjoy the cool air around the canal. Marie declined, claiming she had papers to correct before the morning, but encouraged them to go without her. After a brief conversation in French, Adèle said, "Let's go."

They were almost in front of the White House before Kory could think of something to say without appearing too anxious.

"The White House," he said, pointing as they drove west, passing in front of the north portico. He could visualize Lyndon Johnson holding his pet beagle by the ears as he talked to reporters, assuring them they would be the first to hear of any change in the war in Vietnam—like pulling out.

"Johnson. He is a cowboy, no?"

"Uh…yes."

"Do you like the waterside?" he asked in Latin.

"*Oui*…yes, I like."

Just three blocks south of the White House was the waterfront. In the summer, because of the smell, you could always tell when you were getting close to the wharf—*eau de* fishmonger. To the south, the Tidal Basin was surrounded by historic landmarks like the Jefferson Memorial, which housed a statue of the slaveholder-author of "All men are created equal." And across the water was a place that rented paddleboats in which to drift around the perimeter in the moonlight, which they did that night.

Kory had a hard enough time containing himself with Adèle getting in and out of his sports car in her miniskirt, but her legs, going in and out or up and down on the pedals, were pushing him to his limit. They had pedaled once around the entire Tidal Basin when Kory stopped; he put his arm around her and gesticulated in Latin, French, and broken English. She did not seem to be paying attention to his rambling as much as to his eyes. Adèle placed a finger on his lips.

"I want to kiss you," Kory said.

"Kiss me!"

From such a delicate girl, he never would have expected such a passionate kiss—a kiss that seemed to last for at least ten minutes, for when they parted lips, they fell back against their seats, breathless. So they just drifted across the moonlight, lying in each other's arms, until the floodlights blinked and the boathouse operator announced the closing of the dock over the public address system.

"Would you like to go for a drink?"

Adèle looked at her watch. "I have a class in the morning."

"Just one drink at Tassos, and I will take you home."

"Okay. Just one."

By the time the two of them arrived, the band was putting away their instruments. There were more candles than people in the still-smoke-filled back room.

Kory was in luck. His favorite waitress was still serving, and he hoped she would bring them two cognacs without asking for ID.

"Would you like a Hennessy?" he asked, holding her hands across the table.

"Hennessy?"

"Cognac!"

"Ah, *oui!*"

The strong liquor did not dampen Kory's desire. It just removed the last inhibitions he had in trying to tell her how he felt.

"Adèle, you make me feel like yelling to heaven that it truly does exist. I have never felt this way before."

"*Moi aussi*...me too."

Someone dropped a dime in the jukebox and played "Michelle." Adèle came around the table and sang the lyrics in French. When the song ended, they did not speak as they walked arm in arm to the car.

The ingenuity of youth is boundless: in a parking lot just at the end of Adèle's apartment building, they explored each other's bodies and got into rubbing positions that would have made a contortionist shy.

"I must go."

Kory's hand tugged at her panty hose. "Just a little bit longer!" he pleaded. Adèle pushed his hand away as he pulled again at the waistband.

Finally, she said, "Let's go out Friday. Marie will be out of town."

"Are you sure?" Kory entreated.

"Yes."

Kory kissed her one more time and opened the car door. At the front door, the banging of their bodies against the glass awakened even the night desk clerk, who usually slept through his shift. He pretended to be placing undelivered messages in mailboxes as he spied them out of the corner of his eye.

As Kory pulled out of the parking lot, he knew a cold beer, a glass of wine, or even a cold shower would do little to quell the heat tonight. In his bedroom he took out writing paper and wrote the words his heart sang:

My heart is so heavy with love for you that I may die before first light. Kiss me once again so I may drift with feeling forever.

The next afternoon, Kory stood in front of Dale.

"So, how did the wine go with dinner?" Dale was gluing the final piece of *lapis armenus* to a board that must have been intended for a display. Kory could not imagine playing with such distraction.

"They loved it—at least that's what they said. We were drunk by the second bottle."

"You don't look happy."

"I think I'm in love."

"Lucky you. I've forgotten how to spell the word."

"I can't stop thinking about her. I need some advice from an older person like you."

"I'm not that much older than you. Why don't we play a couple of games to get your mind off her?" Dale set the ebony-and-ivory board between them.

Dale and Kory played for about two hours, but Kory was not able to concentrate. He foolishly passed up opportunities to control the game; instead he built a fortress around his queen and allowed all of his other pieces to be captured in her protection.

"That's three straight games you have lost to me. When I was your age, I fell in love with a girl who sat two rows in front of me in my freshmen English literature class. For two months, I watched in agony, as she was within arm's reach, but I didn't have the nerve to tell her how I felt. One day we bumped into each other in the library. I was looking on the shelves for more research material for my term paper, when I saw her standing on one of those little stools that always rocks just when you've spotted your book, only to realize it is on the opposite end of the shelf. I said hello to her, and when she turned, she lost her balance and fell right into my arms. It was then I was convinced there is a God. Looking into her eyes, I admitted I was secretly in love with her."

"What did she say?"

"She had been watching me as well. Since I hadn't returned her smiles and asked her for a date, she thought I was not interested. Now she was dating a guy who promised to marry her after graduation."

"Is that a true story?"

Dale winked. "It could be!"

"So what should I do?"

"From what you told me about last night, she already sounds like she's in love with you."

"But you haven't told me what I should do next."

"I don't mean to sound corny, but you should let your feelings for her guide your actions. But in the meantime, you now owe me seventy-five dollars."

"How about double or nothing?"

"You really think you're that good, young man?"

"What can I say? I'll probably get to the middle game, and the moment you attack my queen, I'll become overly protective." Kory dropped his head.

"Well, since I like you, I won't do what you did and run off without giving you another chance."

Kory could see greed in Dale's smile. They had played only ten minutes. "Dale, I believe you are in check."

"Dammit! You did it to me again. You suckered me with that crap about being distracted."

"No, I really was. Thanks to your advice, I have regained my confidence. You're such a wise older person," said Kory, as he counted the money on the edge of the table.

"Mr. Burke, Mr. Haddad is here to pick up his board. What should I tell him?"

Dale glared at his employee standing in the doorway. "Tell him to go to h… Never mind. I'll tell him. Be out in a minute."

Kory handed his winnings to Dale. "How about two bottles of wine and we call it even?"

Dale extended his hand. "Deal!"

CHAPTER 14:

Love 101

Kory spent most of the afternoon polishing his Austin-Healey and thinking about his date with Adèle. When he was dressed and sitting behind the wheel, he put his head in his hands, as if praying. "Please let it be tonight." Minutes later, wind rustled under his ears as he caught all seven green lights for the first time.

Leaning with her back against a taunting gargoyle, there she was, smoking a cigarette and looking like a model right out of the latest edition of *ELLE*. Instead of flashbulbs popping from paparazzi, late-summer sunshine bathed the evening with streams of orange, allowing Kory to see Adèle for the first time in natural light. The color of her hair, her eyes—her everything—made him weak in the knees as he held open the car door. She was even wearing hose with fine vertical strands of gold, which seemed to emanate from a place he could only imagine—but hoped to be before the night was over.

"Where we going, Kory?"

"Do you like seafood?"

"*Oui*, not here, America."

"Oh, you haven't had Amerian seafood yet. That's good because I know of a great place in Southwest Washington where you can pick your own lobster from a large tank. Do you like lobster?"

"Lob-sterr?"

"*Homard!*" he said before they entered the underpass under Thomas Circle.

"*Oui, beaucoup.* Lob-ster!" The wind rushed through her hair as they drove at high speed to the end of the tunnel.

"*C'est bon.*" Kory's French vocabulary was nearly exhausted.

The Market Inn Restaurant was a well-kept secret by residents of Southwest Washington and those who worked on Capitol Hill, hoping to steal a few minutes of romance out of camera shot from local reporters.

Besides their reputation for excellent food, the real attractions of this hideaway were the candlelight that dazzled lovers' eyes and the crooning piano player who always seemed to whisper the right song. Although the restaurant was small, the tables were placed far enough apart that only the invisible, highly tipped waiter would have been able to repeat the words of the unfaithful, trying to recapture the thrill of a newly made love. For a few hours when people entered this romantic eatery tucked under an abandoned railroad bridge two blocks from Congress, they could experience the sweetness of love they thought came only once in a lifetime.

Kory and Adèle's passion mounted as the waiter filled their glasses with champagne. Few words needed to be said. They just looked into each other's eyes, hypnotized by expectations.

"Would you like to order now?" whispered the waiter.

"Yes. Two cold showers!"

"Would you like them with scented or unscented water, sir?"

"Unscented, of course. I don't want to miss anything."

Kory looked at Adèle. "Tu *faim?*" (Are you hungry?)

Adèle smiled. "*Mais oui!*"

The waiter rolled a crowded lobster tank to their table. He recommended two enormous lobsters with large banded claws, but Kory suggested to Adèle that the older lobsters were tough, whereas the smaller bottom-feeders, were sweet and tender. They settled on two three-pound Maine lobsters with all the usual side dishes.

Adèle put butter-drenched pieces of lobster in Kory's mouth while he searched unseen places with his hands. When the waiter asked if they needed something more or maybe dessert, Kory winked and informed him they had dessert waiting for them.

An early moon followed them as they drove around the circle below the U.S. Capitol, which was undergoing renovation. The dome, primed in orange paint, with little imagination, appeared to be a suntanned breast with a protruding, erect nipple longing for a gentle nibble.

"Where would you like to go?"

"Home," she said as she nuzzled her head against his shoulder.

Eros favors those in love; not only did Kory drive faster than usual, he went through three yellow traffic lights, hoping they would be the only thing trying to stop him tonight.

It took less than ten minutes to get to Adèle's building, and when the elevator reached her floor, buttons were already popping and zippers were being undone in concert.

The hallway door had barely closed before Adèle's hand went inside his shirt; she ran her fingers over his hairy chest while Kory buried his head in her breast. Round and round they went as they undressed each other, until Adèle's panty hose, now around her ankles, caused them to lose their balance and land in a pool of cushions.

Kory was about to enter her when she closed her legs tightly and confided, "I...virgin."

"So am I. I've never really made love before."

With each gentle thrust, Adèle dug her fingernails into Kory's back just below his shoulder blades. Streams of sweat stung each scratch she had made but only increased his passion. Adèle, moaning and very wet, pushed her hips so hard that Kory had to cup her buttocks with both hands, until instinct showed her how to wrap her legs around his waist and take them to another level. They made love for the next four hours, breaking only long enough to take a few breaths apart and start again; all the while, in the background, Isaac Hayes's "Walk On By" played again and again. Before morning, they had explored every inch of each other; neither eyelid nor toe had gone uncaressed. They had sworn their love with rhythm—over and over again.

Morning arrived with a call from Marie inside a phone booth at the boarding gate of La Guardia Airport. She had missed her flight. Adèle was relieved. The apartment was in shambles, and Kory was in her bed. Now that she had extra time, she woke Kory, who needed little encouragement to rise.

Hours went by before Adèle stumbled to the kitchen and returned with fruit, cheese, and Evian bottled water. No sooner had they recovered for the umpteenth time than Marie was putting her key in the hallway door.

Kory remained in Adèle's bed while she went to the living room to talk to Marie. Kory could not understand what they were saying, but by their laughter, it was obvious they were celebrating something. Adèle returned to bed. It was about six o'clock when they awoke in each other's arms. Without saying a word, they began making love again. They had forgotten Marie had returned until they heard knocking at the door.

"You two need to think of something else to do. How about dinner?"

Kory was busy under the sheets.   "Just…give…twenty…twenty… minutes…to…shower," Adèle cried out.

It was closer to an hour before they dragged themselves to the dining table. Marie, who loved to lose herself in the kitchen, had prepared coq au vin, melted Brie topped with truffles, and goose foie gras. A 1965 Pommard breathed in the center. Sitting directly across from Marie, Kory saw a fresh bandage on the same wrist he had noticed at Tassos, and playing again on the stereo was her favorite sad song. She ate only one cracker with cheese before she excused herself from the table. Despite the music in the background, Kory heard Marie retching in the bathroom. Her face was pallid when she returned, but she managed to smile as she reached for another cracker.

"So, what did you two do while I was gone, besides exercise?"

"Well, I tried to get your roommate to attend a lecture called 'Morality in the Sixties,' hosted by the Washington Ethical Society, but she insisted she was already a paragon of virtue—something the nuns beat into both of you before you graduated from the parochial school outside Besançon."

"That is a big lie you just told her. He took advantage of an innocent girl from a small town in France." Adèle tapped glasses with Marie.

CHAPTER 15:

The Choice

For the next two years, whenever possible, Adèle and Kory spent time together. Whether sunning in the Circle or just reading Camus or Proust together, they were becoming lost in each other: Kory became more French, and Adèle got soul.

Adèle was approaching her twenty-third birthday, which was just ten days before Kory's nineteenth. Lately she had begun pointing out children in strollers while they sunned. At first he marveled at the idea of having a child, but Kory knew he was not ready. They had spoken about marriage one day, but Kory's family, although they liked Adèle, did not approve of the union.

On April 4, 1968, Martin Luther King was assassinated. When Kory heard the news on television, he immediately walked to the heart of the black business district at the intersection of Fourteenth and U Streets. Within minutes the first brick was thrown through the window of Sam's Pawnbrokers. It was quickly followed by the breaking of the fifteen-foot plate-glass window in Peoples Drug Store. By the time the first squad car arrived, it was as if the cap had been removed from a hot bottle of Coca-Cola. The police did not attempt to make any arrests; in fact, as one very large woman climbed through the broken glass and pulled a six-foot-wide color television to the sidewalk, the policeman standing by walked up to her and said, "You should get your husband to help you take it home."

Hours later Kory was glued to the television when the phone rang. "It's Adèle. You have not called. Is everything all right? I heard the police shot people. Why did you not call me?"

"Sorry. Because of my family's involvement in civil rights, we have been concerned with my grandfather's safety, and there are other things on my mind as well."

"Like what?"

"Yesterday I joined the Student Nonviolent Coordinating Committee to help some of the people who've been arrested in the revolt. We're also trying to force the president of the school to resign. He's just too much of an Uncle Tom."

"Uncle Tom? Who is he? Since you transferred to Howard University, I hardly know you anymore."

"It's not who but what. The president of the college is always giving in to the white establishment."

"I'm white!"

"That's part of the problem."

"So that's why...You Americans are so concerned with race."

"There are many things going on in this country you don't understand."

"Such as?"

"A revolution is coming. A lot of people will probably be killed."

"Do you mean whites killing blacks?"

"More like blacks killing whites."

"Does that mean you might have to kill me to protect your people?"

"Uh...I don't know what it means. I need time to sort my life out."

"Well, take all the time you need. I am leaving for France in two weeks. I will be gone for a year."

"Why didn't you tell me sooner?"

"You stopped calling. What did you want me to do, draw a picture or something?"

"Adèle, you know I love you. When I look in the mirror, I need to be sure of who I am."

"I know who you are. You are the guy I fell in love with two years ago."

"Would you like to have a drink with me tonight?"

"Sure. Marie is out of town. We can be alone here tonight."

"I'll see you after the rally on campus."

"Do you want me to go with you?" Adèle asked.

"I don't think that would be a good idea right now."

Early that evening, Kory went to a rally on campus featuring Stokely Carmichael as its keynote speaker, followed by the vitriolic H. Rap Brown.

"*Black Power! Black Power! Black Power!*"

"Kill the pigs! Get a gun and free your people from the oppressor." Those were the words from speaker after speaker.

Kory unknowingly raised his fist in the protest salute and repeated the slogans that had become the mantra of the crowd.

"My brother, will you join us at the meeting after the rally?" asked a very serious-looking student wearing an African dress. Kory had met her a few days ago.

"No, Sister-Lady. I have some family business to attend to."

"Sorry to hear that. We need all the brothers we can get now. Black blood is flowing in the street. It should be white blood running into the sewers. I'll be looking for you tomorrow at the march."

"I'll be there. Stay strong, my sister."

Kory drove down Georgia Avenue from the campus. Every block showed the anger and frustration of his people. The air was filled with smoke and tear gas, and on every corner he could see young and old black people shackled like cattle and forced to lie face down on the pavement. There was even a handcuffed pregnant woman who was struggling to lie on her side to take the pressure of the hard cement off her unborn child.

As he got within a few blocks of Adèle's building, with the exception of the cordon of police cars protecting that part of the city, the streets were bereft of people. The intersection of Fourteenth and Massachusetts Avenue was also deserted. The city had become polarized again. Kory wondered if what was happening was really a lurch forward or a stumble back to the days of blatant Jim Crow.

"I didn't think you would come," said Adèle as she hugged him at the door.

"I almost didn't. Sorry, but I can't stay. I just wanted to say good-bye to you before you left for France."

She stepped back from him. "Is that all? Good-bye?"

"I don't know what else to say right now. I want to be here with you, but I feel I have a responsibility to be a part of what is happening in the streets."

"You could get yourself killed."

"Maybe. But if I do, I will have died for a good reason."

"Am I not important to you anymore?"

"Of course you are. Are you expecting me to make a choice between my people and you?"

"If you really loved me, you would."

Kory grabbed his car keys. "I was afraid you would say that."

"So you are just going to walk out on me without an explanation."

"There's no explanation I could give you to make you understand."

"Then leave!" she screamed.

Kory reached for her. "Adèle!"

"Don't touch me. You are breaking my heart."

"I'm sorry. I never meant for things to end like this."

"Get out. I never want to see you again."

Kory grabbed the doorknob and looked at her for the last time, he thought. "What happened to the world we once had? One day you will understand why I can't ignore this opportunity to be more than I am now."

Once behind the wheel, he looked into the rearview mirror, as if he were trying to see if someone had followed; there was only his reflection. After placing a red, black, and green headband over his blooming Afro, he drove his car toward his identity without an occupant in the passenger seat.

CHAPTER 16:

Lost in the Mirror

America survived the sixties. Chains of slavery became grudging fetters of racial tolerance to stave off revenge. Back doors were supplanted with welcome mats at main entrances as sepia-hued Washingtonians exercised their rights to be treated as sentient taxpayers, as opposed to Stepin Fetchit doppelgängers shuffling their feet as they walked backward to moronic invisibility.

It was a typical hot evening in Washington, DC. After a long hiatus from his studies, the summer of 1972, Kory completed another year of college and in the evenings finished a two-month modeling course in Bethesda, Maryland. The last day of the course ended with a fashion show at the Statler Hilton Hotel, just one block from Richard Nixon's White House.

After the show, he asked the director of the school about his modeling prospects. She was unexpectedly candid: opportunities for black models were very limited; he could stay in the Washington area and work the local shows or move to New York. With only two years to complete his undergraduate work, he was not ready throw all that away to take a chance on finding a job where signs still read FOR WHITES ONLY in the minds of casting agents.

An ad appeared before the end of summer in the *Washington Post* from a local modeling agency. With only three fashion shows to his credit, Kory convinced Carol Collingsworth, the head of casting, that he had the look her agency was trying to find. She told him there was a cancellation that day if he could make it there that afternoon. Kory took the two thirty opening without a second thought.

It was already 1:50 p.m. as he rushed through the house. After slamming the front door shut, he nearly fell down the granite front steps when the wooden heel of one of his shoes slipped on some of the smooth pebbles that always seemed to collect there after a storm.

Today he was in luck, though. A cab was cruising down Sixteenth Street when he reached the sidewalk. The driver was Yale Lewis, a jazz station disc jockey at night and cab driver during the day. He was having a slow day, so he was more than glad to accept a five-dollar tip to get Kory on time to the Cinderella Modeling School and Agency at Thirteenth and G Streets in ten minutes.

Yale earned his tip. His passenger's heart raced as the taxi just made it through the yellow light in one intersection after another. When the cab pulled up in front of his destination, Kory took a deep breath, put on a smile that started from his toes, and stepped inside the make-believe world of fashion modeling.

The lobby was all white, with the exception of the glass reception desk, where a very tall blond wearing a blue designer evening gown was seated behind a large telephone console that a hummed every time another line needed to be answered.

"Hi! My name is Kory Vanon. I have a two thirty appointment with Carol Collingsworth."

"So *you're* Kory Vanon. Nice suit! I was wondering what a Kory would look like. She's expecting you. The phones are not too busy. If you'll follow me, I'll take you to her office."

"I'll follow you anywhere you want. What's your name?"

"I'm Heather."

"So you're what a Heather looks like. It was worth the wait."

She smiled and strutted in front of Kory like a runway model, brushing her ankles as she walked. He wondered why such a lovely lady was simply answering the phones. Maybe she had just finished her course.

As he followed her down the spongy carpeted hallway, head shots of agency models covered the wall. Kory imagined his face among others in a world more interested in what was on the outside than what remained of a person after the youthful smile had faded to wrinkles.

"Carol, Kory Vanon is here for his two thirty interview."

"Thanks, Heather." As if someone had flipped a switch, Carol extended her hand to Kory and smiled as though she were looking into the lens of a camera. "Glad you could make it. Please make yourself comfortable. Now, this is our agency's application. While you're filling it out, I need to check on a photo shoot upstairs. It will only take me about ten minutes. You are actually about fifteen minutes early. I hope you don't mind," she said as she checked her makeup in the mirror on her desk.

"I'm sorry. I have a habit of always being a little faster than the hour. Ten minutes will be more than enough time for me to finish." Kory watched her swivel past him into the hallway. She still had the smile, but her body would do little for a designer's svelte evening dress.

He could easily imagine Carol Collingsworth when she was at the top of her game, before she crossed over into the business side of fashion modeling. She had fading good looks, now propped up by heavy makeup, which smoothed the etched lines around her mouth from years of smiling on cue. Although she was still quite attractive, the bright lights, countless applications of professional-grade face foundations, and, most likely, a hectic lifestyle, caused her to have an air bereft of genuineness. Maybe it was just his imagination, but in some ways she reminded him of some of the worn-out madams whom he had met during his days in the nightlife. Perhaps what he saw was the face of one who had become jaded by life's overconsumption—or perhaps life had consumed her and had its fill.

"All finished? Sorry it took a little longer than fifteen minutes. The photographer couldn't make up his mind which models he wanted for the fall spread in the Woodies catalog—so I had to throw my weight around." Carol exhaled as sat down, as if she had been holding her breath. She rechecked herself in the mirror before looking at Kory again.

"I've seen their ads. Never guessed they were your models. One would think the largest department store in Washington would only use models from New York City."

"We have contracts with most of the major clothing stores in the area. In fact, I'm proud to say we have lost very little business to New York models lately. Local advertisers are happy to use our graduates and sometimes our more promising students at the discount rates we give them."

"Ah, the persuasive power of money will do it every time. Washington is finally getting the respect it has been denied."

Carol smiled as she reviewed Kory's application. Her heavy blond false eyelashes blinked in approval; all the while, Kory wondered if she would be able to complete the interview before one row of her lashes stuck to the other and caused her to smile with one eye closed.

"Kory, I can see you don't have a lot of experience, but time in the business isn't necessarily a guarantee of success. You've many talents for a model. In fact, you appear to be better educated than most of the people who apply to our agency."

"I hope that's a plus."

"Well, we're actually two businesses. As you know, there's Cinderella, our modeling school, and Central Casting, the professional segment of the business. Please tell me more about the kind of work you're looking for."

"I'm still a little green, so I'm open to anything."

"I'm glad you said that. The school has considered launching a male modeling department. Did you know there's not a formal course geared exclusively to training male models?"

"Well, I don't know about the whole country, but obviously a place to get the proper training is hard to find around Washington."

"Have you ever considered teaching a course in modeling?"

Kory could not believe his ears. The speed he had taken before he left his house was hard at work. "Yes, in fact, I have. I've been working on a curriculum for the past six months. I only wrote it to remind myself of what I had learned and maybe turn it into a book one day."

"That's amazing! I would like you to meet the director of our school, Bill Wiltzer. You've probably never heard his name before, but he was one of the first Ronald McDonald clowns. Excuse me for a minute. I'll see if he has a minute to pop in." She rose from her chair, this time without checking her makeup.

Looking up at the fluorescent lights in the ceiling, he thought, *Now you've done it, Kory. What have you gotten yourself into this time? Showtime!*

The meeting with the director lasted only ten minutes. He asked Kory very little about his experience. Kory knew performers are always looking for an audience, so he sat through the highlights of the director's career as an actor and model. The last thing he asked Kory was whether or not he had a girlfriend. Kory understood why Carol wore her makeup, but the director's makeup and dyed hair left some unanswered questions in Kory's brain, now in overdrive.

When Kory was in high school, he had told his typing instructor he didn't need clerical skills, since he would certainly have a secretary to type all of his letters. Well, it was good she had threatened to fail him, because his meager typing skills came in handy when he had to come up with a complete male-modeling curriculum in seven days. In less than a week, he became familiar with every modeling format, as well as personal makeup, fencing, basic acting techniques, etiquette, and Smiling 101. The school invested thousands in advertising. Two weeks later, there were thirty eager male-modeling students who ran the spectrum from unusual to ridiculously ugly.

CHAPTER 17:

Routine

By the second week of class, Kory had become comfortable enough with the curriculum to step out of himself and onto another precipice. There he was again, dangling by a thread. Before he had made the commitment to the Cinderella Modeling School, he had already scheduled a full load of college classes in the fall, and maintaining both required a regimen of coffee, cigarettes, and speed. At nineteen, Kory believed himself indestructible.

Things began to change after one year, when Kory's lack of experience allowed him one act of poor judgment: being only twenty and teaching etiquette to a classroom of aspiring female models proved to be a great temptation for the very young pedagogue.

One student in particular, who was all of six feet tall, with Elizabeth Taylor–like violet eyes and a body as svelte as a seal's, nearly cost him his job when another student, who had a crush on Kory, reported their liaison to the school's director, Bill.

The former Ronald McDonald clown said in a not-so-funny fashion, "Beth was seen entering your house on a number of evenings. There's a rumor you are sleeping with her. Before you answer, be aware this is a very serious accusation with consequences."

Guessing his accuser could provide proof or at least another witness, Kory resigned himself to confessing to the terrible deed. "I don't know how she found my address. She started showing up under the pretense of needing some additional coaching. I thought I was being a good teacher by offering support outside the classroom. I never expected her intentions were anything more than those of a student seeking guidance. Now that I look back on it, it was very naïve of me, but it just happened. And it only happened once. I wish I had never let her into my house."

Looking very serious—and still very un-clown-like—Bill said, "So tell me: How was it?"

"Excuse me!"

The clown smile had returned to the director's face. "Was she good in bed?"

"All I can say is, sometimes the prettier they are, the more disappointing they are in the sack. She was young and inexperienced. It was as if she still had the scent of Carnation milk on her breath."

"Thank God you're only one year older than she is. But one year of growing up in Washington is equivalent to five years in a town like Wilkes-Barre, Pennsylvania. I've already talked with her, and luckily she's not going to say anything to her parents. It might not be a bad idea for you to pay a little more attention to the young lady who turned you in."

"Yeah, I should have known better. I was hoping she would just lose interest in me and focus her infatuations on another teacher. My experience with scorned women in the past should have taught me better." Kory was recalling the time when a drunken young woman in a nightclub, whom he had not asked to dance, had stuck a loaded gun to the back of his head.

"Fat chance! These are girls trying to become women. You need to call her into your office and do everything but take that little bigmouth to bed. I can see why you didn't before. She's dreaming if she thinks she'll ever make it in the modeling world. The girl doesn't have it."

"Well, I greatly appreciate your understanding. I was almost expecting to be fired."

"If I ever hear about something like this again, you can count on it." The big clown smiled a final time before checking his nails, which were better manicured than most women's.

The rumors around the school died down after two weeks. Despite the imprudent incident with one of his students, things were going well. There he was, at his age—the director of male modeling and the author of a new program that was going to become a part of the curriculum in all the Cinderella Modeling Schools in the country.

But after a year and a half had gone by, boredom began to rear its ugly head. Kory knew the feeling too well; it would not be long before another transition would force him ahead.

One afternoon, while he was storing the fencing equipment, the teacher of the next class arrived before Kory had a chance to rearrange the classroom. Jennifer, the new ballet instructor, had been a principal dancer with the New York City Ballet before taking a position with Cinderella. She had given up her career in New York to start a family in her hometown of Washington, DC. Since they were the only people of color on staff, they had developed a quick friendship and shortly had begun to trade professional information.

"Kory, I've watched you teach your fencing class. Have you ever had any dance training?"

"Well, nothing formal, but I pick up steps easily."

"Tell you what: I need to get more hours here, and if you teach me modeling, I'll teach you ballet, if you're interested."

"I already have a sword; all I need are the tights, and I could be the black Rudolf Nureyev," Kory said jokingly, as he went up on his toes and thrust his foil at his reflection in the studio-length mirror.

"So, you have been to the ballet," Jennifer said.

"Not as often as I would like. I recently saw the Washington Ballet, but they could not share the same stage with the Bolshoi Ballet, which I saw last fall at the Kennedy Center. I guess I could see myself carrying some beautiful lady in a tutu around a stage."

"When would you like to start? I really need to make some extra money. It's hard getting by on just five classes a week. My fiancé and I are trying to buy our first house. I'm really serious if you're interested in the trade."

"Sure! I'm free until four o'clock. And at this time of day, we shouldn't be disturbed. I really don't want any of my students seeing me make a fool of myself."

"Come on, now! I've watched you move in your fencing class. I know you'll do just fine. Now, we only have about forty-five minutes before my next class. I usually take this time to warm up and give myself a barre. Why don't you just stand behind me and follow what I'm doing?"

Jennifer took off her baggy warm-up suit and displayed a body devoid of the slightest hint of fat. She rested her left hand on the ballet barre, stood with her feet on the same plane, pointed her toes in opposite directions, and proceeded to bend her legs into a plié.

"Wow! You don't really expect for me to get my feet like that!"

"Don't think about your feet. You're trying to turn out your hips. The worst thing a dancer can do is force turnout from his or her feet. It will ruin your knees. Just visualize the top of your leg where it inserts into the hip socket. I want you to see those bones rotating to the direction of your little toe."

"You make it look so easy. This is really hard work!"

"This is what we do to look good onstage. Okay, let's try the other side. This time I'm going to watch you. Just relax."

"Sure. That's easy for you to say."

"That's it. Squeeze those thighs, and keep your butt perpendicular to the floor. Now press on your entire foot, and push through your hips to rise. After you feel you're in the correct position, I want you to check yourself in the mirror. But I must warn you not to become a prisoner. I only want you to use it to develop an inner reflection of what your body is doing. Now look, and tell me what you see."

"Well, I'm not sure what I should be looking for, but I do notice I appear to be leaning forward." Kory grabbed the ballet barre for balance, sensing fatigue in his ankles from standing on the balls of his feet.

"I'm glad you noticed that first. All movement involves some direction of falling. To compensate for that, I want you to offset it by directing your energy up through your spine. The opposing energies allow you to balance and reduce fatigue in your body, and furthermore, it extends the illusion to the audience of not being limited by gravity. It's not just about strength; finding balance is more important than developing big muscles."

"Wow, just thinking about letting my energy flow upward has given me a rush. This is amazing."

"That's good, Kory. What you have learned today is something some dancers take years to understand. You've picked it up in just twenty minutes."

"It's your teaching. You're able to break things down so it's easy to understand. That's a gift few teachers have in any field."

"I can tell you are getting a little tired, but I want you to try again. This time, keep your head up. Don't look at the floor. The floor won't help you. Just try to expand the picture in your mind of what your body is doing. There are no mirrors onstage—just critics."

"This is incredible. I can't believe I'm sweating."

"As the ballet master moves around the classroom, he or she frequently checks to see who has the biggest puddle of sweat. Classical dance is probably the greatest challenge to the body. Every muscle in your body is used to give the illusion of floating above the stage. Your goal is to direct all your energy up."

"Whatever you say."

"And, Kory, you don't know it yet, but you have what we call in the business 'natural turnout.' Your hips naturally rotate from their sockets without your forcing them from the feet. Do you have any idea how many dancers would kill to have that ability?"

"I barely have a clue what you're talking about, so no. I've always been flexible. If having natural turnout means there's some hope of my ever progressing beyond the basic level, then I guess I should thank my parents for their genes the next time I see them."

CHAPTER 18:

Another Audition

Within a month, Jennifer and Kory were exchanging teaching skills three times a week. Since she had experience applying her own stage makeup, it did not take much to extrapolate it to Makeup I for modeling. He also added etiquette to her teaching repertoire.

They bumped into each other four months later in the teachers' lounge, "Hi, Kory. What are you doing Friday night?"

"Uh, just the usual. Are you asking me out? I thought you were engaged."

"Get a grip on your hormones. My fiancé is all the man I need."

"I just thought I was getting lucky."

"You are, but not where you're thinking. There's a dance audition for a new production of *Music Man*, and I think you're good enough to make it. Do you sing?"

"You can't be serious! I barely know dance terminology."

"Don't worry about that. You pick up steps like a seasoned dancer. All you have to do is copy what the dance captain does."

"Hey, I'm willing to try anything once. Do you really think I have a chance?"

"Honey, I've danced all over New York and have been to hundreds of auditions. You have the look choreographers want, in that you are the right height to partner and you have a soft, butch look, which will please the women and the men in the audience."

The audition was held in Cramton Auditorium on the Howard University campus. The stage must have had over a hundred dancers, in all sorts of attire, ready to show their stuff to the barking dance captain. Kory was more than a little intimidated by some of the dancers when he saw them practicing double and triple turns; being able to complete one good pirouette without losing his balance was challenge enough for him. Little did he know he was auditioning with people like Debbie Allen and other soon-to-be-famous dancers.

"Hello, everyone, my name is Mike Malone. I am the director. To my left is Clyde, my dance captain. He'll be giving you the dance routines and helping you with questions. I want everyone to relax and have a good time. Not everyone will make it, and if you're not called back, it's not that you don't have enough talent, but maybe you don't have the look for the particular part available at this time. We'll be having further auditions for other parts as they become available. So make sure we have your name and telephone number. Break a leg, everyone!"

"Break a leg? Why did he say that?" Kory said it loud enough for the dancer beside him to hear.

"Where are you from, Miss Thing? Is this your first audition or something?" said a very feminine-looking guy in purple tights wearing his leotard on top of his tights, instead of under them like most men did.

"Is it that obvious?"

Throwing his head back before he answered, the dancer said, "Yes, honey—very."

"This is my first audition, and I'm nervous," Kory said.

"This is my hundredth, and I'm nervous. You're supposed to be nervous every time you step on the stage. It's what you do with that nervousness that separates the divas from the dogs. Just stand behind me and follow me. And don't get any ideas. I already have someone."

"That's comforting; I mean…I'm glad you have someone."

"Everyone, we'll do this routine three times en masse, and then we'll break into three groups for the elimination. Any questions?" Mike asked, turning his back to the stage. "Clyde will give you the first routine," he said as he walked across the stage like a cat prancing on its toes, but his heels hardly left the floor, despite the fact that he looked as if his next step would be a leap.

Clyde was only about five and a half feet tall, but he had legs like a gymnast. "Five-six, five-six, seven-eight, and one-two-three-four triple turn, hold two-three-four and contract left-right, and chassé and hold," he barked.

"Did you get that, Mr. Black? I don't know your name, so I'll call you that."

"It's Kory."

"I like 'Mr. Black' better. You look mysterious. What are you hiding under those tights?"

"Just the usual stuff. Didn't you tell me you're with someone?"

"We like a ménage à trois every now and then."

"I don't share. Maybe some other time when you're free."

"Good answer, honey. Just playing around."

Clyde, with clipboard in hand, walked around the stage and directed timorous, similarly clad, svelte bodies into three groups.

"Group One—five-six-seven-eight, and one, two, three, four; two, two, three, four; and stop. Group Two—five-six-seven-eight…" the dance captain commanded.

When Group Three was called to the stage, Kory managed to get behind the guy in the purple tights. He did all the steps correctly and even managed to do a double turn that he had never done before. Jennifer had told him if he could see the step in his mind, he could do it onstage. He just had to relax and let it happen.

Mike Malone was now sitting about seven rows from the stage in a seat that had a small lamp and microphone. He said patronizingly, "All right, everyone, thanks for coming. From Group One, if I point to you, that means you get a callback. The rest of you, watch the bulletin board for our next audition."

And on it went until he reached Group Three. By the time the director had eliminated most of the dancers in Group Three, Kory considered avoiding the humiliation by leaving then, but his ego would not let his feet move. When Mike Malone finally got to the back row, he looked directly into Kory's eyes and said, "And you in the black headband—Monday at three o'clock."

"Well, Mr. Black, I guess I won't see you on Monday. You must have the look. Even though you're green, you'll make a good third leg for one of the girls."

"Third leg? Are you talking about—"

"Don't even go there, as hot as I am right now. Mr. Black, what I meant is the female dancer will use your body for balance when she's going en pointe or balancing on one leg. One word of advice, though."

"What's that?"

"Don't let some of those queens turn your head around before you get with me."

"Excuse me!"

"Never mind, Mr. Black."

It was a shame his conversation with the epicene dancer in purple ended so soon; Kory was just beginning to understand what the hell the guy was talking about.

Later that evening, while he was relaxing on the sofa, the doorbell rang. Kory cracked the blinds just enough to recognize Beth holding a bunch of flowers and a bottle of wine. He turned up John Coltrane on his stereo and fell into a deep sleep. "Transition" was playing on the record player.

CHAPTER 19

The First Fall

Nightime was falling earlier in Washington, DC. The air had become nostalgic waves of decaying, sweet maple, and oak leaves. There was something about autumn in this city that calmed Kory. Maybe it was that in the colder months, he often spent more time at home with his thoughts, or perhaps it was because during the cooler days, he had less trouble with the stiffness in his legs, which nagged him with increasing frequency. Regardless, tonight he pondered what to do with his life, now that the director's job at the Cinderella Modeling School had lost his interest.

A few weeks earlier, on Jennifer's advice, he had enrolled in a beginners' ballet class at the Washington School of Ballet. The first night, most students were middle-aged women trying to take the ballet class they had missed as children; he was the only male.

After the fifth week, two students from the daytime academy joined the class. They were both on scholarship and already had the look of classical dancers. The girl had lissome legs and looked like she had not eaten in days, whereas the guy had a look of aloofness Kory found imitable. During the middle of class, Mavis, the thirty-something instructor, stood behind Kory at the ballet barre and with her hips pushed his pelvis forward to show him how to best use his turnout. When he finished the exercise, she whispered to him to see her after class.

"Mavis. You wanted to see to me?" Kory said as he adjusted his black thigh-length leg warmers and adjusted his belt around his tights.

"Kory, it's time for you to move along. I and some other teachers have been discussing you. We believe you would benefit from more challenging classes, although I want you to continue my class until the end of the term. Are you able to take class on Tuesday and Thursday evenings?"

"Sure!"

"There's an advanced beginners' class on those nights. You'll get a chance to see if you're ready for more complicated work. I believe you can handle it."

"I don't know what to say. You really think I can keep up with that class?"

"Believe me, if I didn't think you were ready, I wouldn't risk damaging my reputation by sending you to another teacher."

"Thank you very much. This is very encouraging. I really want to become a good dancer."

"I can see that. You've got a lot of potential—particularly, your turnout is excellent for a man, and if you were a woman, you would do well to have the amount of natural turnout you possess."

"When can I start?"

"I'll speak with the instructor tonight. Class starts at six o'clock. Will you be able to start that soon?"

"I usually teach a fencing class then, but I think I'll be able to get away with changing the hour. Nothing is more important to me now than ballet." Kory looked at the poster on the wall of Arthur Mitchell in the role of Puck in Balanchine's production of *A Midsummer Night's Dream*. Mitchell had been the first black male to become a principal dancer in a major dance company in the United States.

Kory flourished in the more advanced class. Within two months, he was allowed to take the company's evening class, held in the largest studio in the building. It was about the same size as the stage at the Lisner Auditorium on the George Washington University campus, which was where the Washington School of Ballet performed *The Nutcracker* every year during Christmas.

Now he was challenged: he saw students who made him look as if he had just learned to walk. They performed the floor routines as if they were performing in front of a paying audience; even the accompanist sounded as if she were playing a command performance. At this level, it was assumed students had obtained more than a nominal command of ballet. More emphasis was placed on pulse and styling. Working at the barre was the time for students to hone their technique, whereas in the center of the floor, the routines were meant to show them how to put it all together into what is known as "the dance."

After his adult ballet class, Kory was usually the only person in the men's dressing room, but after the first company class, he found himself having to wade through ten or more guys changing into their street clothes.

"Tonight is my night," said a very skinny guy with long blond hair.

"I beg your pardon, you non-turning queen, tonight they're mine to do," protested a short guy with very hairy legs and an earring in his right ear.

"I'll decide who'll wash my dance belt tonight," said a tall guy with blond hair, straddling the bench naked, who was also the principal male dancer of the school.

"But you promised me!" whined the guy with the hairy legs, now standing with his hands on his hips and turning red.

"No, I want the new guy to do it. You over there with the black headband—catch, and make sure you use lots of fabric softener."

The sweaty dance belt fell at Kory's feet. With the toe of his shoe, he flipped the dance belt into a trash can at the end of the bench and walked out of the locker room.

"Who the hell does he think he is?" Kory heard as he walked down the hallway. He wasn't always sure about a lot of things in life, but he knew he wasn't gay. And if he were, then the principal male dancer would be washing *his* sweaty dance belt, not the other way around.

Soon after leaving the dressing room, Kory was sitting on the bench in front of the school, waiting for his bus, when he saw a familiar face walking in his direction.

"They tried to give you a hard time in the locker room, but I see you didn't let them get to you," said the only other black male dancer he had seen at the school. "My name is Charles."

"I'm Kory. I didn't see you when all of that hazing was going on."

"Yeah, I usually take a locker as far away from those queens as possible. Mind you, I like to kid around, but after a hard class I need to wind down without the drama of those sluts," he said, taking a chocolate bar and cigarette out of his dance bag and offering Kory both.

"No, thanks! I'm trying to cut down on those cancer sticks. I never developed a taste for chocolate, though. Would you care for an organic McIntosh apple instead of the chocolate?" Kory asked.

Charles examined the apple as if it were something he had never seen before. "So this is one of those organic things. Looks like a plain ol' apple to me."

"Well, you know what they say: it's what you don't see that'll kill you. I guess you have to make a choice between pesticides and horseshit when buying fruit," said Kory, taking a bite out of his apple.

"Well, you got to die from something. I like my cigarettes and pesticides." Charles adjusted the sport strap around his gold-rimmed glasses.

Kory pulled a napkin out of his dance bag. "I watched you in class. You've obviously been studying for a while. You seem to have the floor routines down pretty well."

"I've been at it about three years now. It doesn't take long before you develop a dance vocabulary you can use wherever you go. When I'm not dancing, I teach," Charles added.

"You're a teacher?"

"Not a dance teacher, though. I teach the sixth grade at Martin Luther King Elementary School in the ghetto, as they call it."

"Wow! I would have never suspected you would be a teacher of future welfare recipients," Kory quipped.

"That's what everybody says. Most people see me as a short and balding guy with big glasses who most likely works in some basement government office without windows and has no future."

"Well, I believe I see my bus coming. Do you live downtown?"

"I share an apartment about a block from Dupont Circle."

"Oh, the Circle! That used to be my hangout."

"Why did you stop?"

"The crowd changed a bit. It's gotten a little too wild down there."

"You're talking about the wild children. Do you have a problem with gay people?"

"Just the ones who hung out at my house and got too drunk to walk. I just finished doing *Music Man*, and since I was one of the few dancers with a car, many guys in the cast stopped by to catch a ride to the theater."

"So I see," said Charles, as they boarded the southbound bus on Wisconsin Avenue.

When they were about three stops from where Kory usually walked the rest of the way home, he said, "Charles, I noticed you don't come to class regularly."

"That's right. I usually take class at the Capitol Ballet. You may know it as the Jones and Haywood School of Ballet."

"Sure. It's been around for a long time."

"It certainly has. And I believe you should audition there. I told the directors about you, and they're interested in taking a look at you—unless the Washington School of Ballet has offered you a scholarship, which is not likely, since you're black."

"Are they talking about a full scholarship?"

"Full, with a stipend if you're good enough."

"May I think about it for a week or so? I still have a lot of other commitments."

"Take as long as you need. Here's my telephone number. Call me if you have any questions—or not," Charles said, placing the folded piece of paper in Kory's dance bag.

For black dancers in the United States, the Jones-Haywood Capitol Ballet was legendary. It had produced such world-renowned dancers as Chita Rivera, Sylvester Campbell, and dancer-choreographer Louis Johnson. Before the emergence of Black Identity, the Jones-Haywood School maintained a regular Yellow Pages ad that read: *Classical Ballet Training for Talented Colored Children.* Luckily, by the time Kory stepped into the classroom, the school had begun to accept the idea of people being called black.

Of all the challenges Kory had encountered, nothing compared to what he experienced at the school of Doris Jones and Claire Haywood. Even students who didn't become dancers after leaving the school had an indelible look of confidence that let the world know they had sweated gallons of effort on the classroom floor to receive the instructors' approval. These students were either born with the features the school preferred or the son or daughter of some influential person—if not, they simply did not get in.

There was a yearlong waiting list of parents hoping to place their children, mostly girls, in the school that would bestow the Capitol Ballet's stamp of snobbery on their persona. Kory was already somewhat of a snob; he just needed the training.

CHAPTER 20:

The Real Audition

Minutes before his audition at the Capitol Ballet, already feeling nervous after getting the "quick and dirty" about the directors' idiosyncrasies from two students in the dressing room, Kory resigned himself to finding the least conspicuous place at the barre, from which he could follow some of the other students. This plan was quickly thwarted. The codirector, Miss Haywood, known for her scathing criticism, took one look at Kory and dispatched him in front of their exquisite prima ballerina. To make matters worse, Miss Haywood stood within a heartbeat and watched every movement, in between making corrections to his posture and placement.

"I want everyone in the class to watch this new boy and see what I don't want you ever to do in my class."

She had Kory repeat the last routine while the whole company class watched.

"He's doing just about everything wrong, but what he has also done is correct everything that I have told him so far tonight. This young man thinks—something most of you have forgotten to do. Too many of you have the audacity to come into my class every night and give just enough to get through it—as if you think I don't know what you're doing. Half of you children should go into the dressing room, put on your clothes, and never return to my sight again. *Have I made myself clear?*" She slammed her highly polished oak cane on the black, studio grand piano.

"Yes, Miss Haywood," the class said in one fawning voice.

"Young man, I want you to demonstrate a grand plié for the class."

"That's not too bad for a beginner. If any of you older students don't perform a grand plié better than he just did, *I will send you home.*"

Kory heard himself answering in unison with the others, "Yes, Miss Haywood."

In order for Jones-Haywood students to know what the next exercise was going to be, they needed to know how to translate the very contained movements of a teacher who demonstrated mostly with facial expressions, abridged movements of her body, and rapid hand gestures. Her grand pliés were slightly more than a hint that the body should move in that direction, whereas the difference between her demi-plié and grand plié was determined by the size of the wrinkle in the pink tights she always wore. If you didn't understand her dance shorthand, you were in danger of receiving castigation deadlier than a stiletto soaked in garlic. Any student preferred death to the vituperations she could inflict with just a raised eyebrow. Ironically, Miss Haywood, unlike the other director, Miss Jones, who was a trained dancer, had never danced a day in her life before opening the school with her lifelong friend. Miss Haywood was a painter. She understood from an artist's perspective the capabilities of the human body. It wasn't long before Kory figured out she was not the favored teacher. Miss Jones had a more even personality. But Kory loved Miss Haywood from the first night he arrived at the school until the day he left.

CHAPTER 21:

Things Unravel

After completing a bachelor's degree in psychology, Kory entered a master's program. Over the next two years, when not researching his thesis, he took dance classes at every local school, including the company class at Jones-Haywood, and when not being a student, he taught ballet at three studios and choreographed for his own dance troupe. Despite the extra time he spent in the studio when others had gone home, he slowly admitted something was amiss. Though only he recognized it, his sense of balance was diminishing. A month earlier, he had been able to perform a quadruple pirouette with the greatest abandon—now it had become a challenge to complete a triple turn without the feeling of losing control at the end of the movement. He tried everything: yoga, meditation, more drugs, more classes, more rest, and even prayer. None had a lasting effect on the problem that grew steadily within.

Kory ignored his symptoms as best he could. He believed he was born to dance, and, as with everything else he had encountered that had tried to dissuade him, his determination would not let him abandon his greatest pleasure in his life. His will to control his body grew stronger, despite his growing weakness within.

Sylvester Campbell, one of the most successful male classical dancers Jones and Haywood had trained, took a sabbatical from his position as premier danseur of the Royal Dutch Ballet and returned to his hometown to add a new ballet to his alma mater's repertoire. Kory could hardly believe one of his idols was coaching him. Anyone who has never seen a top male dancer soar across the stage has never seen someone who has discovered how to defy gravity and propel himself into the air, if only for a few seconds. Sylvester Campbell was an air lord of distinction. He also had the ability to elevate the dancing of those who had the honor of being in his presence. Sylvester took a special interest when he saw Kory's jumping ability, along with his *quatre battements en l'air* (four beats in the air) while remaining fully turned out. Usually known for his aloofness, Sylvester shared Kory's mind-set about ballet. His explanations on the flow of energy answered many questions that the two female director of the school had not been able to answer.

Six months later, the Capitol Ballet had its annual performance at the Kennedy Center. Sylvester Campbell's new ballet received great reviews. Kory had only a minor role, but just to be onstage with this icon made him realize he had accomplished a lot in his short time in ballet. Eerily, the brevity of his experience did not account for the tremors that struck him during the performance. It was as if his body did not want to stay in the same position for more than a few seconds without constantly being reminded that it was not time to move yet. What he had worked so many years to incorporate in his muscle memory had become a frighteningly conscious effort. He had not forgotten how to dance on an intellectual level, but his body needed constant prompts.

Two weeks after the performance, Kory resigned from the Capitol Ballet. It was not the first time he had left the school, but this time he knew he would never return. Miss Haywood was furious. But he did not know how to tell her or anyone else, for that matter, what was going on inside his body. He had no idea it was all in his head. Never would he have suspected his brain was having problems communicating with his body. He assumed it was the other way around.

"Kory, I've spent years training you, and now you have the nerve to walk into my office and tell me you are leaving." Miss Haywood lit a cigarette from the one still burning in the ashtray.

"I'm really sorry, but I have some personal problems I would rather not discuss with you."

"Well, I'd rather you did. Kory, I have known you for almost five years. I've seen hundreds of dancers with all kinds of problems. I doubt there's something wrong with you I've not heard before."

"Miss Haywood, I wish to God I could tell you what's going on in my life, but frankly, I don't understand it myself."

"Then instead of you leaving, why don't you take a break from us for a while? Maybe during that time you'll be able to work out whatever is troubling you."

"I'll think about it for a couple of weeks, but I doubt I'll return. The only reason I would even consider coming back is because of you, Miss Haywood. You believed in me, and I'm deeply grateful. Of all the teachers I've met, you have taught me to think about dance like no other."

Tears welled in her eyes. He felt his own heart breaking as well. She was the teacher he had come to love. Now he was forced to give up a part of something and someone who had made him understand there was something greater than he.

As he closed behind him the door that led to the walkway outside the boys' dressing room, he turned to take one last look at his locker. He had made sure to empty it so there would be no reason for him to return.

He spent the two weeks Miss Haywood had given him ensconced behind the twelve-foot oak doors in his grandfather's house. During that time, he did not talk to anyone except the voices in his head. They all said the same thing: *you have gone as far as you can go.* Kory cried at times and considered suicide, which to him had always been a coward's way out. He resolved to deconstruct himself again and discard the broken pieces as he found them, if possible. But the shards of his nervous system could not be cast aside or mended. This time he would not be able to fix himself, and he feared that a diagnosis from a doctor would dispel any hopes of his ever finding a cure from within.

Many days later, he emerged from isolation—vowing never to return to the Capitol Ballet. Although he felt more in control of himself after his self-imprisonment, what he had discovered this time meant the end of his dream. Handicapped, he would never be the dancer he had fought so hard to become. And the frustrating cycle of building up his body only for it to fail him again was a roller coaster he no longer wished to ride. It seemed a choice had been made for him.

He also still had a thesis to complete. So, two weeks later, he registered for fall classes without giving much thought to dance until there was a conflict with his schedule. Advanced Psychological Statistics was filled, which left him with only one class for Tuesday.

CHAPTER 22:

A Different Step

Modern Dance I was the only class still open to fill vacant time in his schedule. While waiting in line to pay tuition, Kory met another student who had just registered for the same class. During their chat, he discovered that the dance department had a new instructor, who had plans for a major winter dance production.

Having never formally studied modern dance, Kory hoped it would be less stressful than classical ballet. At the very least, it might fill some of the emptiness inside him.

The next morning, Kory walked the six blocks from his grandfather's house down Sixteenth Street to the Fine Arts building. Before he had made the decision to take modern dance, he had known the university had recently leased this annex, which had been the Jewish Community Center for more than fifty years.

"Hi, everybody! I'm Lynne Edwards. To make sure you're in the right place, this is Modern Dance One. I want to go around the studio and have everyone give their name and any dance experience they may have. We're supposed to have two football players here, so I guess it must be you two guys with the big muscles by the window." She had a strikingly white smile silhouetted by beautiful brown-sugar skin. It was obvious that this was her first teaching position—she had the ebullience of a recent graduate. Her modern-dance training was evident from the wide second position she stood in while addressing the class, which was vastly different from that of classical dancers, who strove to balance on a finer pointe.

Most of the ten students in the college class lacked any formal dance training, but some were physical education majors. If nothing else, Kory thought, he could at least keep his body limber and maybe have some fun at the same time.

"What are you doing here? You could be teaching it," Lynne declared after class.

"I've had a lot of ballet and some jazz training, but this is my first time trying modern."

"That's what I thought. Where did you study?"

"Some in New York, but mostly in DC. Are you familiar with the Capitol Ballet?"

"Sorry. No, I'm not."

"What about Jones-Haywood?"

"You studied at Jones-Haywood! I've seen Chita Rivera and Sylvester Campbell. All of you have a similar carriage."

"That's the Jones-Haywood look. They don't let you out of there until you have your nose high enough in the air."

"You've certainly mastered that. Just kidding! They must have spent years working on your turnout."

"Actually, I brought that with me to the audition. I think that's what got me into the school. My ballet was horrible at that time."

"I bet this was the only class available to you."

"Good guess. I'm always up for trying something new."

"This may be a little too easy for you. Are you sure you won't get bored and drop my class?"

"That's up to you. If nothing else, you could help me develop a beautiful second position like yours." Kory admired her body, particularly her large breasts—something he seldom saw in classical dancers. He recalled Miss Haywood's telling one of the girls in the company her large breasts were grotesque. They interfered with her lines and balance en pointe, according to the director.

"We could trade technique. My ballet is very weak," Lynne said. She dried her face with a red, black, and green towel.

"Why don't we start with lunch? There's a great Kundalini restaurant off Dupont Circle," Kory suggested as he stretched his leg on the top bar.

"Kundalini! Is that Middle Eastern?" asked Lynne.

"Right side of the world, but too far south. It's health food with an East Indian flourish, served by people who worship their bodies more than we do," he said while extending the heel of his foot to his right ear.

"Wow! I've never seen a man with that much extension. And you released your hand and it didn't drop. That's why I took only one semester of ballet. My legs will never stretch that much, regardless of the number of years I study."

"And I will never have a second position as commanding as yours," Kory replied.

"Commanding? Well...thank you, I guess. Anyway, that came easily to me."

Kory looked at his watch. "My stomach is telling me to put something in it."

"Just give me ten minutes to drop some papers with my secretary, and I'll meet you in the lobby."

"The lobby in ten!"

Now alone, Kory realized this was the first time he had seen himself in a studio-size mirror since he had left the Capitol Ballet. The average person spends only a few minutes a day grooming; a classical dancer uses the mirror as an audience to check every detail of his body. It does not take long for this practice to become an obsession. As Kory checked his positioning while practicing an allegro routine, he watched the person in the mirror for indications of his new encumbrance; he made no mistakes, but the fun and abandonment were gone. For a moment, he thought he saw a ghostlike image just behind his reflection making an adjustment after the last step, instead of his being frozen in time.

"Sorry to take so long. I jumped in the shower," Lynne said as she met Kory in the lobby.

"Well, that's not fair. It's difficult for two sweaty people to smell each other," Kory jokingly complained.

"Then I'll try not to get too close to you." She pinched her nose.

"I like your humor. That comment just added dessert."

"You mean I wasn't getting it before?"

"I know how weight-conscious you female dancers are."

"Not me. I burn everything I put in my mouth."

"I won't touch that one until after lunch."

"You have something planned after lunch?"

"Not necessarily today."

"You may not like me after you've seen me eat."

"For some reason, I doubt that."

CHAPTER 23:

Shiva Shingles

The Golden Temple restaurant was five blocks from the dance studio. Lynne had been in Washington only a few weeks, so Kory pointed out some of the lesser-known landmarks as they walked. When they approached Eighteenth Street and Massachusetts Avenue, just a few doors away from his old prep school, an early autumn gust blew through Lynne's massive Afro hairstyle. He imagined all those luscious curls pressed against a pillow and sweaty again.

When they came in view of the Circle, they saw how the second shift had replaced the workers of Embassy Row. Soon this island, less than a mile from the White House, would be filled with those who exchanged what was going on inside their heads as casually as the weather.

"So this is the infamous Dupont Circle," Lynne said as they passed the Hubbard House, which, when not serving lunch to workers from Embassy Row, was a hangout for high-school kids skipping class and runaways skipping out on life.

"I spent many days and nights in the Circle and in between drank lots of coffee in the Hubbard House." He pointed to the green stools facing Dupont Circle through the smoke stain–blocked glass windows.

"Was that a man or woman who just passed in that flowing white linen robe?" asked Lynne, as she turned her head to get a second look.

"That was androgynous. Sometimes they don't even know. That's a great thing about this area—no one cares if you don't have a label for yourself."

"We don't have this street life in Chicago."

"Has the consciousness three movement overlooked the Windy City?"

"A lot of things happening in this country haven't even reached the Midwest. There's a different mind-set there, especially on the Southside. Also, compared with Washington, DC, most people there don't have the money to experience this cultural movement. Many are just getting by—if you know what I mean."

"Believe me when I say there're places like your Southside just across the Anacostia River in Southeast Washington. Some neighborhoods are so disenfranchised, you'd think you were in some shantytown in South Africa."

"I'll bet you don't know much about that part of town."

"No, I don't," he said, looking at Lynne. "That had a slightly accusatory tone to it."

"Kory, you have *prep school* and *black elite* written all over you."

"And I doubt you were brought up on pork and beans. I heard someone mention while I was waiting in the lobby that you graduated from Columbia University."

"I went there on scholarship. Times were hard for my parents."

"Every family had to struggle at one time or another. Here we are," he said, opening the door. "I hope you're hungry."

"Starving!"

"Good. The pork and beans are popular on the menu here!"

"Sure, that and blood-red steak in an Indian restaurant."

"Why not? Obtain instant enlightenment by eating the brains of a recently evolved Brahmin in a tangy curry sauce."

"That's gross. I'm starting to worry about you."

"Don't worry. This is a strictly vegetarian place. And I haven't eaten meat in five years—although a plate of brains might be just what the doctor ordered." Kory looked at his blurred reflection in the mirror behind the cashier.

"You almost sound serious. You must have been kidding. What about seafood?"

"Well, I might make an exception for seafood on special occasions. I spent most of my summers at Highland Beach on the Chesapeake Bay. We had a family cottage near the pier."

"As I was saying," she said with satisfaction.

Kory greeted the cashier and asked for a table next to a window overlooking the Connecticut Avenue sidewalk and the Dupont Circle fountain. It was late afternoon, so they had the restaurant to themselves. The air was filled with Indian spices, and Ravi Shankar's music played softly in the background from bookshelf speakers, which were partially hidden behind an overgrown rubber plant and a tranquil portrait of Lord Vishnu.

"Hi! Would you like one of our special fruit drinks while you look at the menu?" asked a very pale and gaunt young woman dressed in the traditional all-white Kundalini habit, which included a large, turban-like headdress.

"Their fruit smoothies are great." Kory tried to rub away a slight numbness in his left hand.

"Whatever you suggest. I've never had a fruit smoothie."

"Two strawberry and yogurt smoothies, please."

"Is your hand bothering you?" Lynne asked as she took a sip from her water glass.

"It's weird. First it's numb, and then it's stiff. I probably hurt it when I was weight lifting."

"How long have you been having problems?"

"About two weeks. I'm sure it's nothing." Kory put his hand under the table. "So, do you see anything that strikes you on the menu?"

"The Mandala vegetables sound yummy. Have you tried them?"

"Good choice. I had that last time I was here. Maybe I should have the Lord Shiva Matar this time."

"Hmmmmm, brown rice, tomatoes, cucumbers, and tofu in a coconut-milk sauce—that sounds good," said Lynne, taking a sip of her pale-pink, milk shake–like drink.

The urge to rub his hand made him uneasy. "So tell me: I understand you're planning a winter performance. Have you decided on a theme yet?"

"Oh, God! I have a thousand ideas, but I'm not close to making a decision. Maybe you can help."

"When I have problems like that, I start thinking about the dancers I plan to use."

"That's definitely a big part of the problem. I really don't have any good dancers to choose from. Any chance of your performing?"

"To be honest with you, I'm still under contract with the Capitol Ballet. Maybe you could convince me to break it."

"You're kidding, right? Why would you leave the Capitol Ballet for a college dance production?"

"It's a long story and filled with soap opera drama. I'll spare you the vapid details. Suffice it to say, I have personal reasons for breaking my contract with the venerable Capitol Ballet."

Lynne considered what Kory had just said while she scanned the menu. "I guess we should just leave it at that. But if there's any way you can be a part of the production, I would be honored to have someone with your experience."

Despite being in the presence of a gorgeous woman and the relaxing atmosphere of the restaurant, Kory felt out of sorts. The numbness in his hand had migrated to his entire arm, and now his left foot was starting to twitch. The plans he'd had for after lunch were beginning to evaporate.

"You're awfully quiet. I hope I didn't put you too much on the spot," said Lynne shortly after the food arrived.

"No. I'm just thinking about how I can make it work. I really think we could produce something fun together."

"I know we can if you'll just give it a chance."

"If I seem to have reservations, it's all about some of my personal situations. And please don't think of me as another self-absorbed dancer."

"The thought had occurred to me, so I assume you're referring to a relationship."

"I wish it were something that simple."

"You consider relationships simple?"

"I'm sorry. That didn't come out right. I meant existential challenges can sometimes inconveniently get in the way of a sunny day."

"That's a bit ethereal. I think you're saying you are not in control of yourself. Sharing can sometimes lighten the load." Lynne reached for Kory's hand.

"Or further complicate the problem." Kory quickly withdrew his hand and rubbed it under the table.

"I can't believe you're this negative. Maybe we should talk about something else." She lifted her nearly empty fruit smoothie with the rejected hand.

"Yes, we should. It's…transition…" Kory struggled to regain his composure.

"I've got only ten minutes to get back. What about later?"

Tingling sensations had moved up to his neck. He briefly closed his eyes. When he opened them, Lynne's image was blurred—as if she had an aura. "I think I should clear up a few things in my life tonight before I do anything else."

"Sure! Are you feeling okay?"

"I hope you don't mind if I sit here and finish my tea."

"Will I see you in class on Tuesday?"

"If I'm still here!"

CHAPTER 24

Will to Survive

Kory had no idea how long he had sat motionless in the chair before he had realized that Lynne was gone. He took a sip of his cold tea, then wished he hadn't. His hand shook violently, and soon after a chill ran from his trembling lips to the blocks of ice that had once been his feet. He looked around for his Kundalini waitress and asked for another cup. With his hands around the hot earthenware mug, he closed his eyes and envisioned the connection from his brain to his lost legs; meanwhile, flashes of yellow light streamed down his spinal cord, searching for life. Determined to stand, he pressed hard into the floor with all his might and stumbled to the register. The cashier appeared to be meditating, for it was a few seconds before she acknowledged his presence. While she counted his change, he looked in the mirror behind her. His reflection was at first blurred and then inside out.

Once he was outside on the sidewalk, late-afternoon sun blinded him. He quickly grabbed a parking meter for support and tried to think of what to do. There was a coffee shop with an alfresco eating area on the corner. Pretending to be a window-shopper, he leaned against the protrusions under the storefront windows and felt his way down the street until he bumped into a table with an empty chair and sat down. The tingling in his legs subsided—only to be replaced by a deafening ring in his ears. But within the clang, there was a familiar sound.

"*Ommmmmmm!*" The voice sounded far away amid the cacophony only he could hear. It was the mantric voice of his spiritual friend, who was announcing to the universe his reverence for the sacred syllable of Brahma.

Kory struggled to focus his eyes. "Mac, I thought you were in India."

"I've been staying at the Krishna Ashram on P Street since I returned two weeks ago. You look at sea," Mac declared. He took a seat across the table and pulled his chessboard out from his multicolored madras knapsack.

"I'm not sure what I am. It's as if I'm fluctuating between two universes. I don't think I'm up for a game right now, unless we're playing on a four-dimensional board." Kory tried to fix his eyes on the vermilion *bindi* on his friend's forehead, below the massive white turban he was wearing.

"I see it, Kory. Your aura is white and brown. This is not a good sign. Did you take some new drug?"

"No. I haven't tripped in six months. To tell you the truth, lately I've been too afraid to take anything. The last time I took acid, I got so lost, I spent eight hours trying to recover my soul. Mac, something is happening to my body. I may need to see a doctor."

"Are you still meditating and fasting like we used to do together?" Mac placed his hand to his forehead, as if he were trying to focus on Kory with his pineal eye.

"Everything! The only thing that helps is long hours of sleep," he heard himself shout through the roar inside of his head. "Mac, I need to get home and into bed, but I doubt I can walk that far."

"No problem. I borrowed the yellow VW van parked at the corner. It's usually I who's in need of *your* help. Do you think you can walk to the van? I will carry you if you want."

"No. Just let me lean a little on your shoulder."

Mac chanted as they drove. Too weary to ask for silence, Kory focused on the rhythm of Mac's mantra, which helped him ignore the ringing in his head. Once they got inside, Mac offered to stay, but Kory insisted he was feeling better and declined the offer of a prayer and further chanting. No sooner had the front door closed than Kory's head hit the pillow. The mattress immediately imprisoned his body. Now that he was lying in his bed and unable to move, his limbs were as useful as Kafka's overturned dung beetle. Sleep quickly overtook him. It would be three days before he woke again in the same universe.

"Kory, it's Mom! Are you in there?" The knocking got louder. "I know you're in there. If you don't call me tonight, I'll have someone break down this door. Did you hear me?" She rapped one last time before he heard the front door close. Thinking about making sure she had left was the limit of his mobility. She was the last person he wanted to see him in this helpless state. And the last thing he wanted to hear from her was "I told you so." She would blame his condition on his "reckless lifestyle" instead of a medical problem beyond his control. Her constant vituperations were why they had not talked for more than a month. Strangely, his mother had the uncanny ability to know when something was wrong with him, regardless of where he was or whether it was his own doing.

Vainly, he tried to sleep. The thoughts of taking on a new challenge, only to be forced to abandon it, made him wonder what sin he had committed to deserve a place in purgatory. Theological self-reproaches had never been one of his lifelong virtues; long ago, he had given up believing in heaven and hell, which had happened shortly after his grandmother died in a fire trying to save him and his brother. God had ignored his infant pleas to return her to life then. What would it take to raise his legs from the dead?

CHAPTER 25

Piecing Together

Consciousness returned to Kory as an ambulance screamed down U Street. There was still an hour of daylight, enough time for him to gather himself before calling his mother. Kory closed his eyes and began to meditate. To walk again, he needed to find his center.

All meditation techniques he had learned began with the same kind of breathing exercise. He blocked everything from his mind except the sound of his breath.

Death was better than being crippled. He had to walk again, even if it meant first crawling on his hands and knees, which he did all the way to the kitchen. A wheeled kitchen stool sufficed for legs as he made a cup of sassafras tea.

Once he had drunk it, he dialed.

"It's Kory. I found your note under my door. It was somewhat dramatic threatening to break down the door."

"Are you all right? I've been having a feeling for the past two weeks you were not happy."

"When did my happiness become so important to you?"

"That's not fair. You know I love you."

"Actually, I don't. You say you do when the urge hits you. Mom, I don't feel like arguing now. What do you want from me?"

Before his mother responded, he heard the sound of her cigarette lighter. She took a long draw and exhaled. "You're an insolent child. I don't deserve this kind of treatment from you."

"First of all, I'm not a child. You made sure my childhood was so bad I couldn't wait to grow up. Now you are telling me that you're not satisfied with what your nurturing wrought. It's a little late in both of our lives for that."

"How did you ever become so spiteful?"

"I had you as a teacher. Be proud of your tutelage."

"I'm sorry I wasn't the parent you needed. I did the best I could do."

"That glib answer is supposed to mitigate everything? I don't believe you did the best you could do. You did your best to make *your* life as comfortable as possible."

"I was always there for you."

"It's true you were usually there, but your door was always closed. You treated our dog better. I guess I didn't learn enough tricks to amuse you."

"Well, I can see this conversation is going nowhere. I just wanted to know if you were okay. Call me if you need anything."

"I will—if I ever do." Kory hung up the phone before she had a chance to reply.

Usually Kory tried hard to be civil to his mother. It hadn't been until he had experienced genuine affection from his girlfriends that he had realized how much she had cheated him. He doubted if he would ever be able to forgive her, but he had more important problems. As it had always been, he had to take care of himself; never had someone been there to dry his tears when he was growing up. Now that he was too old for tears, silent cries replaced closets until the hurt had passed.

After two weeks of practice, he was walking normally again. He refused to believe he would have another attack. For now, he needed to deny the possibility to keep his sanity. Only in his dreams was he able to be honest with himself: The applause for his dancing had been replaced by the clapping sound of a wheelchair moving slowly offstage.

CHAPTER 26

No Encore

Blue gels glowed on opening night from the stage of Lisner Auditorium after Lynne's modern-dance students exited the wings. Kory breathed a sigh of relief for her. Hours of rehearsals had produced an illusion worth the price of admission.

The second offering began with a blinding light from the backdrop. A distant pan flute slowly grew in volume and searched for pitch. Its nascent sound played a single note for one minute and then echoed all possible tones until a high note morphed into a cacophony of meaningless noise, like that produced by a Moog synthesizer playing every sound discernible to the human ear. Then it ceased. Despite the silence, sound resonated within the listeners. And before memory could fade, thunder and lightning announced another beginning.

"Abraxas" was the first number Kory choreographed for the concert. When trying to come up with a theme for his solo to tie into the rest of the evening, he had stumbled upon the mythological character while doing research for a thesis paper on the schools of prepsychological thought that followed the Ionian School of Philosophy .

Some Gnostics believed Jesus Christ emanated from a phantom called Abraxas. This view threatened to consider more explanations of God than the accepted biblical dogma. It was Kory's objective to force the audience to entertain alternative views of creation and the creator.

When the spotlight hit him, his only prop was a tree bereft of leaves. Dressed in a loincloth, his body glistened as it wound around the tree like a primordial reptile stalking its tail.

The serpentine dance lasted about two minutes, until Kory coiled his way back to the base of the tree. There his body writhed and turned until hands, then arms, spastically sprouted from his body. Even with new appendages, he was able to walk and stand. After falling many times, his body transformed again. This time legs grew from what had once been his tail.

Free to explore, Protoman became frightened when his shadow appeared. At first he thought it was another animal pursuing him, until he realized what he feared most emanated from him, not from something floating above the clouds.

For the finale, Kory choreographed a one-act satirical ballet to Leonard Bernstein's latest inspiration, "The Mass." This closing piece contrasted sharply with the opening number: it strove to translate the unbridled fears and passions of the soul into a sensual experience directed at the collective unconscious of the audience.

Lastly, the primitive fear of God was dumped into the laps of those who had paid the price of admission. Toward the end, the music was replaced by twenty-one noiseless dancers with light streaming from candles they cupped in their hands. For brief periods they appeared as one, only to be replaced by another dancer from the rear taking center stage. When all had lain on the floor of the stage, the first to fall ran to the center of the stage, followed by the rest of the troupe, until they formed concentric circles, the innermost of which represented the Judas ring.

The audience was redeemed at the end when a dancer, dressed in snow-white papal attire and barely visible through a cloud of smoky incense, absolved the audience with the signing of the cross. Tension deflated into hope that those summoned to judgment would be spared damnation and an interminable stay in Hell.

After accepting kudos and kisses, Kory and Lynne retired to their shared dressing room backstage. They had done other, lesser performances before, so they had become comfortable dressing in front of each other. But tonight was special. They were both still sweaty and scintillating from the elysium of the performance.

"Can you believe what Jean Beatty Lewis said?" Lynne stood before Kory with just a smile.

"Not from the toughest critic in town. I just hope she prints in *The Washington Post* what she said backstage." Kory rolled his dance belt down his legs and kicked it into the air. He caught it before it hit the floor and tossed it into his dance bag. When he turned around, Lynne was just standing there, admiring him. He reached for her. "We should celebrate. Do you have any plans later?"

Feeling his sweaty body pressed against her, she suggested, "Let's open that bottle of champagne and have a party here."

Kory, wearing just a gleam, grabbed Lynne's hand and pulled her onto his lap.

"Where's this going?" Lynne asked.

"Right in the middle, where it belongs." He directed her body on top of his.

"I can't believe I'm doing this. You know I just got engaged."

"You certainly did! Let's make the most of it."

"I was wondering if you were gay." She placed her hands on his shoulders for leverage. "You're the first male ballet dancer I've met who likes women."

"And it's great most women believe that," he said as he grabbed her tight buttocks and drove her harder on him.

"I bet you've taken a lot of girls to bed by making them think they've made you stray from your nature."

"Is that why you're riding me now? Rescue me! Rescue me!" Kory said as he squeezed her buttocks harder and bit her hard on the neck.

"Right now, I don't give a shit if you're gay. If all gay guys make love like this, then I've been missing something."

"There's only one male body I obsess over, and you're looking at it. The female body is the perfection of evolution. And when I'm making love to someone who means something to me, I'm a complete man."

"What took us so long to get here? After our first lunch, I thought we'd never get any closer than that. When I tried to suggest something, you always seemed to change the subject to dance."

"Don't you see? I can only be close to someone through dance. Without it, I'm an unnamed town without streets for others to walk down. You probably think me a bit odd, but that's who I am."

"Kory, you're like no man I have ever met before. I know now a sustained relationship with you is impossible. If this is the most you can give, then I'm grateful to you for showing me a side of me I never knew existed. If this never happens again, always know I love you the way you are."

"Then this is a most perfect moment. I doubt we'll ever be this close again. We've gone as far as we could, and it was beautiful. Tonight was my last performance."

CHAPTER 27

Unexpected Guest

Weeks after his last curtain call, Kory had time to think about life outside theater and academia. Although mornings often required his scouring library tomes for esoterica to support his thesis, his evenings were open, provided his advisor did not have an early-afternoon assignation with a coed seeking extra credit.

In the past, friends stopping by had been a welcome break. Lately they had become more of an annoyance, especially if their visits involved revisting existential challenges, an excercise he likened to a scratched LP of John Coltrane's *Transition* skipping back and forth in the same rut. Those resistant to change increasingly found their doorbell rings unanswered and the music coming from inside louder than when they had arrived. It was time to broaden his circle, or least to replace overly familiar faces revolving around his life with personalities asking questions he had not already answered about them or himself.

Living in Washington usually meant residents were accustomed to hot air constantly rising from Congress. But in the fall, even the most long-winded legislator could not compete with nippy autumn winds sapping green from countless trees lining most streets of the Nation's Capital. One such fall gust of winter's prelude blew a flyer at Kory's feet one fortuitous October afternoon. The *Quicksliver Times*, a Washington antiwar newspaper, had rented an abandoned warehouse for a Halloween party. Invitations were never sent; the publication assummed that people who took time to read countercultural literature floating down the street or pasted on lampposts were already on its guest list.

Having worked briefly as a researcher at the *Washington Free Press*, Kory had stayed in touch with activists near the heart of social change. Although he did not always agree with their methods, consciousness three political functions often attracted liberated women looking for an experience, as opposed to a manogimous relationship. The era of free love meant changing lovers as often as ones sheets; the former was easier than hanging the latter out to dry or getting change for the laundromat.

Besides having seen James A. Michener's *Hawaii*, Kory knew as much about Polynesia as he did about being modest backstage. All of that changed in a black-lighted room with psychedelic posters of acid-rock groups covering the walls; antiwar protestations spewed between familiar-sounding coughs.

"Where's your costume?" she asked.

"Yes, it does appear natural." He sank into a beanbag chair among casually strewn milk crates and bales of hay. "This is a Kory outfit."

"And who the hell is Kory?"

"I'm glad you're so eager to know. He's the tall, dark, and handsome guy dying to know your name."

"Well, whoever you call yourself, considering that I'm an undercover FBI agent, telling you would mean I'd have to kill you."

Kory feigned a shiver. "Would it come quickly, or would I suffer for hours?"

"Until you begged for mercy, if I'm in the mood."

"Well, in that case, tell me."

With a smile, she lit a joint and then exhaled. "It's Eseta." She turned the wet end of the plump marijuana cigarette his direction.

Kory tasted a fruity sweetness mixed with the expected smoky resins. He savored her lips a few seconds before inhaling.

"Hmm, tasty..." Kory's mind went blank for a few seconds before he could think of something to say. "Is your name Hawaiian?"

She snatched the joint out of his hand and rolled her eyes.

"*Ufa!*"

"And what does that mean?"

"It means 'go screw yourself.' I'm no goddamn Hawaiian. Ever hear of Samoa?"

"Pago Pago?"

"At least you don't pronounce like it a mainlander."

"Allow me to show more of my ignorance. What's the difference?"

She took another drag and blew it right into his face. "Do you really want to know, or are you just pretending to be interested so you can get into my pants?"

Kory sank deeper into the beanbag chair. "I was hoping you would see that I was not pretending to know how to get into your pants."

"That's an interesting answer. This is Samoa 101: We're pure Polynesians. Hawaiians were for the most part until World War II. Now they're mostly people of Japanese descent calling themselves native."

"Sounds tribal...Does that mean Samoans only marry Samoans?"

"Marrying and dating, if you live on the island. That's why I left."

"So you don't follow the old ways."

"Haven't seen a Samoan since I left California two years ago. I prefer to bow when I'm in the mood and not when some stupid tradition turns a woman into her husband's slave."

The rest of the night was a blur by morning. Somehow a small group from the Halloween party was passed out around Kory's grandfather's house at daybreak. Eseta must have changed her mind about killing him, because she was fast asleep on his recently changed sheets.

Kory was usually relieved when overnight guests went home. But there was something different about Eseta. After a week she seemed to fit perfectly into where his life was at that moment.

Having someone around who was always available but not intrusive required few adjustments. When it was time for him to study, she busied herself in another part of house. And when he was ready to play, she appeared with her perfect smile behind pillow-soft lips, which he expected to taste of crushed banana and sweet pineapple juice; the rest was edible from head to her tiny toes as well.

Until now, Kory's relationships had been like drug highs: there was nothing like the first time. But now that notion changed; it was possible, after all, to reach extended moments of self-abandonment. For the first time in his life, Kory was not afraid for another person to discover who he really was: not yet the person he wanted to be. Repeated shedding of old personas and donning the latest iteration of himself had been his path to self-mastery.

Two years earlier, Kory had been a self-centered ex-dancer looking for a new identity. Of all the labels he could have envisioned, father was not one of them. But the next Halloween came with a trick and a life-changing treat: Eseta was pregnant.

The idea of moving from his grandfather's house had seldom come to mind until Eseta started wearing maternity clothes. Kory had been a prisoner in the jail that had given him the freedom to explore life without the fetter of needing to earn a living. Despite his grandfather's eternal indulgence, it was time to make a life without the safety net he had often fallen into when he lost his footing trying to make sense of where he was after another transition. Parenthood would be permanent.

Finding a home in the same neighborhood was easier than getting the blessings of their families to marry. Kory and Eseta took revenge by eloping and announcing the birth of their son weeks later. Estrangement satisfied old scores with their parents but did little to ease the challenge of paying rent and going to biweekly checkups.

Being raised by a single parent with limited resources had taught Kory early about the value of money. Instead of buying a new car with his savings, he rented what he thought was the perfect place for a dance studio in Adams Morgan.

Teaching dance did not require the sustained exertion of a performance, but trying to find enough paying students to stay ahead of mounting bills became harder than rehearsing a troupe for an evening performance. Even the extra money Kory got from subletting the extra space in his studio was not enough some months.

One evening, while he was cleaning the studio mirrors for his morning class, an old acquaintance stopped by. Kory's back was turned when the studio door creaked open. Before he could turn around, an old school chum was easing across the floor. Doc, to his friends and others, was the son of a prominent heart surgeon whom Kory had met on the Howard University campus. Originally, this friend had gotten the moniker Doc because everyone assumed he would follow his father's footsteps. Later he was known as Doc for being the guy who knew everything there was to know about drugs. Whatever mind-altering substance people wanted, they could count on him to have it on hand or to know where to find it. He was so successful at dealing illegal drugs that he boasted he made more money getting people high than his father did saving lives.

"So this is where you've been hiding yourself." Doc looked many years older than Kory, despite his expensive clothes.

"I wouldn't call it hiding when I'm trying to get as many people as possible in my studio. Where have you been hiding? The last I heard, you had run into a little trouble with the law."

"It was more rumor than fact. They never found anything, but I decided to move to New York to let the hearsay die down. How's business?" Doc surveyed the empty studio.

"Well, not bad, but to tell you the truth, with a new mouth to feed, I'm just getting by." Kory resumed cleaning the last section of the mirror.

"That's no fun. There's always plenty of money out there."

Kory tossed the sponge into the bucket. "Yeah, out *there*, maybe, but not in here."

Doc wiped his nose with a handkerchief from the pocket of his dashiki. "Is there something I can do to help?"

"Want to buy a dance studio?"

"That's not my style, but maybe I can lend some help in another way."

"Such as what, Good Brother?"

"I think you know what I'm referring to. You made a little money with me back in the day, as it were," Doc said.

"That was a long time ago. Nobody wants weed these days. Anyway, I don't know if I have the balls to get into that again."

"Well, I'm not referring to smoke. Everybody wants 'the lady' nowadays. Besides, once you've been in the business, it's easy to do it again. I've got some really good product if you're interested in trying some. You look like you could use a pick-me-up."

"Maybe…Let's go into my office. I better lock the front door first."

Doc pulled out a clear plastic baggie of uncut cocaine. It had been more than five years since Kory had taken any.

"Try a couple lines of this stuff, and forget your troubles."

"It'll have to be more than good to do that." Kory sniffed the white powder with Doc's rolled-up hundred-dollar bill.

"Well, what do you think, Professor?"

"You know I hate that nickname. This stuff is pretty good."

"I can give you a real good deal on weight," Doc added.

"Such as?"

"Five hundred an ounce, and you can step on it three times."

Kory wiped his nose. "Give me your number, and I'll let you know tomorrow."

The next day Kory met Doc and left with two ounces on consignment. It was not long before he sold his dance studio, paid his overdue bills, and had more time to spend with his family.

CHAPTER 28:

Snow-blind

Money ceased being a challenge by early winter 1980. The Vanon family had a new townhouse, tasteful furnishings, and enough to send their son to private school.

Kory had developed a loyal clientele for his wares. Just a few years earlier, he had been selling product to anyone who was willing and able to afford it. But now he had promoted himself to the wholesale level, where he saw only dealers. Having made enough money, he now considered ways to convert his unreported cash into a legitimate business.

Fish comprises more than 80 percent of the diet of most Samoans; his wife was no exception. Her favorite was lobster. Early one morning, Kory hoped to miss the crowd at the wharf in Southwest Washington by arriving just as fishmongers were opening their stalls. While he was waiting for his favorite, he spied a character wearing a long white apron, like butchers wear, and thigh-high black boots. The sign on his truck read LOWELL'S LIVE MAINE LOBSTER. Kory's father had once owned a seafood market in Upper Northwest Washington. It was there he had learned about seafood, including that much sold as Maine lobster was actually from the Gulf of Mexico or Australia, lacking North Atlantic flavor and large claws.

"Hi there! Your sign says MAINE LOBSTER. Is it really Maine lobster or mixed with varieties of crawfish?"

With a look of annoyance and the accent of the Gorton's fisherman, he said, "I don't have time to waste on trying to cheat the public. I own my lobster pounds and fishing rights in Bangor, Maine. There're many imitators out there, but my family has been in this business for four generations. I'm Tim Lowell." He extended his hand, which was the size of a bear trap. Kory told him about his experience in his family's seafood business and his desire to open his own. The lobsterman gave him his business card and a list of products. After giving Kory a few lobsters from his truck, Lowell asked to call him when he was ready to get the lowest-priced Maine lobsters on the East Coast.

The next morning, Kory made calls around the city to find out the range of wholesale and retail prices. By 1:00 p.m., he had compiled a list of more than one hundred wholesalers and obtained prices for retail lobster from all the local supermarkets and specialty shops. The average retail price most supermarkets offered was about $9.45 per pound, and the average wholesale price was about $4.35 per pound. Tim Lowell offered Kory live lobster delivered three times a week at $1.50 per pound. The math was simple. Now he needed to devise a distribution strategy and delineate a market.

Days later he struck agreements with ten restaurants that guaranteed to purchase one hundred pounds each at $3.25 per pound. After expenses, his profit was a little over $900 per week—not a lot of money, but certainly a good beginning. Three months later, his business more than quadrupled to weekly profits of $4,000 or more.

During his seafood venture, Kory's other business brought in regular profits, but there was not a lot to do there. His relationships with clients and dealers worked seamlessly.

It was still hot in Washington, D.C., in the early autumn. While waiting for his takeout order at the Rib Pit on Fourteenth Street, Kory ran into a person from his childhood—someone he had never wanted for a friend.

Harry lived on the other side of the avenue, where coveralls dried on clotheslines, compared with the freshly starched white shirts spinning in the clothes dryers on Kory's street. Harry's parents were blue-collar workers with only cursory education and fewer social graces. It was no wonder many of his crowd came from similar backgrounds and, for the most part, traveled in gangs. Kory's initial encounter with him had been the first week of school, during recess. Harry's cousin, the playground bully, tried to steal one of Kory's new cat-eye marbles after losing two rounds. Although not the greatest boxer, he learned early in life he was more afraid of being called a coward than taking on the best fighter in the school. Assuming this bully was not as bright as his skills, Kory foamed at the mouth while he repeatedly "joaned" (disparaged) the bully's mother in front of the crowd. His bluff worked, because shouts 'that he's crazy' from the crowd convinced Harry's cousin he had a madman on his hands. He was right about one thing; he saw it in Kory's eyes: something snapped when Kory got into fights. He was ready to kill when his opponent was expecting only a fistfight.

"Is that you, Kory? Man, I haven't seen you since Roosevelt High School. One day I saw you hitting on some fine 'hamma' in the cafeteria, and then you disappeared. What happened to you?"

"Uh, Ha…rry? Hey, man! How you been? It's been a while. Whatcha been up to?"

"Same ol', same ol'. What about you? You haven't changed a bit."

Harry had certainly changed. As a teenager, he had been fat, with shiny ebony skin; now he was a very plump, blotchy-skinned young adult with a receding hairline. And even though the restaurant's air-conditioning was set on low, he was sweating as if he were running a high fever. Moreover, there was a certain urgency about him, in that he repeatedly searched the same empty pocket and bit his lip when his hand came out empty.

Kory folded his arms in front of him. "Just doing my family thing. What about you?"

"Hey, man, I got four kids—all girls," Harry said as he fumbled with his cigarette lighter.

"Just one boy so far."

Harry dropped his cigarette on the floor and reached inside his pocket again.

"Well, looks like they got my order ready. It was good seeing you, man."

"Kory, my man, we should hook up. I got a few things going on you might be interested in."

"Really! Like what?"

"Do you get high?"

"I toot a little bit every now and then."

"Man, I got the bomb if you want to check it out."

"Tell you what: here's my telephone number. How about buzzing me around eight o'clock tonight?" Kory wrote his number on the receipt for his pound of ribs.

"Sounds like a plan. Later!"

Kory was always looking to increase his market—except to some people, he should have remained a ghost. Unfortunately, male egos had a way of supplanting good judgment.

After taking a short nap, he laced his running shoes for an afternoon run in Rock Creek Park. It was when he was running that he processed many of his problems. Now there was more than usual to consider. Kory was usually overly cautious and low key. Something told him he had made a very serious mistake.

Harry arrived an hour late. Kory ignored the possible reasons and lack of a phone call from him saying he was delayed.

"Man, this is a nice spot. Looks like you're doing pretty well for yourself, Kory."

Kory went behind the bar. "You up for a Rémy Martin?"

"You know it," Harry said as he took the barstool closest to the wall.

Kory poured two large snifters of cognac. "Here's to the old neighborhood."

Harry reached inside his suit jacket pocket and produced a small, neatly folded packet. "Man, I told you that I got the bomb. Check it out." He placed his sample of drugs on the bar.

Kory reached underneath and placed a long dental spatula on the bar.

"Whatcha got there, Kory? It looks like something my dentist uses."

"Very good. This dental instrument makes the best coke spoon I've found. Give it a try."

"Since I brought this for you to check out, you go first."

"Sho 'nuff," Kory said as he took a one-in-one. "Nice shit there, Harry," he said, after taking two quick inhalations to stop any extraneous powder from falling from his nose.

"Man, I only sport the best," Harry said, leaning back against the wall after taking a big gulp from his snifter.

"I've a little something here for you to check out, too, there, Brother Man." Kory reached under the bar.

"Bring it on!"

Kory placed a tightly folded white packet on the bar; it dwarfed Harry's meager offering.

"That looks like a quarter ounce there, my man."

Kory handed the spatula to Harry. "Check it out. You won't be disappointed."

"Goddamn, Kory! This is some thorough shit, man. Where did you get this monster?"

"I got a brother that's pretty deep. The best shit I've seen in the city."

Harry took another sniff. "Where can I get some of this shit?"

"How much you looking for?"

"Well, I'd like to cop about an eighth—just to let my people check it out."

"No problem. Got that right here," Kory said.

"Hope you don't mind fronting it. I wasn't expecting to be picking up anything tonight. I thought you would be checking me out. But it seems like you the man."

"I'll be honest with you: I don't believe in fronting anything, but since we go way back, I guess it can happen. When are you going to tighten me up for this shit?"

"No problem. I'll get it back to you tonight if you want."

"Solid!"

There was a buzz from the front-door intercom.

"Speak!"

"It's Stu."

"Hey, man, I'll buzz you in."

Stu was a fairly new friend. They had met on campus three years earlier. Their friendship had been immediate, after they had discovered Stu's father had been Colonel Toile's adjutant before making colonel as well. Stu was not a very tall man. To compensate, he had spent years overdeveloping his body.

"What the hell is this muva-fucker doing in your house?" Stu said, taking a crouching position like a praying mantis ready to attack his prey.

"What's up, Brother Stu?" Harry stuck the packet in his sweaty breast pocket.

"You two know each other?" asked Kory.

"I ain't your brother, Harry. Kory, you need to get this devil out of your house before God strikes your family."

"Kory, I'm splitting. I don't feel like going through any shit with him tonight." Harry sniffed another spatula before he stood up.

"Okay, I'll see you later." He walked Harry to the door.

"Kory, you don't need to have someone like that in your house with your family around. Harry is not to be trusted. He's a base freak."

"Base freak?"

"I'm not surprised you don't know about freebase. Those people use the product to turn it into a concentrated crystal and smoke it."

"So what's so terrible about that?"

"Freebase is the breath of the devil. It only takes one puff of that shit for someone to become addicted and sentenced to a lifetime in the worst part of hell. I've seen some of my friends renounce God and sacrifice their families for another hit from the base pipe."

"How do you know so much about this?"

"I...er...tried it a couple of times. Kory, I'm begging you, for your family's sake, keep Harry out of your house. Nothing good can come of it."

"I think I can handle Harry."

"Don't say I didn't warn you. Just watch him. He's poison. Nothing can stop one of those zombies from destroying anything or anyone that stands in the way of his next hit."

Stu's admonishments were prophetic. Around 10:30 p.m., Kory got a call from Harry.

"Kory, I got everything, but I've got to go and pick up something else. I can get there in an hour."

"That sounds a bit complicated. Don't sweat it. Can you make it here around one o'clock tomorrow afternoon?"

"Sure. Thanks, man. I'll have everything together...then," he said with a choking cough.

"Sounds like you're coming down with something."

"Ah, it's nothing. Gotta cut out all those cancer sticks," Harry declared.

Kory had a sour taste in his mouth. "Okay, see you tomorrow."

CHAPTER 29:

Stu Was Right

The only furniture Kory had brought from his grandfather's house was his favorite wingback chair. Sitting there tonight, Kory listened to his son's giggles and Eseta's singing as little Kory played in the tub. No matter how hard he tried, he could not remember having felt such joy when he was a child.

His son was in bed by the time he got upstairs. As was his evening pleasure, he read one of his son's favorite stories until he was fast asleep on his shoulder. Kory looked down at his sleeping boy over his heart and thought how lucky he was to have the chance to give his son the childhood he had never had. He stroked little Kory's hair as a lone tear streamed down his face into his moustache.

Eseta was sitting at her vanity, braiding her hair, when he entered their bedroom. "Something bothering you? You said little during dinner, and now your brow is furrowed. Is there something going on I should know about?"

"I hope not. My intuition is telling me to be on guard. It may have something to do with running into someone I've not seen in many years."

She looked at him in the mirror. "An old friend?"

"Not quite. More like the ghost of someone I hardly knew."

"Sometimes you worry too much. Why don't you go out and catch a few jazz sets tonight? You haven't been out in weeks."

"Sounds like a good idea. Sure you won't miss me?"

"I always miss you when you're gone, but I know if you don't have time to yourself, you'll withdraw anyway."

He hugged her shoulders and looked at the two of them in the mirror. "How did you get so lucky to fall in love with such a moody guy?"

"I've never thought of you as moody. You have a way of letting me know what you are feeling. With the exception of our son, I doubt few people have a clue what's really going on inside that wild brain of yours. And by the way, if you keep rubbing my neck like that, I'll find some homework for you to do," she warned.

Kory loved jazz. Whenever he could, he toured the jazz clubs in Dupont Circle and Georgetown. His favorite was Arnold's Jazz Bar, just one block south of Dupont Circle. Here, the old, dark, and seedy jazz clubs of the fifties and sixties had been replaced by a modern pub catering to jazz aficionados looking for a comfortable place to tap their feet or sit at the bar and listen to the performance in the next room. Regardless of who was playing, before the night was over, the owner, Dr. Arnold Katz, a Georgetown psychiatrist in the daylight, would convince the pianist to let him sit in on one set. After all, it was his nightclub.

"Hi, Kory. The usual?" asked Mae as she poured a healthy snifter of Rémy Martin.

"How you doing, gorgeous? Is Nell working tonight?"

"You should know. What did you do to her last night? She called in late. Arnold is pissed since this is the second time this month. He's going to fire her if she doesn't tighten up."

"Is this *Peyton Place* or something?"

"What's *Peyton Place?*"

"I keep forgetting you're so young and tender. It was a soap opera during the late fifties and early sixties."

"You drank that one fast. Ready for another?"

"Sure, hit me. I'm going to the men's room to powder my nose."

She smiled as she poured another cognac. "I've noticed a lot people have been powdering their noses around here lately."

This early in the evening, when many non-regulars were in the bar, Kory and those who were members of the bar family would powder their noses out of view until the bar closed. It was a different world then, and closed to outsiders. As soon as the front door was locked, the music resumed and the real party began. The privileged regulars enjoyed their private world until the ones who had to work regular jobs left to stop home long enough to change clothes before rejoining the conservative world of those who only saw the outside of the jazz culture.

Kory checked his reflection in the mirror before returning to the bar. It was considered bad taste to walk around looking like you had just inhaled a powdered doughnut. There was a disadvantage to sniffing cocaine in a men's room: the smells were amplified, but this early in the evening, the only scent was that of the camphor disk in the urinal. There was a new joke on the wall: *Welcome Reagan Back to Bonzo*, or *Ketchup does not take the place of vegetables, but someone should put a cap on Reagan.* John, the dishwasher and a former researcher for the Department of Defense, with high security clearance, had probably written those. The aphorisms by some of the pot-smoking musicians were usually the most interesting: *What is the sound of one hand clapping? The applause after Arnold's last solo.* Actually, Arnold took a lot of undeserved ribbing from people around his club. He was actually a very good musician. During the few occasions Kory had seen or heard Arnold "free" (in the zone), he could play with the best of them. Arnold knew when he had crossed the threshold. Kory could picture a young Arnold in his orthodox Jewish home, yearning to play something besides the etudes required by his pedagogy. His whole body would gyrate with the rhythm of the music. Not bad for someone from a diaspora not known for letting it all hang out in public.

The scintillating sound of Dave Brubeck's "Take Five," a jazz standard, was the first selection of Tim Eyerman and his East Coast Offering. Tim, an eclectic flutist, like so many other white jazz musicians, was colorless and "Kool." Their Koolness was all that remained of the beatnik area.

Kory had cracked the door to the music room just wide enough to catch Tim's eye, when he heard, "Nice ass. How's the rest of it?"

Without turning around, he knew it was Nell. "It's all good. Just break off any piece you want."

Kory nodded to Tim and turned around. "The word is going around that Arnold is going to sack you because of my bad influence on his most popular waitress."

"Arnold is always complaining. He's not going to fire me. I know where all the bodies are buried in the green room. I guess you've heard the rumor that we're hot and heavy."

"Let them think whatever they like, as long as we know we're just close friends."

"It doesn't have to be that way, you know. I don't mind sharing you with your wife."

"Nell, we had a good thing going on before I got married. Why should we take a chance spoiling all those good memories?"

"I miss what we once had. I'm glad you have settled down with one woman—something you found hard to do when we were dating."

"You told me then that you liked the challenge."

"Okay, you've got me there. But if you ever change your mind, you know the number. There's Arnold. I'd better get to my tables. Talk to you later."

Kory enjoyed seeing Nell. She reminded him of times when he had been carefree and lived life like there was no tomorrow.

"All right, everyone, last call! Want one for the road, Kory?" Mae reached for the Rémy Martin.

"Sure, but make it an Irish coffee, sweet lady."

Even at two o'clock in the morning, Dupont Circle hosted a sizable group of people. When Kory was in high school, the Circle was populated mostly with hippies and similar groups of that time. Now it had become a meeting place for the gay community, which was fine with him.

Most houses were dark by the time Kory got home. He quietly went to the kitchen and made a cup of chamomile tea before heading to bed. Years of surviving all types of challenges had taught him to listen to impressions of things just below the surface of his consciousness. It wasn't that he could foretell the future; he had learned to trust his instincts to guide him when deliberate thought wrought only indecision. Stu's admonitions were just flashes of light in a dark room of intermittently discernible bodies without faces. Something was about to happen.

Just before dawn, Kory woke to a church choir warming the audience to open their wallets for a beseeching TV evangelist sporting a pompadour taller than the lies he would tell. He quickly pressed the OFF button on the remote and quietly made his way upstairs to the bedroom to find that his son was already sleeping on his pillow next to his mother. Not wanting to wake them, Kory closed the door and went to the spare bedroom, but as hard as he tried, he could not fall asleep. Stu's words of warning resounded. With his eyes closed, he sensed the presence of his grandmother standing at the foot of the bed. Someone was going to die.

CHAPTER 30

Depth After Death

While Kory watched a Redskins football game, his wife came into the bedroom to grab her sunglasses from the armoire. "We're going for ice cream. Would you like a quart of rum raisin?"

"No, thanks. I'm fasting today."

"Are you feeling okay?" She felt his forehead.

"Just a lot on my mind right now."

The Dallas Cowboys had just intercepted a Redskins pass. It was Washington's last chance to tie the game. Just as he was about to change the channel, he heard a crash downstairs. Kory's wife screamed.

"Who are you? Kory!" she screamed.

Instinctively he ran to the closet, loaded his Smith & Wesson .38 competition revolver, and raced down the stairs. Before he reached the bottom landing, he saw Eseta in front of the fireplace and their son hiding behind her. Standing in the living room was Harry, holding a gun at his side. Harry's cousin, looking very nervous, was holding a similar weapon.

"What the hell is this, Harry?" Kory demanded. His gun was at his side and out of sight.

Harry raised his gun. "Give it up, Kory."

"Give what up?" Kory demanded as he pulled the hammer back.

"Don't play dumb. You know what this is about."

"I'll give you something, you piece of shit," he said as he shot above Harry's cousin's head. "Get the hell out of my house!" Kory yelled.

The bullet shattered the plant hanging from the lintel above the second intruder's head. "Fuck this shit, Harry. I told you this muva-fucker was crazy," he said as backed out the door with his pistol pointed in Kory's direction.

"You bitch-ass punk," Harry screamed at his cousin. "I said give it up, Kory." He pushed Eseta into the fireplace. She struck her head against the granite mantel and fell to the floor, dazed. His son reached for his mother, but Harry grabbed him as a shield.

"Put him down, Harry. We can work this out," Kory said. He was leaning over the railing but not enough to give Harry a good shot.

"Don't hurt my baby," his wife begged.

"You're all going to die," yelled Harry as he held their son with his left hand and fired at Kory with the other.

Because of the angle, Kory was unable to return fire. He could only duck when he saw Harry's finger about to squeeze the trigger.

"Harry, put your gun down, and let's talk about this. You know the cops will be here in a few minutes."

Harry ignored the offer and fired again. By now, Kory had counted three shots from the coward holding his son. He noticed that every time he did, he would partially lose his grip on his little boy, who was frightened by the sound of the gunshots and flinched with every *boom*.

The next seconds seemed like minutes, and each gunshot sounded louder than the one before. The smell of burnt sulfur filled the air. Kory looked into Harry's eyes and saw desperation and something worse—fear. He knew Harry had no intention of letting them live. Even if Kory were to lay down his gun and give him everything he demanded, they would all certainly die.

"Harry, I'm asking you for the last time to drop your gun."

"I'm going to kill you and blow your son's brains out."

"Take whatever you want. I beg you. Please don't hurt my child," his wife pleaded.

Kory said a silent prayer. He thought of all the hours he had spent honing his marksmanship skills on the range. For three years Kory had devoted ten hours or more per week earning his Distinguished Expert rating from the National Rifle Association, but this was not a paper target. In his mind, he saw what he hoped would happen. "God, don't let me hit my son," he repeated to himself again. Harry's next shot missed his head by inches. Kory first crouched and then quickly stood before the sound of the last shot had died down.

"Eseta, get down!" Kory screamed. He leaned over the iron railing and aimed for the spot he begged God to send the bullet to. His son's head was now below Harry's waist.

The sound of Kory's gun was like a shotgun. The size of the barrel and the special load of the bullet gushed fire and smoke that blasted Harry's body into the glass coffee table and onto his back.

Kory rushed down the last two steps and through the dining room in the direction of the living room. All he could see was Harry, still clutching his son by his shirtsleeve. His gun was still in his right hand resting on the floor by his leg. Just as he was within five feet, Harry tried to get a stronger hold on Kory's son, who was now crying and trying to reach his mother's outstretched hands.

"Stay down!" Kory yelled to Eseta again as he entered the living room. Harry struggled to sit up. He pointed his gun directly at the back of the child's head. Without hesitation, Kory put a second bullet beside the other in Harry's heart. He collapsed this time, grabbing his chest. Eseta crawled across the floor, grabbed their son into her arms, and turned her back to Harry, who was now motionless.

"You piece of shit," Kory said as he kicked Harry's head until blood and saliva spattered the two holes on his white shirt and the carpet around him. Soon after, Harry expelled his last breath: a putrid miasma of his wretched humanity.

"Are you two all right?" Kory asked, putting his arms around his family. "It's over. He's dead. You'd better go upstairs. The police will probably be here in a minute."

Seconds later, uniformed police officers cautiously entered through the French doors with guns drawn. Kory was sitting at the bar, swallowing a large cognac, with his back to them.

"Put your hands up, and turn around slowly," they ordered.

"Where is the shotgun?"

Kory put his hands up. "I'm the owner. The man lying on the floor tried to kill my family. There's no shotgun—just these." He pointed to the weapons on the bar.

The older officer with graying temples spoke. "Did you shoot him, sir?"

"Not soon enough. I should have killed him twenty years ago."

"Is there anyone else in the house?"

"Yes. My wife and son are upstairs."

"Jim, I'll call this in. You go upstairs and check on them."

"Sir, just sit here until the detectives get here."

"Okay, but I'm going to call my attorney."

"If you think that is necessary. This looks like a case of home invasion and self-defense."

Kory ignored his comment and called Josh David. "This is Kory Vanon. I need to talk to Josh immediately."

"Sorry, but he's with a client. Can I have him call you when he's free?"

"This is an emergency. *Get him on the phone now!*"

"What's the problem, Kory?" Josh asked.

"There's been a shooting at my hocuse. I need you over here."

"Is anyone hurt?"

"We're okay, but there's a dead man on my living-room floor."

"Do you know him?"

"Yes."

"Don't say a word to the police until I get there."

For the most part, Kory remained in control. After his attorney arrived, when asked by the investigating detective to describe what had happened, Kory had to run into the powder room and throw up.

"Detective Fishburne, we know each other. He's in no condition to answer any questions right now. You have my word that I'll bring him and his family to the station in an hour. Would you do this for me?" asked Josh, as if he knew what the detective's answer would be.

"Sure, Josh. You've always been straight with me. This is sticking my neck out, so I don't expect any half-stepping from you."

"We'll see you in an hour," Josh assured him.

"Thanks for getting here right away, Josh," Kory said as he wiped his mouth with a paper towel from behind the bar.

"This may be a bit rough on Eseta, but I need for you to go upstairs and go over what happened before we go to the station,"

"Is there any way she can come in tomorrow? She's terrified, but I'm more worried about my son. That animal put a gun...he put a gun to my child's head. I wish the bastard would come back to life so I could kill him again." Kory looked at Harry's still body on the living-room floor.

CHAPTER 31

The Inquest

Harry's body lay cold on the living-room floor as members of the forensic team dug out bullets inches from where Kory had stood. Bulbs flashed outside as TV stations' roving anchors gathered fodder for the evening news. A mile away, Kory and Eseta had just finished two hours of separate interrogations.

Kory held the door for Eseta as she slid into the backseat of Josh's black Mercedes. "We're never going back to that house. Never! Do you hear me?" She began to sob as Kory put his arm around his wife. Their son slept on the shoulder of Josh's wife in the front seat. Josh drove to his house west of Rock Creek Park, where they stayed until the coroner's inquest.

Kory was watching the news days later in the family room when Josh's wife came in, carrying the cordless phone. "Josh is on the phone for you."

"Thanks." Kory closed the door before he got the words out. He took a deep breath. "Is this going to be good news?"

"We may have a problem. They're saying this may be a case of overkill."

"What the hell does that mean?"

"There must be some anal-retentive wannabe investigator with a burr up his ass, because they're positing that the second shot may not have been in self-defense."

"He threatened to blow off my son's head. Did they expect me to give that bastard mouth-to-mouth resuscitation? I shot the son of a bitch a second time because he was about to shoot my son in the back of his head."

"I know that, and I think the lead detective believes it as well. We need to convince the grand jury, even though the lead detective has the final word. You can never be certain if someone else in the detective squad is trying to make a name for himself. There may be a cop on the force with a grudge against your family."

"I can't see—"

"Your father's close tie with the chief doesn't help us with those with a grudge against the brass."

"Well, can't worry about that now. What's our next step?"

"Just a sec! I'm trying to make this light. Listen, I've got a friend in the coroner's office who owes me big-time. If anyone can help, he's the guy."

"How soon can you reach him?"

"I'm now within a block of the city morgue. I'll call you in a few."

"Man, I just want this thing to be over. Eseta can't sleep, and little Kory won't take his nap; he even cries now in his sleep."

"Little Kory is like his old man. He's a strong kid." There was a pause while a bus passed by Josh's car. "Kory, we've been through a lot together. You know I've got your back and I'll do my best."

"Josh, you *are* the best. I guess that's why everyone calls you Silky."

Kory went upstairs to the bedroom and put his arms around Eseta, who was stroking their son's head as he fought sleep. The three of them eventually fell asleep, with their arms around one another, until evening.

There was a knock on the bedroom door. "Kory! It's Josh. You awake?"

"Give me a minute," he said as he untangled himself from his little sleeping family.

Kory went to the bathroom to wash his face before going into Josh's study. After he dried off, he looked closely into the mirror for the first time since the shooting. Despite his long nap with his family, the bags under his eyes looked more like welts from punches to his face.

"He's the man!" said Josh as Kory came into the study.

"What did he say?"

"Thank God you're a good shot, Kory. The first one hit the left ventricle, and the second obliterated the aorta. In other words, both shots were fatal. The second was, as they say, academic. It's still not over. There's a grand jury hearing in the morning. You and Eseta have to come to the courthouse, but I'll see if they'll let me keep you in the hallway while I do my thing."

"You look confident."

"I am. This is just a formality. You two will be back by lunchtime."

"Okay. I'd better wake Eseta and tell her."

"Tell her everything is going to be all right."

"Thanks, Josh. I'll see you in the morning."

The grand-jury hearing went just as Josh predicted. Hadassah, his wife, prepared a festive lunch for them in the conservatory, a piece of Eden filled with her plants.

That evening, when the men were in Josh's study, Josh said, "Kory, the legal part of this is over; therefore, I trust you know there're still some loose ends you need to deal with before you and your family can safely sleep at night. The cops haven't found the accomplice. We don't know if he has left town or is waiting for an opportunity to get revenge. I know you're the type of man who does not like to leave things to chance. I'll leave it there."

"No loose ends," Kory said as he looked inside himself.

Never again would he leave his family's security to chance. He tried to tell himself the worst was over, but deep inside he knew it was not. Something had died inside him. Burying the corpse was difficult without leaving a part of him to rot in the ground.

CHAPTER 32

One Too Many

The marketing success of Kory's seafood business was partially due to an investor, who had a lot of cash that needed to be put into a legitimate business. She was a strikingly beautiful woman of Sicilian heritage, whom Kory had met at a dance concert many years before Eseta moved in with him. They had dated only a couple of times before they'd admitted that their friendship was natural, but as lovers they might last only six months. When she got word of what had happened, she arranged for members of her family to provide security for Kory's.

They were old-fashioned Sicilian: the old men still wore their shirts buttoned to the chin without ties, and the matrons dressed in black and carried rosaries as proof of their perpetual oblation. So wherever Kory and his family went, a car was always far enough away that he could not read the license plates, but close enough to make anyone else following think twice. One of the few times he looked out the window to see if his protectors were on the job, he saw one of them who had a neck the width of an average man's head and the countenance of a mother elephant.

Six months went by. One evening the TV anchorwoman announced the name of Harry's accomplice. "Tyrone Robinson, who was wanted for kidnapping by the FBI, was found floating facedown two miles from Point Lookout, Maryland." Kory made a note in his ledger and went into the family room.

"*MNOPQRSTUVWXYZ*—that's perfect. There's Papa."

Kory took a seat in the easy chair. His son jumped into his lap.

"Your namesake has earned a new book. He wants to recite his ABC's for you."

"Well, young man, let's hear them," Kory said, giving him a hug.

His son recited as his mother clapped a rhythm.

"That's perfect, Kory. Your mother says you earned a new book. Let's go to Borders bookstore and then to Chuck E. Cheese for pizza afterward. Would you like that?" Kory kissed his son on the forehead, which made him giggle.

"Yes, Papa. May I ride in the spaceship?" His little arms were still around his father's neck.

"Of course you can. You may go on any ride you want today." Kory lifted his son in the air and moved him as if he were flying.

Life in suburban Virginia was a world far away from in-town Washington, D.C.: lots of sprawling lawns and overly pregnant women with other children in strollers who ruled the street. For nine months the Vanons stayed in the home of Kory's investor, Lani, and her fiancé, Manuel, who was the Cuban version of Engelbert Humperdinck but with better teeth and a natural stage presence that made the ladies in the audience send him their panties with their room numbers written in lipstick on the crotch. Their Ozzie and Harriet–style house in Virginia was far enough from the other side of the Potomac River to make Eseta feel safe. She spent most of her days teaching their son while Kory made phone calls to keep his seafood business afloat. Life was quiet for the most part, but Kory was starting to have problems sleeping through the night. He usually slept peacefully for about three hours and then was awakened by the looping video of the police drama that had changed their lives. Nothing seemed to work, including sleeping pills, herbal teas, and lots of alcohol.

By the end of the year, Kory was back to hanging out at jazz clubs and taking anything to numb the pain. He could not overlook the nagging feeling that something inside him had died the day he took another life—even in self-defense.

Unable to relax one Sunday afternoon, Kory told his wife he was going for a drive to clear his head. She reminded him to be careful and kissed him good-bye.

It was just a quick ten-minute drive in his Jaguar across the Key Bridge to Georgetown. Early Sunday afternoon was the best time to see the area. The multitude of sightseers had not yet made their way there from touring popular attractions like the Washington Monument and the White House.

As Kory drove, memories of Georgetown during the late sixties reminded him of the time when he had had few worries and almost no responsibilities. Continuing east on M Street, past the specialty shops with their quaint-sounding names and bistros with alfresco tables, he approached the One Step Down jazz nightclub.

This was one of his old haunts from his high school days and recent past. As he drove by the entrance, people waited in line to walk through the narrow doorway to one of the best jazz clubs in town. At Washington Circle it occurred to him that on Sundays there was a jazz workshop, where those who loved jazz could hear young musicians and the older ones who were willing to pass on their legacy. The sagacious ones shared their deftness in drawing inspiration from their river of creativity, while the aspiring young musicians were eager to catch some of the droplets released from the steady-flowing currents created by those who had found the soul of jazz, and, for some of them, the perfect key of life.

One of the older musicians brought his girlfriend to the club that afternoon. Kory found her impossible to ignore. She had fiery red hair, flawless, milky-white skin, and a voice that would have made even Lauren Bacall sound like Minnie Mouse.

Elizabeth made the hair on Kory's neck stand on end with every syllable he heard from two booths away. The musicians went through countless scores while Elizabeth absorbed their energy and used it to sketch everyone who walked onto the stage.

After a few drinks, Kory walked to her booth and introduced himself. "Hi, I'm Kory. Would you mind if I take a look at some of your finished sketches? I'm a bit of an artist myself."

"Oh, really! What do you work in?"

"Tights and sweats! I'm a dancer and choreographer."

"I'm Elizabeth. Not Liz or Lizzie."

"Enchanted, Elizabeth. May I buy you a drink?"

She took a deep drag from her cigarette and blew it across the table. "Sure. Grand Marnier with a shot of Cuervo Gold on the side."

"That's heavy-duty. Tequila would put me to sleep this early." He waved for to the waitress.

"It keeps me in the mood," she said as she closed her sketchbook and took another deep drag on her cigarette.

"Have you been coming to these workshops long?"

"That's kind of corny for an opener." Dual plumes of smoke flowed from her nostrils.

"I guess I'm a little out of practice."

"Hard to get away from the wife, huh?" She grinned as she looked at his wedding band.

"Not really. She suggested I go out and have some fun alone."

"She sounds like a secure woman."

"We've been together for almost ten years. There's nothing I can do that would surprise her—except not being home by daylight." The waitress brought their drinks and winked at Kory. He wasn't sure if she was the one he had slept with many years earlier.

Elizabeth upended her glass of tequila. "Ta kill ya!"

"What?"

"That's what I call it."

"Do you do anything else?"

She took out another cigarette. "Are you writing a book?"

"Just like to find out more about you. I love your voice."

"Yeah, yeah, yeah! I've heard that before. Can't you come up with something more original than that?"

"Was that a question?"

"Do whatever you wish with what I said," she replied.

"Well…er…when I'm drinking heavily, I like to take something to keep me humming."

"I'm already singing inside. You're talking about blow?"

"Indeed!"

"I like a one-in-one now and then, but not now." She opened her sketchbook.

"I'll be back in a minute. Need to powder my nose." Kory got up from the table and headed for the men's room.

Elizabeth checked over her shoulder the direction Kory went. She smiled to herself as she started another page in her sketchbook. As the next group took the stage, she took another look to see if the door to the men's room was still closed and quickly walked to the bandstand.

"Steve, do you know the guy who just walked by dressed in black?"

"I think his name is Kory or something like that." He started to clean his trumpet. "He used to hang with Marshall Hawkins, the bassist. You know that says a lot."

"Thanks for the info," Elizabeth said.

"Anytime, Liz!"

She quickly turned around. "You've been blowing the wrong end of that thing or something. You know I hate for anyone to screw with my name."

"Chill out, baby!"

"And I ain't your baby, asshole," she said, walking away from the bandstand.

"Okay! Okay! I'm sorry. You get so serious sometimes. Listen to the music and relax."

Now back at the table, Kory was able to overhear parts of the exchange. Her boyfriend nodded his head in the direction of her table. She said something in his ear and walked back to the table.

"I'd like a hit if that offer is still good," said Elizabeth as she slid across the leather seat into the booth.

"Here, help yourself. There's plenty."

Elizabeth briefly held Kory's hand as he passed the packet to her under the table.

"I'll be back in a minute. Don't go anywhere," she said as she stuck her sketch pencil in the crown of her hair.

"Just grooving with the music, E-liz-a-beth."

The last musician was one of Washington's local treasures. Andrew White, a prodigy, was well known to the true lovers of jazz and scholars of musicology. As a teenager, he was the first person to chart all of John Coltrane's work. This would have been a challenge for the most prodigious adult musicologists today. Andrew White went further than placing those screaming sounds on a piece of paper; he allowed John Coltrane's spirit to take over his soul. He looked and dressed like Trane, including the high-water pants and clean white shirt. When he spoke—it was the great master pressing the keys on his alto saxophone.

"Good afternoon, everyone. 'A Love Supreme'!" he said, announcing the next piece.

"That was nice." Elizabeth handed Kory her business card with the packet underneath.

"So you are a graphic artist as well!"

"At least in the daylight, when everyone is watching. This is my Sunday to have dinner with my folks. My number is on the card. I should be home around nine o'clock if you want to continue."

"Should I pick up something?"

"We already have all we need."

"Just out of curiosity, is that guy playing the trumpet your boyfriend?"

"When I want him to be." She placed dark sunglasses on the tip of her very British nose.

"Okay, E-liz-a-beth."

She looked into his eyes and squeezed his bicep, then disappeared into the late-afternoon sun. Soon after, Kory stepped onto Pennsylvania Avenue and sat at one of the alfresco tables the lunch crowd used on weekdays. He looked at his watch. His wife would have dinner ready around six. He thought about calling Elizabeth to cancel their plans later that night, but he didn't.

"Okay, you two. I'll finish cleaning up while you put Kory to bed."

"What would you like to read tonight?"

"Read *The Cat in the Hat*, Papa!" Little Kory jumped into his father's lap.

It wasn't long before little Kory had fallen asleep against his father's chest. He looked at his son and remembered the promise he had made to himself when he was his son's age. Nothing would stop him from giving little Kory the love and security he had missed so dearly as a child.

"Looks like you're about ready to do your thing tonight. Just be careful, and remember we're going out to dinner tomorrow at my aunt's house in Reston." Eseta resumed brushing her hair in the vanity mirror.

"No, I won't forget. In fact, I look forward to seeing Mina tomorrow night."

CHAPTER 33:

Devil's Breath

It was a short drive up Route 1 to Old Town Alexandria, a medium-size, close-in community of two-hundred-year-old townhouses. Just twenty years earlier, it had been the home of low-income blacks and whites, many the descendants of freed slaves and indentured servants; despite having lost the shackles of institutional slavery, they were far from being free enough to realize the American Dream.

Elizabeth had an end-unit row house just off Patrick Henry Drive with an obstructed view of the Potomac River and the constant roar of National Airport. The redbrick construction was typical for the neighborhood. And, like most of the other houses, it was totally renovated inside, with all the modern amenities that made any new-millennium earthling comfortable.

"Hi, come on in." She was standing in the doorway wearing a purple pullover dress, suggesting it could be removed just as easily.

"Nice place. You must have done the remodeling yourself."

"I like to see myself wherever I turn. Please make yourself comfortable." The living room was small, but so were those in most of the houses on the block. Elizabeth had produced a capacious illusion by raising the ceiling three feet, which made the second floor more of a loft, accessible by the spiral staircase off to the right. She glanced in the direction of a brocade loveseat with assorted patterned pillows. A glass-and-chrome coffee table was littered with design and art magazines.

"So, what's a nice guy like you doing in my place?" She drew her feet under her and placed a pillow on her lap.

Kory noted the defensive posture. He feigned surprise at her comment. "Excuse me?"

"Do you think I invited you here to admire my artwork?"

"As a matter of fact, yes."

"Bullshit! You'll have to come up with something better than that if you want to get to know me better." She reached for the pack of Marlboro cigarettes sitting in a bowl filled with matches.

"Give me a few nanoseconds to get my thoughts to mesh with your style. You're definitely not your garden-variety person. I would venture to say you created yourself."

"Now you're trying to get into my business. But I like it, coming from you. What else you got?" She took a quick, deep drag from her cigarette.

"I've got what you need."

"Really?"

"Of all the guys you've met recently, I'm sure none of them have been able to reach inside your soul, so you can be free of all of the bullshit you've been carrying around with you since that day."

"Who are you? You must have been checking up on me!" She pulled the pillow up to her breast and feigned discovery.

"Just you!"

"Oh, you're good. What's next—a séance or something?"

"We could start by holding hands, if you like," he said, sensing he had really put her on the defensive again.

"I know your type. You think you can get inside my head and steal my heart." She leaned back on the Queen Anne love seat and replaced the pillow on her lap.

"Elizabeth, believe me when I say that I'm not looking to fall in love. I've a wife and son that I adore, but there's a part of my life I can't share with them."

"So you're just trying to get a little on the side?"

"On the side. On the top. On the bottom. And particularly in the middle."

"Pretty sure about yourself! I like that. What does your wife think about you hanging out all night?"

" She loves me despite my faults."

"Sounds like you have your cake and you have other people feed it to you, too."

"It's more like I have dug a hole for myself, and occasionally I'm attracted to the surface by sunlight bouncing off the foreheads of those who feel I can give them something they've failed to find for themselves."

"So, are you a missionary or an interloper looking to steal my soul?"

"If you're not careful, I'll visit you in your dreams for the rest of your life."

"That's a long time for you to keep knocking on my door."

"Time shouldn't mean that much to you. I noticed you have a print of Salvador Dalí's *Persistence of a Dream*. One would think you would consider time to be a concept wherein you reside at your pleasure."

"I'm impressed. You're the first guest to recognize that print so quickly."

"Choreography is similar to painting, except I use bodies instead of canvases to place what's inside me in a time-space continuum."

"What did all that mean?"

"Excuse me. I tend to ramble in the evenings and particularly in good company."

"I'm sorry. I haven't offered you anything to drink. Do you like white wine? I have a Châteauneuf-du-Pape blanc you might enjoy."

"Now I'm impressed. That happens to be one of my favorite wines. How did you discover it? Most people are only aware of the red."

"Serendipity, as my grandmother would say. Actually, I dated a wine importer for a few months. I met him at one of my shows in Georgetown. He was married as well."

Kory noticed she did not appear to be wearing panties as she walked toward the kitchen. She returned with the bottle and a corkscrew. "How did you find it?"

"Oh, I lived in the north of France for a while with a girl from Besançon. She introduced me to some of the finer points of French cuisine and culture."

"So I should add *world traveler* to your dossier?"

"Do as you will. It was just another wrinkle of my eclectic education. Now I look forward to learning from you."

She leaned back against the love seat and twisted her hair. "Would you like to see the rest of my house?"

"Sure. Do we take the spiral staircase, or is there an elevator in that closet?"

"Sorry, the elevator is stuck on the fourth floor, so we'll just have to climb to the top. Just follow me."

When the idea of a spiral staircase was first conceived, it is doubtful the inventor took into account the effect of the high risers on the view produced by a woman wearing a short skirt.

In the center of the bedroom ceiling was a large skylight, which provided more than ample light in the daytime for the studio. The back had a bedroom alcove behind a Tuscan column painted on a four-panel screen.

"This is where I spend most of my life. You're lucky today. This is one of the few times this year my studio had gotten so messy that I was forced to clean it up. When it gets so bad I can't even find my brushes, it's time to start over."

"You mean you didn't clean it for me?"

"Don't flatter yourself so soon. This space is all about me."

"So, by that you mean you may be borderline manic-depressive?"

"That's a very personal question."

"Well, you have invited me into your inner sanctum. I assume you're still testing me, so that was a demonstration of my powers of observation."

"Kory, I find your comments overly inquisitive: with every word, you seem to step more inside me. I'm feeling both intrigued and apprehensive. There's a fine line between sharing and intrusion."

"I feel I might be looking over your shoulder while you're painting. Please forgive my impetuousness. I foolishly rush into rooms despite the warning signs announcing Personal Construction in Progress."

"You didn't read the small print that says Those Who Try Hard Stay That Way."

"That's because I wasn't looking into your eyes."

Kory continued to stare into her eyes and at the same time pulled her to him. She wrapped her arms around his neck. When Kory tried to put his hand between her legs, she started to unzip his pants. They both lost their balance and fell against a blank canvas. The easel toppled to the floor, and brushes, pens, spatulas, and a host of other creative instruments produced a cacophony of sounds that made their heavy breathing inaudible.

"Wow, I needed that," Elizabeth said as she rolled over to her side. "Would you like a cigarette?"

"I'm really a pipe smoker, but this would be a good time for a cigarette. Where are they?"

"They're still on the coffee table downstairs. Why don't you move over to the bed while I retrieve them and get something else for you to try?"

"I forgot there was a bed up here. When you get back, let's try it there," he said, standing up and still erect.

"Just hold that position until I get back."

"Was that a command, Mistress?"

"You don't want to go there with me."

"Why not?"

"Unless I misjudged you, and I may have, I believe you may be out of your league if you go in that direction with me."

"I hope I am. As I said earlier, I look forward to learning from you."

"All right. Get into bed and lie on your stomach until I get back."

"On my stomach?"

"That was not a question. You have been given an order by Madam Elizabeth," she barked, winking as she wound down the spiral stairs.

Elizabeth returned before Kory had a chance to survey the room for more clues into her personality.

"Here are the cigarettes, and I just happen to have a pipe. It may be a little different from what you usually puff."

"Hmm," Kory said, holding it up. "Well, I've smoked pot from a glass pipe, but this one has a shape I've never seen before."

"It's called a base pipe."

"A *base pipe*!" Kory held it by the stem and turned around.

"Have you ever heard of freebase?" She reached inside the top cabinet above the sink and produced a glass beaker.

"Isn't that the stuff that makes you go crazy?"

"I've been smoking it for a few years. My sanity has always been questionable—if you were to ask my family."

"So you're saying the stories I've heard are untrue?"

"I'm saying drugs do not create psychological syndromes; they only release what's already there—at least that's what my shrink says."

"All of us carry around demons. Most of them are probably best left chained to the dungeon walls in the deepest recesses of that part of our psyches labeled too painful to remember."

"I'm not trying to convince you to try it, but if you have a little of what you had this afternoon, I would like to transform just a sample of it into freebase to see how well it smokes."

Kory handed her the packet with the spatula. "Take as much as you need for your experiment, E-liz-a-beth."

She eyeballed about half a gram and put it into a solution of water and ammonia sitting in her beaker.

"Are you going to smoke that stuff mixed with ammonia? That combination alone could get you high—not to mention it could be lethal."

"Of course not! Once the chemical change has taken place, I rinse it until all of the ammonia is gone."

"How do you know that?"

"The smell, baby, and the consistency."

She continued to swirl the mixture until what had once been a powder had turned into a solid ball that audibly rattled against the sides of the beaker.

"That's amazing. All the time I spent in chemistry class, and an art major demonstrates alchemy before my eyes."

Elizabeth took the now-spherical substance over to the sink and rinsed it in fresh water. She returned with it wrapped in a paper towel and then placed it on a rectangular mirror, where she chopped it into six pieces. Kory picked one up and admired the density of freebase.

"This looks like a piece of mothball. You're right. I don't smell any ammonia."

Elizabeth took a piece from the mirror and placed it in the bowl of the glass pipe, which she had half-filled with water.

"Are you ready to see my demons?" she asked, putting the pipe to her mouth. The Bic cigarette lighter she used caused the crystalline section to vaporize into smoke and a rainbow of colors. When she had inhaled all of the smoke that was briefly visible in the bottom of the pipe, she placed the pipe on the table, threw her arms around Kory's neck, and breathed like she had had an orgasm.

"How do you feel?" He felt her heart racing against his chest.

"Man, too good for words. Try a small hit, and you'll know what I'm talking about."

"Okay. My demons aren't strangers to me."

Kory took a smaller piece and lit it. He took a long draw on it. When he exhaled, every neuron in his brain came alive. It was similar to the hot, engrossing feeling he had during an orgasm—but he hadn't, at least not the kind he'd had before she had gone downstairs to retrieve the cigarettes.

"This is some dangerous stuff. I can see why a person would become addicted. You have all the residual effects of intimacy without the need for another person."

"That's one way of looking at it. Now let's take that 'almost' feeling and add some real sex to it." She started licking around his navel and continued down until he reached an orgasm of an intensity he had never experienced before.

"If I take another hit of the pipe, will I have another orgasm?" He lay on his back, not sure whether the stars he was seeing were coming through the skylight or were inside his brain.

"Not sure. I guess you'll just have to try and see," she said, handing him the pipe.

"Shit! I think my balls just exploded, or I just had a heart attack. It can't be possible to experience more pleasure and live to tell about it." His heart pounded.

"Welcome to my world. You stay as long as you can handle it."

"This feeling is scary. I feel a little guilty betraying my body with a trick."

"What are you talking about, baby? I thought you liked what just happened."

"I liked it too much, and that's the problem. This drug is asking me to relinquish control to it—totally against my nature. I can't completely enjoy this unless I know I'm in control."

"As long you're the one lighting the pipe, then you're the one in control."

"I don't think it's that simple. If you feel compelled to do something, then you're not in control. Elizabeth, if that is what you truly believe, I have some bad news: you may be addicted."

"I'm addicted to my art. The pipe is just a reward after a good day's work."

"How often do you smoke this stuff?"

"Couple of times a week," she said, reaching for the pipe again.

"Hmm, that could become expensive."

"I have a lot of friends who don't mind sharing." She lit the pipe again.

"Perhaps—they may be sharing imprisonment. Let's drop it for now and enjoy what we have. I believe there're a few pieces left. I've had enough. Would you like to finish the rest?"

"Fire me up!"

Kory visited Elizabeth for another two weeks before her addiction became an issue. Every visit, she seemed to be falling deeper into the pipe, where finding the next hit made her mouth water, and she began searching for slivers of freebase that may have fallen into the carpet. Moreover, she had supplanted her palettes and brushes with numerous bottles of ammonia and razor blades in preparation for the next puff of smoke.

Seeing her demise should have been enough to dissuade him, but his arrogance about his ability to have modulated his usage in the past gave him false confidence when he climbed into the pipe stem in search of that first feeling of euphoria. Now he faced a substance stronger than he was.

CHAPTER 34:

Recovery Is Recall

Along with stacks of drug-powdered money, Kory was literally going up in smoke. Though not physically addicted, dominion over his dealers and users had become more satisfying than the first puff from a pipe filled with the "rocked lady."

People who smoked base cocaine became transmogrified like the rocks they dropped frenetically to the bottom of the bowl; adult self-control and responsibility vaporized into infantile whines for immediate gratification. Regression was also evident when users crawled on all fours for that seldom-found piece of base among the loops of a shag carpet, although chemicals used to make cheap rugs were known to elicit a high, as well as the destruction of brain cells already in short supply.

Sympathy was in supply for those who had hit bottom. It was not unusual for Kory to succor those who smoked up money for their mortgage payment or, sadder, to buy groceries to feed their children. But once they received help, there was no returning to the pipe with his product. Saving someone else was easier than looking in the mirror.

Another year went by almost as fast as the drugs melted at the end of a propane torch. He spent days sleeping, followed by nights haunted by zombies who came to life for another hit—only to return to their grave addictions before morning. There seemed to be no end to the cycle.

But, as with everything else in the real world, there were limits. The quiet suburban life in Virginia that Kory escaped to every morning disappeared the day his wife had a violent argument with his investor after she took little Kory for an ice cream cone without Eseta's permission or knowledge. The next day, his family stayed in a hotel while Kory searched for a house and security in Chevy Chase.

Walking away from the nightlife was not so simple; he still needed to go out every night to make money and to see his sycophants. Fortunately, there was one thing stronger than using crystallized cocaine and its lifestyle. Kory needed only to keep the promise he had made as a child to reach past the drugs and guilt to reclaim his humanity.

"Hi, Papa!" little Kory whispered. His father was still groggy from being out all night. "Are we still going to play basketball today?"

Kory struggled to get one eye opened. He barely focused enough to see his son holding a basketball almost as big as he.

"Sure, what time is it?"

"It's three o'clock, Papa."

"Give me an hour, and I'll be up."

Little Kory knew better. Today he was looking forward to playing with his father, who had told him the night before how much fun they were going to have, though it seldom happened.

"But, Papa, you'll fall back to sleep and not wake up in time." His son forced a smile as he held back his disappointment and tears.

Kory looked at his son, and now it was he who could barely hold back the tears. He remembered when a similar promise had been made to him and broken. Although he was still hungover from the previous night, he was not blind to the truth. His behavior was counter to the oath he had made with God when he was a child—when he had still hoped a God existed.

He did not know how long it had been after his son closed the door to his bedroom before he woke again. There was a warm breeze coming between the dark drapes. Kory smelled the storm predicted later that evening.

It was late in the afternoon when he finally stepped into the hallway. The house was quiet. He peeked into little Kory's room to find him napping with the basketball beside his pillow. His wife had fallen asleep in the family room with a book. Only his white shepherd, Ramses, was aware of his seldom-seen presence that afternoon. And even he just wagged his tail a few times and turned over on his other side, not expecting a pat on the head.

Clouds were gathering into a tightness to release the day's heat. Kory sat down on the chaise lounge in the solarium and watched the storm rush to what seemed to be just above his house. He looked into the distance and remembered the similarity of this afternoon to the many times he and his brother had waited for their father, who had often failed to show up to take them to all the wonderful places he had promised.

Kory picked up one of his son's books lying on the wicker table beside the lounge. Inside it, his son had used as a bookmark a copy of the instant photos they had taken together during their last visit to the Wheaton Mall. He could feel his son's warm cheek against his and smiled at the ring the chocolate ice cream cone made around the boy's mouth. He even noticed for the first time that he had a chocolate ring around the fringes of his moustache as well. The joy of this moment was quickly replaced with shame. He could not forget the promise he had made. It was as heartfelt now as it had been almost thirty years earlier when he had waited on his mother's front porch and cried when the first hour passed, the time his father had promised to pick him up. That day, Kory had not moved from the porch for almost three hours, until his mother had called him in for an early dinner. He had told her he was not hungry and gone to his bedroom instead. It had been the last time he had tried to make excuses for his father.

He had tried hard not to believe all the disparaging remarks his mother made about his father's character, but he had done little then but cry in the darkness of his bedroom and accept the truth about his father and the reality of his childhood.

Even now, during the coming storm, he could not remember how many times his father had broken his promise, but he did recall the tears he had shed when he finally resolved that his father would not show up again. Before nightfall, Kory had made a promise to himself and to the son he hoped to have one day. Then the tears from that day returned. They flowed as if he had become ten years old again. He could see himself sitting on the front steps of his mother's house and walking to the end of the walkway every five minutes, hoping to see his father's big black Cadillac turning the corner; it never did, and Kory never forgot or forgave.

It was now raining so heavily that he could no longer see out the jalousie windows. He dried his eyes, went to his closet, and found the bag containing all he wished to keep hidden from his son. Kory flushed thousands of dollars' worth of drugs down the toilet and broke every piece of paraphernalia. When the last bit had disappeared into the commode, he felt the curse had been lifted. He went into his son's bedroom, kissed him on the forehead, and stroked his curly hair.

"Papa, you're awake. Can we go now?"

"Yes, Kory. I just washed my face. By the time you've washed yours, the sun will be out again. I'll be the father I promised to be. I'll never break a promise again."

CHAPTER 35:

Reinvention

There were a few times Kory visited the drug world after remembering his promise. They were dares. He had conditioned himself to feel shame every time the thought arose to ring the doorbell to Hell. The transition back into the conservative world was difficult, considering he had not held a real job since his early twenties, and even then, he was teaching dance and was free to make his own schedule.

The next day he walked to the 7-Eleven and purchased *The Washington Post*. He searched the Help Wanted section for something he could handle. Dance was out of the question. He needed something fast, where few questions would be asked about his lack of a recent work history.

Ads for drivers said they were paid cash daily. It turned out to be a cab company looking for new people to get behind the wheel of their blue-and-white taxis. Two days later he was driving the streets of Silver Spring, searching for fares.

He barely made twenty dollars the first day, compared with the thousands he used to make in a night.

Within two years he stopped driving and became the evening manager and dispatcher. In another six months, he was the highest-paid dispatcher in the county. To Kory, this was no great accomplishment. The money he was paid was just enough to pay the bills, but at least he slept well at night.

The cab company was only a few blocks from Montgomery College. Frequent fares in the past there went to the admissions office. One day during his lunch break, he walked into the lobby and browsed the summer class schedule. He had already taken all the psychology classes the school had to offer, but he made an appointment with an admissions counselor before his evening shift.

"It's been a while since I've been on a college campus," Kory said as he sat before the counselor.

"Then you've come to the right place. We have a varied student body here. Most are right out of high school, but lately we've had an increase in applicants from your age group. Why don't you take another look at our updated schedule while I review your application?"

The only class of interest to him was Computer Programming 101, and it was still open.

The counselor peered over her glasses. "I assume you know we don't offer any postgraduate studies. You indicated that you have a bachelor's and a master's degree in psychology. Perhaps Maryland University would better suit your needs."

"Psychology was good when I was still filled with idealism and a need for self-discovery. I'm looking for something entirely different now. There are predictions of computers being used in every facet of life in the future. I believe they're right, and I want to be prepared for their arrival."

"Well, then, this will be easy for me. Most applicants don't have a clue where they're going. You seem like you've already been there, and probably more. Just take this to the cashier's office. You'll need to have copies of your degrees and a transcript sent within thirty days to my office."

"No problem. Thank you for your time."

Having to concentrate on something new was just what he needed. The course was not difficult, but the lab work did cut into free time he preferred to spend with his son.

Dr. Namdern, head of the computer science department, could have been dreamed up by a writer on *Saturday Night Live*. Never had Kory seen anyone with glasses as thick as his computer professor's. He always began lectures with some inane news flash that suggested politicians were not as capable of running the country as a scientist like him.

"Good morning, everyone! Today we're going to learn about DOS. What do the letters *DOS* stand for? Well, it's not an acronym for *dogs only shit*." The professor was the only one in the classroom to laugh at his attempted humor. He cleared his throat, which he often did. "Anyway, in order for a computer to operate, like a child, it must be told what to do next. That's what DOS does. It tells the computer which part of the memory to read next, or what piece of the hardware to turn on or off. This was a major advancement in computer science, considering that prior to 1980, it was necessary to manually access different parts of the computer's memory via a teletype, using esoteric commands that sometimes even people like me could not remember. Now DOS has standardized those commands so that all computers can use the same operating system and easily communicate with one another. The latest version of DOS is now in what we call a personal computer, named the IBM 5150. This machine makes it possible for more people to have access to the power of computing. You'll all be glad to know that Montgomery College is one of the first colleges in the state of Maryland to have this milestone in technology. Please take out your textbooks and turn to chapter two."

Dr. Namdern spent the rest of the class explaining the features of the IBM 5150. Despite his efforts to demonstrate the computer's functions on the board, many students had that dazed look from trying to digest the flow charts of a computer program, which looked more like an extemporaneous jigsaw puzzle than a sequential blueprint of abstruse instructions—both of which made little sense to the overwhelmed students.

"Okay, everybody. I know we've covered a lot of material today. We've got about five minutes left. If there are no questions, I'll see you Thursday."

Kory raised his hand. "Dr. Namdern, in Isaac Asimov's *I, Robot*, man's quest to facilitate communication between computers almost led to his destruction. They became better organized than their inventors and soon recognized mankind was imperfect. Later they sought to cleanse the planet of annoying human infestation. Do you see anything like that in our future?"

Dr. Namdern grinned. "That's quite a revision of the story, but you pose an interesting question. The same question has been asked by those government agencies funding my research. Before the possibility of anything close to that occurs, we scientists will have to make major advancements in artificial intelligence. Today our computers are little more than fancy toasters. This may sound a bit strange; frankly, I looked forward to talking to my computer."

Kory could barely resist laughing when he tried to visualize his professor trying to talk romantically to his wife; she was probably waiting for a robot to be built with the feelings her husband lacked.

CHAPTER 36

Last Chance to Forgive

Midterm exams were starting the next day. Following a long night of study, Sunday morning a cold cup of mint tea splattered to the floor before the last ring from the phone sitting on the nightstand.

"This better be good!"

"Kory, it's…Arthur…Sorry to call so early, but I knew you'd want to know…Your mother is sick."

"What's wrong with her?"

"An ambulance took her to the hospital this morning. I'm at Holy Cross Hospital, waiting to talk to her doctor. I don't think it's anything serious."

"I'll ask you again. What's wrong with her?"

His stepfather took a deep breath. "You mother fell the other day in the basement. When I tried to get her up, she refused to let me lift her. She said she wanted to lie there until she was ready to get up."

"What do you mean she refused? Had she been drinking again?"

There was a longer pause this time. "Uh…she begged me not to tell you she had fallen off the wagon."

"How long was she on the floor?"

Arthur choked. "I let my wife lie there for two days. She begged me not to call for an ambulance. I should never have listened to her."

"Well, listen to this, Arthur. If anything happens to my mother, there's no place on this planet I can't find you."

"There's no need for that kind of talk. I was only doing what your mother told me."

"My mother seldom drank liquor before she met you. You turned her into a drunk like you."

"Your mother knew I had a drinking problem when she met me."

"Actually, she didn't, but I did!"

"I see the doctor coming down the hall. Why don't you call Ephen and—"

Kory hung up before Arthur could finish. He quickly dressed and headed for the hospital, forgetting to call his brother before he left. The drive was only two miles, but he had to stop at every light.

This was not the first time his mother had been hospitalized for alcoholism. Just a year earlier, Kory had found his mother in a drunken stupor, wandering around his neighborhood because she was too intoxicated to remember his address. Despite her objections and his stepfather's, he'd had her hospitalized at Suburban Hospital. Even though he had never forgiven her for neglecting him and his brother, seldom did a day go by without spending his break or study time visiting his mother.

The day she was discharged the first time, trees in Rock Creek Park were displaying autumn splendor as they drove to her house in Kensington. Along the way she promised repeatedly never to drink liquor again, except an occasional glass of white wine with dinner. It was too nice a day to argue with her about the dangers of drinking any alcohol again. Before he left, the last thing Kory said was that he would never come to see her again when she was drinking. His mother did not respond; she went into the den and returned with an old leather valise containing most of the poetry and essays she'd written since her teenage years.

"So they'll be safe, I want you to take this with you."

Kory was too overwhelmed to refuse. "I thought you liked to look at your old work to inspire you to write your life story."

She threw her arms around his neck and just held him for what seemed like the last time. "There's nothing more for me to say."

The light at Forest Glen Road turned red just as the car in front of him slowly crossed the intersection. Kory ran it. Unable to find a parking space right away, he ignored the No Parking signs and left his car near the entrance to the emergency room.

"Can you help? I'm looking for Elaine Halloway. I'm her son."

The nurse at the desk scanned the computer. "Did you say 'Calloway'?"

"No. Halloway. *H-a-l-l-o-w-a-y*. First name Elaine. That's *E-l*—"

Cutting him off, she said curtly, "I can spell 'Elaine.' She's in a cardiac intensive care unit."

"And he said it was nothing serious—that lying bastard!"

"Excuse me!"

"Sorry, that was not directed at you. Which way to ICU?"

"It's in the yellow wing, but you can't go there right now."

Before the last words had left her mouth, he was following the painted yellow ribbon on the floor to find his mother. It did not take him long to locate her room. There was no one else there when he arrived. His stepfather had gone down to the hospital cafeteria. Seeing his mother lying there unconscious and on a respirator, he felt fortunate that his stepfather was not there. During the first year of her second marriage, before she had married Arthur, her third husband, her second husband had raised his hand to strike Elaine. Kory had beaten him so badly, he had been hospitalized for two weeks. Predictably, his first stepfather had refused to enter the house, convinced he would receive the same or worse if he ever threatened his wife again. Six months later, Kory had moved into his grandfather's house. Strangely, his mother's second husband had never been heard from again.

Kory left his mother's side and went to the nursing station down the hall. "Excuse me. I'm Elaine Halloway's son. I need to talk to her doctor about her condition."

"Halloway? Halloway? Oh, yes, here it is. Her doctor is Thomas Barnard. Would you like me to page him for you?"

Kory forced a polite tone. "If you would be so kind."

Dr. Barnard, a very tall man, picked up his mother's chart from the station, walked in Kory's direction, and asked, "Mr. Halloway?"

"No. My name is Vanon. Halloway is my mother's third husband."

"Mr. Vanon, please follow me to my office so we can talk."

As they entered, Kory asked, "Is she going to be all right?"

The doctor pointed to one of the chairs in front of his desk. "It's too soon to tell. Your mother is very ill."

"What's her condition?"

"Your mother has pneumonia, congestive heart failure, and cirrhosis of the liver. That's a poor mixture."

"Did lying on the floor for two days contribute to the heart failure?"

"According to the ambulance report, your stepfather said she was there for almost a week."

Kory cracked his knuckles. "I'm going to kill that asshole."

"Calm down. Blaming your stepfather will not make your mother better. I would guess your mother has been drinking heavily for years. Were you aware of her problem?"

"Yes. It was almost a year ago that she was in a detoxification program at Suburban Hospital. She swore to me she would never drink more than a few glasses of wine."

"Alcoholism is just like any other addiction. They need a lot more than promising to leave the bottle alone. Alcoholics need the support of a group such as AA or psychotherapy to stay sober."

Kory thought what it had taken for him to achieve his own sobriety; it should have been obvious to him she was incapable of denying herself anything for the benefit of her loved ones.

"Dr. Barnard, tell me candidly: What is her prognosis?"

"As I said before, Mr. Vanon, it's too early to speculate. The first thing we need to do is to wake her up. Then I can assess whether or not there has been any permanent brain damage."

"And what is the worst-case scenario?"

"I don't wish to alarm you, but your mother may never leave this hospital alive if she does not respond well to treatment."

"So, there're things you can do?"

"Yes, but we're hampered by her advanced cirrhosis. Every drug we need to administer may weaken her already-fragile liver."

"It sounds like you're saying all we can do now is wait."

"I do not discount the benefit a close family member can have in the recovery of my patients. On some level, your mother may be able to hear you, even in her coma." He glanced again at the chart. "There's one very interesting thing, though."

"And what's that?"

"Your mother's EEG shows unusually high activity. We sometimes see this in brain-injured patients, but in your mother's case, it may suggest a sustained dream state."

"Are you saying this is a positive sign?"

He touched the tip of his nose with his forefinger. "I'm saying there've been cases where the voice of someone talking to an unconscious patient becomes incorporated into the dream. If that voice is someone the patient really cares for, it may inspire consciousness. There have only been a few documented cases of this phenomenon. In your mother's condition, I think it's worth a try."

Kory shifted in his chair. "Then can the reverse be true?"

The doctor scratched his bald pate. "The reverse?"

"Well, suppose she wants to avoid the person talking to her. Could that push her deeper into the coma?"

"I'm not a psychiatrist, but I suppose it could. As I said, very little is known about this type of intervention."

"Then my stepfather should be kept from her."

"I must caution you: he has a legal right to visit her, unless it can be proved his presence has a deleterious effect on her recovery."

"He spends most of his time swimming in a bottle of vodka." Kory folded his arms. "I doubt he'll visit often."

The doctor began clicking his ballpoint pen as he took another look at Elaine's chart. "I want to closely monitor your mother's vital signs when you're with her. The head nurse will be directed to note her readings at the beginning of your visit, after thirty minutes, and just before you are about to leave. Can I rely on you to tell me the moment she reacts to the slightest verbal command?"

"Absolutely!"

"Here's my card. If you have any questions, please feel free to call me."

When Kory returned to his mother's room, his stepfather was holding her hand as he bowed his head, as if he were praying. The smell of alcohol emanating from Arthur struck Kory's nose as he crossed the threshold.

"You lied to me about how long she was on the floor."

Arthur's eyes were bloodshot when he looked up. "What difference does it make now? It's not my fault. I did what she told me."

"The difference it makes may determine whether or not you see your next birthday. You'd better pray she lives. I've already decided how I'm going to kill you. Would you like to know how, you insignificant piece of shit?"

Arthur stumbled to his feet. "I'm not afraid of you." His stepfather barely came up to Kory's shoulder.

Kory grabbed him by his collar and whispered in his ear, "You're too stupid to be. *I'm* even afraid of me. Once you've taken one life, the next one comes easily—something you should keep in mind when you go to sleep tonight. There's no one and nothing that can protect you from me. If she dies, I'll only give you enough time to say good-bye to your children, if you are lucky. The smartest thing you can do now is to stay away from her—starting now." Kory let go of his stepfather's shirt. Arthur fell into the chair beside the bed.

"But she is my wife. Kory, even you aren't that coldhearted," he whimpered.

"Arthur, I'm going down the hall to call Ephen. Even I don't want to be around him when he's angry. And when he gets here, if you're still sitting there with our mother, he will not say a word before he breaks that window over there and throws your worthless ass to the parking lot below."

"I could see you doing something like that, but not your brother. He likes me."

"My brother doesn't like anyone. The only emotion he's capable of is anger."

"He's not like you, Kory. He'll understand I was just doing what your mother wanted."

Kory did not answer. He turned around before the urge to beat his stepfather to a pulp took control.

He tried to reach his brother, but, as usual, Ephen did not answer his phone. He even tried his brother's ex-wife. Ephen had just dropped their children at her house an hour earlier. Elaine had never liked Ephen's ex-wife; therefore, no need to tell Ephen's ex about her former mother-in-law's condition.

Later that evening, Kory was able to reach his brother. He gave Ephen all the salient details of their mother's condition, but he did not tell him about their stepfather's delay in calling for an ambulance. Since his childhood car accident, Ephen had dreaded doctors and hospitals. Seeing her unconscious was too much for him to handle. Even though he loved his mother, sadly, he, like her, was incapable of showing it. Kory had learned to live with his scars, whereas his brother was hopelessly dammed and trapped inside himself forever.

At one o'clock every day, Kory sat by his mother's bed. He would talk to her about her grandson, recite poems she had composed before she married her third husband, and read to her some of her favorite novels, such as *The Scrolls of Lysis*, by Barnaby Ross, which had some pretty explicit romantic scenes for the early sixties. He was just about to start the chapter where Myrrha is having a tryst to spite her husband, Simon.

"My...rrha is such a bitch," his mother whispered.

"Mom!" he said, kissing his mother on the cheek and ringing for the nurse.

"Where am I?"

"You're in the hospital. Do you remember falling in the basement?"

"I remember being on the floor. My legs wouldn't move."

"That's because you made yourself sick again. You promised me you'd never drink liquor again."

"Arthur refused to go to the store and get wine for me, so I started drinking his vodka instead. I guess I overdid it."

"You overdid it for at least a month."

"I feel so sleepy. Let me go back to sleep." She did more than fall asleep. By the time the nurse arrived, her blood pressure had dropped dangerously low. As soon as the nurse placed the stethoscope on Elaine's heart, the monitor gave off a chilling alarm.

"Mom! Mom! What's happening to her?"

"Code blue!" the nurse yelled.

Two more nurses and Dr. Barnard rushed into the room with a crash cart. "She's going into cardiac arrest. Sir, I need for you to wait outside," said the doctor as he started CPR.

"I'm not going anywhere." The doctor looked into Kory's eyes and did not ask again.

After a long needle was placed directly into her heart and two shocks of the defibrillator were administered, Elaine Halloway's heart signs beeped across the monitor.

Kory's mother did not regain consciousness until the next morning, while he dozed in a chair. Just before dawn, a muted cough awakened him. Because of the tube in her trachea, Elaine was unable to talk. Later that day, he purchased a few writing pads. At first her messages were just an illegible word or two. She even tried to communicate using nods, but they made little sense in response to his questions.

On the third day, she wrote, *Don't.*

"Don't what?" Kory asked.

Arthur, she wrote.

"Don't Arthur what, Mom?"

Don't hurt him.

"He left you to die!"

No...no. Then she closed her eyes.

"Mom, are you all right? Should I call the nurse?"

She opened her eyes again. *I didn't want to get up because I wanted to die.*

"But why?"

Three strikes.

"Three strikes?"

He tried to steady the pad as she wrote, *Marriages! Three marriages! I'm tired of trying. I want to be free.*

"It's still about you. What about your family?"

You would be better off without me. I've always let you and your brother down.

"Nobody is perfect."

Tears welled in her eyes. *I know you resent me. And I would not blame you if you hated me.*

"I don't hate you. I just find it hard to love someone who doesn't love me."

Her left arm began to shake as she struggled to write. *Kory, you're wrong about that. I've always loved you. I'm sorry I was too selfish to show it.*

His mother dropped the pen and reached for him. He was too far away, so she fell back into the pillow and quickly turned pale. This time she fell into a deeper coma. And, to make matters worse, her kidneys were beginning to fail. Kory asked if dialysis would help, but they told him she was too weak. Every day that he came, more fluids accumulated in her body. She looked at one point as if she were going to explode. And now her coma was so deep, her eyes had to be taped shut. When her bulging, bloodshot eyes were open, she looked like someone from Kory's worst nightmare. Even still, for another week, he refused to believe his mother would never wake again.

Kory had just finished reading the first line from one of her sonnets: *On a bed of roses in heaven's field we sleep…,* when suddenly it seemed as if she were trying to sit up. She took one large breath and gasped for the last time. Her doctors and nurses tried for an hour to revive her. "I'm sorry, Mr. Vanon. There's nothing more we can do," Dr. Barnard said. He placed his hand on Kory's shoulder.

The nurse asked if he wanted his mother covered with a sheet. He motioned for her to leave him alone. He laid his head on Elaine's breast until the last warmth of her body was gone. He finished reciting her favorite sonnet from memory as his hot tears fell onto her cooling body.

At the gravesite he looked over his shoulder at his stepfather. He had resolved that his mother had wanted to die and that her husband was only a convenient partner. Kory had seen his stepfather only once since that day, while waiting at a red light. His first urge was to floor the accelerator. Instead, he honked the horn as Arthur crossed in front of his car, and then he rolled down the window. His stepfather froze at the sight of him.

"I told you I'd find you. Enjoy the rest of your life." His stepfather stood in the middle of the crosswalk as if he were worse than dead.

CHAPTER 37:

Ignoring the Truth

It was all of one hundred degrees outside when Kory rushed into the Holiday Inn. He tugged at his sweat-soaked polo shirt as he approached the front desk.

"Please direct me to the nearest men's room."

The desk clerk scrutinized him and hesitated for a second. "Room mumber, please?"

Kory gripped his stomach muscles. "I'm not a guest. This is an emergency."

"Just past the elevators, sir. Take a right turn and stop."

"Thank you very much."

What a relief it was he did not have to walk farther. A few more steps, and he would have embarrassed himself by showing in public how not age but infirmity had taken residence in his mostly youthful body. It was ironic for someone who had spent most of his life sculpting his body to have the inconveniences not present in the typical McDonald's hamburger–eating Joe Blow waddling down the street.

He tried everything: Stop It, Wet No More, Control, and Confident. He even tried a sample pair of Depends; however, none of these stopgap measures could return him to his carefree days of not worrying about pissing in his pants. Seldom did he have an accident in public; nonetheless, there was always a clock ticking, reminding him to get into and out of where he was before he did. Despite the constant uncertainty, Kory felt blessed after meeting recently diagnosed multiple sclerosis patients, who were having problems walking and—worse—recognizing their reflections in the mirror of their doctors' examination rooms.

Just a year ago was the first anniversary of his divorce from Eseta. After he had put up with her drinking and outbursts for years, she had agreed to an amiable legal separation, giving him sole custody of their son—then fourteen years old.

What started out this day as a typical autumn morning, a ten-mile run down and back up the steep hills of Sixteenth Street, became one of the worst days of his life.

Kory had been running six days a week for nearly ten years. Not the usual weekend runner, he was one of those crazy, die-hard runners who even ran in the snow wearing only shorts, a woolen cap, mittens, and, of course, the latest in running technology on his feet. He enjoyed the stares he got from motorists when he darted across an intersection while they waited for lights to change or, even better, when he crossed the path of a walker, whom he would catch mumbling something like, "Health nut," "Mr. Natural," "Crazy man," or sometimes just "Damn…" Maybe the onlookers were annoyed with the fact that he was raising his level of health while they were snailing in traffic between bites of a trans fat–infused doughnut and sips of an expensive cup of Starbucks hypercaffeinated coffee.

Shortly after he began the final half-mile sprint to his house, he stumbled on the hard, inclining sidewalk.

As with many runners, tripping in a pothole now and then had become a liability of trying to stay healthy, but this time Kory had trouble getting back on his feet. Every time he tried to stand, his legs collapsed like an ironing board that was not locked into place. So he crawled over to the grass and sat against a tree while rush-hour traffic roared by, now uninterested in him.

He waited for his legs to communicate with his brain, and after ten minutes or more, they did. Although marginally weaker, Kory managed to slowly trot the remaining five blocks to his modest four-bedroom colonial nestled in Woodside Park.

Later, while soaking in the Jacuzzi, he thought he just needed to stop pushing himself so hard, but that was the way he had always been—as soon as he reached a new level, he pushed himself to the next. Secretly he prayed this would pass, except he knew this time he had done more than just "hit the wall" too many times. He had awakened a family curse that had been silent in him for almost twenty years. Kory Vanon was about to meet his shadow under clinical light.

That night and in the early hours of the next morning, Kory wrote the following message to his body:

speak to me only of my dreams,
for I have grown weary of today.
show me not the unfinished moments of yesterday.
but with clean hands, start again.
my breath is of new air.
the stench of yesterday I refuse to let linger in mind.
cast out all that tries to darken the dawn light of today.
I will run through the thrushes,
drink the sweet nectar of the calla lilies
and make my bed by the riverside,
so that I may never return to yesterday.

On the next page, he wrote:

Stop, thief! You have taken from me that which I never knew was my greatest treasure. You have left me with *thoughts of movement, where before I could think or not and still arrive. Now I contemplate from a chair which foot to will first. Somehow the conscious conversations between my brain and legs have become a feud between strangers. Alas, I still have my ego and pride. They have been servants to give me a push when I thought I could go no further. Kick me now, for I am weary. Kick me so hard that I can forget my mortality. It is no longer my body that walks. My will now casts the shadow over where I have been. Hello again, my constant friend. Let's walk together, or shall we run another mile?*

Kory woke with his head on the desk and his hand still holding the pen. When he had gathered his wits, his first thought was to get some definitive answers on his condition.

A fellow runner had once told him about a neurologist in Silver Spring who specialized in sports injuries. He was not difficult to find, since his ad in the Yellow Pages blared, *We treat sports-related injuries* in large, bold type. He called the office of Dr. Bradley and told the receptionist it was an emergency. Unfortunately, their earliest opening was the following week, but they said they would call him if they had a cancellation.

He spent the next two hours calling other doctors to find one willing to see him that day. As he considered going to the hospital emergency room, his cell phone rang. It was the receptionist from Dr. Bradley's office. Kory had mistakenly given her the number to his cell phone instead of his home phone. They had just gotten a cancellation for a three o'clock appointment. He gladly accepted that time slot.

At ten minutes to three, Kory pulled his Jaguar into the parking lot of the oldest office building in downtown Silver Spring. Since he had moved there, he'd never had a reason to go inside. As he approached the large revolving door, something about the building's facade reminded him of an era when he would not have been welcomed there.

"May I help you?" asked the security guard, whose belly hung over his belt buckle.

"I'm going to suite 911, Dr. Bradley's office."

"This is a secure building. You'll need to sign in."

He turned around and walked to the lobby desk. The security guard did not hand him the clipboard—he threw it on the counter. Kory noticed a large Confederate flag tattooed on his bicep and asked, "Do I need to put the time on here, or is that your job?"

"If you want to go upstairs, you better put it on there!" he snapped.

"I *better*? Are you a security guard or just an everyday fascist?"

"A fas…cist?" he asked, displaying yellow gap teeth.

"Ask your Grand Wizard to break it down for you at your next Klan meeting this weekend."

"You've got a smart mouth on you."

Kory stared directly in his eyes. "And I can back it up, too! Listen, I don't have time for your racist bullshit. You guys lost the war. Here's your clipboard. Enjoy your day." He dropped the clipboard on the counter and walked to the elevator.

"Mr. Vanon, you're on time. Please fill out these forms and let me know when you've finished," said the sterile-appearing receptionist, matching the perfunctory voice he had heard over the phone.

Filling out the forms took him longer than he expected. He was having trouble controlling the pen. When finished, he asked where he could find the men's room. The receptionist gave him a key attached to a floppy piece of wood.

"Oh, Mr. Vanon, I'm glad you're back. Dr. Bradley will see you now. His office is to my right."

The door to his office was open. "Mr. Vanon, I'm Dr. Bradley. Please have a seat. I just finished reviewing your brief medical history, and I'm surprised to see someone like you in my office. Please tell me a little more about what your legs are doing."

"Well, to say it succinctly, I can no longer run. When I take one step, it's as if I'm running in deep sand with heavy ankle weights."

"I see. And when did this start?" he asked, as if reciting from a script.

Kory told him about the incident the day before, and as he did, he felt the urge to run out of the office and forget everything that had happened. But now he could barely feel his feet, so he sat there as the neurologist continued down his clipboard of questions.

"Well, there are many things that could be causing this. We need to run a battery of tests to be sure what's causing your problems. If you have the time today, we can perform most of the tests in about two hours." He clasped his well-manicured little hands under his chin.

"I had other things planned for today, but I need to know what's going on with my body. Please run whatever tests you need to fix me!"

Dr. Bradley got up from his desk. He was not a very tall man. In fact, he appeared a bit effeminate. His handshake was mushy, and there seemed to be no obvious sign of physical strength emanating from his arms or from the rest of his body. But maybe, Kory reasoned, he was just trying to find fault in the doctor if the test results were not favorable.

After about two hours of prodding, poking, and shocks over every inch of his body, Kory was directed back to the waiting room, which he was glad to find empty. Unconsciously he reached for his cell phone. He scrolled through his phone book and tried to think of someone to call. His son was still in class, and he wasn't sure if he would tell him what was going on anyway. So he just looked at numbers as they scrolled faster down the screen.

"Mr. Vanon, the doctor is ready to see you again. Do you need some help getting there?"

"Why would I need help?"

"Just checking. Do you remember where the consultation room is?"

Kory did not bother to answer—he just walked in the direction of the doctor's office.

"Mr. Vanon, we've performed every test we have available at this office." Dr. Bradley did not look up from his clipboard.

There was a certain detachment in the doctor's voice that unsettled Kory. It was as if what he was about to say were coming from someone else in the room. "Mr. Vanon, nothing is conclusive so far. Based on your symptoms, though, I suspect you have suffered a stroke, are in the early stages of a brain tumor, and, lastly, are perhaps in the early stages of multiple sclerosis. Do you have a family history of any of these conditions?"

"Uh...I...I mean, I think there's MS in my family. My first cousin has suffered from it for nearly ten years." Kory recalled his older female cousin struggling on crutches to attend the wedding of another cousin a few years ago. Most relatives looked upon her with pleasant and detached expressions of sympathy. Illness was very rare in the Vanon family.

"Mr. Vanon, it's not been clearly established that there is a genetic link, but I believe MS might be the area to consider first," the doctor said as he added notes to his chart.

"Are you sure?" Kory could feel his legs tremble and his hands clamp into fists.

"As I said, we cannot be sure at this time. We'll need to run additional tests to be certain. I'd like to schedule you for an MRI at another office, if you wish to proceed. I know this is a lot to take in."

"Yes, it is. To tell you the truth, I'm feeling a bit light-headed. I need to go home and digest the menu of causes you gave me this afternoon."

"I completely understand. Would you like my nurse to call a family member to help you home?"

Kory pushed himself from the chair with the strength of his arms. "No, I'll be fine. I just need to get outside and breathe some fresh air."

"Okay. Just give me a call after you've had a chance to decide what you want to do. And try not to worry. We still don't know for sure what we're dealing with."

The hallway seemed smaller than before, more like a tunnel blinding him to everything but despair. He ignored the security guard's request for him to sign out. He did not even have an internal monologue to distract him as he drove home.

When he got to the front door, his white shepherd, Ramses, greeted him with an extra whine, as if he knew something was wrong. Kory slammed the front door and collapsed on the hall landing, just before he put his arms around his dog and began to sob.

"How could this be happening to me? What have I done to deserve this? I've done everything asked of me in this lifetime." He jumped to his feet, drove his fist through the wall, and continued with both hands until the foyer was dappled with blood. With each punch, he yelled, "I won't give in! I'll beat this shit! I can do anything!" Ramses howled at his rage and tried to lick his hands as he slid down the wall and hunched on the landing. He tried to calm his dog, even though every pat turned his white fur the pattern of the blood-spattered wall.

After what seemed like an eternity, he stumbled to the kitchen, where he ran cool water over his hands until the bleeding slowed enough for him to light the kettle. While he waited for the water to boil, he soaked his swollen hands in a bucket of ice.

Now sitting at the kitchen table and shivering, he struggled to get the hot liquid to his lips. With the cup now sitting empty before him, he closed his eyes to find his chi. More inside himself now, he took off his bloodied shirt and headed down the narrow stairwell to the basement, where he spent an hour every day sculpting his body.

Most exercise sessions started on the heavy punching bag. But with both hands still too swollen to pull on the gloves, he began with the lat machine to raise his pulse and encourage a sweat. Thoroughly spent after forty-five minutes, he sat on the workout bench and wondered to whom he owed this ostensible reprieve and how long it would last.

The next day he chose not to call the doctor to make an appointment for the MRI; instead, he read everything available at the local library and on the Internet about multiple sclerosis. The more he read, the more he tried to convince himself there was nothing amiss. As far as he was concerned, if he didn't believe it, then it wouldn't come true.

Within five days he was running again on the path that flowed beside Rock Creek, where he often went when he needed to heal or just enjoy the sound of the water instead of that of horns at the fingertips of anxious motorists.

Kory was "in the zone" as he cruised down the deserted path, when it dawned on him. At infrequent times during his early teens, he'd had symptoms of multiple sclerosis—except then, and until his personal research, he had not been aware that this was the shadow in the wake of his life. For a few days after his thirteenth birthday, he had not received muffled health bulletins from his body. His family had thought he was just obsessing over his body and maybe bordering on hypochondria.

For the next eleven months, Kory immersed himself in a busy schedule, performing real estate appraisals; for which he had received his license three years earlier. He schedule most appointments early in the day, which allowed him to attend a ballet class in Bethesda, followed by an hour of private coaching from two Russian Gold International ballroom dance champions. By three o'clock every day, he was at home, eating a quick vegetarian dinner before his two-hour nap. He needed the early rest before his evening workout, followed by going out to enjoy his latest passion—international ballroom dancing.

The Hollywood Ballroom, also known as Bobbi's Ballroom, was his favorite place to practice. Larger than most studios in the area, it had over five thousand square feet of floating maple hardwood floors, with dancers of all levels eager to show off their latest steps. No one liked to show off more than he.

"Hi, Kory! Glad to see you tonight. Just you, or do you have another one of your dance partners coming in later?" Gretchen asked in her heavy German accent.

"Yes, Alejandra and Jillian will be coming tonight."

"Both of them the same night? My, my, my!" She winked as she smoothed her tightly coiffed pale-blond hair.

"Well, they like…each other. There's no need for me to keep them separated. Jillian dances with me on the smooth pieces, whereas Alejandra comes to life when Steve puts on the swing and Latin numbers."

"Sounds like you got it all worked out, young man."

"I think you forget we're about the same age." He blew her a kiss as he headed for the main ballroom.

After the premature ending of his ballet career a few years after the birth of his son, Kory had abandoned dance to make a living completely estranged from the art world. Fortunately, after the divorce from his wife of twenty years, he had rediscovered his old love on the dance floor.

Just on a whim a year earlier, he had decided to try social dancing after seeing an ad in the Singles section of The *Washington Post*. Never had he done anything close to ballroom except some steps like a balancé that mimicked the waltz. His visions of ballroom dancing were limited to Ginger Rogers and Fred Astaire gliding across an art-deco ballroom floor. Tonight that same ambience had been resurrected by an enormous mirrored revolving globe that cast mini-spotlights on every couple as they floated across the floor hip to hip.

"Good evening, everyone. My name is Steve. I'll be your dance instructor for the next hour. This class is only meant to be an introduction to one of the ballroom dances. If you're interested in further instruction, please see me after class." Steve looked like a dancer. In fact, he had the good looks that could have taken him to Hollywood or more if he had wanted. The rumor about him, among the many others in this small community, was that he'd just gotten comfortable one day and stayed at Bobbi's Ballroom.

"I like him," said Helen, a woman with salt-and-pepper hair. She, like many of the women in the class, was recently divorced. The rest were widowed; therefore, men were at a premium in the class.

"I heard our little ticket girl, Brenda, at the front desk—the cute blond who wears those tight mini–ballroom dresses and does the demonstration with him—is also his secret girlfriend. I can't see what he sees in her," said Joan, trying to copy Helen's cha-cha-cha step.

"Well, the men here can certainly see her talents. Did I forget to mention I heard she has a bit of money?"

"Are you saying she has to pay for it?"

"What do you think?" she said with a throaty giggle.

"Okay, let's change partners. If you don't have a man to dance with, I'll be there in a minute to try it with you," Steve said as he strutted around his barnyard.

"Let's try the first sequence again. One-two, one-two-three. One-two, one-two-three. Try to relax your hips over there in the blue dress."

"He's always getting on her. The problem isn't her hips. She's so vain, she refuses to wear her glasses to see what Steve is doing. Poor thing. I understand she lost her husband two months ago," Joan added.

"Joan, is there anyone here you don't know something about?"

"Helen, I just like to know what's going on. There's no harm in that, is there?"

"Who cares? I just hope I can at least get in a few dances before the night is over."

Joan looked over to where Kory was standing. "Helen, do you know the young guy dressed in black at the other end of the class?"

"No, I don't. Never seen him before, but he looks like a dancer. Maybe he's a dance teacher from another studio. Steve is always having some of his friends stop by."

"Since we don't have enough men here tonight for everyone, would you gentlemen please try to make sure you move around to the women who haven't tried the routine with a guy?"

"Hi! I'm Kory. This is my first time doing ballroom. Something tells me you two are regulars."

"For ten years now. Hi, I'm Joan, and this is my friend Helen. I was just saying to her that you look like a dance teacher. But you say this is your first time doing ballroom?"

"Well, I did a little dancing in college. I guess some of the steps I learned then are similar to what we are doing tonight."

"Okay, everybody, let's try the routine one more time before we add another step. Back-forward, cha-cha-cha, then forward-back, cha-cha-cha. And one more time for good luck."

"Gee, this is fun! I haven't done the cha-cha-cha since I was twelve years old," Kory announced.

"I can't remember that far back. Anyway, we didn't dance in my family," Helen said.

"What about you, Joan?" Kory asked.

"Well, I'm Jewish. We're not as uptight as those Southern Baptists like Helen," Joan smirked.

"Are the batteries running low in your hearing aid again, sweetie? I keep telling you that I'm Presbyterian. Or did you forget to take your memory pills tonight?"

"Oh, just hush, Helen, and keep dancing. Kory doesn't want to hear about ancient history from two old ladies."

"You two don't look old to me. I thought we were about the same age. I just turned fifty." Kory was actually lying; it was just his way of being kind, because he wanted to make the ladies as comfortable as possible.

"What's your secret? You look like you just hit forty."

"Good genes and wicked thoughts will keep you young forever, my grandmother used to say. She was ninety-five when she passed. She had a boyfriend until she was ninety. But after he died, she said she was tired of men because they kept breaking on her."

"Well, bless her heart. She sounds like she had a lot of spunk."

"That she did. She was a pretty good dancer as well. At the nursing home, she would dance at the Christmas party. Even at ninety-two, she could still manage a little two-step."

"Okay, class, we've run out of time. Sorry we didn't get to the last sequence, but at least we practiced the first sequence enough that everyone should be able to dance it during the open dance party tonight. And remember, if you want private lessons, see me after class."

"Joan, I hear he charges one hundred dollars an hour. That's a little high, even for a cutie pie like Steve."

"I'd pay one hundred dollars for something else."

"Helen, you're awful. You're almost old enough to be his mother."

"I am not! I just turned fifty-five."

"For the seventh time, you old battle-ax! But you might have more luck dancing with Kory."

"I wonder if he's going to stay for the dance party."

"Well, I'm certainly not afraid to ask. Watch me!"

Kory was talking to Steve about the class when he saw Helen coming their way.

"You'd better look out. Given that you're the new guy in the ballroom, you're going to have all of them after you," Steve said, patting Kory on the back.

"Uh, Kory, I have a favor to ask you. My friend Joan is a little shy. If you're going to stay for the dance party, would you mind doing a couple of dances with her?"

"It would be my pleasure. That makes it easier for me. I'm also a little shy. I'll see the two of you on the dance floor in about twenty minutes."

Helen walked back to her table with a smile of victory. She was wearing a gown that revealed her age, despite the dim lights that faded the telltale signs of having lived a full life.

Kory turned back to Steve. "Is this really how it is here?"

"Welcome to Bobbi's. You've just entered middle-age heaven. A guy like you will need to quit your day job to keep up with all the dinner invitations you'll be getting."

"How many of them have you dated?"

"None. Bobbi, the owner, has a strict policy of no employees dating customers."

"Why is that?"

"I think she's trying to protect herself. But actually she's done me a favor. When the ladies ask me out and I refuse, they know I'm not rejecting them but am obeying company policy."

"I get your point. Who's your assistant? You two dance like Fred and Ginger."

"Oh, that's Mary. She's one of my students. Listen, it's time for me to start the music for the dance party. Great meeting you, Kory. Have fun!"

"Thanks. I will!"

Kory had never expected to enjoy dancing again. He took three classes with Steve every week. The rest he picked up the following two years from regulars willing to share their joy of ballroom dancing during the open dance party. Learning the steps to the different dances was relatively easy for him. Within a few weeks he had learned enough to dance the basic routines of every dance style: cha-cha-cha, fox-trot, mambo, waltz, quick-step, rumba, and his favorite, the East Coast swing, which he had done as a teenager. Perhaps his love of that fast dance reminded him to stay a few steps ahead of his shadow—waiting to trip him up again.

Chapter 38

Having a Ball

"Good evening, everyone. My name is Steve. I'll be your DJ tonight. If there's something you would like me to play, just come over to the booth and let me know. Let's start tonight with a fox-trot. *Dancers to the floor!*" The musical introduction of Natalie Cole's remix of her father's "Unforgettable" brought the first couples to the floor. Kory walked to his regular table next to the DJ's box.

"Hi Kory! Where's Alejandra? I thought we were sharing you tonight," Jillian quipped as she smoothed the stockings on her long legs.

Kory placed his black dance bag on the table. "Don't fret. She called me on my cell phone a few minutes ago. Her lecture ran a tad over tonight."

Jillian took a brush from her bag to clean her shoes. "What dance class is she taking? Rumba One, maybe…"

"That's a rather feline remark from my favorite partner. Just for your information, she wasn't taking a class. I thought you knew she was a professor at Maryland."

"Hmm, I had no idea. She looks like a secretary."

"Well, you don't look like a published author or college instructor with those beautiful long legs of yours. You could be a panty hose model. I would certainly buy a pair if I saw you standing in front of me wearing just Hanes."

Jillian raised an eyebrow. "Yeah, yeah, yeah! You had your chance and turned me down."

"You told me you were dating that hairy-looking guy, What's His Name."

"His name is Oscar, and we're just friends, for your information, Mr. Vanon."

"So there's still hope for me?"

"I don't think you could handle me with your other women. I would wear you out." She stood in front of Kory, forcing him to admire her legs in the short dress she was wearing tonight.

"Promises…Look! There's your sister Alejandra, coming this way."

"What do you mean by *sister*?"

Kory ignored the question. "*Hola*, Alejandra. *Me gusta!* That dress you're wearing is going to force one of the old guys to take a nitroglycerin pill before the night is over."

"Jillian, how are you? Like your dress. What is it?" Alejandra asked.

"Just something I dragged out of my closet from my Gold Competition days."

"You competed in Gold?"

Jillian took a seat beside Kory. "He didn't tell you?"

"Uh…no. He just said you were a good international dancer. I like international, but not as much as rhythm."

"Well, Alejandra, your legs may not be long enough to dance smooth with Kory."

"Yes, maybe, and perhaps yours are too long to do the jive."

Before Jillian could retort, Kory jumped to his feet. "Well, ladies, anyone for a cold drink before we get started?"

"Too early for me," Jillian answered.

"I stopped for a Pepsi on the way," Alejandra said as she bent over to buckle her four-inch-high dance shoes.

"He always disappears. Where do you think he goes?"

"Where do you think—looking for other women?"

Jillian handed her shoe brush to Alejandra. "He's such a flirt. But at least you know where you stand with him. He's the only man I've met here who doesn't lie. Half of them are still married but looking for a little something on the side. The rest fabricate what they do. The guy by the door with the ridiculous toupee told me he was an attorney. Gretchen saw him stocking shelves at Home Depot. Why do they all have to lie?"

"It's a guy thing, I guess. They're born lying." Both of them sat back and laughed.

Kory returned a few minutes later, carrying a large bottle of Pepsi and three chocolate bars.

"How do you manage to stay so thin with all the chocolate you eat?" asked Jillian.

"I burn it up dancing with you ladies. I give all I have to you two."

His two partners looked at each other in a silent acknowledgment of why they thought he was always tired. He had not told either of them about his MS. The times it got so bad that it affected his coordination, he fabricated a running injury.

"Oh, Steve is playing a fox-trot! Are you warmed up yet, Kory?" asked Jillian. She rose to her full height of six feet one in heels.

Kory grabbed Jillian's hand. "He's playing Frank Sinatra's 'Fly Me to the Moon.' Let's stretch those legs of yours. See you in a bit, Alejandra."

Jillian and Alejandra were professional women with little time for dating. Jillian had been divorced for three years; Alejandra's marriage, according to her, was just a union of convenience until they could work out the details of separation. Kory had heard little about her husband, except about his possessiveness and his insecurity about his wife's success and independence.

For the next three hours, Kory stayed busy alternating between his two partners. He made certain the other ladies in the ballroom knew he was there to dance exclusively with Jillian and Alejandra. When an outsider was brazen enough to come to their table and ask Kory for a dance, he would direct her to his partners for their permission.

Regarding favoritism, he went out of his way to make sure neither felt he preferred one over the other; it was just a matter of style that determined whom he would dance with next.

Alternating between partners went well until one night during the hot summer. It was his routine to walk each of his partners to her car and kiss her good night on the cheek. One night, a kiss went past platonic.

After returning to the lobby from seeing Jillian to her car, he said, "Alejandra, you really had me going tonight." Kory hugged her as they walked to her red sports car. "You've gotten so good that I think we may be ready for competition."

"Really!" Alejandra threw her arms around Kory's neck and kissed him on the lips. Instinctively, their tongues found each other. Their bodies pressed together so hard that they bent the radio antenna on Alejandra's recently purchased BMW.

"Wow. That was a hell of a kiss." Kory straightened his tie.

"I thought you were kissing me," she replied.

"Well, uh…what difference does it make? It was good." He put his hands on her bottom and pulled her to him again.

"Where's this going?" She felt his erection through his loose-fitting trousers.

Kory put his knee in between her legs. "Wherever it goes."

She pushed him away. "You know we can't go to my place."

He pushed her against the car again. "But you're still married."

"Just legally. He knows it's over."

"Are you sure?"

"I'm very sure."

After waiting for him to grab his dance bag, she drove him to the other side of the building where he had parked.

Kory rolled down his window. "Just follow me. I hope you drive fast."

"If I knew where you lived, I would be sitting on your porch when you pulled up in your car. You know a BMW can outrun a Jaguar any day of the week." She raced her engine.

"I know people who drive BMWs think so. Just try to keep up with me when we get on the Beltway."

Alejandra floored her accelerator as soon as she came off the ramp. Kory let her get a quarter of mile ahead before he pursued her. She was about a half mile from the Georgia Avenue exit when he pulled alongside her and honked his horn. She must have mistakenly engaged the overdrive, because the only thing she could see of Kory was the exhaust coming from his dual tailpipes and his turn signal to exit the highway.

He thought to himself, *People who drive BMWs don't know they're no match for a Jaguar at high speeds.*

Kory lived only ten minutes from Bobbi's Ballroom; they made it to his door in seven.

"Would you like something to drink?" he asked, helping her out of her jacket and motioning to the living room.

"A glass of white wine, please," she said as she sat down and placed one of the hand-stitched pillows on her lap.

Kory disappeared into the kitchen. "Coming right up."

"This is a nice room. I like the painting over the fireplace. Who's the artist?"

He handed her a glass of wine filled almost to the top. "Oh, that was painted by a young artist I met at a show a few years ago."

"What's the title?"

"He told me it had more than one. His favorite was *Last Chance to Begin Again*."

"Hmm, *Last Chance*. I like that. And this wine is delicious. What is it?"

"It's a Châteauneuf-du-Pape Blanc, one of my favorites."

"Didn't know there was a white Châteauneuf. The red, I've had many times."

"Here's to dance." He tapped her glass with his.

"Here's to dance and more," she said. "How about a tour?"

"Would you like the quick tour or the extended walk?"

"I never like to rush things," she said.

"You can bring your glass if you like." He poured a little more wine into her glass.

Kory turned on the floodlights in the backyard. "I love this Florida room. And your garden is gorgeous. Who tends it?" she asked.

"I have someone come by every other week. The garden was my ex-wife's passion."

"And where's she now?"

Kory ran his fingers through her wavy black hair. "She's thousands of miles away on the other side of the planet. After the divorce, she returned to her country and, thankfully, remarried."

"What about your son? I thought he lived with you."

"He does. And like most teenagers with a car, he has a full social life. Tonight he's staying at a friend's house. I checked with the parents to make sure. A parent should never forget the things he did at that age."

"It must have been difficult at times being a single parent."

"Actually, it's been the best time of my life. I've been blessed to have a level-headed son who has a clear idea of himself. Most young adults his age are trying to imitate someone else. He sets his own standards, pretty much as I did at his age."

"Our lack of children is a major problem. I want children, but Raoul's too obsessed with his fragile ego to be a good parent. And as far as he's concerned, child rearing is the job of the mother." She took a large sip from her glass. "I wish he'd go to the other side of the planet, or at least back to Spain."

"Should we talk more about it?"

"As far as I'm concerned, that's all there is to it."

"In that case, shall we continue the tour? You haven't seen the upstairs yet."

CHAPTER 39

Forgot the Whipped Cream

The upstairs tour began with Kory's son's room. Alejandra remarked on its neatness. He pointed out that it looked habitable only two or three days out of the week.

"And this is the master bedroom."

"What a big bed!" she said, referring to his king-size bed with its hand-carved mahogany headboard. The lamps were set low. There was also the faint scent of his cologne and pipe tobacco in the air.

"I think of it as the playground," he said, taking her drink and placing it on the nightstand.

Alejandra was wearing a red spandex dress that Kory had already removed in his mind. When he turned around, she had pulled the dress over her head. He bent over and pulled it completely off while she unzipped his pants.

"You've to go easy on me. It's been almost a year since I had sex."

"It's been a while for me as well," he said as he pulled down her bra and began kissing her hardening nipples.

"Oooooh...It's throbbing like a drum. It's been so long. And talking about long, where did you get that thing?"

"It was a part of my inheritance from my father, may he burn in hell. Professor Alejandra, you're very wet."

"And you! You're as hard as a baseball bat. Give it to me now."

She lay back as Kory worked his way below her navel. Before he could go farther, she pulled him on top of her and thrust him inside her wetness.

He pushed deeper. "I've been dreaming about this."

She held her knees to spread her legs wider. "Ooooh, that feels so good. Don't stop."

"All night long, babyyyyyyyyyyyy!"

"Go deeper. Fill me…up."

The bed creaked and the bedposts beat the walls like the Latin dance rhythm they had danced to most of the night. They fell to the floor and made love until Kory's knees were raw and Alejandra's bottom blistered.

"Mmmmm…yeah! More! You?"

"He's getting cold."

"We can't let that happen. Oh, yes," she said as she mounted him.

"Do your thing, baby. Get wild. Just don't break it. We're just getting started."

Her body was trembling. "I'm cumming. Kory, I'm cum…ming."

"I'm cumming with you. Shittttttttttttttttttt, that's good!"

They made love until she was too sore for more and Kory was too flaccid to give. Exhausted, they fell asleep in each other's arms for about two hours. At the first light of the morning, Kory got up to go to the bathroom. While he was gone, Alejandra jumped up and started to dress.

"What are you doing?"

"I've got to get home."

"Why? I was looking forward to spending the rest of the day with you."

"That's sweet, Kory. Have you forgotten that little matter of my being married?"

"I thought you two had an arrangement."

"We do, but I don't want to rub his nose in it until he's out of the house. With his temper, he might do something stupid, like—"

"He wouldn't hurt you, would he?"

"He's a Latin man with a big ego."

"Then you should stay. I'll call him and—"

"That's crazy. I'd rather go home and face him if I have to."

"Are you sure?"

"No. But it's the right thing to do."

As Alejandra repaired her makeup, Kory could barely restrain himself but gathered her jacket from the hall closet.

"Drive slowly, baby. I'll be waiting for your call."

After she had gone, Kory poured another glass of wine and took it upstairs. The bed was still damp. He smelled her intoxicating scent as he buried his head in the pillows and wondered why she had not called.

An hour later, the phone that he had placed beside his pillow rang.

"Hi. I just wanted to let you know I made it home and I'm in bed."

"I was worried about you."

"I'm okay. He's sleeping in the spare bedroom."

"I wish you were here in my bed."

"And if I were, what would you do to me?"

"I would start kissing your eyelids and work my way down to your toes, with a rest stop halfway."

"Forget about my toes," she demanded.

"Did I mention I was going to stop just long enough to get some whipped cream from the kitchen?"

"*You're going to put whipped cream on my wife! Who is this?*"

"Oh, hell. I thought he was asleep. Listen, I'll call you later."

"No. I'll come and get you."

Kory heard a loud thud that sounded like a door being thrown open.

"Who the hell was that?"

"What are you doing in here? Get out!"

"This is still my house, and you're still my wife."

"Raoul, it's over and you know it."

He grabbed her clothes across the chair and smelled them. "I'm not going to let you get away with this, you fucking tramp." He threw her clothes on the floor.

She clutched the phone. "Raoul, you don't own me. You've not wanted me in more than a year."

Her husband picked up a large table lamp and threw it against the wall behind her.

"Get the hell out of my bedroom before I call the police, you crazy bastard," she yelled.

"I don't give a damn who you call. When I find the guy you were talking to, I'm going to kill him. Tell me where he lives, you fucking bitch." He tried to grab the phone.

Alejandra put the phone under her as Raoul jumped on the bed. "I want to talk to that son of a bitch you were screwing." He grabbed for the phone as he bellowed, "If you can hear me, I'm going to cut your dick off and stick it up your ass when I find you."

"Raoul! Stop it! You're hurting me!"

"Alejandra! Alejandra! Are you all right?" Kory yelled into the phone.

Now there was just a dial tone. Kory started to dress, but he got only as far as putting on his briefs. He sat on the edge of his bed and felt powerless. There had never been a need for him to know any more than that Alejandra lived somewhere in Chevy Chase, which was only a few minutes away but an expanse without an address. He decided to dial 911.

A female dispatcher answered his call. "Nine one one. This is operator 2145. My name is Betty. Is this an emergency?"

He hesitated for a second. "Yes, this is an emergency!" He heard typing and radio calls in the background.

"What's the nature of your emergency, sir?"

"My friend's husband is beating her up."

"When did this happen, sir?"

"About two minutes ago."

"Did she ask you to call the police for her?"

"No, her husband took the phone from her, and then the line went dead. I heard her screaming for him to stop just before that, and I heard breaking glass as well."

"Are you there now, sir?"

"No. I said I was talking to her on the phone when it started. I'm in my home."

"What's your name, sir?"

"Kory Vanon."

"What is the address where this assault is happening?"

Kory paused, "I...uh, well, I don't know where she lives."

"Okay, sir. How do you expect us to dispatch an officer if we don't have an address?"

"I have her phone number. Can you at least have someone call her? If there is no answer, I know you have a way to match telephone numbers with addresses."

"Yes, we do, sir. What is her name and telephone number, sir? And can you tell me why her husband is threatening her? Are you involved in any way with the argument?"

"What does all that have to do with it? He may be killing her as you ask me these needless questions. Sorry. Her name is Dr. Alejandra Banderas. The number is 301-993-2902."

"Sir, I'm just following procedure. If we have to send an officer over there, we need to have as much information as possible before we send someone into a volatile situation."

"Okay. I understand. Please do something before he hurts her."

"I want you to hold on while I have an officer call."

Kory imagined the worst. He paced from the bedroom to the hallway and back while he tried to dress.

"Mr. Vanon, Dr. Alejandra Banderas is all right. Her husband has left the house. We're sending a unit there now to take a statement. There is another problem, though. She said her husband has threatened to kill you. Does he know where you live, sir?"

"Not to my knowledge. But if he shows up at my door, you'll need to go to the nearest hospital to arrest him."

"Sir, if you assault him, we'll have to arrest you, too."

"Not if it's self-defense!"

"Sir, we've just issued a lookout for her husband. There will be an officer driving through your neighborhood. If Mr. Banderas tries to approach your house, please call 911 again."

"Thank you, Betty. You have been very professional."

Chapter 40

Dancing in the China Shop

When Kory was troubled, exercise usually distracted him enough for a solution to reveal itself. He had just finished his workout on the heavy bag when the phone rang.

"Kory, it's Alejandra. Sorry to drag you into my marital problems."

"You didn't drag me into it. I feel responsible for what happened. Did he hurt you?"

"Raoul is all talk—it's one of the problems with our marriage. And no, he didn't really hurt me. As soon as I started screaming, he stopped. When they find him, he'll probably have a cut on his head. I threw so many things at him, he ran out of the house."

"So you're tough as well as beautiful."

"I don't feel so pretty now. I haven't had much sleep, and to make matters worse, I've a staff meeting in two hours."

"Can't you reschedule it?"

"If only I could. We have two orals scheduled this afternoon. There's just no way."

"Are you sure you're going to be all right? I could come by and pick you up."

"That would just make things worse. And I know you've got other things on your mind besides my teaching career, and I like that."

"How about stopping by and I'll make breakfast and give you a massage?"

"Sounds good, but I'm not going to fall for that one. All you would have to do right now is look at me, and I would have my panties on top of your curly head in two seconds."

"Well, forget about breakfast. I've got a full bottle of organic honey I could lick off you."

"You're incorrigible. You know I would die if you did that to me."

"If you've gotta go, can you think of a better way to cum?"

"That's cute, but I really have to go. I'll give you a call from my office."

Kory made a slurping sound. "Okay, Dr. Banderas. Have it your way. I guess I'll just cry into my pillow until you call."

"You're too much." She hung up laughing.

Still lying in bed, Kory wondered why he had broken his dating rule; every time it happened, he lost a good partner. The few times he had, he blamed it on the necessity of having sustained and regular physical contract, which often caused the perspiration and scents of his partner to linger in his clothes long after practice was over. Now that the damage was done, he knew there was little he could do except make the most of it and keep his eyes open for a replacement, if the worst happened.

The doorbell rang around ten o'clock. He rubbed his eyes, looked out the window, and expected to see a Spanish American man wielding a machete, but it was just a UPS driver leaving a package on his doorstep.

The phone rang: "Good morning! This is Terry with the *New York Times*. This is your lucky day! You can get a subscription for two months free if you sign up today."

"Does it come in Braille?"

"Braille?"

"I'm blind!"

Again, he heard only a dial tone. Unable to fall asleep, he resigned himself to the shower and placed the phone on the counter. He sat on the shower floor and enjoyed the feeling of warm water hitting his still–highly aroused body until the phone rang.

"Hi, Kory."

"Hi there."

"What's that noise?"

"I'm sitting in the shower. Want to join me?"

"Don't tempt me. I just got out of a long meeting with one of my doctoral candidates."

"I need to see you. Can you meet me for lunch?"

"Sure! But it'll have to be something fast," she added.

"Do you like seafood?

"Love it," she answered.

"How about Crisfield?"

"I've heard about that place."

"Can you make it at one o'clock?"

"I'd like to leave now and get in the shower with you."

"I could fix lunch here instead."

"I don't think that would be a good idea. I'd never make it back to the office."

"And I may not let you go back home."

"We need to talk about that. See you at one."

"Ciao!"

Crisfield was only a five-minute drive. *What luck*, Kory thought; being able to find a parking space near the entrance was rare. He'd save a step here and use it later in the day when his MS got restless.

There were two Crisfield restaurants in Silver Spring: a new one, on Colesville Road, where the decor created more of a Euro-trash atmosphere; and the original, just past the B&O Railroad Bridge on Georgia Avenue.

The old guys behind the counter looked like old watermen who had traded in their crab pots to display their deftness at shucking clams and oysters. There were no fancy tablecloths and fake plants covering up unused spaces and cheating couples. If you were a regular customer, you sat on one of the stools at the bar and enjoyed the best seafood to be found this side of the Chesapeake Bay.

"Mr. Vanon, good to see you again. The usual?" asked Dave, a very pale, friendly man, probably seventy years old or more, who worked the counter like an eel.

"Hi, Dave. Just a Pepsi for now. I'm expecting company in a few."

"Take your time. Just let me know when you're ready," he said as he uncapped a bottle of Pepsi and poured it in one movement.

The walls of the restaurant were covered with the photos of notables who had actually eaten there: presidents to prostitutes, doctors to lawyers, and actors to assholes. Crisfield was so renowned, many tour buses put a glossy of its famous crab cake sandwich in their travel brochures. Kory was admiring the youthfulness of Senator Ted Kennedy's prejowl days, when he saw Alejandra out of the corner of his eye.

"There you are. I was afraid you weren't going to make it." He gave her a light kiss on the lips.

"Sorry. Raoul called every half hour and left somewhat threatening messages with my assistant. But let's not talk about that now. I'm starving. What's good here?"

"Everything. Would you like to see a menu, or would you like me to order for you?"

"Both," she said.

Kory caught Dave's eye. "Two orders of my usual, please."

"Coming right up."

"What's your usual?"

"I would like it to be a little bit of loving early every morning from you, but in lieu of that, one dozen raw Chesapeake Bay oysters; a cup of New England–style clam chowder; the Norfolk special (lobster, crab, and scallops drowning in a savory butter sauce); baked potatoes with sour cream; and Crisfield's coleslaw. I usually skip the kaiser roll. And if you are still able to keep your pants buttoned, a chilled piece of key lime pie will top the meal."

"Are you serious? I can't eat that much."

"You don't have to. It's not about stuffing yourself as much as it's about the panoptic flavors and textures created on your palate."

"Okay, but you have to make one promise."

"Say it."

"If I tell you I'm sleepy after eating all that food, you have to promise you'll not let me sleep with you this afternoon."

"I promise!"

"Why are you doing strange things with your eyes?"

"I can't cross my fingers while I'm kissing your hands."

She pinched his cheek. "I'm serious."

"So am I!"

Dave's timing with the food could not have been better.

Alejandra let an oyster slide down her throat. "Is it true what they say about oysters?"

"I hope so," said Kory with a mischievous grin.

"If I eat all of this chowder, there won't be room for the Norfolk Special."

"I love the way you slide the spoon between your lips. Do whatever feels or tastes good to you," he suggested.

"You should have warned me. Yum, it's heavenly. I had chowder in Maine that wasn't this delicious. Have you tried everything on the menu?"

"Let's see. I've been coming here about twenty-five years, and I guess I've had everything at least twice—all served by Dave."

"He looks like part of the woodwork. I envy people who've found their place in life and enjoy it."

"Don't you enjoy what you do?"

"Usually. But I swear there are days I feel like trading in my dean's chair for a quiet house on the bay and spending the rest of my life writing. After twenty years of having to publish in academia, I'm ready to have some fun and write a novel."

"Sounds great. What would it be about?"

"You really like to push things along. I like that."

"A few years ago, I had a runner's injury. Since then I've tried to live more in the moment. Every day I look forward to a new experience." Kory took another sip of his Pepsi. "In the meantime, get ready for real decadence. This is the Norfolk special."

Dave deposited their entrees on the counter.

"This looks like a small metal skillet filled with sizzling butter containing seafood for embellishment. Do I need to call a cardiologist after eating here?"

"Only if you don't exercise within two hours of your meal."

"And what kind of exercise would be fitting after a meal such as this?"

"How about dance?"

"Dance?"

"Yes. Like the horizontal mambo! Sorry, it's the oysters."

"Kory, every other word from you has a reference to sex. Are you really like that?"

In a faux-contrite voice, he answered, "I'm afraid so. Just can't seem to find a pill to dampen my drive."

"And I thought Latin men were the oversexed ones."

"I can't speak to their sexuality, but I'll blame my constant arousal on you. Alejandra, you are one of the most attractive women I have ever met. Combined with your mind, you are the complete package only God could have conceived. And if no one ever told you before, you have some kind of sex gland under your right ear that exudes a scent that is irresistible."

"You're sweet," she said as she took a large forkful of lobster and put it in his mouth. She licked the excess butter that dripped along the sides of his lips.

"Mmmmmmm. What time did you say you had to get back?"

"I didn't. Is there a coffee shop nearby? It's too noisy in here to talk seriously."

"Sure. Dave, would you bring the check, please?"

"Was everything okay, Mr. Vanon?"

"Superb, as usual. We're on a tight schedule," he said, placing a hundred-dollar bill on the check.

"Thanks, Mr. Vanon. Come back soon."

"I know an intimate English-style teahouse tucked away not far from here. Would you like to follow or ride with me?" he said, holding the door for her.

"No, I think it better that we take separate cars until we've talked."

"Okay. You sound so serious. Whatever you have to say will not change what happened last night."

Alejandra looked into Kory's eyes and melted into his arms.

"I'll never forget last night. Regardless of what I have to say, promise not to hate me after we've talked."

"I promise to always cherish the woman I made love to last night."

Scones and Scoffs was a secret except to the residents of Woodside Park. Almost hidden from the road by willows and other draping trees, this quaint, five-table establishment did all the business the owner wanted: just a few good friends dropping by for a cup of tea and a slice of her freshly baked wisdom.

"Kory, I've driven down this stretch of Seminary Road for years and never guessed there was a place like this here," Alejandra said as they walked under the trellis.

"Yes, and we hope to keep it that way."

"Are those scones in the display case?"

"Real ones, at that. Not the stuff mixed from a box at Starbucks. Mrs. Hempton, the proprietress, used to run a similar tearoom in Yorkshire."

"You sound like you've visited there."

"As a matter of fact, I lived not far from there in another life," he answered as he pulled out a chair for her at the table behind the partially ivy-covered window.

"I've searched my mind and my heart. What we had last night was something I've never experienced, even after ten years of marriage. And there the problem lies. I can't be duplicitous with Raoul without guilt."

"Alejandra, that's natural—"

"Please let me finish before you say anything. I've been thinking about this since I left this morning. We can't...I mean...let's not go further until I'm free from Raoul. If you still want me then, I'll be all yours, instead of a spiteful woman destroying the man she once loved."

Kory lowered his head and rested his chin on his folded hands. "I'm relieved in one way that you feel guilty. But I guess I'm being selfish and maybe immature when I say I want you so much. Are you sure about this?"

Tears ran down her cheeks. "Yes, I am...I'd better go while I still have the strength."

Kory grabbed her wrist as she reached for her keys. "I understand even though I don't want to. Please know if we never go further than what we did last night, I will treasure those hours and always remain your friend—whatever happens."

"Don't see me to my car. I'll call you soon."

"I'll be waiting," he said to himself, as she disappeared to the other side of the overhanging branches of the willow trees.

Mrs. Hempton placed another pot of tea in front of him.

"Looks like you could use this. I've seen you with that look before. Cheer up, love—there are worse things in life than being alone."

Kory looked at her etched face and sparkling blue eyes. "And what might those be?"

"Not having any memories of having once loved at all," she said as she filled his cup.

Kory did wait. When the clock struck ten on his nightstand, he dressed in black and headed for Bobbi's Ballroom.

"Good evening, Kory. Two partners tonight?" asked Gretchen.

"Only Jillian tonight. Alejandra is on sabbatical."

"The ladies will be pleased. Have fun tonight," she said, handing him a ticket.

"Thank you, Gretchen."

"Maybe I could get on your dance card tonight," she said, smoothing her hair.

"I look forward to doing a waltz with you tonight," he said as crossed the threshold of the main dance floor for another night of make-believe.

"Hi, Jillian! You look unusually stunning tonight," he said, giving her a kiss on the cheek.

Kory waved to Steve. He gave him the two-thumbs-up signal.

"And now our next number for you Latin-dance lovers: 'You've Got to Change Your Evil Ways,' by Santana."

Jillian, as usual, was wearing the wrong shoes for a rhythm dance. But the song was not wasted; a ruby-red Latin shoe dangled over the well-developed thigh of a Jennifer Lopez look-alike on the other side of the ballroom.

"Hi, I'm Kory. Mambo or cha-cha-cha?"

Chapter 41:

The Brahmin's Opinion

The cycle continued: springtime in Maryland was a repeat performance of lavender crocuses bordering the walkway with their arms stretched from Persephone's bower, while sanguine azaleas unfurled below the bow window to confirm the end of her long nap.

Despite the promise of a new beginning, Kory always greeted spring with trepidation. In his childhood, this had been the season when he'd frequently had hives and an array of undiagnosed allergies. Since he'd had no one to tell how miserable he felt, learning to live with discomfort became the only option.

Two days earlier, it had become evident spring had still not forgotten him. After a morning run, his skin started to itch. And later, unsquashable insects eluded detection on his back. Although over-the-counter allergy medicine did modulate his immune system and reduced his scratching, it left him wondering, *How bad is it going to be this time?* Preparing for the worst, he canceled his appointments for the day in the hope that he would feel well enough to dance at Bobbi's Ballroom that night.

Because his mother's death had occurred during the middle of the semester, Kory never had finished his computer programming class, but he had finished reading the textbook. And with additional self-study, he had taught himself enough about programming and computer hardware to need the services of a computer geek only when he had more money than time. With that in mind, he decided to spend the rest of the day making sure his computer continued to operate at its peak.

Just as he had deleted his last old appraisal files, the computer screen blurred. At first he thought the video card had malfunctioned, but as he looked around the room, images merged in the print of Salvador Dalí's *First Days of Spring* hanging on the bedroom wall. The only character clearly discernible was in the foreground, an androgynous figure with no eyes, sitting on a bench, with its feet pointed in opposite directions.

In the past, Kory had been spared the optic neuritis many MS patients experienced. Most of his recent attacks had been fleeting and inconvenient. But today he yelled at the universe and cursed his fear.

While he lay in bed, hoping for his vision to clear, the doorbell chimed. Instead of ignoring it, he jumped out of bed and immediately had an uncontrollable urge to urinate. Two steps later he fell while haplessly reaching for the bookcase, which overturned, leaving him under a pile of his favorite books and wetting himself like a child. Being pinned was bad enough; worse were the voices at the front door, Jehovah Witness missionaries hoping to proselytize a sinner like him, who never doubted hell and paradise existed solely on Earth.

Even though control of the muscles below his navel was gone, he still had enough arm strength to push himself from under the bookcase and crawl to the bathroom like an animal that had been run over by a bus. After rolling into and out of the tub, unable to dry himself, he just dragged his wet body back to bed, ignoring the mess and too tired to care.

Hours later he stirred to his son's knock on the door.

"Pop, are you all right? Aren't you going dancing tonight?"

Kory tried to gather his thoughts. "I'm...not sure."

"I thought something was wrong. Ramses hasn't been fed, and he relieved himself at the back door."

His son waited for a response, but Kory just lay there, not knowing what say.

"Okay for me to come in?"

"It's not locked."

When he entered his father's bedroom, there was just enough ambient light from the window to see the overturned bookcase. As he crossed the floor, the smell of urine struck his nose. "Pop, what happened? Did you have another fall? Tell me the truth this time."

"Leave the light off. I'm not feeling well. The big one finally happened."

"The big one?"

"We've talked about the possibility of my having a major attack one day. This afternoon that cursed MS monster raised its ugly head and bit me right on the ass."

"How did the bookcase turn over?" His son picked up the large photo of them standing at the entrance to Constitution Hall the day he graduated high school.

"I tried to answer the doorbell. As soon as I got to my feet, my bladder started to empty. And before I got two steps toward the bathroom, I started to fall and grabbed the bookcase on the way down."

"Did you hurt yourself?"

"Just my overgrown pride!"

"Pop, sorry I wasn't here."

"Actually, I'm glad you weren't. I'd rather you not see me so helpless."

Young Kory's voice choked before he could speak. "Pop, I love you. It doesn't make any difference to me. Please don't shut me out. It's been just the two of us since Mom left."

"I hate this! I'd rather die than stay like this for the rest of my life."

His son reached over and turned on the lamp beside the bed. Never had he seen tears streaming down his father's cheeks. He threw his arms around his father's neck. "Pop, everything is going to be all right. You're too strong to let anything beat you. And I'll always be here to help you."

"Kory, I'm so ashamed right now. I never imagined I would ever be this helpless. You have to make one promise to me now."

"Just name it, Pop."

"If I don't get better, I think you know what I'll do."

His son tried to wipe away his tears. "Don't talk like that."

He grabbed his son's hand and pulled him close to his face. "If I'm unable to do it by myself, I want you to help me. Promise me!"

"I promise, Pop, but I know we're going to get through this. Just tell me what I need to do to help you get back on your feet."

"Just leave me alone until the morning. You know I'm in touch with my body in ways few people can imagine."

"After all those years you spent studying yoga and other meditation techniques, if anyone can, you can. I've never known you to fail at anything."

"I wish at times failure could have been an option for me. This life didn't bestow that luxury on me."

His son stood up at the sound of their dog barking. "I'd better let him in. I know he wants to see you."

"When he gets a whiff of the air in here, he may prefer the backyard."

"What are you talking about?"

"Never mind! You should let him in before he wakes the whole neighborhood."

His son lifted the bookcase. "I'll be back in a minute to clean up."

"You'd better bring a bucket, gloves, and a clothespin for your nose."

"It's not that bad. I'm sure you smelled worse when you had to change my diapers."

"If it ever gets that bad, I'm out of here."

"I hear you," Kory said as he ran down the stairs.

The house was quiet. His son was in his room, and his dog was sleeping just outside the bedroom. Kory did not sleep. He meditated until his will to control his body took over again. This time he knew he had come close to permanent damage, but he convinced himself he would walk and hopefully dance again.

While he contemplated the future, he wondered if he and his son would ever again enjoy the times they spent together doing things like elbowing each other on the basketball court, racing twenty miles on their bicycles, or smashing tennis balls at each other late at night. Competition to them was about father against son, and the gloves were always off. They even bragged about the cuts and bruises they frequently took home. Kory had done everything with his son he had dreamed of doing with his father. When he thought about regaining what he had lost from this latest attack, not being able to dance again paled in comparison with not being able to nurture his son into manhood.

Within ten days, he was regaining his balance while his son attended class. He still needed the walls for balance as he went from the foyer to the kitchen, through the dining room, and across the living-room floor to the foyer again, which became a part of his therapy to walk again. It took only another three days before he was able to walk five times around the course without the aid of the walls, which by now needed serious washing. He still didn't know if he could drive. One day when his son was not around, he found out.

Around eleven o'clock every day, his neighborhood had little traffic and few people walking about. He sat on the front stoop for a few minutes, took a deep breath, and stumbled to his dirty car. Quite satisfied with himself, he sat on the hood for a few minutes and just enjoyed being in the sunlight again. Once inside, he was not sure if his brain remembered how to operate the pedals; therefore, he sat there alternating his foot between the accelerator and the brake with all his might.

Just as he put a Brandenburg Concerto in the CD player, the Jehovah Witness brigade headed in his direction. Kory checked his mirrors and placed the selector in drive. When they were within ten feet, he floored it, leaving them baptized in a large plume of sooty black smoke. *God certainly moves in mysterious ways*, he thought.

His dog greeted him upon his return, wagging his impressive tail with the usual excitement. Somehow he knew Kory could drive again, and that meant resumed opportunities to stick his furry head out the window as they sped around the Beltway.

Following his afternoon meal, Ramses usually needed to go out to the backyard to fertilize the grass. While Kory waited, he heard his son open the door.

"Pop, have you been driving?" he yelled.

"I'm in the sunroom. Yes, I took it for a quick spin."

"Well, how was it? You didn't run over any little old ladies, did you?"

"Now that you mention it, I did assault a group of support hose–wearing grandmothers today."

"Really? How so?"

"Well, you know if the car sits for long periods, carbon accumulates in the injectors."

"Pop, you didn't!"

"I floored it just as the Jehovah Witness doorbell ringers were approaching the car. I feel so guilty now."

"Pop, you're terrible."

"I'll have extra bags for Charon to carry across the River Styx."

"I thought you didn't believe in hell."

"I don't. I've already lived in it."

"Glad you're in such a good mood, because I need to confess something."

"Time to get the old belt out, huh?"

"You never hit with a belt. In fact, I can remember only the one time you whacked me on my butt, when a bigger kid chased me home. You told me I could go inside and face you or stand up to the kid down the street and take my chances there."

"And I believe that kid still crosses the street when he sees you coming his way. So, what did you do that requires a confession, young man?"

"Pop, you know I respect your knowledge of physiology and natural healing, but there are times when modern medicine may trump herbs and spiritual healing."

"Go on..."

"I've been researching MS. Everything I've learned so far, despite the disagreement about its causes, suggests there are therapies like Betaseron that have proven to be effective in bridling the progression of the disease."

"In order for me take it, I'll need a prescription from a doctor, and you know how I feel about them."

"That's what I want to confess: I made an appointment for you with the best neurologist in the area. He was recommended by the Multiple Sclerosis Society in Bethesda."

"You had the audacity to make an appointment without asking me first?"

"I knew you would be angry, but can we at least talk about it?"

"So, I had one bad attack, and now you are ready to take over my life?"

"Not at all! You seldom admit it when you are wrong. I think you may be gambling with your health if you don't at least get a professional assessment."

"You have grown up. Where did you get such big balls?"

"They run—or, should I say, they hang—in the family."

"Very clever. And when is the appointment?"

"Friday, at eleven o'clock."

"I must confess something, too."

"And what's that?"

"I'm afraid of running around in circles."

"Huh? I don't follow you."

"If you have done as much research as you claim, then you should know the latest drug, Avonex, is derived from the ova of a Chinese hamster. I don't relish the thought of injecting the DNA of a brainless rodent into my veins."

"Don't worry, Pop. I'll find the coolest cage money can buy."

"If it doesn't come with an exercise wheel, then forget it."

Shady Grove Hospital was about a thirty-minute drive away. After filling out the requisite paperwork, Kory and his son waited for the receptionist to call him to meet with one Dr. Raj Siddhartha.

"Well, at least I like his name. I wonder if he's really from a Brahmin family in India."

"Why so?" his son asked as he flipped through an old copy of *Sports Illustrated*.

"You told me you read Hermann Hesse's *Siddhartha*."

"I never finished it, but I recall it's the Indian version of the Prodigal Son story."

"More like the Prodigal Son story is the Judeo-Christian version of *Siddhartha*."

"I believe you once told me the best stories in the Bible are plagiarisms."

"The only stories that are not told and retold are those about outer space. Now that I think about it, many of Gene Roddenberry's stories are becoming passé."

"Are you referring to *Star Trek*?"

"The one and only! I remember an episode where the landing party encountered a being that had the ability to heal itself. Doctors did not exist on his world."

"Isn't that the one where they had infinite life expectancy but, ironically, they were unable to reproduce?"

"The crew visited many worlds that came close to being Utopia. It seems one can obtain peace in Utopia, but not necessarily happiness. There's something untold about that paradox."

"Maybe conflict is necessary in order to appreciate what you have," his son posited.

"Well said. I'll try to remember that after I've talked to Siddhartha."

"Mr. Vanon?"

"Yes!"

"I'm Dr. Siddhartha." He extended a long, thin, brown hand from his white lab coat.

Kory made an extra effort to stand erect. "I like your name."

"Many people comment on it. It is not uncommon back home. If you would follow me, we can get started with your examination."

Most of the questions and tests were similar to those in Dr. Bradley's office. Kory had prepared himself for the tedium.

Two hours later, he was sitting in Dr. Siddhartha's office. "Mr. Vanon, you definitely have symptoms of MS. Have you had an MRI recently?"

"I've never had one."

"In order for me to give you a proper diagnosis, I need you to have a high-contrast MRI with gadolinium."

"I read a little about the mechanics of the MRI. Please tell me more about gadolinium. The name sounds a little ominous."

"Gadolinium is a natural rare element. Because of its unique properties, it is well suited to enhance the images of the body."

"What is so unique about gadolinium?"

"Without going into a dissertation of light waves, let me say that because it has high magnetic properties, gadolinium has the superior ability to light up abnormal tissues in the body."

"That doesn't sound very complicated."

"You ask interesting questions, Mr. Vanon. Do you have a background in the sciences?"

"I have the background of a Neo-Renaissance Man. Seriously, I just like to know how things work. And my knowledge of light theory is limited to the Müller-Lyer Illusion."

"Let's see. If I recall, that is a study of the effects of perspective on the brain's interpretation of distance."

"That's one example."

"What is your education, Mr. Vanon?"

"I'm your typical underachieving postgraduate-school dropout."

"You listed your occupation as a real estate appraiser. Obviously you have experience in other fields."

"As I said before, I'm a Neo-Renaissance Man. I've done so many different things in my life, I'm starting to forget some of them."

"Getting back to where we were, have you experienced any memory problems?"

"Thankfully, no! I've always had a great memory. The possibility of losing some of my cognitive functions frightens me more than not being able to walk normally."

"I can tell from our conversation so far you do not exhibit any symptoms in that area. But that could change one day. We need to find out how far your MS has progressed and where it is located. Judging by your present symptoms, I know already where in your spinal cord we should look."

"And where is that?"

"The spinal cord is broken into many regions, sectors, and levels. The deficits you are showing suggest plaques in the L1 through the L5 regions. But as I said before, we need a laboratory diagnosis before we can be certain."

"And that is opposed to a clinical diagnosis, which is deductive."

"It's refreshing to have a patient who has more than a cursory understanding of medicine."

"I can read a thermometer," Kory said.

He ignored Kory's flippancy. "Do you have any bladder problems?"

"Oh, yes! But they're few, though there have been times when I did not make it to the bathroom in time."

"It is not unusual to see urinary and bowel problems in conjunction with walking problems. This would suggest that, in addition to your having plaques in the lumbar region, you have them in the sacral area."

"Is that good or bad?"

"Until your MRI is read, we can't know. A lot depends on the number of plaques and their level of activity."

"Correct me if I'm wrong, but I assume the level of activity refers to whether or not plaque is causing swelling in the respective area."

"That's the short answer. What is important now is whether or not you want to proceed with an MRI."

"Well, as said I before, I like to know how things work. So let's get started before MS gobbles up more of the little myelin sheath I have left in those areas."

Kory had heard all the stories of claustrophobia one can experience in the MRI tube, but he slept for most of the scan.

"So, Dr. Siddhartha, did I pass?"

"The results confirm my suspicions. You do have active lesions in the areas I mentioned. I might point out I have seen people with plaques in many areas who do not display any clinical symptoms at all."

"The Pygmalion Effect is one of the reasons I was reluctant to get an MRI from the start. It's like saying now that you know on an intellectual level you have something, you have to display the symptoms."

"That is an interesting interpretation of that phenomenon. Regardless of how you look at it, I want you to consider some of the new therapies we have now."

"Are you referring to Avonex?"

"Avonex is one possible protocol."

"I thought the latest study showed it to be superior to its predecessor, Betaseron."

"You have done some homework, I see. Yes, Avonex provides the most effective treatment at this time. You should consider starting a regimen as soon as possible."

"Before I agree to put a foreign substance like that in my body, I need to think about it more."

"I understand. The reported negative side effects are more than manageable. Here is some literature that might help you."

Kory perused the pamphlet. "This doesn't tell me anything. I place little trust in a pamphlet and research provided by a drug manufacturer like Biogen. Reporting all of the negative side effects may be a conflict of interest in producing the maximum profit for its shareholders. That is Biogen's *raison d'être*, is it not? I prefer to rely on my own research."

"I detect a degree of cynicism in you, Mr. Vanon."

"Dr. Siddhartha, what you see is a man who prefers to take the blame for his errors. If I decide to try Avonex, it will be because I've arrived at that decision on my own and not because of your recommendations. Besides, if I have a bad reaction, I promise not to increase the premiums of your malpractice insurance."

The doctor stood and forced a smile. "Mr. Vanon, if I can answer any questions about the therapy, please let me know."

His son stood when he saw his father enter the waiting room. "How did it go, Pop?"

"They said I was missing a brain and nine months pregnant."

"The first part, I might believe. You, pregnant! I didn't know it could happen at your advanced age."

Kory grabbed his son and put him in a headlock. "You'd better watch your mouth. I'm thinking of revising my will next week."

"Okay already. You're not that old yet. Have you thought of a name for my new brother or sister?"

"Yes: Replacement!"

On the way out of the doctor's office, Kory grabbed literature published by the Multiple Sclerosis Society. Among the ad nauseam choices of information, he spotted a schedule for the next meeting at the local chapter for recently diagnosed patients. He showed it to his son.

"Pop, six o'clock is not a bad time for us. From our house, it's only a ten-minute drive down Jones Bridge Road."

"For us?"

"Well, if you don't want me to go with you, how about if you come there with me for moral support?"

"I'm too hungry to think about that now. Where would you like to go for food? I don't know of any decent place around here."

They looked at each other, and they said at the same time, "Crisfield!"

He took his watch out of his pocket, which had been removed for the MRI. "It's only three o'clock. We could be chugging down chowder in twenty minutes."

"Sounds like a plan to me," his son said, unlocking the passenger door for his father to get in.

"Pop, there is one good thing about your recent attack."

Kory sensed he was being set up. "And what is that?"

"This is the most I've ever driven the Jag."

"Don't get too comfortable behind the wheel. The master will return."

At Crisfield, Dave looked up from shucking oysters under the counter and saw them come in. "Mr. Vanon and Mr. Vanon, I know what you two want."

"Bring on the chowder, Dave. We're starving."

When they returned home, Kory tried to take a nap while his son fed the dog and loaded the dishwasher.

"I thought you were going to take a nap," his son said.

"I tried but couldn't stop thinking about the questions I want to ask the support group at the meeting tonight."

"What questions did you come up with?"

"The main one is whether any of them have considered alternative approaches to therapy, such as vitamins and herbs."

"It should be interesting to hear what they have to say." His son looked at his watch. "It's almost time to leave."

"Give me five minutes to shower and another five to dress."

CHAPTER 42:

Fellow Inmates

The Recently Diagnosed MS Patients meeting was held on the second floor of Building 20 on the National Institutes of Health Bethesda campus. And tonight of all nights, the elevators were out of service.

"Good evening, everyone. My name is Cathy Sutton. I'm a registered nurse who has treated MS patients for over ten years. Before the evening is over, we'll be joined by Dr. Eaton Myelintovich, who just called to say he's running a little late. So why don't we get started by introducing ourselves? Please state your name and the date of your diagnosis."

An anxious-looking, overweight, middle-aged guy in a shiny black wheelchair was the first to speak.

"Hi, everybody! My name is Aaron Greenberg. I found out I would be having a close relationship with this wheelchair three months ago. Our marriage will probably end in a divorce. I hope to be back on my feet and return to my job in six months."

Next was a fit but sullen-looking woman dressed in black. Kory wondered whether she had once been in the arts or, like him, in a state of perpetual mourning.

"Hi, my name is Madelyna Huberte. As Cathy can tell you, this is not my first meeting. It's been two years since they found plaques in my brain. Three months ago I took my first Avonex shot. Well, I'm happy to say my last MRI showed no new plaques and a reduction in those I had," she said in a very slow monotone.

After she spoke, no one seemed eager to continue. Cathy Sutton broke the lull. "So we don't run overtime, how about if we just continue clockwise from Madelyna?" She pointed to a young woman sitting next to a man about the same age. Their features were so similar, they could have been brother and sister.

"Good evening. Peggy Spivak here. And this is my husband, Peter Spivak. We're recently married. I'm the one with MS. We found out about my immune system problem when I started having problems with my pregnancy last month."

All eyes moved to Kory's son. "My name is Kory Vanon. I'm here with my father, who, incidentally, has the same name. He's the one with MS. I'm here to find out what I can do to help."

The senior Kory smiled and looked around the room before he spoke. "Since you already know my name, I'll get on to my condition. I had my first major attack about a year ago, but I didn't have a conclusive diagnosis until my MRI this afternoon. Regarding Avonex therapy, I have a few concerns."

Cathy broke in. "We all have concerns about our conditions and the medications we're taking. Dr. Myelintovich will be able to address any questions you have about medications."

The three remaining patients had been diagnosed within the past year. The meeting was supposed to last only one hour. Dr. Myelintovich arrived ten minutes before the end.

"First of all, please accept my apology for being so late. There was an accident on the American Legion Bridge. Those of you who came here tonight from Virginia know what I'm talking about." He reached inside his briefcase and pulled out a large leather folder that bore a Biogen company logo. Before he continued, he whispered something in Cathy's ear.

"Many of you here tonight are recently diagnosed. The good news is, we now have ways to slow the progression of your condition. While Avonex isn't a cure, it's the best thing we can offer you at this time." He passed around literature on the benefits of taking the latest release of the Betaseron family. "Because of the little time we have left, I would like to go to your questions. Who would like to start?"

Kory raised his hand. "Dr. Myelintovich, I've read, in addition to site reactions and stiffness, there have been reports of increased depression associated with Avonex."

"Every drug has side effects. We're still evaluating the increase of reported depression. It's not clear yet whether it's the drug or just an emotional response to MS."

Kory broke in, "So you're saying whether or not I take the drug, I should expect to suffer depression?"

The doctor hesitated. "What I'm saying is, we just don't know at this time."

The recently married young woman raised her hand. "I have been pregnant for two months. Are there any dangers in taking Avonex during pregnancy?"

"At this time, we have not collected enough data in that regard. There are always risks associated with any new drug. Biogen does plan to study this, but we've not been given a commencement date. You can, of course, consider starting the protocol after you deliver."

"If I decide not to take Avonex until I deliver, what can I do to reduce the frequency of attacks during my pregnancy? I don't want to take anything that might hurt our baby."

"If you have a serious exacerbation, we can safely give you medications to reduce the severity without harming the fetus. Does anyone else have a question about Avonex or MS in general?"

A teenage girl in jeans and wearing wire braces on her teeth raised her hand. "Now that I have MS, what is my life expectancy? Also, my parents were considering changing their insurance company, but I heard if they do, the new insurance company may refuse me and possibly deny coverage for my parents as well. The last thing I want is to become a burden to them. They're both retired."

"Insurance is an area the foundation is looking into. This may involve legal action to keep MS patients from losing their coverage. Now, wasn't there another question?"

Before the girl with braces could continue with her first question, Cathy Sutton broke in. "Everyone, unfortunately, we've run out of time, and there's another group waiting to use this room. I would like to thank Dr. Myelintovich for coming tonight. Our next meeting will be in two weeks. I hope to see all of you then. By the way, you'll be glad to know the elevators are working again, especially you, Aaron. It took three of us to get you and your wheelchair up here. Anyway, again, see you in two weeks."

When Kory and his son were in the hallway, waiting for the elevator, young Kory said, "Pop, that guy was full of crap."

"Serving two masters can be difficult." He leaned against the wall after pressing the elevator button again. "I thought they fixed these darn things!"

"Which masters are you referring to?" his son asked.

The elevator arrived with two people aboard. Once they were off, Kory continued. "The one he swore to when took his Hippocratic Oath, and the master who signs his check."

"I'm surprised you didn't ask about natural remedies for MS."

Kory used his hand to bend his left leg as he was getting into the car. "I thought it would be a waste of time. Did you notice the logo on the portfolio he was carrying?"

"No. What was it?"

"It was the logo of the maker of Avonex."

Kory buckled his seat belt and checked his father's. "And therein the duplicity may lie—something you might say, Pop."

"Well said, young man. Was that a modification of 'there's the rub'?"

"I like to think of it as an improvement," he said, winking at his father.

"You must be analyzing that scene for English Lit."

"To sleep, to dream…is what most of the class did yesterday."

"I know how he yearned. Let's go home. That meeting was depressing. Most of those people were scared to death. Multiple sclerosis no longer frightens me; it angers me to no end."

As in the past, the more his symptoms abated, the less he considered a drug protocol. Instead, he began taking megadoses of evening primrose oil, grape seed extract, and vitamin D with calcium; all had high anti-inflammatory properties.

The morning after the MS support-group meeting, Kory returned to a full day of completing the stack of appraisals waiting on his desk. Around five o'clock, his shepherd nuzzled him with his cold nose to remind him it was time for his dinner. Kory rubbed his tired legs, and as he did, he thought about his diminishing ability to walk. He wondered if one day he would be too weak to earn a living. Hours later, when he finished the last appraisal after dinner, he answered the phone on the third ring.

"Kory! Mark Foley of Mortgage 123. Any chance of getting those appraisals tonight? I know you just did the inspections, but you're one of the fastest appraisers in the area, so I thought there was a chance they'd be ready," he said in a nebbishy tone.

Kory seldom talked to clients after six o'clock, but he tried to sound cordial. "Finished the last one about an hour ago."

"As always, I'm impressed with your turnaround time. Uh...I know you've been in business for yourself for more than twenty years. And as you know, I'm still growing mine. Is there any chance you would tell me how you got so many clients? I guess what I'm asking is, what's the best way to promote my business? I still have the first flyer I got in the mail from you last year. Would you be willing to help me develop a marketing plan based on some of the techniques you have developed? And, of course, I'll compensate you at whatever rate you charge, or maybe we could swap information."

Mark's voice reminded Kory of some less-than-masculine dancers he had known in his former life. "Information such as what?"

"Well, even though you've never been in the mortgage business, I'm sure you could do well. You'd be surprised how much money can be made. What do you think?"

"Hmm, what kind of split are we talking about?"

"Most loan officers are at thirty percent. How about fifty percent?"

"Okay, two loans at fifty percent. After that, let's talk again."

"Only two? Okay...when would you like to start?"

"I have a few hours free the day after tomorrow."

"Okay. I think after I explain the loan application and some of the loan programs, you should have enough to get started. And by the way, how are your computer skills?"

"Excellent. I build computers sometimes to relax, and I write computer code as well. As far as the loan process is concerned, I'm a little more than familiar with it. I used to sit through some of my clients' training programs while I waited to give my lecture on appraisal interpretation to their new and seasoned loan officers."

"So maybe you just need a refresher course."

"I'm sure you'll be able to tell me what I need after we sit down."

Kory met with Mark at his modest Chevy Chase home. Even though Mark had been one of his clients for more than a year, this was the first time they had met face-to-face. He was surprised to find Mark actually operated his mortgage company from his basement. After the meeting, it was clear why Mark had so few customers. In addition to having poor eye contact, he seemed to lack a natural feel for business, despite having a degree in business management.

Two months later, Kory closed two loans. But then his relationship with Mortgage 123 came to an end when he began suspecting Mark of being a pedophile.

By chance, while searching file cabinets for an old loan application, he discovered child pornography hidden in a folder. Although Kory had always thought of himself as broad-minded, he had no tolerance for any adult fantasizing about sexual pleasure from a child. With little evidence, his thoughts about turning Mark in to the police never went far, but he did consider that a wretched piece of human detritus like Mark should have been castrated with a dull razor blade soaked in fresh garlic and left for sewer rats to feast upon.

CHAPTER 43:

Just in Case

After dropping Mark as a client, Kory researched the requirements for a mortgage broker's license. Perquisites were based on financial worth and credit, which he had in ample supply.

Nexus Mortgage came into existence a little more than thirty days after he removed Mortgage 123 from his Rolodex. Despite Mark's sordid proclivities, he was right about one thing: originating mortgages was easier than climbing stairs for a home inspection. Now when clients called, they found one-stop shopping. Nexus offered appraisal service, real estate sales, and most recently home mortgages, all under one roof.

Less than a year went by before there was an inkling of trouble. It began the day Kory spent showing more than ten houses to a couple who had already gone through two agents. Kory relished the challenge to get this couple to the settlement table, despite their finicky tastes.

The neighborhood of the last house lacked the right ambience for his buyers. Fortunately, they wanted to revisit the second Cape Cod, on a corner lot with a secluded wooded area in the rear. By then Kory's legs were weary from all the stairs. Since the house, which they had seen three hours earlier, was on the way back to his buyers' apartment, he added up the commission and broker's fee as he drove, and pushed the pain and stiffness out of his mind.

"We really like this one, but we wonder if the owner would drop the price."

"Hmm, maybe…Let's see: This house has been on the market for two months. And I heard from the widow next door the sellers are carrying two mortgages because their new house was completed three months ahead of schedule." Kory scrolled his cell phone for recently called numbers. "I'll give the listing agent a call. And while I'm talking to her, you may want to take another look at the garden. According to public records, the lot is larger than what is on the printout. The listing states fifty-seven hundred square feet, but I believe the agent transposed the first two numbers. Tax assessment has the lot size at seventy-five hundred square feet."

"So maybe we can put in the pool after all," the husband said in his heavy Russian accent.

"I think so. Just give me about ten minutes to negotiate with the agent and her sellers. If they come down ten thousand, can we write tonight?" Kory got out his calculator and legal pad.

"We'll sign the purchase agreement now if they agree to our offer," said the wife.

While his purchasers were in the garden, he sat on the window seat in the kitchen and negotiated the new offer. Surprisingly, their bid was accepted after only two counteroffers.

After he hung up, he felt a strange burning sensation in his groin, and his neck felt as if someone had directed a sun lamp at its nape—the same feelings he'd had before his last flare-up. But Kory closed his eyes for a few seconds and told his body it would just have to wait.

The back door opened, and in stepped his buyers. Kory shoved the pain out of his mind and replaced it with a smile.

"They accepted your offer. But the good doesn't end there: they're willing to pay all of your closing costs if you will settle on the first of the month instead of the thirtieth."

The wife rubbed her young husband's back. "We could settle sooner, but they don't need to know that. We like the garden so much, we would have paid the listing price. We're impressed with the way you work. Can you prepare the paperwork in half an hour? We have guests coming for drinks at six."

"I'll have you at your door by five fifteen." Kory pulled a purchase offer from his briefcase and began filling in the blanks. The pain in his groin had waned to intermittent palpations.

An hour later, back in the comfort of his home, he placed the signed purchase offer in the fax machine and called the listing agent. The sellers were waiting to sign, the agent said. Thirty minutes later, the ratified contract spewed out. Kory poured a snifter of cognac, took two sips, and quickly fell into a deep sleep. When he awoke three hours later, he had to rush to the bathroom again, but this time he did not fall. The tingling in his legs did forebode the displeasure he would have with his body for a couple of days.

By the end of the week, he was on the low side of the seesaw again. This flare-up did not result in a major attack, but it did leave him weak and less coordinated. It was not until he was halfway through his grocery shopping at Snider's Market that he first became aware of his left foot dragging. But since he was pushing a shopping cart, it was probably noticeable only to him.

"Hi, Mr. Vanon. Paper or plastic?"

"Hi, Carmen. The usual—paper bags, please. How's your new massage-therapy business coming along?"

"I thought after I got my license, I would have customers coming out the yin-yang. I've got only two full-body massages scheduled for Saturday."

"That's great to hear. I'll bet this time next year, the owners of this store will miss you, as well as the customers. I know I will."

"You're so sweet, Mr. Vanon. When are you going to let me give you a massage?"

"I would love to, but my girlfriend would feel threatened by another woman giving me a massage."

"It's all professional." She leaned over to place his bags in the cart. Kory imagined her leaning over him with her top off while her firm breasts bumped against his tired legs with every rub her hands made.

"I'm sure it is. Maybe sometime in the future," he said as he signed the credit card receipt.

Kory was glad he had been lucky enough to find a parking space so close to the door. The foot dragging was getting worse. As he drove home, he thought about the massage offer. He was sure he would enjoy it, and what was more, he needed one. But there were already enough things going on in his life; the last thing he needed now was the sexual vivacity of a younger woman to deplete the little energy he had left. After putting away the groceries and feeding his dog, he limped over to the rocking chair in the living room. Episodes like this usually lasted a few hours. What was angering him now was unpredictability. He imagined having to limp off the ballroom floor in embarrassment while those who had once thought him the epitome of health whispered sympathies behind his back, if they knew the truth.

It was not long before he limited going out to work and shopping. As long as he did not see anyone from the dance community, he felt confident he could fake it long enough to get back to his car and return home.

"Hi, Kory. It's Clara. Someone told me the other day they saw you limping in Staples. Are you all right? You remember I'm a nurse, don't you?"

"I'm okay. Well, actually…Listen, can you keep a secret?"

"Sure, Kory."

"You're the first person from Bobbi's I've told about this." Kory cleared his throat. "I've got multiple sclerosis."

"Jesus Christ, Kory. I'm so sorry to hear that. We have MS patients on my ward. I assume you're only in the relapsing-remitting stage?"

"Yes. I had an MRI some months ago. I have a few active plaques."

"Are you going to start on one of the Betaseron drugs or the synthetic version, Copaxone?"

"To be honest with you, Clara, I've decided to treat my symptoms with herbs and vitamins at this stage. Until I'm certain what long-term effects they could have on my overall immune system, I can't risk my health on a drug that lacks a protracted study. They may find a few years from now that MS was slowed but cancer and the problems of aging were accelerated in patients taking one of the ABC drugs."

"Kory, self-medication can be risky. But you probably know your body better than most people. And I venture to say by now you probably know more about MS than I do. Is there anything I can do to help?"

"No. Everything is going fairly well. I do have flare-ups, though."

"I guess you know the drugs are supposed to reduce flare-ups," she said.

"Of course! I know that you as a nurse have seen instances where the cancer-killing drugs eliminated the tumor and the patient as well. I'm just not ready to inject a foreign substance in my body. My instincts tell me to wait."

"What can I say? You know what's best for you. Will I still get a dance with you this Friday?"

"I hope so. You know how much I love to dance the Sway with you. I've never found another who fits as well as you for that dance."

"You're so kind to say that. About this Friday, don't push yourself. If you can't make it, I'll understand."

"Well, Clara, thanks for calling. I know eventually the word will get out about my condition, but for now, I appreciate your discretion."

"You know you can count on me. Take care of yourself, Kory. You'll always be my special friend."

"You as well." Kory hung up the phone.

He never found the source. After a two-week hiatus, Kory ventured one Friday night to Bobbi's. Two of the older ladies stopped at his table to express their sympathies. Even Steve, the DJ, told him to "hang in there." Soon after he finished an East Coast swing, a fast and athletic dance, he could not feel the floor as he returned to his table. He waited for the lights to dim during one of the slow dances and exited unnoticed through the side door for the last time.

Over and over again later that night, he listened to the message on his answering machine from Emily, his long-distance girlfriend, whom he had met during his vacation in England two years earlier. Two months had passed since they had spoken, and nearly a year since they had held each other. Of all the women he had met since his divorce, she was the only one he seriously considered marrying.

Although they were a natural fit, he was unable to share his pain; now he could only offer despair. Bringing heavy baggage into a relationship would have been selfish, in his mind. So as long as she remained on the other side of the Atlantic, he could keep putting off ending the relationship or telling her the truth.

Another transition was needed. No longer able to dance, he had to reinvent himself again. He thought out loud: "Regardless of whether or not those around can accept me for who I am, can I accept myself, limp and all?" Unable to answer that question, he was certain the more people knew about his condition, the less his phone rang. Even when he met someone shopping, he sensed a degree of hesitancy not there before. It was as if they thought shaking hands with him would make MS run down his fingers, causing them to limp all the way home. At first he was enraged. Now, with his circle of friends shrinking, he was relieved of not having to give daily updates on his condition to those too dull to understand that multiple sclerosis does not one day go away like the flu. "How are you feeling today?" Self-deception was less painful than the truth. The last thing he wanted was pity or sympathy, since there was nothing in his repertoire that could respond to either one.

CHAPTER 44

Another Way Out of Here

Fall's sweet, redolent message smelled of decaying leaves, so warm and musty. Trees in the backyard shrugged off their veils of green for warmer coats of browns and gold and everything in between. Tank tops and scanty halter tops had been replaced with sweaters, overwhelming the senses with cedar from trees long turned to dust. The pace of the world slowly wound down.

Too apprehensive to think about dance, Kory spent time visiting art galleries, searching for additions to his growing collection of originals. Most Friday evenings in the past, he had prepared for a night of self-abandonment; tonight, he looked through the Weekend section of The *Washington Post* for gallery openings and art shows to visit instead. An announcement for the Arts Club of Washington caught his eye. A chamber music concert and an exhibition by a local artist, open to nonmembers, were being held Sunday afternoon. He knew about this club through his uncle, a semiretired architect who had been elected club president the year before.

The Arts Club of Washington, the oldest of its kind in the city, had a membership that ran the gamut from artists and patrons of the arts to rank dilettantes. After he spoke to his uncle about the admission requirements, Kory was assured his application would be little more than a formality. The next admissions meeting for prospective members was the following Tuesday.

Upon entering the club's foyer, he first noticed beautiful colonial antiques once owned by James Monroe before he was elected president of the United States. Kory was given a brief tour of both houses before the admissions meeting.

There were many private clubs in Washington, D.C. He had been a guest to most. What distinguished the Arts Club from others was more than its mission of promoting the arts; members did not have the affectations of the people he met sipping champagne in some of the better-known private clubs.

Elections for new committee chairs were held one month after he joined. He easily won chairmanship of the Dance Committee, since he was the only one who had ever danced professionally. Three of the members had danced in college, and another two had stage movement in pursuit of acting careers. The rest had unfulfilled dreams.

From behind her very thick glasses, the secretary read the minutes of the last meeting. "The first order of business is to review suggestions for the dance series to be presented this winter. Who would like to start?"

"I would like to see an evening of flamenco dancing. Everyone loves it. And I think it would make for a fun evening," Beth said. She had never danced in college nor had stage movement.

Kory looked around the table. "I understand a night of flamenco was done about two years ago."

"That's right, and it was very entertaining. We may want to have something a little more interactive this year. Some members wished they could have tried some of the steps," Laura said. She twiddled her gold-filigreed Mont Blanc pen with every syllable.

"I like the idea of getting the members out of their chairs. We may want to consider a different dance, though. Flamenco dancing takes years of study just to perform it fairly," Kory noted.

"Keeping in the same Latin vein, how about tango? That's a dance everyone loves to do, and it's not as difficult to fake as the flamenco. I did some in college," Judith said as she knitted her fingers, which showed evidence of extensive nail biting.

Laura broke in. "Well, maybe the flamenco wasn't such a good idea after all. I certainly would vote for an evening of tango. What are your thoughts on this, Kory? Do you dance the tango?"

"The Argentine tango is not in my repertoire. But I can more than hold my own on the dance floor with the American and International styles. There's a local professional couple who could give us a half-hour performance and then teach the basic tango for an hour at a reasonable rate. I might add they came in second at the Blackpool Competition last year."

Jeremy fingered the waxed edges of his handlebar moustache, which diverted attention from his heavily pomaded, combed-over pate before he spoke. "No pun intended, but that sounds like a winner to me," he said. He also sported an attractive bow tie, which blended with his mauve vest.

They spent the rest of the meeting working out details for the winter tango evening and deciding if they wanted red or white wine at next month's meeting. Kory was beginning to feel tired.

"Well, if there's no further business to discuss, I motion we close this meeting." Kory shuffled his feet under the table.

The cochairman seconded his motion, and the meeting came to an end—not a minute too soon. His feet were numb, and spasms ran down his back into his thighs.

It was a quiet evening later in Kory's home. His son was already in bed. Ramses was in his usual place on the rug by the front door. A comfortable fire burned in the hearth while Kory sat in his rocking chair, writing in his journal. He had just finished entering his thoughts for the day when he looked at the date. Tomorrow was October 18, Emily's birthday. He poured another cognac, picked up the phone, and dialed. There were many changes in the tone before he heard it ringing at Crestwood Hall.

"Emily York here!"

"You're not here. You're there."

"I beg your pardon. Who is this, please?"

"Happy birthday, my sweetest."

"Is that you, Kory?"

In his deepest baritone, he crooned, "Happy birthday to you! Happy birthday to you!"

"You have a great voice. It is so deep."

"Hmmm, I'll let that one slide for now."

"You're delightfully incorrigible. The last time we spoke, you seemed to be in the doldrums. What has meliorated your spirits?"

"In the doldrums…That could also mean that place where the winds are in perfect balance between the Atlantic and the Pacific Oceans. Hearing your voice puts me in such a place."

"You always say such sweet things. When I woke this morning, I was afraid you'd forget. What a great surprise. Where are you? Tell me you're in London, about to drive out to Crestwood."

"I could tell you that, but it wouldn't be true. I'm sitting in my rocking chair, imagining all the fun things we could do back and forth."

"If you keep talking like that, I won't need to apply any blush to my cheeks."

"I prefer your cheeks uncovered…"

"Unless you have figured out a way to touch me with your computer skills, I'll finish dressing, if you don't mind my doing that while we talk."

"Now *you're* being incorrigible."

"Just trying to assist you in maintaining global balance, my dear."

"You're so thoughtful," he said, looking at his watch. "I hope I didn't call too early. It's four o'clock here, so it must be just about nine there."

"I was just about to go down to breakfast with Katherine."

"How is she faring?"

"Every time her doctors tell me she has only a few days left, she bounces back stronger than before. I don't know what keeps her going. Maybe it's just utter stubbornness or defiance of God that motivates her to open her eyes every day. She's a medical marvel: bad heart, high blood pressure, glaucoma, and colitis. You name it, she probably has it. If I were she, I would have died years ago."

"Send her my love. Tell her she still owes me a waltz. Did you know she was a gold-rated ballroom dancer in the fifties?"

"How did you know that?"

"Katherine is allowed to tell me things she'd never tell you. She told me things about her youth that I promised never to divulge to a living soul."

"I'm slightly jealous but heartened the two of you got along so well. She really looks forward to seeing you again—as do I."

"I would be there now if it were possible."

"Indeed. Now tell me—how are you? The last time we spoke, you said you were having problems with your legs. I thought it may be arthritis that developed from the broken leg you suffered in the car accident the first day you arrived in Wytherton."

"Today is your birthday. I'm feeling quite well."

"Okay, so you don't want to talk about your health. What have you been doing lately? Are you preparing for a competition, maybe? I've been hoping you would compete and come to Blackpool; then, perhaps, I would have a chance to spend some time with you."

"I've been so busy lately, I seldom dance. Between business, my book, and the activities at the club, I've little time to do anything else."

"And what club is that? I thought you didn't join groups."

"Normally I don't, but this is the Arts Club of Washington."

"You must be kidding!"

"Why do you say that?"

"I'm a member of the Arts Club in London. They're reciprocal clubs, if memory serves me."

"Is that the one on Dover Street, near Piccadilly Circus? This is a coincidence. Well, not really, I guess. Our interests are so similar that I'm not surprised you're involved with an arts club there."

"When did you become a member?"

"Last fall. My uncle suggested I join after he was elected president. He's hoping I'll show the same level of interest and succeed him."

"Just like a Vanon. You're so dynastic."

"I think the club would benefit from a little color added to its cheeks."

"Back to the cheeks again, are we? Sorry, I couldn't pass that one up. You have such a bad influence on me," she said.

"I? You seduced me!"

"Are you sure you're feeling well? You are projecting your lustful personality on me."

"Must you aristocrats always have your way? You lured an innocent American man into the moonlight. It was your idea to go to Blighton Bay," Kory remarked.

"Balderdash! Maybe so, but that did not mean for you to rip my knickers off."

"I beg your pardon, m-lady. I gently rolled them down."

Emily chuckled. "That you did."

"Many nights when I'm writing in my journal and I remember that night, I get so excited that I have to take a cold shower."

"I think I need one now."

"That would be fun," Kory said. "So, tell me, how are things with you?"

"It's hard to believe a year has gone by since we last saw each other. Please trust that my feelings for you have not changed. Every day I wish you could be here, but I know you said you had obligations at home, and I understand your need to ensure your son gets the support he needs from you. In many ways, I envy you."

"With the life I have led, you must be kidding."

"Despite the tumultuous periods in your life, you've maintained your conviction in believing in yourself and those few who are close to you."

"My options were limited when I was a child. So it was no great accomplishment to believe in myself; the few were the feat."

"To have self-awareness and humility must be a cosmic juggling act."

"Emily, if only we had met sooner."

"Then we wouldn't be the people we are now."

"Hmm, there're philosophical answers to that question that support both sides of your argument."

"Which side are you on?"

"I like Plato's *Allegory of the Cave,* except I would remove the puppet roadway and lower the bonfire behind the prisoners so the only shadows they would see would be their own."

"Your Plato was an elitist who repudiated the facility of those not of his class, thereby denying their ability to make the connection between what is believed and what really exists."

"My dear Lady Emily, if you were to look into a mirror and deem what you see to be true, I would rely on your wisdom and consider your compliment to be fact."

"The only reality I acknowledge is the empathy we have to understand that which is not emanating from our minds."

"Then you're certain if you were to close your eyes forever, the universe would continue without you."

"I haven't thought about that until now. So I'll not be so presumptuous as to believe anything more than that I'm just a permanent element of what was and shall always be."

"So you accept existence on some level that lacks form?"

"I suppose I do."

"Then I could die today and still exist with you forever."

"Yes, if you put it that way."

"Always know I cherish the closeness I experience from being alive. Having form supports what I think and feel."

"I couldn't imagine a world without touch," she said.

"And I would not want to be in a world without you."

"I don't wish to sound mundane, but our relationship needs more form. When am I going to see you again?"

"There're too many things going on here right now to say when. I'm so busy tending to new challenges, there hasn't been any time to do something just for myself. What about you?"

"You'll be happy to know I donated land for a summer-stock theater. We expect to break ground after the first thaw. A visit from an American choreographer one day would be stellar."

"If I'm able, I would love to come."

"Well, I'd better go down now. Love you and miss you."

"So do I. We'll talk soon about everything."

"I look forward to your call." She hung up.

Kory thought about calling back and telling her the truth, but it would open a door to a room with no place for her to sit.

CHAPTER 45

Pick Your Poison—
Pins or Needles

Always moving the goal post had been one of the few constants in Kory's life. After heading the Dance Committee for nine months, he set his sights on the Admissions Committee's chair. It was an easy win because the only person running against him was Jeremy, who sported a new toupee, which made him look more like an Afghan hound having a bad hair day than an odd-looking fellow with a waxed moustache and hair bought off the shelf. At the end of any evening, no one would have been surprised to find him under President Monroe's writing desk, licking his loins into delirium.

Chairing the Admissions Committee was more fun for Kory than overseeing the Dance Committee. Except when the members' few pet projects were voted down, drama was rare as challenges to his authority.

Two weeks before his birthday and halfway through interviewing prospective members, Kory felt that all-too-familiar and ominous pain at the base of his neck. He did his best not to draw attention to himself as he tried to think away the throbbing now covering the left side of his face. Ignoring the discomfort as best he could, he refocused his attention on asking additional questions of the prospective member sitting directly across the table. "Eric, the narrative in your application states you travel a lot. With your busy schedule, how are you able to contribute to the club? That is not to say there is a minimum amount of hours a member must donate to the betterment of the club. We would just like to…like to…like to know a little more about you." He mumbled his last words.

Until that night, he had been spared the cognitive deficits frequently associated with MS. Kory needed to get out of the meeting. He furtively reset the ring tone on his cell phone to sound like an incoming call.

"Sorry, everyone! There's an emergency at home. Please excuse me while I deal with a small crisis." That was the best excuse he could come up with to get out of the meeting. He rushed down the stairs to the basement level and quickly closed the door to the men's lavatory. Fortunately, there was no one in the only stall. Kory closed and locked the door. As soon as he sat on the commode, he felt a violent urge to void. He just barely got his pants down in time without soiling his clothes.

As he stood at the basin to wash his hands, he wondered whether this was MS or a minor stroke brought on by his licorice-root regimen. A multitude of causes went through his head.

Despite the trouble he had enunciating, he still had the meeting to finish. He looked into the mirror and recited Lady Macbeth's soliloquy from Act V. The words flowed effortlessly. When he returned, the quorum had just excused the last applicant. The only thing left was to vote yea or nay. All the applicants were voted in, with the exception of the dullard wearing the serge leisure suit, who had put on his application that he wanted to improve his social standing by joining the club.

Later, at home, Kory perused all the information he could find on dyspraxia and other neurological disorders with slurring, like multiple sclerosis. Maybe it was time to rethink taking one of the ABC drugs before his condition got worse, he considered. Not able to make a decision, he decided to sleep on it.

Days later, a light rain pelted the window behind his computer. After an hour of surfing the Internet for more information, he heard the phone rang.

"Kory, it's Pat. How are you?"

"My, my, my! Patricia, a voice out of the blue…Well, to answer your question, I'll be honest: some parts of me are perfect."

She giggled in way that reminded him of when they had played together as children. "And which parts are those? Dare I ask?"

"Do you have a boyfriend right now?"

"Absolutely!"

"In that case, I can't tell you."

"You must be feeling okay, because you're still full of shit."

"Good things seldom change, my dear. How are you doing? The last time we spoke, your neuro was about to put you on prednisone again."

"That was only a brief flare-up. Actually, that's the reason for my call. I saw an article in The *Washington Post* about the start of a new study comparing the latest MS drugs. They're still looking for participants."

"Which drugs are they comparing?"

"They're comparing Avonex to a new drug called Rebif. Have you ever heard of it?"

"I've read a little about it. It's not approved yet in the United States. The maker claims it's more effective than Avonex, and, better still, you have to inject yourself only once a week, as opposed to jabbing yourself with a large needle three times a week."

"I'm worried I may be getting worse. Maybe it's time to try one."

"Funny you would call today. I'm musing over whether I should try one of them as well."

"Have you gotten worse?" she asked.

"Well...I slurred my words during a meeting at my club a few nights ago."

"That's nothing. I do that all the time."

"It was a first for me. For a while I wondered if it was a stroke."

"Honey, it's just the MS."

"'Just the MS' scared the crap out of me."

"Kory, if you'll join the study group, I will."

"Hmm, tell you what. Give me the telephone number and any information you have, and I'll find out as much as I can and call you back this afternoon."

"Thank you, Kory."

"No, thank *you*. I've been waiting for your call all day."

"Whatever!"

The study was being conducted at the Center for Neurological Study in Fairfax, Virginia. Kory's call there was transferred to the program director, Dendra Axson.

"Well, Kory, tell me a little about yourself and your MS," she said.

"Frankly, it's hard now to separate myself from my MS. Lately I seem to be spending most of my waking hours and a lot of my dreamtime dealing with my symptoms. The most recent episode was a slight slurring of my speech during a meeting."

"Nothing to be too concerned about. What you're reporting is very common. Have you ever taken any of the MS drugs?"

"Not so far."

"Good. Have you taken prednisone in the past sixty days?"

"I've never taken prednisone. I control my symptoms with herbs and vitamins."

He heard her turning a page. "Tell me what you're using. I need to make sure you're not taking anything that might conflict with one of the drugs we're testing."

"Let's see...I take evening primrose oil, pycnogenol, or grape seed extract, and lately I added licorice root to the cauldron."

"That's an interesting olio. I know of other MS patients who use primrose oil and grape seed extract. I'm not familiar with pycnogenol and the use of licorice root. What are they supposed to do?"

"Pycnogenol is chemically similar to grape seed extract, but it contains a more potent version of procyanidins, which have high anti-inflammatory properties. I recently found licorice root has a modulating effect on my immune system as well."

"Very interesting! I had no idea licorice root had any real medical benefits except soothing a scratchy throat. I see you've taken a proactive approach to your condition."

"I'm determined to control my health as long as possible."

"That's good to hear. Now, we're conducting a comparison study of Avonex versus Rebif. Have you heard of Rebif?"

"Yes, I have. It's made by Serono, is it not?"

"That's exactly right. We're doing the research for Serono. Some of those chosen for the study will receive Avonex, and some will receive Rebif."

"You mean no one will be receiving a placebo?"

"No."

"That's unusual for a drug study."

"Not at this stage. The efficacy of both drugs has been demonstrated to the FDA. We're just trying to find out which works better. The drugs are free of charge, and you'll be given monthly MRIs if you are accepted into the program."

"What's the next step?"

"Can you come in tomorrow at eleven o'clock for an interview and physical?"

"I can move a few things around to make it. How long will all of this take tomorrow?"

"About three hours. We need to be absolutely sure you fit the study guidelines."

Kory called Patricia after his telephone interview. He told her about his appointment the next day. "Pat, it sounds like a good deal for me."

"How so?"

"I think I told you my health care insurer refused to renew my policy when I admitted I have MS."

"You never told me about that. Thank God for the District of Columbia government. They have a good health-care plan for all their employees—even the ones with MS. Is that why you've not tried one of the ABC drugs?"

"It was more of an excuse not to. I make enough money to easily afford them."

"I have staff training for most of tomorrow. How about giving me a call at home tomorrow night and telling me all about it?"

"Should I tell them I know someone else who's interested?"

"Sure, but don't give them my name and telephone number yet."

"So, when you called me this morning, you were looking for a guinea pig?"

"Don't say it like that. You're just more adventurous than I am."

"That's a good answer. And you told me I was full of crap!"

"Be nice. Remember, I'm the big sister you never had."

"That's right! You're older than I am," he said with a snicker.

"I'm going to smack you the next time I see you."

Kory feigned a puppy pant. "*Hah-hah-ruff-ruff.* I thought you had a boyfriend."

"You're so crazy. What's that got to do with it?"

"Never mind. I'll call you tomorrow night."

The Center for Neurological Study was in the same building that cast the afternoon shadow over the house where he stayed in Virginia. Kory signed in and waited. There were ten other people strewn around the room. His attention was immediately drawn to a man who could not sit straight in his chair. And when he talked, his wife used a tissue to blot saliva that ran down the sides of his mouth.

Just about halfway through an article in *Time* magazine about Monica Lewinsky's allegations against President Bill Clinton, he heard his name softly called.

"I'm Dendra Axson," she announced, extending her hand.

Kory stood to shake her hand. "How did you know me from the rest of the people here?"

"Our receptionist told me to look for the muscular guy dressed in black. My office is just around the desk. Please follow me."

The width of her office was slightly more than a closet. It was filled with charts, books, and photos—of her family, he guessed. She reached above her desk and grabbed a binder marked Serono. "I just have a short battery of questions for you before your physical."

He lifted his sunglasses and rested them on the crown of his head. "Let's get started. I would like to make it back to Route 66 before rush hour begins."

"I can't promise that, but I'll do my best to get you out of here quickly."

After the usual questions about his health history, she asked, "Have you ever consumed illegal drugs, such as marijuana?"

"I'm a product of the sixties and seventies. During those years, I tried just about everything once—except injecting heroin."

"What about now?"

"I'm a moderate pipe smoker."

"Pipe tobacco? My husband smokes a pipe. I'd never have taken you for a pipe smoker."

"That's the story of life—breaking stereotypes."

"I see. What are your eating habits?"

"Very healthy! Lots of fruits and vegetables, I'm happy to say. I also drink about a half a gallon of distilled water every day."

"Most people drink spring water. Why do you prefer distilled?"

"That's easy to answer. The EPA classifies any water as spring water so long as it originates from a spring. The chance it may have passed through a toxic-waste dump or a mercury-laden mine does not compel the bottlers to change the name."

"I'm sure that does not happen often."

"Why take a chance when you can get pure H_2O? The trace minerals in spring water are negligible. If you eat just a few leaves of lettuce, you have consumed more minerals than you will ever find in a case of what they call natural spring water. Drinking distilled water has worked for me for twenty years."

"I can see that. Your skin glows. I try to drink more water, but it is usually in coffee."

"Caffeine is harmful to the nervous system. But you are a medical professional who already knows that."

She rubbed her wedding band as she spoke. "We must have some vice, or there would be nothing to repent for on Sunday."

"Was that a question about my religiosity?"

"Absolutely not. We only want you to believe in the importance of this study."

She turned the page on her clipboard before she continued. "All we need to do now is to record your height and weight. After I get those, I'll need samples of your blood and urine. I can weigh you now."

Kory took off his shoes and stood on the scales. As she adjusted the sliding bar, he could smell her perfume, mixed with coffee and stale cigarette smoke.

"You weigh one hundred eighty-five pounds. I'm surprised. I would have guessed one sixty-five. It must all be muscle," she said as she grabbed his right shoulder to guide him off the platform scale.

Kory was getting bored. I work out every day. And I go ballroom dancing when I have the time."

"I love the waltz; unfortunately, my husband has two left feet."

"There are many studios in Virginia where you don't need a partner."

"I would feel awkward dancing with another man. My husband would be jealous if he found out."

"Maybe that would encourage him to try a few steps," he said as he sat down to replace his shoes.

"I never thought about it that way. Anyway, here is a specimen cup. The bathroom is down the hall to the right. When you return, I'll draw your blood."

Kory glanced at his watch. "Okay, down the hall to the right."

After Kory returned to program director's office, she gave him the results. "Everything looks fine up to this point. It will take two days for your blood work and urine analysis. If you don't have any questions, I think you'll make it to Route 66 before rush-hour traffic begins."

"What's the next step?"

"As long as you don't have any conditions, such as heart disease or liver problems, that would preclude your taking one of the drugs, you should expect to hear from us by this time next week."

"I have just one question before I leave."

She placed her hands on her hips. "I'm here to answer all your questions."

"If someone in your family had MS, which drug would you want them to take?"

She folded her arms. "I would have them take the stronger of the two, Rebif."

"What about the other drugs?"

"There hasn't been a follow-up on them in years."

"Just curious."

Five days later, Kory was working out in his basement when Dendra Axson called.

"This is Dendra from the Center for Neurological Study. I have good news: you've been chosen to participate in the study."

"That's…uh…great! Which drug will I be taking?"

"Sorry, it's going to be Avonex. I know I told you Rebif was better. As soon as the study is over, you can continue on Rebif at Serono's expense."

"Let's see. If I have a flare-up, it could possibly be avoided if I were taking Rebif. Since it's not available by prescription yet, and since I was fortunate enough to get into the study, then my choices are to accept what is being offered or get nothing at all."

"That's putting it bluntly. I guess that's true. Do you have a problem with it?"

"Not at all. I love clarity. When do I start 'shooting up,' as they say?"

"There's one last thing to do before you take your first shot, and that is to get an MRI."

"I'm surprised I was not given one before."

"Because of the cost, MRIs are always done last. Unless you have a malignant tumor or something life-threatening, you will have your first month's supply of Avonex by this time next week."

That evening, Kory felt inspired to go to Bobbi's. It had been almost a year since he had danced. Although he didn't anticipate any problems, he felt his shadow struggling to keep up with him as he left his house.

"Hi there, stranger. You must be dancing at another studio these days. All the ladies have been asking about you…Someone said you were sick," Gretchen mentioned as she counted his change.

"That's what I miss about this place—rumors and gossip." Kory leaned against the counter and pursed his lips. "And I've really missed seeing you every week. Are you free this weekend to go to the Pocono Mountains with me?"

"I've got a fully packed overnight bag in the car," she said.

"Then again, maybe not. I might fall in love with you, and then you break my little heart," he said.

"I might break something else."

"That's what I love about you, Gretchen. You're undaunted by anything I say."

"I knew guys like you in my younger days. They had problems keeping up with me."

Kory reached over the desk, softly touched her hand, and kissed her cheek. "I'll bet they did."

"What was that for?" she asked.

"Because you're a sexy lady. I just realized you're one of the reasons I come here."

Before he crossed the threshold to the ballroom, he heard her yell, "Don't forget I have an extra toothbrush in there as well."

Kory waved to the regulars as he walked toward his old table. Jillian was being escorted to the table as he approached the DJ's stand. "Oye Como Va," by Santana, was coming through the sound system, bringing all the Latin dancers to the dance floor.

Jillian rose and kissed him. "I didn't think you would show up tonight. How are you feeling?" she asked as she started to rub a pressure point on his hand.

"Is that a new reflexology point? It's making my toes tingle."

"I've got a whole battery of things in my reflexology library I could do to make you feel better, but you never come by my house so I can help you. There are many pathways I could stimulate to mitigate some of your MS symptoms."

"Jillian, you know how much I love smooth dancing with you. I just do not want to do anything that would jeopardize that relationship."

"What makes you think I would let it go any further than professional therapy? I'll charge you at my highest rate, if it would make you feel more comfortable."

"I don't think I need any therapy except your long legs between mine when we sail across the floor."

"Whatever you say. Just remember, I'm your friend as well as your dance partner."

"Let's show these people how it's done."

Kory decided not to push himself too hard that night, so he danced with Jillian only one hour before calling it a night. On his way out, he didn't check to see if Gretchen actually had a spare toothbrush. Ten minutes later, he pulled up in front of his house. His son's Toyota was parked just behind where he usually left the Jag. There was also a car parked on the other side of the walkway, belonging to one of his son's girlfriends. Since 1:00 a.m. was the usual time for him to return from the ballroom, he did not expect to find his son in an embarrassing situation. As he stuck his key in the lock, his son opened the door. "Hi, Pop. I was hoping…I mean, I thought you might be staying out tonight."

"Do I need to get a hotel room, or do you?"

"Neither. We won't make any noise; we're just watching movies in the recreation room and playing video games. How was the dancing tonight?"

"I actually had a lot of fun tonight. The ol' legs cooperated and didn't leave me stranded on the floor without a way to get back to my table."

"That's good to hear. Are you still going to start the MS drug?"

"I'm going to think about it tonight."

"Having second thoughts?"

"Of course I am! Taking that stuff could make me worse."

"I don't know what to say. I guess that's a decision that does not require my input."

"Quite the contrary, actually. Sometimes I trust things you say more than mine."

"I didn't know that."

"In that case, this has been a good day for you."

"How so?"

"You learned something new."

CHAPTER 46:

Reason to Lie

Tonight had been a sham. Bobbi's Ballroom–goers had been duped. A ghost had danced across the floor. Each step they witnessed was choreographed in Kory's mind before the next, because his muscle memory had tattered. For him what had been in the past an evening of joy had become a prideful masquerade. Pretending to be someone he no longer was left him exhausted.

While his son entertained in the recreation room, the top floor was his alone. His thoughts turned to relaxation. Showers had worked in the past, but recently hot ones exacerbated his symptoms, leaving his legs unresponsive to thoughtless desires of placing one foot after the other.

After drying himself, Kory closed the bedroom door and got comfortable watching one of his favorite movies, *The Lion in Winter.* Around three o'clock, he considered telling Emily about his MS. At the end of the movie, King Henry II waved good-bye to his exiled wife, Eleanor of Aquitaine, as she sailed down the Vienne river to her confinement for another year. Kory decided to end his procrastination.

The connection to her cell phone was immediate. "Good morning. This is Emily York."

"Good morning, Lady York. This is Henri Plantagenet of Scones and Moans. We have your baker's dozen of currant scones ready for delivery."

"I beg your pardon. I've never heard of you or Scones and Moans." He let out a muted chuckle. "Kory, is that you?"

"Have you finished breakfast?"

"No. Scones and Moans—really, Kory. Sometimes you are—"

"I'm sorry. Did I catch you at a good time?"

"No. I was just about to pull on my Wellies for my morning walk."

"Should I call you later?"

"Oh, no! We had a heavy rain last night, so the later, the better. So, King Henri, how art thou? I must say that I'm surprised. I thought the Plantagenets spoke only French!"

"*Je suis fatigué, ma chérie*, perhaps because I haven't slept."

"Is there something wrong?"

He hesitated before answering. "Emily, I should have told you sooner."

"So there *is* another woman after all."

"Nothing that prosaic."

"Then what?"

"I have M...that is, I have multiple sclerosis."

"If this is another one of your jokes, the humor escapes me."

"I wish it were a joke; it's quite true."

"When did you find out?"

"Well...about a year ago. I—"

"And you're telling me about it now. Why have you hidden this from me? Don't you trust me enough to share this with me?"

"I'm sorry, Emily. Being silly and selfish seemed a better choice than burdening you with my problems."

"That's a paltry excuse. How's your health now? Is that why you stopped calling me regularly last year? I knew something was wrong, but I never expected something like this."

"I'm supposed to start one of the MS drugs in a week. I want to tell you about my health before I begin."

"That's very considerate of you to tell me one week before you're to begin treatment for something you've had so long."

"Emily, you have every right to be angry. I told you when we met how difficult it is for me to share my pain."

"You and your infernal selfishness. Don't you know I love you? Stop shutting me out."

"I'm doing the best I can. Maybe it was a bad idea to tell you."

"I'm sorry. With what you must be going through, the last thing you need now is a heavy dose of my anger."

"Actually, I find it liberating."

"Does that mean you feel guilty for not telling me?"

"Exceedingly."

"At least we're making some progress there. Tell me the truth: How ill are you?"

"Lately I've not had any flare-ups of consequence. More than a year ago, I had a major episode that left me unable to walk for about two weeks."

"That must have been demoralizing for you in your solitude."

"It was ugly. But let me go on. I had other flare-ups that affected my walking, but not as badly. About two months ago, I slurred my speech during a meeting and experienced what is known as word loss."

"Katherine started having the same thing after her second stroke, but you sound fine now."

"As long as I'm not too tired or stressed—they're fleeting and predictable."

"Then the solution is simple: pack your bags and enjoy the country living here with me."

"So often I've dreamed of that. As you know, there are still obligations here preventing me from doing more than wishful thinking."

"Such as?"

"We've discussed this. My son still has college to finish and a career to start."

"He could do all of that here. Need I mention, British education is far superior to what your students suffer through in the States."

"I'm surprised you didn't refer to here as the colonies. Never mind that… You know it's easier said than done. I should have moved three years ago. Now I'll just have to see things through."

"You're right. I'm thinking with my heart. Tell me more about the treatment."

"Well, if I decide to go ahead with it, I'll be taking a drug called Avonex, an immune system–modulating drug, to slow down the progression of the little white cells dining on my nervous system."

"Have you considered the possibility you may be carrying the muted Delta 32 gene that saved your great-great-grandfather from the plague?"

"That's why I love you so much: you're able to draw connections most people could not dream of. As a matter of fact, I believe my unusually strong immune system may be at the root of my condition. There is some cosmic irony in what saved my great-great-grandfather may be my demise a hundred years later."

"Shouldn't Avonex help?"

"If it works, the best it can do is buy me time until a cure or treatment for the damage is found."

"What damage is that?"

"Every time I have an attack, little scabs, or what they call plaques, are left on the affected nerve. Eventually the buildup will affect nerve transmission on a more permanent basis."

"So what affects the frequency of your attacks?"

"The Big S."

"The Big S? Is that some American slang?"

"Maybe. Stress, my dear."

"Considering the multiple lives you have led, stress should be something you have grown more than accustomed to. I couldn't dream of doing a fraction of what you have done and still have my sanity or health."

"My inability to handle stress now, as in the past, is an indication of my disease. Stress activates the immune system. When it can't find foreign bodies to attack, it defaults to the fatty myelin sheath on my nerves and makes them swell."

"My scant readings on MS have told me people with it have weakened immune systems. From what you just told me, it sounds more like you are being hit by friendly fire from an overcompensating army."

"Nice one! I'll post it on the MS website."

"Why the sarcasm?"

"Just the opposite, my clever one. What you said shows more understanding of MS than some of the neurologists who pretend to know what they're treating. And those in the medical profession outside of neurology don't have a clue about what they're not treating."

"I know you prefer a natural approach to healing the body. So what are they saying in that arena?"

"Tragically, the recommendations from those in the alternative-medicine area suggest strengthening the immune system with echinacea, megadoses of vitamin C, and garlic capsules, and recently everyone is raving about 'Noni' juice."

"Noni juice. Now that's a darling name. What does it mean— no need to take anything else?"

"If you have MS, you don't need anything else, because it will probably kill you after one month. The rest ramp up the immune system so high, the makers should offer a free wheelchair to those crippled from using them."

"So, there is nothing natural that works?"

"Glad you asked. I've been experimenting with licorice root."

"There's an old woman who lives alone in Midsomer Wood who uses licorice root to treat arthritis. Most of the people in the village think she's a witch or a loon."

"She may be onto something. We now know some forms of arthritis are caused by the immune system's doing to the joints what it does to the nerves."

"I thought it was just the body wearing out. Why are so many health professionals so ill-informed?"

"Here's another slang term: the Big P."

"Profit?"

"You've got it, babe!"

"I love the way you're able to switch from one vernacular to another. I find it sexy."

"Was that an entreaty to talk dirty to you in Ebonics?"

"I don't care what language you use; just make sure you keep the door open."

"I'll do my best."

"Given what you have told me about the different treatments, are you going to try Avonex?"

"There are few options. So far I haven't found the correct dosage of licorice root my body can tolerate to effectively modulate my immune system."

"You know better than I."

"I have an appointment for my MRI tomorrow. If the scan shows active lesions, I'll proceed with the drug."

"Will you call me with the findings?"

"I promise."

"I love you even though you drive me crazy."

"I love you because you drive me crazy."

"Okay, it's time to ramble," she said.

"In America, *ramble* means *aimlessly talk or walk*. You English mean walking across private land that has a century-old common law allowing the serfdom to trample the shrubbery of the evil landowner. Since you owned the land, maybe you're just going for a walk."

"Must you parse everything? How about I'm going to meander over my flora and fauna?"

"May I be the satyr in your luscious glade?"

"As long as you have firm horns and soft ears!" she said.

"It's time for another cold shower."

"Cheers!" Emily giggled as she hung up the phone.

CHAPTER 47

Now You've Done It

The MRI was performed at Health South Radiology, about two miles from the Center for Neurological Studies. After the scan, Kory stood in front of the locker where he had placed his jewelry and anything attracted to the powerful magnets of the multimillion-dollar General Electric Magnetic Resonance Imager. Mary, the redheaded technician, handed him the ear stud from her pocket that he had forgotten to take it out just before the scan.

"Since you're in the study, Dendra will have your scans in about an hour."

"Did you find any active plaques?"

"I'm just a technician, so you'll need to speak to the radiologist. She's on her way. Would you like to wait?"

"No. I need to make a few phone calls on the way back."

Kory was back in the waiting room of the center. It was empty except for the glare of the fluorescent lights and the constant hum of the switchboard. Dendra came out after ten minutes and directed him to the neurologist who would evaluate him for the duration of the study.

"I'm Dr. Charles Charon. Please have a seat, and we'll review your scan."

Kory took a seat and looked around the well-furnished office as Dr. Charon reviewed notes from the radiologist.

"The good news is, you don't have any active lesions in your brain. But there are some dark areas that may require a higher contrast to determine their significance."

"That was the good news. Should I grab the box of Kleenex on your desk to hear the bad?"

"It's not so bad. You do have lesions from L1 through L5, which explains your symptoms."

"So that means I'm still in the early stages with the MS monster?"

"You could say that."

"What would you say?"

The neurologist folded his arms and then scratched the back of his neck. "I think you would benefit from an Avonex regime. It should keep you from descending into more debilitating symptoms."

"Are there problems transferring from Avonex to Rebif?"

"We've not seen any problems so far. Notwithstanding potency, there's little chemical difference between them."

"So where do I sign my life away?"

"We hope you're giving us permission to improve the quality of your life." Dr. Charon stood and extended his hand. "Dendra has all the requisite disclosures for you to sign and your first month's supply of Avonex." He handed Kory his card. "If you have any questions about your treatment, just give me a call."

The last two times Kory had been in Dendra's office, she had left the door open through the entire interview. Today she closed it after he sat.

"Congratulations. You have only to complete the disclosures so I can show you how to inject yourself." She placed a stack of papers with yellow flags.

"There's quite a lot here to read." Kory put his half-rimmed glasses on the end of his nose.

"Most people don't read all of that. Most of it is in legal jargon."

Kory thumbed through the stack. "I can handle legalese and speed-read as well."

Dendra made a few phone calls while he read the disclosures. All in all, they exonerated the center of any injury, death, progression of MS, etc. With the exception of the participant's natural aging, they disavowed responsibility for anything. They were willing to treat him outside the program at a discounted rate if he needed treatment for a potential problem resulting from the study. Kory was not surprised by what he read. If they had said anything else, he would have been suspicious. Before Dendra finished her second call, Kory handed her the signed disclosures.

"You do read quickly." Dendra checked the signature areas below the little yellow flags. "Are you ready for your first shot?"

"As ready as I'll ever be."

Except intravenous drug users, few people look forward to sticking a sharp needle in their bodies; Kory was no exception. He could feel his breathing deepen as Dendra opened the white box marked AVONEX. She deftly laid out the syringe with the drug and distilled water, which must first be mixed into the desiccated powder of Chinese hamster cells. Dendra coached him through the preparation.

"You'll need to drop your pants. This injection must be made in your thigh."

Kory casually dropped his pants.

"Mini-briefs! I took you for a boxer-shorts guy."

"I need the extra support."

She pointed to an area midway on his quadriceps. "This would be a good place to inject. Just take one of the cotton swabs and clean the area first."

Kory cleaned an anterior spot on his thigh. Dendra handed him the filled syringe. For what seemed a long time, he held the needle above the target area. It must have been a signal from the reptilian area of his brain that seemed to stop him from injecting himself at first. He told his hand to pierce his skin with the needle, but his arm seemed to be caught in midflight.

"Do you need some help? The first shot is the hardest."

"I can handle it." Kory took a deep breath. It was as if the needle were going into someone else's leg. He did not feel anything more than a slight tightening of the large muscle as the tip of the syringe disappeared below his skin.

Dendra handed him a cotton ball to stop the bleeding. "Congratulations! As you see, it's not so bad after all."

"You're right. To think I passed up an opportunity to share a bag of heroin with Janis Joplin at Woodstock," he said with a grin of satisfaction.

"Were you really at Woodstock? I was too afraid to go."

"That's what a friend told me. The whole experience is little more now than a sea of unwashed bodies banging against one another while ear-shattering music made our brains number than the smoke coming out of the hashish pipes passed around the multitude."

"You should write a book about your experience," she said as she handed him a Band-Aid.

"I would if I had the writing skills to make sounds and smells sensible from reading a page."

"I see what you mean."

Kory winced at her reply; then he looked at her high-buttoned blouse and smiled.

Dendra reached under her desk and produced a green, multi-pocketed shoulder bag. "Inside the pocket is an injection chart for you to record the time and date of every shot. It's very important that you choose a schedule and maintain it as best you can. Do you have any questions?"

"No. Everything seems straightforward. I'm slightly anal at times, so I doubt there will be a problem maintaining a schedule."

"Okay. Then you're all set. Your next appointment is a month from today. The MRI will be at ten o'clock, and then your examination will be at noon."

The sun had burned away the remnants of the heavy morning fog as his Jag hugged the roadway heading northeast on Route 66. Kory's mood was so light, he missed his usual exit, which would have taken him across the Memorial Bridge over the Potomac River. Instead he took the next exit, for the Fourteenth Street Bridge. After passing the Bureau of Engraving, he saw on his left tourists lined up to view the city from the Washington Monument, and, two blocks farther, another line formed to take the daily tour of the White House.

As he made the turn for Lafayette Park and turned onto Sixteenth Street, his spirits dimmed for a few seconds as he recalled the night he had returned from England and how much his life had changed: the things he had lost and what he had gained in understanding about himself and the people who were an important part of his life; the rest fading into unanswered calls and patronizing hellos, meaningless relationships compared with the growing closeness he now shared with his son and Emily. Even though his ability to walk had become shackled by multiple sclerosis, Kory ran along flowering pathways beside those who continued to unfurl.

CHAPTER 48:

Acceptance

Perhaps it was all in his mind. Everything seemed farther away than when he had left. By the time he returned from taking his first shot and reached the crest overlooking his street, the place he called home seemed out of reach.

Something was wrong. Beads of sweat flowed over the rim of his sunglasses, despite the air conditioner being turned on high. Dendra had told him to expect "a little discomfort," but she had not prepared him for feeling disconnected by the time he stuck his key in the door.

Fully prepared for the worst, with a glass of water and two ibuprofen tablets sitting on the nightstand, he reached for the remote control and started the CD *Gymnopedie*, by Erik Satie. The ambient and ethereal sounds of the solitary piano reminded him of hours working alone on choreography in the dance studio a lifetime ago. The soft adagio transported him from reality into a fugue until the allegro section began, or maybe it was the phone ringing beside his bed.

"I couldn't do anything today but wonder what you had chosen to do," Emily declared.

"I did more today than decide to participate in the program. I'm feeling the side effects of the drug. If this is the worst, then I'll be fine by the morning."

"What made you decide to give it a try?"

"You were a major part of my decision. I'm certain you wouldn't relish pushing a grumpy ex-dancer in a wheelchair during his next visit."

"Kory, I would push you around on a gurney if necessary. Although I love your body, it was your soul I fell in love with. You've helped me unlock doors to questions about life I thought were unknowable. If we were both to die today, I have no doubt we would find each other and roam the cosmos arm in arm."

"What a wonderful thought: you and I traveling the galaxies in the morning, creating stars in the afternoon, and searching the boundless dark matter of the universe for other souls. Sounds like the life of a Q."

"A Q? What might that be?"

"I keep forgetting *Star Trek* wasn't the hit in the UK that it was in the States. Qs are immortal beings that roam the universe in search of fun and games—frequently at the expense of human omnipotence."

"They don't sound like the nice entities that you and I would be. Human beings have enough things in their lives to remind them there is something greater than the void between their ears."

"I noticed you didn't say 'someone greater than them, like a vengeful old man with a white beard.' But anyway, what you said is quite true. And, I might add, we as a species are compelled to improve ourselves, and at some point, a complacent and arrogant self-actualized biped will decide he or she has reached the zenith of being, at least until that biped runs into someone who says, 'My zenith is bigger than yours.' Are being alive and having true spirituality mutually exclusive?"

"I suppose they are. Are you suggesting death is preferable to the cycles of the human experience? If you are, that frightens me."

"If we consider the afterlife from a Judeo-Christian perspective, what are we waiting for?"

"Kory, are you considering suicide?"

"Are you referring to today?"

"Anytime!"

"I've considered it so many times that I have to keep reminding myself why I haven't…"

"What stops you?"

"Besides the people I would leave behind, such as you and my son—and this may sound a bit self-absorbed—I suppose it's ego. I want to die when I have reached a point in my life when I'm so certain of being hopelessly jaded, there's nothing left in this timeline to experience. Right now, I refuse to let MS rob me of the right to end my own life on my terms."

"If I had recorded the words you just spoke, you would hear the pronoun I repeated over and over again."

"Regardless of how close you come to anyone in life, you will leave as you entered—wrapped in your own arms."

"That is frightfully cynical. You may be having reactions you are unaware of. I did some more research: depression is a very common side effect of Avonex."

"Thanks for reminding me. I do feel a little more inside myself than usual—nothing that a good night's sleep can't cure."

"I'll be in London overnight. Promise me you'll give me call in the morning or sooner if you start to feel worse."

"You have my word."

After two weeks, his body and mind had not adjusted to Avonex. Despite the drug's acclaimed ability to reduce MS flare-ups, the side effects still left him with debilitating stiffness for two days and the fear that he had violated his body. Not only did his walking worsen, his sense of well-being declined as well. Even his shadow had trouble maintaining its shape. And when he looked in the mirror, his reflection did everything it could to admonish him that something was terribly wrong. He used to look forward to escaping in his dreams, to the times when running and dancing came as effortlessly as breathing; now the runs in the park had been replaced with fleeing an unrecognizable force, chasing him from one unlockable room to another place not granting sanctuary. No matter how hard he tried in his dreams to turn around to see the face of his pursuer, it always managed to turn its head to the side.

Halloween was here again. It was also the day to jab himself with another needle. Kory decided to postpone his Avonex injection until after his evening workout. An hour later, as the shower ran, he mixed distilled water with the bottle of dried Chinese hamster ova, so that it would be room temperature and less painful to inject into the iced area of his thigh.

While shaving, he thought about Bobbi's Ballroom and the costume party that would be held there tonight. Months had gone by since he had last danced an hour, before he had gotten too tired to maintain his shape as a dancer. Maybe tonight his shadow would fare better, but his inability to maintain his balance long enough to dry his feet while he stood should have been a warning. And when he stepped on the uncarpeted section in his bedroom, he slipped and ended up face-first on the bed. After gathering himself, he sat on the edge of his bed and reached for the prepared needle, ready to inject, but it was bent.

Instead of getting another needle from the refrigerator, he went to his closet and looked to see what he could put together for a costume. Buried under memories of happier days were an old black cloak, a large fedora, and a smart pair of old riding boots, but there was something missing: the mask. Being in disguise would have the added benefit of allowing him to limp off the floor without shame if his legs failed him. He imagined the comments: *Who was that masked man with the limp?*

CHAPTER 49:

Last Dance

Long before Halloween, a mask had become skin; it was a veil between memory and giving in to his condition.

"Good evening, love," he said to Gretchen, imitating an East Ender's London accent.

"Your voice sounds familiar, but the accent doesn't fit," she said.

"This is my first time here. I must say, your ballroom reminds me of a similar hall in Leeds."

She patted her hair, as usual, before she replied. "I'm Gretchen. I'll bet I can guess your favorite dance."

"My dear, it's the waltz."

"I was hoping it was. Would you put me on your dance card?"

Kory kissed her hand. "Of course, love."

It was like old times: he thoroughly enjoyed himself. His legs and timing were as they had been before his last major attack. The only thing different was that he had forgotten to take his Avonex shot.

The next evening, the admissions meeting at the Arts Club was just about to start when he got a call on his cell phone.

"Kory! It's Dendra from the center. I have good news for you."

"I love good news, but I'm just about to go into a meeting. Is it something you can tell me quickly?"

"The results were so encouraging, Serono has decided to stop the study and put everyone on Rebif. When would you like to pick up your supply?"

"I don't have much planned for tomorrow. How about eleven o'clock?"

"Eleven it is. I look forward to seeing you then."

Kory's study group was scheduled for evaluation after one month. As he waited in the anteroom, an alarm rang between his ears. He could not believe his eyes at first, but second looks confirmed his original angst about pumping the DNA of a rodent into his veins. Most of the people who had started the study with him looked different. One of the guys, who had also been an athlete before getting MS, was noticeably gaunt, and his hair had turned gray since he had started Rebif, one year ago. And Kory heard one woman sitting across from say to another that she was experiencing menopausal symptoms, even though she was only thirty-five. Besides the physical symptoms, which seemed to manifest differently, the one common complaint he heard from all with whom he spoke was paranoia and depression. He listened to their stories and then had second thoughts about accepting his next supply of drugs.

Dendra convinced him to stay on Rebif for another month. When the time came for him to take his shot on Friday, he decided to leave it in the refrigerator. Thoughts of a major episode were constantly on his mind. He looked for the slightest change in his symptoms. There were changes by the middle of the next week: the stiffness that plagued him had all but disappeared, and his sense of well-being returned to normal in his drug-free body.

Two weeks later, Kory was in the kitchen, cutting vegetables for the dinner salad, when his son came in from his late-afternoon class.

"Dinner will be ready in about half an hour," he yelled to his son over the jazz solo echoing throughout the house.

"What are we having tonight?" his son asked.

"Brown rice and tofu."

"Disgusting...I hope you're kidding."

"How does couscous with chicken marinated in cumin and garlic sound?"

"Sounds like dinner to me."

Kory's son had long ago gotten used to his father's unusual eating habits. He ate only one meal a day, although he sometimes snacked on dried fruits and raw seeds when needed.

The two of them had just started eating, when Kory asked, "Pop, did you get an extra supply of Rebif?"

"No. It's the same box from last month."

"When did you stop taking your shots?"

"About three weeks ago, and I feel better."

"You've seemed more like your old self lately. But aren't you worried about having a major attack?"

"Well, not worried but certainly on the lookout. But as you said, I seem more like my old self. I stopped injecting myself because I was becoming a stranger to myself, not to mention, my walking had deteriorated."

"I hope you know what you are doing."

"So do I. In the meantime, I'll do everything to stay healthy."

Eventually, he did have a few minor episodes. They left him weak and wondering if he had made the right decision. But he was determined to let his body heal itself, even if it meant having worse symptoms every time he had a flare-up. Now that the study was over, he no longer had to make monthly trips to the center for checkups and regular MRIs. He just waited for the FedEx person to bring him his supply of drugs the second Monday of every month. The last time he looked, there was a six-month supply of Rebif in his refrigerator—just in case he changed his mind.

"Hi, this is Jane from Serono. Just calling to see how you're doing. We're now required to make this call to you every six months for you to continue receiving the Rebif from us."

"I'm glad you called. I'm doing well, but I've decided not to continue on Rebif."

"Why not? Have you been having problems with your injections?"

"Nothing like that. I just want to cleanse my body of all drugs and allow it to heal itself. I know it's risky, and I could be setting myself up for a major attack, but I want to try."

"Are you sure you want to do this? You need to be aware, if you stop now and change your mind, you'll have to pay full price for something you were once getting for free. Also, Rebif is very expensive, and according to your file, you don't have medical insurance."

"Certain. If it turns out I made the wrong decision, then I'll just have to live with the consequences."

"Kory, we'll keep your file open seven days for you to reconsider. If we don't hear from you before the end of that period, you will be permanently removed from the program."

"There's no need for a trial. Please remove me today."

Kory did not wait for her reply. As he leaned back in his chair, he knew he had made the right decision.

CHAPTER 50

No Pretense

In the fall of 2004, a welcome-back letter arrived from the Arts Club for members who had not attended functions within nine months. Kory tossed the enclosed New Year's Eve invitation into the same trash can with the same alacrity as the other invitations he had received from friends and family. He often thought about going out for social affairs, but his pride would not let him unnecessarily exhibit his diminished state without chagrin.

Until a year ago, he had still been able to get around without a cane; now there were times he even tottered while trying to keep his balance—despite his constant walking stick at his side. He did not blame his present state on his decision to stop taking Rebif; it was the stress from running three businesses that left him totally exhausted by the end of every day.

After his son earned his appraisal license, seldom did Kory have to inspect houses, which had usually involved stair climbing; now all he had to do was review his son's reports for errors and omissions. Like a sponge, his son had absorbed his father's many years of experience in the appraisal business and his penchant for accurate detail. He approached every job with the same degree of concentration, which seldom led to errors; therefore, Kory was left to deal with clients only over the phone, and he did everything to provide service no other appraiser was able to give. That level of service often meant spending six or more hours providing pre-appraisal information to his clients—something many appraisers refused to do. When it came to selling real estate, his son also did most of the legwork, while Kory wrote the contracts. The energy required to do both of those jobs would have been a lot for a person half Kory's age without the health challenges. And when he was not reviewing appraisals or writing contracts, he squeezed in loan applicants for appointments in his office for people who were often the purchasers of the houses he was selling. Yes, the money he was making was considerable, but he was literally killing himself seven days a week. Now there were times when even the cane was not capable of keeping him on his feet. Kory was afraid to slow the pace of his self-destruction. He simply did not know how much time he had left, but he was certain he would soon find out if he did not take a break.

Though they may have been infrequent, there were times, particularly in the winter, when business slowed enough for him to relax and spend a little time remediating his health. It was during those periods when he knew he had made the right decision to stop the drugs. Usually after two consecutive days away from the stress of his businesses, his strength and balance improved; he dreamed of one day when he would just walk away from everything and find the level of health he had once enjoyed.

On Christmas Eve, for the first time in his career, Kory turned down any new appraisal assignments or loan applications until the first of the next year. Most of the free time would be spent with his son and visiting family he had not seen in years. They had no idea he had ever had some of the mobility problems he was now able to hide during the timed visits. His regained confidence in hiding his disability even allowed him to consider another outing: he decided to take his son to the New Year's party at the Arts Club.

It was a quiet and early Christmas morning when he slowly drove through downtown Silver Spring. Silent falling snow in the rearview mirror covered his tracks as he made his way north. With the exception of a lone police car, there was not another soul to be seen. He turned the windshield wipers to high and thought to himself, *This is the closest man gets to peace on Earth.* As expected, Dunkin' Donuts was one of the few businesses open that day. He ordered a freshly baked raisin-bran muffin and a medium cup of decaffeinated Earl Grey tea from a counter person with seasonal bloodshot eyes. Abdul, the tired man, greeted him with an obligatory "Merry Christmas" in his heavy Pakistani accent. Kory did not return with the same greeting; instead, he wished Abdul the peacefulness of the day. Abdul just smiled and stuffed the dollar bills into the overflowing till. Obviously, he was more interested in the piece of money than in peace. If Kory could have heard his thoughts, they probably would have been *If I wanted peace, I could have stayed in Islamabad.*

Outside, blustery wind chilled Kory as he sat his hot breakfast on the roof of the car while he searched for his keys. His cell phone rang just as he got behind the wheel.

"Merry Christmas!"

"Merry Christmas to you, Lady York. Did you receive my gift?"

"Yes. I'm wearing it now, but I long for something in a larger box."

"A larger box? I was always told size did not matter," he quipped.

"You seldom pass up an opportunity. I wouldn't touch that one with a ten-foot pole. No pun intended, love. With your piercing sense of humor, it wouldn't have surprised me if you'd had yourself wrapped and delivered to Crestwood, thereby giving me the present I've been waiting for."

"Give me a second to write that down. Let's see—send one scantily clad dancer with big muscles to Crestwood Manor in a very large box," he said.

"Don't forget to strategically place garlands of mistletoe over areas of my interest," she added.

"This conversation is apropos, considering the temperature outside," he remarked.

"The temperature is rising here as well. Now, on a more seasonal note, since you don't celebrate the birth of Christ, what are you doing for Christmas?"

"I'll celebrate the esprit de corps of Christmas with the usual dinner at a cousin's house, where I'll see other family members whom I've not seen since last winter. We'll say how we will try to stay more in touch until we see one another next year, except tonight I'll insist it's not likely I'll call, in light of we have only some similar DNA in common, and that is not enough to compel me to hypocrisy without two more cups of eggnog."

"You're a bit cynical so early in the day."

"Maybe, but I feel fantastic. Hearing from you may be the highlight of the day. What are you doing for this holiday, besides talking to a misanthropic man on the other side of the ocean?"

"The best of it, I enjoyed in the chapel last night. The boys' choir was unusually good. Katherine even felt well enough to attend."

"The best of my holiday is yet to come. I decided to be unemployed until next year."

"Overdue but good to hear. Speaking of next year, what are you doing New Year's Eve?" she asked.

"Going to the Arts Club with my son to have a fun night. What about you?"

"What a coincidence—I made reservations to do the same; that is, I'm going to a private party at the Arts Club in London. I intend to cajole some of the inebriated impresarios into promoting my little theater next year."

"Sounds like fun. Shame we're not ringing in the new year in the same city."

"That and a larger box will be added to next year's Christmas list," she said.

"Now that another year is about to end, I think we should talk more about us."

"Since I've already expressed my desires, I'm all ears."

"First of all, I'm sorry things did not work out for us in the way I had hoped. Wishfully, I envisioned us together, savoring life through the prism of our affection. It saddens me when I think of how my life has become so diminished from the constraints of my condition."

"Kory, your soul has not changed—just your body. Why not build upon what you have and make the best of it?"

"I suppose...I'm stuck in self-pity and delusion, with no clue how to break the cycle. Can it be folly for me to believe one day I'll fully recover and be the person I once was?"

"You know one cannot return to the past. What's more, most of your pain is in the past. Maybe it's time for you to be the most of who you are now."

"I thought you were a professor of literature. Maybe you should add psychology to the brass nameplate on your office door."

"Kory, I can't ignore your equivocation. You know I'm only trying to point out the obvious. Is there nothing I can say to help you get off your carousel?"

"Sure. Tell me when I'll be able to stand unaided and grab the last brass ring."

"I expected your carousel to have a gold ring."

"Is that your way of saying what I'm reaching for is not worth the effort?"

"Do you remember when you were a child that if you constantly looked outside the merry-go-round, you became dizzy?"

"I must be missing the metaphor, because if I look to the inside of the carousel, I remember all the mirrors. You can't think I need to look inside myself more than I have. My self-absorption is already borderline manic-depressive!"

"Maybe that was a bad example."

"Maybe I'm a poor model of actualization. Forget I said that. Today is not a good day for an existential conversation."

"Why not just enjoy the holiday?" she said in exasperation.

"Sorry, but most of my life I experienced Christmas with ambivalence. Since adolescence, I've always been dismayed at the utter hypocrisy of those who are so friendly one week and then ignore the same person seven days later. Why must we have excuses to acknowledge the validity of others? I guess if there's any value in religion, it is to force those lacking natural humility to display it. Is the purpose of Christmas to show how charity should be exhibited regularly? Maybe it's just another example of how the sins of character—even displayed under the auspices of a religious holiday—can be absolved by the recitation of a contrite Hail Mary."

"Is there any social custom you accept at face value?"

"Yes, and only when I'm among strangers."

"My sweet, there are some social conventions that are intended to allow people the opportunity to be silly and gay."

"But I do not want to be 'allowed' to be anything. I want to be an ass when I want to be an ass."

"You're certainly being one now."

"Thank you. I guess I had that coming."

"Before I ring off—did you get my gift?"

"Not yet, I'm afraid."

"Blast it! Amazon.com assured me it would arrive before Christmas."

"Hearing your voice is the only gift I'll ever need from you."

"Kory, what do you really want?"

"At this moment, I want to take you into my arms and hold you until the world stops shaking."

"But I would need to be there for that!"

"I can wish, can't I?"

"And I can see if I can satisfy your wish," she added.

"What does that mean?"

"You'll see. Ta-ta! "

"Bah, Humbug" had not always been Kory's appraisal of Christmas. Like most children, he struggled to sleep the long hours before the tree was relit in the morning and holiday paper was ripped off carefully wrapped gifts. The last time he had felt the same excitement was the year before his son had figured out Santa Claus was actually his father and mother. Removal of the myth never seemed to dampen his son's holiday cheer. With maturity, he began to appreciate the best of the holiday, as his father did, the time when people forgot about their problems and stuffed their biases and prejudices in a drawer for a few days, or at least until the liquored glow wore off.

Days after his conversation with Emily, Kory reflected on her well-intentioned comments. Maybe she was right: he did have symptoms of depression, although they were more a response to reality and not the machinations of an unbridled imagination. In the end, as far as he was concerned, happiness and effectiveness in dealing with others were the true barometers of mental health. Never did he plod along, chanting, *Woe is me* as his mantra; instead he cursed his condition when necessary and blamed not himself or God. His unusual immune system was the real culprit of his plight and not some amorphous figment of cognitive dissonance. Yes, the quality of his life had changed, but his determination to beat MS had not. He mourned for those who prematurely had given up the fight against the thief that would one day rob them of their dignity; the capitulation of others bolstered his conviction.

Loneliness was never a problem with MS by his side. Sometimes he thought of it as his evil twin who always tagged along, despite entreaties to make a life of its own. But the umbilical tether was inseverable; while his doppelgänger test-drove wheelchairs, Kory wondered if he would be forced to give up the independence he still enjoyed every time he flipped the ignition switch in his car.

Getting dressed for the New Year's Eve party was arduous. Kory's tuxedo still fit well, but it took almost fifteen minutes to insert all of the gold studs in those starched slits in the formal shirt. MS did not affect much of his body above the waist, except when he needed the synchrony of his thumb and index finger, like when buttoning his clothes or handling a pair of scissors to clip those irksome nose hairs. As he stood in front of the cheval mirror and admired himself, with the exception of a few gray hairs, he had changed little on first glance, but his countenance had. Tonight he would have to make more of an effort to be outside his head, instead of constantly monitoring his body for warnings of fatigue or the need to visit the men's room. The demands of being vigilant sometimes muted his spontaneity; nevertheless, he was determined to have a good time that night.

Kory's son appeared in the doorway, dressed in his new tuxedo. His father was taking one last look.

"Pop, are we taking your car or mine?"

"I feel like driving tonight, so let's take the Jag."

His son took his father's place in the mirror.

"I hope there will be someone there born before the invention of the wheel to appreciate how dashing I look tonight." His son checked both profiles.

"Well, that eliminates everyone in my age group. We were just getting used to fire when I was your age," Kory said.

"You mean you can actually remember that far back? I'm impressed, Pop."

"If you're going to spend so much time admiring yourself in the mirror, please make sure you clean the smudges off where you kissed your image.

And tell me, from whom did you develop a narcissistic complex? It must have been your mother!"

He turned in his father's direction.

"Look closely in the mirror, and you'll see your answer."

"Well, at least I remember to clean the lip smudges off the mirror when I'm finished. Try to remember that the next time you spend an hour shaving in the bathroom."

"Interesting story, but I can tell by the smudges already on this mirror that they're from your lips."

"Are you sure? I was certain I removed the lip prints before you came in," Kory said as he picked up his car keys sitting on the armoire.

"You forgot your cane, Pop." He grabbed the foldable black lacquered cane lying across the leather bench.

"I was thinking about leaving it there," Kory replied.

"How about if I bring it along, just in case?" His son folded the cane into its smallest size. "Look, I can fold it small enough that it fits in my pocket under my jacket."

"I guess you're right. It's better to drag the cane along now than to have to hold on to the walls if I get tired later."

Washington, D.C. has unusual winters: one day it is bitter cold, and the next, one can see people in short sleeves strolling in the warm afternoon sun. It was so warm as they drove down Sixteenth Street to the Arts Club, Kory opened the moon roof of the Jag and let in the last rays of the winter sun. They sped south down the five-mile hill, lined with ecumenical churches on both sides of the thoroughfare, until it ended at the north entrance of Lafayette Park. Through leafless trees, the North Portico of the White House reflected an orange tint from the escaping sun. It was only three blocks more before they reached the front of the club, where two cars waited in queue for the gold-vested valets to park their cars. He ignored fleeting waves of fatigue that rose from his legs and tried to push obsession with his health out of his mind.

When they got out of the car, his son offered him the cane. Kory groaned and unfolded it. As they walked toward the entrance of the club, he spotted Beth, who now held his former position as head of the Dance Committee.

"Is that you, Kory?" Beth floated their way and kissed him on the cheeks.

"Beth, you remember my son, Kory, don't you?"

"Of course I do. He's a very handsome young man."

"Please don't say that to him. It took me an hour just to get him away from the mirror so we wouldn't miss cocktails."

"Pop, I was dressed before you," his son interjected.

"You must forgive him, Beth. He's in denial."

"You two certainly have a good relationship," she remarked.

"Excluding some of the other things in my life, I've been very fortunate to have a good son and friend in the same person."

"I've not seen you around here in many months. I heard you were ill. Is that why you are sporting the cane?"

"It's, uh...just a prop. Actually, I have a few problems with the nerves in my legs. Nothing major, though. My son makes me carry it. He's such a nag sometimes," he said as he winked at his son.

"Then I suppose you won't be doing any dancing tonight?" she said.

"If I pace myself, I should manage a few dances tonight. How's your fox-trot these days?"

"You remembered! That's my favorite dance. Maybe I should tell the other ladies you're not dancing tonight. Just let me know when you feel up to a dance, and we'll dazzle them."

"No need. I think I can manage more than one dance tonight."

Beth's attention turned to a van pulling to the door. "There's the band bringing in their instruments. The Dance Committee is sponsoring the party, so I need to go over some last-minute details with their pianist. I'll see you later, Twinkle Toes."

"Twinkle Toes! Is she a member of your fan club?" his son asked.

"Yes, if I haven't been replaced with someone younger."

The front door of the club was opened to the street. Familiar faces mingled with one another in the foyer as they approached the entrance. Kory stopped in the hallway to check his bowtie in the gilded Florentine mirror above the mahogany sideboard; both had once belonged to President Monroe and his family. His refection looked slightly distorted, which made him wonder if his eyes were out of focus, or maybe his blurred image was just the result of more than two centuries of cleaning or of the images of long-departed souls stuck inside the abyss of the mirror. Also in the reflection was the empty dining room behind him, reminding him drinks were probably being served in the garden.

Kory's son leaned over and also checked himself in the mirror.

"Pop, try not to tire yourself tonight."

Noticing his son's tie aslant, Kory turned around to him and straightened the bow. "Don't worry about me. Try to have a good time with some of the younger members around midnight."

"So far, I've only smelled Bengay mixed with perfume. I hope I don't end up standing next to someone's grandmother when the ball drops."

"Don't knock grannies. Some of my best friends wear support hose."

"Gross," his son exclaimed.

"Sometimes age and experience trump youth and vivacity. Wow! I can't believe I said that sober."

"Now that you mentioned it, are you up for cocktails?" his son asked.

"Sure. But I'm going to pace myself and just have a glass of white wine."

"I'm going to try whatever red they have tonight, although it's usually a good Cabernet."

The French doors at the back of the main dining room were thrown open to the garden, sprouting with familiar faces—most whose names Kory had forgotten. It was time for him to turn on the charm again—something he had not done since spring. They crossed the door's threshold, which led down a slightly declining slate walkway to the largest privately owned garden in downtown Washington. And just before the terrace, delicate aromas wafted through the early-evening air as they passed the kitchen. Brennan, the club's treasured chef, waved to Kory and gave him the thumbs-up while he prepared another gastronomical delight for those eagerly waiting palates sipping cocktails in the fading light.

"The Korys have arrived," announced Jeremy, still sporting his awful toupee.

"Jeremy, how are you? I heard you are running for the admissions chair."

"It's time for the committee to have some semblance of direction." Jeremy tried to pull the edges of his vest over his growing paunch. I'll be straight with you: since you left, the only thing they do is rubber-stamp every Tom, Dick, and Harry into the club. I realize we need new members, but they should be properly screened before admission. I think there should be a mandatory waiting period of one month after the interview to check on the claims some of them make."

Kory found a level spot on the pavement to lean on his cane. "Good luck trying to get the board to pass that one. You know the bylaws will have to be amended to further vet applicants. That's not to say I agree with the open-door policy of late. There's always the balancing act of paying the club's bills and promoting our mission. It has been my experience that the ones who don't seem to fit in usually don't last more than a year. As long as they're not chairing committees and disturbing the mirth, I'm fine to let them be."

Jeremy was not satisfied with Kory's answer. "One is running for a seat on the board of governors, and you know what that could mean."

"It's still of little concern. The majority still rules the board. So if they get a seat, which is not likely, they'll spend their term in frustration. What concerns you is usually neutralized by the general social makeup of the older members, who outlast the curiosity seekers."

"Speaking of social makeup, have you met the lovely lady visiting us from our reciprocal club in London?" Jeremy asked.

"No, I haven't. Who is she?"

"She's the tall woman coming our way. Lady Emily York, I believe is her name."

"It can't be!"

Before Kory could finish turning around, the familiar scent of her perfume stoked the embers of his passion; everything and everyone else around him faded into the ether.

"Ta-da! Your genie has arrived," she said as she threw her arms around his neck.

Dumbfounded, he just held her in his arms while his brain searched for his tongue.

"I'm glad you're so happy to see me, but you don't have to squeeze me so hard," she said.

"Who's squeezing? I'm holding on. My knees are so weak from seeing you that I'm using you to stay on my feet."

She whispered, "It's not that bad, is it?"

"Some days…Let's find a quiet place. There's something I've been meaning to ask you."

Emily looked deep into Kory's eyes. "I mulled over all of the things I wanted to say to you during the entire flight. The attendant even asked me if everything was all right when she noticed I was talking to myself as I looked out the window."

The most secluded place in the club was the parlor on the second floor outside the president's office. Emily could see the effort it took him to climb the long flight of stairs, but she said nothing. He pointed to a red velvet love seat and folded his cane as they sat down.

"Kory, there are many things I need to say. Will you—"

He placed a finger on her lips and stopped her in midsentence. "I must confess there have been days when my body was so riddled with pain that I wanted to hasten my end. Many times I sat with my gun in my mouth, ready to end the nightmare. But every time I started to pull the trigger, I had visions of you and my son standing over my cold body, wondering why I didn't at least say good-bye."

"Is this good-bye?"

A spasm struck Kory's arm as he thought about what was inside his jacket.

"My fingers are so stiff, I can't even…"

"You can't even what, Kory?"

"Can't you see! A shadow is all that's left of me. My legs are so stiff, I can't even…"

"It doesn't matter."

"But, I…I can't even get down on one knee to ask…"

"Is this a proposal?"

"It's an entreaty."

Kory reached into his waistband and pulled out a gun. Emily held her breath as his trembling hand placed it on her lap. Tears streamed down her cheeks as she slowly nodded her head.

"Yes—"